Sep. 1960.

LONG PIG

In 1800 the American vessel *Argo* foundered
on a reef among the Fiji Islands, where in
those days cannibalism flourished. Taking
the historical wreck as a starting-point, this
novel imagines the fate of the survivors, a
small group of men among whom are the
stubborn and elderly Captain Berry, his mate
Oliver Slater, the huge seaman Barber and
the surly Solomon Doyle. It is a tale of the
impact of a handful of white men on a
ferocious and primitive society and of the
tensions and antagonisms which build up
among them in their isolation. Few, in the
end, live through the physical and psycho-
logical ordeal.

LONG PIG

RUSSELL FOREMAN

THE BOOK CLUB
121 CHARING CROSS ROAD
LONDON, W.C.2

Made and printed in Great Britain by
William Clowes and Sons, Limited, London and Beccles

Author's Note

There is some history in this tale of old Fiji. Though little is known of the wreck of the American ship *Argo* at the beginning of the nineteenth century, her name is important, for her crew were the first white men to remain for any length of time in these lovely islands, and one of them discovered sandalwood —an accident that led to what was, perhaps, the bloodiest decade in South Sea history.

What we know of *Argo* from old journals and official records is extraordinarily contradictory and in many respects not even in accordance with the recorded natural phenomena of the period. Her wrecking on Bukatatanoa reef—the Argo Reefs of modern charts—has been given variously as in 1800, 1803, 1804, and even 1806, but the comet (in the catalogues of the Royal Greenwich Observatory) seems to fix it definitely as having been in 1800. Not all of what has come down to us can be determined as surely. She has been described as brig and schooner, as being English and French, and even as owned in China. The fact that several ships of the name *Argo* appear on the registers of the time has only added to the confusion. The Fijian tradition that touches her is meagre. In the face of many discrepancies, improbabilities, and contradictions, I have taken the elements of what it would appear did happen, invented an order for them, and made them the basis of this novel.

So far as Fijian words are concerned, I have used the now official Bauan, ignoring differences of dialect in places as far east as Lau and as remote as Bua.

This sight on Loa caused great astonishment. They . . . saw what appeared to be men, but thought they must be gods, as they were biting live fire and had their ears wrapped up. This was because they had never seen pipes smoked nor the red caps the men were wearing . . . and then a double canoe called the *Taivaleta* set off for Loa and brought all the people to Oneata.

After . . . the Oneata people were affected . . . the hair of those dropped off and they suffered from diarrhoea. No medicine was of any use. Some of the people from the ship died. . . . I do not know whether they were eaten or buried. . . . Some of the sick were strangled as they had been ill a long time and had become offensive, and some were buried before they died.

The . . . chiefs first learned the use of firearms from the people of this ship.

—LAVENIA, the last survivor of
Vatutuva, Oneata, in *Namata*, 1893

LONG PIG: The human victim of a cannibal feast—from the terms employed by Maori and Polynesian cannibals.
—*Webster's New International Dictionary*

Chapter 1

HIDEOUSLY, the cry seemed to hang on in the air. It rose over the surging run of the brig through the night, the creaking of her rigging, the working of her hull; it rose over all this movement of water and wood and canvas and rope, and it set the ship alive with a tumbling, wild-eyed press of men.

Oliver Slater, the brig's mate, heard the cry as he put his foot on the bottom step of the poop companion. It seemed so fantastic, so remote and awful a threat that at first he could not believe, but stood there, waiting for it to come again.

Now it was louder.

"Breakers. . . . Breakers a-a-a-head. . . ." An old man's voice that broke on the words, then repeated them.

Slater barely heard it the third time, for he was racing forward. He ran into a man who was pushing groggily out from the fo'c'sle on to the deck. In three strides he mounted the ladder. Thomas Peppercorn, the greying man on look-out, turned, his arm thrown out pointing forward. "Breakers, Sir," he said hoarsely.

"Where away?" Slater called, stumbling in his rush on the spray-wet deck.

"Dead ahead—an' on both port an' starboard bows. 'Tis reef. Ye can hear it thunderin'." As Slater peered into the black night Peppercorn put back his head and called again. Now astern of them came shouts, muffled cries and curses, the uncertain movement of frightened men who ran from one rail to the other, hand over hand, peering forward.

"Ye see it?" Peppercorn asked.

"Aye, Pepper, I do. 'Tis reef—God damn it." Facing aft, Slater called to the second mate: "Mr. Doyle."

"Aye," came the answer from the poop, a sullen sound, pulled at by the wind.

"Message to the cap'n. A heavy break across our bows!"

I

Slater waited until he heard Doyle's answer, then turned forward again to the line of woolly, breaking water that stretched like some gigantic hawser across the brig's course.

Within the minute Captain Berry was up beside Slater, who stood now straddling the heel of the jib boom, his hand clutching a stay above his head. After the brightness of his cabin, Berry was unable to see the reef for a few moments, precious seconds which gnawed at Slater.

Then he saw it. "Jesus, Mister, 'tis close!" he said quickly. Awe, fear, even disbelief filled his old-man's voice. Without looking aft he cried his order to the helm: "Hard aport y'wheel." Then he added to Slater: "Reef", and to himself, "an' no warnin', no warnin' at all." Muttering under his breath, he pulled himself up to Peppercorn, who was standing in the very eyes of the ship.

Doyle repeated Berry's order, but as Morgan, the helmsman, leaned, the helm already starting to move under his hands, Doyle jumped on to the grating, pushed Morgan from the wheel and throwing the whole of his strength behind it sent it spinning round. As they waited those dreadful seconds for the brig to answer, Berry growled: "Damn ye, feel y'rudder." There was a desperate edge in his voice as if he saw already the death of his lovely ship.

'Twas time, thought Slater after, that beat her. He remembered Berry calling for the lead, then ordering the jib to be doused and the topgallant sails clewed up. It was not panic, nor was it indecision on Berry's part—but so rapidly was *Argo* boxed in by reef that minutes after Peppercorn's first cry it was plain there was no way out. Broken water was all about them; even as she went to port more reef showed. It grew out of the sea to port and starboard of them, and as her heading changed it appeared astern of her. It seemed not as if *Argo* had come upon reef, but as if reef had come upon her, had been thrust up from the depths of the ocean by earthquake or volcano.

Berry saw his brig must strike and cried to Slater to have the men down out of the rigging. She was heeling under the pressure of wind and helm when there came the first deadly kiss of the coral, a shudder that danced through her. Some of the men clung to standing rigging, others sought shelter (as if there could be any) in the lee of the poop break; a few, stupidly, grouped themselves about the mainmast and Slater called to them to get out from under and watch for falling spars and gear. Lester Light, the steward, threw himself to his knees and began to pray out loud, hands clasped before him.

Jonas Day, the carpenter, leaped to the launch—the one boat left seaworthy by the hurricane of weeks before—grabbing at its cover, beginning to strip it, calling to others to free the falls. Men stumbled in the dark, cursing, pushing at one another. Then she struck again, a graze as if she had moved on to a greased slide, and then stuck, locked as in a groove. Until this moment Jeremy Tucker, the ship's boy, had stood it bravely, hands gripping the starboard rail capping, eyes wide as he stared into the tumbling, phosphorescent water about them. But with this graze, and the shudder which ended it, setting his feet vibrating on the deck, he broke. He ran from the rail, darting between the men, forward on to the fo'c'sle. Slater heard his cry, and, as the boy reached him, he caught him in his arms and bent to offer a word of comfort.

But the word never came; it was on Slater's lips when *Argo* struck with terrible force. For an instant Slater thought she might run over into deep water, for all about her now the sea was so confused as to mask what might be shoal and what might be deep. But she hit again, and the reef water seemed to rise up and claim her. It poured in over her rail, solid and warm, swirling rope and gear, rushing at her crew as they staggered to hold themselves on her slanting, trembling decks. She rose on a sea, carrying all this water with her, streaming back, streaked with sea fire, from her freeing ports and scuppers. Then with a rending of her timbers she slewed and ground to a stop.

Slater, clinging to Jeremy, was thrown against the inboard end of the port cat-head, Berry against the iron crown of the capstan; everyone was pitched from his place, Peppercorn almost being catapulted into the water. Her mainmast cracked and another sea, driving hard up under her, brought it crashing to the deck. Mingled with the sound of the water rushing across her decks, the thunder of the reef about her, the cursing of the men, was the prayer of Light, pinned now on the top

3

of the after hatch under a tangle of canvas and rigging, his voice breaking, sobbing in his fear. Each succeeding wave drove the brig on harder until, holed in several places, her garboards opened, her rudder wrenched from its pintles, the water rushed into her and she sank to her rubbing strakes and lay trembling.

Berry got half-way to his feet, then leaned against the capstan, a cut on his head running blood down one side of his face. Slater moved, disentangling himself from Jeremy.

"Look to the men, Mister," Berry gasped out. "I've struck m'head. An' the launch, Mister, the launch. We don't know how long she'll stick here—deep water, maybe. She might slide off any minute. *See to it, Mr. Slater.*" There was a tormented edge in the old man's high-pitched voice.

"Aye aye, Sir," muttered Slater. "Jeremy, stay here with Cap'n Berry."

"Are ye hurt any, boy?" asked Berry, looking for Jeremy in the filmy darkness.

"Nay, Sir. Thank'ee, Sir."

Slater started aft, picking his way through the tangle of rigging that cluttered the fo'c'sle deck. *Argo* lay now almost on even keel but was bumping hard, and as Slater moved he could hear as well as feel her timbers grinding against the coral.

"Mister," Berry called after him, "call the roll."

Slater got to the rail and looked aft to the poop. "Mr. Doyle," he cried.

"Aye."

"Ye're on the poop?"

"I am."

"Morgan still wi' ye?"

"Aye."

"I'm goin' to call each man." Now he looked down into the waist of the ship. "As ye hear me call y'name, answer."

"Aye aye, sir," came from somewhere beneath him.

"Who's that?"

"Elisha Hockin'."

"Are ye hurt, Hocking?"

"Nay—be a bloody miracle."

"Good man. Homer Wilkinson."

4

" 'Ere, Mr. Slater." It was Wilkinson's voice, but distorted by the fear in it. Slater paused, wondering if fear showed in his voice too.

"Light, Lester Light?" he called.

No answer came from the steward, and Slater called his name again, and added: "Answer, man, if ye be there."

"He's here, Sir. But jammed under the main riggin'."

"That ye, Barber?"

"Aye, Sir."

"Is he hurt, do ye know?"

"He's still prayin'——"

"Then get him out."

"We're tryin' to, Sir."

"Who's with ye?"

"Me, Sir, Peleg Leadbeater."

"Lend Barber and Leadbeater a hand, someone. Wilky, look lively, lad, jump to it."

Slater heard the movement and saw it, faint in the light of the sea fire which swirled about the brig. He was about to go down when they got Light, who stood from the hatch, rubbing a shoulder.

"Are ye all right, Light?" Slater called.

"Thanks be to God, Sir, I am. Saved."

"Stow that about bein' saved, Les." It was Barber's voice, big, like the man. "For all ye know ye'll be makin' a meal for a bunch o' hungry cannibals afore the day's out."

"Jonas Day," Slater went on, calling them not in any order, but as they came to his mind.

"Take more'n a mainmast to do me in, Sir, or a coral reef."

Day was a talker, but Slater gave him no time to get started. "Pain, Jeb Pain," he called.

"Afloat, for the time bein', God muck it." It was a savage, frightened voice.

"Scared, Jeb?" Morgan's quiet voice floated from aft.

"Nay," returned Pain, and he cursed. "I'm enjoyin' it. Sam Barber's right—we'll be eaten, as like as not. God damn the day I ever clapped eyes on this ship."

Then came Barber's voice cutting in on the last of Pain's

5

words. "Have ye seen the boy, Sir? He don't seem to be no-where hereabouts."

"He's here, Sam. Wi' the cap'n." But though Slater spoke to Barber, he looked to where Pain stood, for he was afraid of the fear he had heard, the panic which might be stirring. He sensed the need to stamp on it lest it grow and smother them. But before he could say anything Berry called to him.

"Mister, I clean forgot about Powell, sick o' the dysentery. See to him. Christ, I'm half stunned. See to it, Mr. Slater—in the fo'c'sle."

Jeb Pain would have to wait. Slater started for the ladder, but Powell's voice drifted up from below him. "I'm out, Cap'n."

"Where are ye, Powell?"

"Here, Sir, be the for'ard hatch."

"Are ye all right?"

"Near enough, Sir," Powell called back weakly. "On me pins, at any rate."

"Don't go movin' about. Stay where ye are until I get done." Then louder, looking out along the deck again, Slater went on: "Silas——" But the rest of the name died on his lips. Silas? Ye fool, Slater, Silas is gone. He stood there, cursing his stupidity, sensing the sudden quietness in the men. *Argo* shivered, as though the mention of the dead negro's name touched her too.

Then Powell shattered the pause with a curious cry, part remorse, part anger, part wonder that such a thing could be. "Look! The dawn."

Slater turned with the rest of them and looked east over the port rail where the faintest glimmering revealed the sea's edge. To the men of the *Argo* it could have been the first of all the dawns that had ever been; a trembling birth to all that was new and terrible, unseen before.

Powell's voice went on. "The day—but what, be Jesus, is the good o' ye?" He paused, as if seeking the strength it took. "Ye've come too late, ye thrice-cursed whore of a day. 'Twould have hurt ye none to glimmer sooner."

In the deadly silence that followed, Berry struggled aft to

Slater and put his hand on his shoulder. "Is that ye, Duke Powell?" he called, a shake in his voice.

"The same, Sir," said Powell, the Englishness strong in his voice. He looked up to the fo'c'sle, where the images of Berry and Slater could be seen against the rail in the beginning daylight.

"We're not done yet, Duke Powell, not be a long shot," cried Berry, and he drew a deep breath. His high-pitched voice issued clear before him. "An' neither ye nor no man here's to think it. With God's help we'll come out o' this. We've the launch. She's still tight, ain't she, Day?"

"So far as I can make out she be, Sir. O' course——"

"Then we're not done yet," he went on, an effort needed now to keep his voice pitched up. "By the livin' God we're not. Other men've overcome worse than this, an' what others can do, we can. Now"—he paused as he moved to lean heavily against Slater—"We'll . . . we'll be abandonin' the brig, lads. See to the launch, Mr. Doyle."

But before Doyle could move, Barber asked: "Might I be sayin' somethin' to ye, Cap'n Berry?"

"Aye, Barber, ye may."

"Then I'd wish ye luck, Sir. All o' the best."

Slater thought that Barber had taken leave of his senses. He looked down and saw him clearly now, his big, black-bearded face upturned. Several of the men looked round to him. Then Slater understood. He turned to Berry, who was regarding Barber with a hurt, bitter expression. "I know what he means, Sir," Slater said quietly. " 'Tis the new year."

Berry remained motionless, letting the words sink into him. Then he said, very slowly: "So it is, aye," and raising his head he looked out to Barber. "Thank'ee, Sam. Thank'ee. An' might I wish ye—all o' ye—the same good luck. The new year. But, nay, be thunder, 'tis more than just the new year—'tis the new century. 'Tis 1800. Dear God, an' to think it saw me losin' m'ship."

Then Berry said to Slater: "We've time, I think; she seems to lie easy enough now. See to an issue o' grog. All hands, afore we make away."

Slater had his foot on the top step of the ladder when Berry

7

said: "An', Mr. Slater, I'll be all right. 'Tis the crack I got on m'head. Quite right in a little while."

Their eyes met in the half-light—Slater's blue and hard and bright; Berry's old and grey-flecked, tired and hurt, the eyes of a man trying to understand why this should happen to him. Slater did not speak; there was nothing he could think of to say. But as he started down the ladder he wondered whether Berry was hurt more than he appeared to be. A hit on the head could do strange things to a man.

The new day slid steadily out to the brig, touching with its light the tangle of gear the men worked in. As it pushed away the night, it exposed by the line after line of breaking water the great size of the trap into which *Argo* had sailed. To the east and north the system seemed to have an end, but ahead of the brig and to the west of it the silver tentacles stretched until they were lost over the curve of the broken ocean.

Now for the first time in weeks the sun rose with the assurance of flying-fish weather. Soon it beat down upon the little brig with a fierce intensity, its beams slanting through the green water about her, glancing off tiny, suspended particles as they washed through the reef and the weed that trailed from the copper of her shattered hull.

Chapter 2

Noon on that first day of the year 1800 found Berry and Slater and Wilkinson standing upon the peak of a tiny islet. Little more than a rock, its only vegetation was a few coconuts, wind-twisted screw pines and a dry, coarse grass. Close by, to the west, lay a larger island, and all about these two islands and away to the north there stretched a vast lagoon, all but linked, so it seemed from that hill, to the system of reef which had claimed the brig.

They were armed, Berry and Slater each with a brace of pistols and Wilkinson with a flintlock musket. Berry had a telescope to his eye and was looking out to the other island. He was hatless, and a crust of dry blood traced the shape of a wound which ran into his scalp above his left ear. In the sea wind of the hill his thin, greying hair lifted. Suddenly he took down the glass and turned to Slater. "I'm damned, Mister, if I can see smoke now. Yet I saw it. I'm positive I did, as we were comin' in here this mornin'."

"Let me try again," said Slater, putting out his hand for the glass. He focused it and began to search the mint-green slopes and dark, mottled valleys.

Slater was a shorter man than Berry, broad and muscular, his skin touched with the darkness that marks any man of thirty-odd years who has been at sea since he was not much more than a child. Like Berry he wore duck trousers, but Berry wore a shirt of some heavy stuff and a jacket with tarnished gilt buttons and Slater only a light shirt, the sleeves of which ended above his elbows. He had on a kind of grass hat he'd bought in China, and its wide brim was pushed back as he held the glass up.

The other island, he judged, was three miles long and about half that wide. Much of its surface was covered by dense scrub, its weather side smothered under vines and creepers which in some places ran to the very edge of the water. The eastern end was furrowed with canyons and bays into which the sea ran. About this end many tiny islets thrust up through the lagoon, mushrooms of limestone, and a spit that ran out into deep water had been carved into fantastic shapes by the wind and rain and the restless, eroding wash of the tides. To Slater it seemed a forbidding place, accentuating his isolation. For the first time he felt the helplessness of the castaway.

He took down the glass. "No sign o' savages," he said slowly, still looking at the island, "but the place looks damp."

"Aye," said Berry, nodding his head, "it does. Boggy I'd say."

"That could mean fever."

9

"I'd not thought o' that. . . . An' ye saw no smoke at all?"

"Nay, Sir."

"I tell ye I saw it, Mister."

"I'm not doubtin' ye did, not for a moment, Cap'n Berry. Ye'll remember that mate's tale in Bristol, how an Englishman named Bligh was chased hereabouts. 'Tweren't long ago—ten, twelve years maybe."

"But Bligh was some way more west o' here when they got after him."

" 'Twas these same islands—Bligh's Islands as they are upon the charts, the Fijis."

Berry said bitterly: "Then I take it that ye'd counsel making off straight away?"

"Aye, I would."

"What about our plan to deck an' rig the launch?"

"Let's find a more likely-lookin' place first."

"Who's to say there is one?"

"There must be, Sir. We know these islands stretch west from here. Surely there's some smaller island where there'd not be the same chance o' bein' discovered by the Indians. Our boat is sound, we've water an' food."

"Ye realise, don't ye," and now there was annoyance in Berry's voice, "that 'tis all o' five hundred leagues from here to Port Jackson?"

"Aye, I do."

"An' that this is the season for hurricanes in these parts?"

"I'm not likely to forget that," Slater said quietly, "not after the storm we went through. But we'd be unlucky, Sir, ye must admit, damned unlucky, to strike another."

"Men've been damned unlucky before this, Mr. Slater. Imagine what we went through in *Argo*, imagine that in a ship's launch, decked or not. An' another thing, while we've water for a v'yage to Port Jackson, we've precious little to go dippin' into while we work at deckin' an' riggin' the boat. Now"—and Berry pointed towards the other island—"there's water over there."

"Be the look of it, too much."

"Even so, but there's water. Nay, Mister, we landed on this bit of a rock to get time to think, decide what was best to do.

I see now two things—one, we've got to get the launch decked; an' two, we've to find some place where we can work on her without broachin' our water casks."

"Where there's water there'll be Indians, ye can bet on that."

"Suppose then that we were to come upon friendly natives. They might be o' the greatest help to us, Mister. With the food they'd let us have, as well as water, we'd sail with our stores untouched."

"You saw smoke; that means savages. An' I'd stake m'bones there's fever there too."

"All I can say, Mister, is that we didn't choose the bloody place. God damn it, we've lost our ship. We could have been drowned be now, or swimmin' for it. At least we're alive—or the most of us are," he added more quietly.

Berry had no sooner finished than Wilkinson swore loudly. Wilkinson had turned from the island and was looking north to where the brig lay. From the hill she looked like some lovely model that a wanton child had smashed. Her foremast still stood, canted as though she were rolling, and from its yards hung a few shreds of tattered sail. Over her decks the litter of wreck was sprawled and in the water alongside spars floated, tangled in gear—sail and rope and wire and chain—and rubbed at her as the waves curled up astern, surged over the reef and rushed along her sides. Ahead, in the lagoon's green acres, moved the fins of slow patrolling sharks, attracted by the salt meat jettisoned from the heavily laden launch.

"She's shiftin', Cap'n Berry," said Wilkinson, and as Berry and Slater turned to look at the ship a wave broke astern of her, a climbing sea that swept up over the reef and buried the starboard rail in a white flurry.

"She'll not be lastin' long," Wilkinson muttered, and he darted small, dark eyes at Berry.

"'Tis the coral. Ships don't last long on coral." And unable to bear the sight of his lovely brig grinding herself to pieces Berry turned back to the island again.

Argo had been built to Berry's order, in Boston, on the North River; he had watched her building, as she grew from timber into a ship. He had seen her frames rise up, of oak, and her knees and breast-hooks adzed from the hackmatack that grew along the river; he had seen yellow pine come in from Ipswich and white oak from Danvers. He had stood morning after morning looking down-stream from the Hanover Bridge. From there he could count eleven shipyards and when *Argo* was building there was a ship in every one of them. At daybreak he would rise and trudge with the shipwrights across the dewy pastures, following the bank of the river, shipyard after shipyard swallowing the men in twos and threes, yards in which they would work from that dawn until the coming dark. Now in the end of his lovely brig all he could see clearly was the beginning of her.

He'd been lucky to get her. It was the result of a fortunate speculation in a voyage that had returned one hundred and fifty thousand dollars on an outlay of thirty-three thousand. Not all his, but enough of it to get him *Argo*. She'd cost him forty-five hundred dollars. His wife, Belle Berry, had wanted her with an orange waist and dark green topsides. And these he had given her, along with lovely quickwork about her bows and stern.

He'd made good use of her; driven her hard into any port that smelled of money and a quick turn-round. This was his second venture through these waters. She was out of Canton now, bound for Port Jackson, the penal colony of New South Wales, and, so far as he knew, was the first ship to make so much easting on the run.

Her cargo was now much the same as it had been on her first voyage south. Rum was the bulk of it—for rum, in fact any liquor, paid handsomely in New South Wales—and she had some gin, and a few pipes of brandy as well, that had run the British blockade. The rest of it was salt meat, yellow nankeen cloth, some sugar and molasses and a few dozen cooking stoves that he thought would be a good speculation in Port Jackson.

From its start this voyage had been bad. *Argo* had been plagued by fluky winds, calms in which she rolled horribly, and storms—sudden tropical squalls which screamed out of hazy horizons and ripped into her viciously. And then, after days of waiting for it, after a weather-glass lower than either

Berry or Slater had ever known, after her crew had been driven near to the limit of what men can stand of a rolling, bruising ship, came the hurricane.

But she had survived the shrieking thirty hours of it, though she had lost two men.

Suddenly Berry shook his head, as if trying to shake off all this of the past. He turned to Slater and said: "But, Mister, ye'll allow we need water. Ye must."

"Aye, I do. But we don't need it yet. We could work on the launch, using the water we have, then when she were decked and rigged make away and the first likely-lookin' land we saw we could water at. We'd be makin' for New South Wales all the time."

"But suppose we are sighted, an' attacked, maybe, while we was waterin'?"

"We're not without arms, Sir. We've the swivel gun, an' muskets, plenty o' powder an' shot. We'd be able to defend ourselves, and, the launch being rigged, we'd be able to put away under sail."

"Ye might have the answer," Berry said slowly. "There are things like this—there's only one right way about them, and if ye're wrong, then ye're dead wrong. . . . Ye might be right, Mister. God only knows."

But looking at him Slater felt that no matter what he might say to the contrary Berry had made up his mind and, having done so, would never alter it. He well knew Berry's stubbornness. He'd seen him hold to a course that had run his ship into dangerous, shoaling water, not because he was a bad seaman, but because he'd said he'd do it in one tack and, by thunder, he was going to. Slater had seen him then, walking his poop, holding on, while the helmsman darted anxious glances at him and a rocky coast came ever nearer; while the watch stopped in their work and looked aft to the poop; while some, gamer than others, left their places, went to the rail and peered over-side for sign of shoal.

Folly or not, there was much to admire in such a man; in that instance the ship had cleared foul water by a cable's length and, squaring away, had left another ship still tacking in a

13

dangerous channel when darkness fell; Berry, with a top-gallant breeze, was driving his ship in fair water and was adding to his reputation as a master who was prepared to take a chance and who, moreover, got away with it. But no man was deceived, least of all Berry, for to sail a windship thus is to flirt with disaster. If the breeze had died, Berry's reputation wouldn't have fetched them clear. But the wind had held, as it seemed it always did for Berry.

Slater had seen Berry carry winds through parts notorious for their windlessness, had seen him make tides that other vessels had missed. He had seen him, with a cannonball from a British frigate through his staysail, standing at the binnacle, cursing in his high-pitched voice, taking his ship close in under Nantucket South Shoals, threading his way with uncanny sea sense through water the frigate wouldn't follow him into. And he had seen him thrash a lateener and then, not stopping to take the vessel, put into Gibraltar and sell his cargo at a handsome profit. Slater knew the man for his luck, but he knew him also for his pigheadedness.

"Very well, Mr. Slater, we can do no more here. We'd best be gettin' down to the men. Wilkinson, ye'll stay here as look-out."

"Aye aye, Sir."

"Keep a sharp watch on the island yonder an' if ye see any smoke, any movement at all, come down and report it at once." With Slater following, Berry walked off the hill.

Wilkinson was a wiry little man with tiny screwed-up eyes. When they had gone he cast about for a shady place from which to keep his look-out. The sun was almost directly overhead, and hot; the sweat ran on him, sticking his shirt to his back. Just over the brow of the hill stood a clump of four or five screw pines. Putting his musket in the crook of his right arm he went to them and set himself down.

The island shimmered in the heat that rose from the lagoon, the water between the islands like still, green ink into which blue had been poured in great, uneven patches. Far out, near the middle of the stretch, birds were fishing, diving upon the water, making tiny eruptions of spray where they hit and disappeared, and rising, moment later, gulping fish. Wilkinson

14

watched, wondering about it all, about being there, about the Chinee silk he'd bought in Batavia for his Lydia. Silk! She'd be bloody lucky if she ever saw her Homer, let alone Chinee silk, or the teapot ye could just about see through if ye held it to the light, an' the tea to go in it—half a chest o' hyson. Aye, be Jesus, hyson, an' wrecked on a cannibal isle, or next to one. There must be Indians, if there was smoke. And the mate said someone'd been chased hereabouts. There was savages all right. What luck! An hour later an' we'd have seen it. Though ye'd need to see it in time, even be daylight, for once ye'd got in there'd be damned little chance of ye gettin' out. Doyle had been right.

It made ye think. Now if Doyle had been cap'n? But, nay, Wilky, if Sol Doyle had been cap'n you wouldn't have been in *Argo*, not after y'first v'yage. That was sure, as sure as ye was in this, up to y'bleedin' eyes. An' what was it that Doyle had said about mutiny to the mate? He and Leadbeater hadn't heard it all, they was too far away from him, what with the breeze blowin', but the word had been used. God Almighty! *Mutiny.*

Well, for himself he'd be with the cap'n, and so would Mr. Slater be. Aye, Oliver Slater'd have no part o' mutiny. Slater had been wild at Doyle, said Leadbeater. So he ought to be, if Sol Doyle had been urgin' mutiny. Now who'd be for Doyle? Jeb Pain. Pain'd always had time for Doyle. But ye couldn't tell; ye didn't know, ever, for sure how a thing like this'd turn out until it còme. Not even how ye'd go yeself, because ye had to look to yeself; ye couldn't be blamed for that.

Wilkinson looked up at a large seafowl, which swooped over the islet and then passed on over the hill, and wondered whether Berry and Slater were down yet. God, but it was hot! Yet there was a breeze, ye could see it ripplin' the water sometimes. The seafowl returned above him and he watched its steady, diving flight. Then it swooped back over the hill-top once more. Looking down, Wilkinson plucked a stem of grass and put it into his mouth. He leaned back against the screw pine, and as his back touched the tree he looked out at the island and saw the canoe.

He leaped to his feet, sending his musket clattering to the

ground, shouting at the top of his voice as he ran back to the top of the hill: *"Cap'n Berry! A canoe! The Injuns, Sir. A war canoe!"*

Berry and Slater were more than half-way down; they wheeled and came running back.

"Just as I was sittin' there," began Wilkinson as Slater ran up to him, well ahead of Berry. "See, Sir." He pointed to the canoe. It stood out clearly against the apple-green water, running from behind the southern end of the island and threading its way between the coral outcrops with incredible speed. It was a double canoe, sixty or more feet long, the two hulls joined by a platform on which it carried its mast and crew. On the mast was set a huge leg-of-mutton sail.

"An' there's y'smoke too, Cap'n," said Wilkinson excitely. "There, from that valley yonder, astern o' the point. Is it them talkin', would ye say, Sir? Once I heard a man say all Indians talked with smoke."

Berry glanced to where Wilkinson pointed. "Cookin' fires, probably," he said disinterestedly.

"Holy Mary," muttered Wilkinson. "Cookin' fires, an' they be cannibals. Here, Sir, we'd best get out o' this, while we can." He looked wildly about, the beginnings of panic starting in him.

"When I said cookin' fires, Wilkinson, I didn't mean that just because they're cannibals they'll be eatin' us, or even want to." For a second longer Berry let his gaze rest upon Wilkinson, then he turned back to the canoe, saying to Slater as he did: "What do ye make of it, Mister?"

Slater spoke with the telescope to his eye. "There's a good fifty or sixty Indians aboard her, armed to the teeth. 'Tis a war party, nothin' surer."

"They've seen the brig, I guess," said Berry, and Wilkinson's eyes snapped to him, a ferrety, frightened look in them.

"Here, have a look for yeself," said Slater, handing the glass to the captain.

Berry swore. He could see the warriors quite plainly through the telescope. Forward of the mast were gathered men who appeared to be armed with clubs, and about the deck of the canoe were piles of weapons. Her sail was made of some mat-like broadly woven stuff.

16

"She's a tricky craft to handle," he said slowly, watching the two men at her long steering sweep.

"Aye, but will ye look at the speed of her. In a wind she'd out-sail a full-rigged ship."

"One thing's clear," Berry said as he looked down the telescope. "To attempt to run from her in the launch is out of the question."

"In heaven's name why, Sir?" said Slater. "We've the swivel. Make away now, while we've time to get the boat into deep water."

Berry shook his head. " 'Twould be to invite attack, Mister. We don't know what sort of weapons they've got."

"To hell with their weapons! Our chance lies in makin' best use of our own. God, Sir, if we wait for them and they come ashore fightin' they'll overrun us, once our first volley's done."

" 'Twouldn't be no different were we to meet 'em at sea."

" 'Twould be all the difference in the world, Cap'n Berry. The swivel's a sea-goin' piece——"

"They mightn't even have seen us, Mister. They've seen the brig, aye, I'll allow ye that, but that don't mean to say they've seen us too."

"Christ, Cap'n Berry"—and anger began now to creep into Slater's voice—"have ye forgotten the launch? If they're makin' for the brig they'll soon see that."

Slater watched Berry as he looked at the canoe. This was the Berry who'd made up his mind, and, by God—uncertain as he might be about the outcome—he wasn't going to alter it. Yet Slater could see doubt nagging at him.

"I was forgettin' the launch," Berry said slowly.

"If they come at us, the noise of the swivel would probably scare them off. But if it didn't and they made to attack us, then a whiff o' grape would soon change their minds. We don't need these people, Sir. 'Tis not as though we were washed ashore without food or water."

Berry stood looking at the canoe. Slater was full of foreboding; again he remembered what that mate in Bristol had told him of the chasing Bligh got. Bligh had thought that the people of these islands were hostile; like a good commander he had played safe and had not tried to discover otherwise. There

17

was the difference between them; Berry, it seemed, wanted to find out, the hard way. Their trump card was the little gun; ashore it would be next to useless, for its effectiveness lay in a concentrated target such as this heavily-manned canoe would offer coming up astern of the launch. Suddenly Slater imagined them trying to use the swivel on a target of savages strung out along the beach and in his anguish and temper he cursed aloud.

Berry glanced sideways at him: "Nay, Mister, we stay. If we can get the right side o' these people they'll be damned useful to us. An' we know there's water over there. I'm not sayin' y'plan to make straight away is not a good one, for it is—'tis just that it seems a mite too risky."

By the living God, thought Slater, a mite too risky! And what of this—meeting these savages on their own ground, when ye could be at sea, armed as ye was meant to be?

"Now listen, Wilkinson," Berry went on, "ye'll stay here as look-out. When the canoe gets off this side o' the point"—Berry gestured with the telescope to the little promontory which made one horn of the cove—"fire y'musket in the air to warn us. But mind it is in the air. No pot shots at 'em. Understand?"

"Aye, Sir, I do. An' can I come down then?"

"Ye'd best. For if Mr. Slater be right, we'll be needin' every musket we've got."

Before Berry's gaze, Slater's anger yielded. He liked and respected Berry and found in the softness of his grey-flecked eyes much that soothed him. "I've told ye, Mister," Berry went on slowly, "there's some things where there's no two ways about it—ye're either right, or ye're wrong, and if ye're wrong then ye're dead wrong. This is one o' those things. But I don't think I'm wrong. 'Tis a gamble, for no man can say for certain. I've ye behind me, Mr. Slater?"

"Ye have, Sir. Forgive me m'anger."

"There's nothin' to forgive. Ye've but spoke y'mind and I admire the man who does. Ye know that. . . . Now we'll be gettin' down to the lads." Slater noticed that the captain stumbled as they started down.

18

Chapter 3

It was a narrow beach upon which the *Argo* men had landed, a shallow half-moon of bright sand. Above it the walls of the cove ran up steeply, scattered over with the thin screw pines and under-nourished coconuts. As they came down the hill Berry told Slater his plan. Slater listened carefully and agreed that it was the only one with any chance of success, now that he had committed them to meeting the savages on the island.

But Slater was far from happy about it. He felt he had been caught out of his element, as if nothing he had ever known had prepared him for what he now faced. Yet as a seaman he had thought of shipwreck often enough; he had never known a ship overdue, never heard of underwriters paying up, but that he imagined himself a member of her crew. He thought of that now, coming down the hill, and wondered if he had stretched his luck too far.

He'd made enough to leave the sea and start a business in Boston. He'd been offered good starts; his friend Paul Revere had offered to take him into his business, and he'd do well there, for Paul was getting help from the Government with his copper mill, rolling sheets for American bottoms. Revere copper was in *Argo*—not her sheeting (that was English) but her fastenings, which had been made in the foundry in Lynn Street. Hartt's yard, close by, could have used him. Boston, all the coast, was booming. And he had many friends well enough set up to help him to a start.

But he had stayed with Berry, a man long past the average age for a shipmaster. Not that he had lost by it, Berry had seen to that. No mate out of Boston did better than Slater. Nor had he squandered his earnings; he was not married, and he owned the house his father lived in on Hanover Street, as well as another next to it.

It was not the fear of death alone that worked in him now. This was something new, and its newness weakened him. At

19

sea, in anything which touched his trade, he did not doubt himself; but it was a confidence born of the sea, and fed by it. As he walked this uneasiness spread in him, draining him, it seemed, of all ability, suddenly, frighteningly. He wondered was Berry touched by it, and whether Berry had seen it in him. He glanced at him, but saw nothing. And there was Doyle, and what he'd said about heaving to. There was that whole bloody business on the poop that night, that thing which proved nothing—except that Solomon Doyle had been right.

They came in sight of the launch. It was partly beached, its stern lapped by the water. Over its bows ran a line bent to a light anchor, one fluke buried half-way up the sand. Slater saw the men seated in the shade of the pandanus trees; Doyle was apart from them, looking out across the light-spangled water to the pattern of reef which lay west of the islet.

In all the crew only Sam Barber was bigger than Solomon Doyle. But Barber was the biggest man Slater had known, outside of freaks. Doyle was a handsome man, dark, and, like Barber, full-bearded. But whereas Barber was generally liked, Doyle was a surly character, hard to know and harder to like. But Slater owned he'd never seen a sharper man aloft, and Berry—never one to praise without good reason—admitted his worth alow, but added, whenever he spoke thus of Doyle, that with no officer had he been less friendly. "I'll put it to ye this way, Mister," Berry had once said to Slater. " 'Tis sailors ye want at sea, not bloody preachers. Doyle's a dull devil, an' a savage one, as well as bein' so silent sometimes ye'd think he was dumb, but put a deck under him an' he knows what he's about.

"But he's a queer cuss. Men dislike him, hate him even, on sight usually. I know I did, or near about, and wouldn't have had him ship wi' me only he'd been strong recommended and I needed a second mate bad, as ye'll remember. But with women? The wenches Solly Doyle has comin' about askin' for him, and down at the wharf to wave him off to sea—tears in their eyes as like as not! Just about the finest women that lie in any port. The man's a marvel when it comes to a woman, damn me if he isn't. An' I'll tell ye somethin' else about him— I'd rather have him a friend than an enemy."

Since the hurricane, Slater noticed, Doyle had been more morose than ever. He had done his work superbly; had earned a word of thanks from Berry and one of praise from Slater, who had seen him secure the shattered remains of the spanker boom, seen him clinging to the stump, disappear under water as *Argo* tore down the back of the sea that took Davidson and Silas; seen him somehow get back aboard (no man could help him without the risk of almost certain death) and passing a line about the boom lash it down. Had the spar not been secured it would have wiped the wheel clean from the deck. Rudderless, *Argo* would have lasted but minutes. To broach would have meant the end.

Now Slater looked away from Doyle as Jonas Day spoke. Berry was wiping his face with a silk handkerchief. As he took it down he glanced at it and saw a little fresh blood from his wound. Day said: " 'Tis hot enough for ye, Sir?"

Berry put the handkerchief into his pocket. "Aye, that she be, Day. An' a steep enough climb down from that damned hill. Now, look ye, lads," and his eyes moved among them. "There's a canoe on the way, and 'tis no use foolin' ourselves, she's a war canoe. Fifty or more warriors aboard her."

One or two of the men shifted uneasily, but none of them spoke. Light turned a frightened pair of eyes to Berry and then bending his head started to mumble a prayer. Doyle turned away from the water and faced the captain.

"Now the plan is this," said Berry, glancing away from Doyle. "We wait here for the canoe. . . ." He paused there, looking from one man to the other as if expecting someone to say something. Except for Light's muttered prayer there was silence. "We don't know, lads," Berry went on, "but the Indians might be friendly, in which case they could be o' the greatest use to us."

Again he paused and Peppercorn, sitting next to Light, said quietly: "Stow that, will ye, Les. Can't hear the cap'n properly wi' ye mutterin' y'prayers in m'ear." Light's voice fell, but Slater saw that he continued to pray, for his lips went on moving.

Berry said then: "There's enough cover on this hill here, as ye can see, an' in all 'tis not a bad place to defend. I've known worse, a damn sight worse, an' any rate we mightn't have to fight. Please God we won't, but we must be ready for it."

Berry took his handkerchief from his pocket and was wiping his face again, when Doyle said: "What about the launch?"

"I was coming to that, Mister," Berry said. "We'll anchor her off, within handy range for the swivel. But that don't mean, lads, that we're spoilin' for a fight. We're not. If fightin' comes, then 'twill be the Indians as'll start it. No man here's to fire until he gets the order. But if the order does come, then for God's sake don't lose y'heads. We've plenty o' powder an' shot, but use it intelligently. Take careful aim and fire for a vital spot—chest or gut'd be best—and don't fire until ye're reasonably sure o' hittin' y'man."

The men were watching Berry intently. Pepper's old eyes were almost closed in the glare; on Morgan's round face was sweat, and his lips were open.

Berry turned back to Doyle. "Right, Mister. See to the launch. Ye'll need three men for her. She's to be anchored about a cable's length off the beach. Mr. Slater, who's the best shot with the swivel—Sam Barber?"

"Aye, Sir."

Barber grinned and got to his feet, nodding his head and showing his teeth white against the bush of his beard. "With pleasure, Sir," he said. Looking at him, Slater was reminded of a picture he'd seen of Henry Morgan, the pirate. But he liked Barber; he was among the best seamen he'd known, a cool head, no man to get rattled.

"But mind, Barber," said Berry, "no firin' unless ye get the order."

"I mind, Sir," answered Barber, suddenly serious.

"Then give him Elisha Hocking, Mr. Doyle. And you, Peleg Leadbeater, you go too. An', Elisha, if it comes to fightin', don't lose y'head. When Barber swings the gun, sponge it cleanly and get out o' the way for Peleg to load. An', Peleg, ram it well."

"Will I leave the grape in her, Sir?" asked Barber.

"Aye, ye'd best. The cove's so small ye'll do more damage with small shot than round. Now, off wi' ye, lads. We've little

22

enough time. An', Mr. Doyle, just as soon as ye see the launch ready get back up here."

Doyle said nothing, but turned and went down the beach, with Barber and Hocking and Leadbeater following him. "Now, Mr. Slater, where's Powell?"

Jonas Day answered Berry. "Along o' that little cliff, Sir. 'Tis cooler there, we figured, and we stretched a sail for him. I said as how——"

"And Jeremy?"

"With Powell, Sir."

"Mr. Slater, fetch them back here. We'll find another place for Powell up on the hill with us."

Of them all in *Argo* Slater had known only Berry longer than Powell. Powell had been bosun's mate in a pretty little topsail schooner that had been dismasted in a typhoon in the China Sea. She'd lost her boats, had her deck wiped clean, and had sprung a garboard seam. Slater was third mate in the *Chanticleer*, out of Boston, when they sighted this dying vessel, almost awash on an unmoving expanse of lead-grey sea. There was no wind and most of that day the old *Chanticleer* drifted, just keeping the schooner in sight. Finally, midway through the afternoon, the master gave the order for two boats to go out to her, fearful that if night came and still not the wind to work *Chanticleer* nearer the schooner, by morning she might be out of sight. Slater commanded one of these boats.

That day he saw men who were unable to pump any longer, who lay about the schooner's decks, looking with dead eyes upon these men who swarmed up out of the ocean to save them from it. The captain of the schooner went in Slater's boat. Half-way back to the *Chanticleer* he took a long look at his sinking ship, put his head in his hands and wept. Beside him on the thwart sat one of his men, gaunt and hollow-cheeked, wild of eye, as were the rest of them. For a full minute he stared right past Slater, out over the boat's stern to the schooner. The boat moved quietly over the leaden sea, but for a slight swish as she passed over it and the rhythmic knocking of the oars in the thole pins.

"Ye've this to console ye, Sir," the man said suddenly to the

23

captain, "there's not a one of us didn't wish ourselves out of it. It had to be, for 'twas God's wish, but bein' as it was, I'd like ye to know there's none among us as would have wanted another cap'n."

The captain stayed with his head down. Then he raised it and looking into the stern of the boat said: " 'Tis the truth ye be speakin', man?"

"Aye, 'fore God it is."

"Then it takes some o' the hurt out o' it."

The man who had offered his consolation was Powell. Four years later, in a Cantonese godown, he and Slater met again. He skipped his ship and Slater signed him on.

Powell didn't hear Slater approach. He was lying back under the shadow of the sail and his eyes were closed. Jeremy was sitting near his head.

Powell opened his eyes. "Ah, Mr. Slater," he said weakly, easing himself up on one elbow.

"Are ye feeling any better, Powell?"

"Not a great deal, Sir. But I can still get up on me pins, that's the great thing."

"Can ye still shoot?"

"I don't say, Sir"—and Powell grinned as he said this—"how I'd be as handy as I used to be when I was a lad in the old country an' I'd go poachin' with m'father."

Powell was the only Englishman in *Argo*. His father had been caught poaching rabbits on a duke's estate and had been transported to New South Wales for the crime. It was Powell's bitterest blow when, on *Argo*'s first visit to Port Jackson, he discovered that his father had not survived the incredible cruelty and hardship of the voyage out.

"Does it look like 'twill come to shootin', Mr. Slater? Have ye set eyes on any Indians?"

"There's a war canoe, comin' this way."

"May the good God defend us, Sir."

"I'm afraid we'll have to be defendin' ourselves, Powell. Now on y'feet, lad, there's no time to be wastin'." Slater started to turn away, but something in the sick man's manner caused him to look back. "Ye heard me, Powell," Slater said. "Or is it ye're too sick to walk?"

"Nay, I can walk, Sir——"

"Then on y'feet, man." But Powell's deep-set eyes had jumped to Jeremy. "Maybe, Sir"—while he addressed Slater he nevertheless continued to look at the boy—"maybe young Jeremy here could run along and fetch a couple o' the men to take down this sail while ye an' me have a bit of a gam?"

Then Powell looked back at Slater, his eyes steady in the skinny hollows of his face. Slater saw the earnestness in him.

"Very well," he said quickly. "Jeremy, run along and tell the cap'n I'm bringin' Powell back and ask would he send a couple of men to take down the sail." As Jeremy raced off down the sand Slater squatted by the sick man. "Now, Powell, be quick. What is it?"

"Aye, Sir, I'll be quick. I, I don't rightly know as how I should be mentionin' it to ye. 'Tis none o' m'business ye might say, but I'll be gone soon—I know that—and I think ye ought to know. Ye've . . . ye've an enemy, Mr. Slater——"

"Doyle?"

"Aye, Sir, Mr. Doyle." Powell's eyes bored up at Slater. There was sweat in the hollows under them; his face had an earthy brown pallor.

"Has he been sayin' anythin' while we were up the hill?"

Powell nodded. "Ye'll remember them words ye had with him afore we left the brig this mornin'? Well, he's back on the same tack again. As how the launch be too deep-loaded and how—if ye'll excuse me the sayin' of it, Mr. Slater—how that murderin' swine the cap'n and his bully mate were for puttin' us on this reef and throwin' us to them as would eat us."

"Who heard him say that?"

"The boy, an' Sam Barber an' Elisha an' I think Johnny Morgan. Jeb Pain were about too, but I don't rightly know whether he 'eard or not."

"And that were all?"

"Aye, Sir, it were. After Mr. Doyle went, Sam Barber said 'twas no good for a sailor to go preachin' that sort of a sermon. I don't think Sam likes Mr. Doyle. Mind, he's not the only one. Jeb seems to get on with him a bit, but Johnny Morgan now, nor Pepper, they won't lie to with him at all. Old Si, Sir —God rest his poor drowned soul—old Si used to say it were a bloody wonder Solly Doyle never went over the side one dark night long afore he ever got aft of the mast. An' he's hard, Mr. Slater, as hard a man as ever I sailed under."

Powell lay back, exhausted with the effort of speaking and keeping himself propped up. Slater watched him a moment, then he stood, speaking as he did. "Powell, I'd ask ye to keep this to yeself; I'd rather the men didn't know ye told me of it."

"I'll keep it to m'self, Sir. I'll take it to me grave."

"We want none o' that," Slater said gruffly. "None o' that talk o' dyin'. Ye'll be with us when we make Port Jackson."

"Ah, Sir, ye've a comfortin' tongue an' it does me good to hear it, but I'll not be makin' Port Jackson, nor nowhere else. I'm done, Sir, like Silas or Tom Davidson, an' a cracked fool of a bawdy-house bottle I'd be to believe otherwise."

Damn Doyle, thought Slater, remembering that morning on the brig. 'Twas a senseless thing to say. 'Twas more—for an officer, 'twas a mutinous thing. But there was his own handling of Doyle. Had he gone the right way about that? He wondered how Berry would have handled it had he been mate; what Berry would have said or done. And would Berry have reported it? Should he report it now? It might be some part of a plan Doyle was hatching to undermine Berry's command, bit by bit —and the first mate's. Aye, be Jesus, his own place! Yet how else could he have handled Doyle? He had had to notice it, for Doyle had spoken in his hearing, plain and straight, with the crew about.

Berry was in his state-room at the time, setting out the charts and the instruments. Slater had been over the side of the brig, peering down through the clear water at her shattered hull, the twisted streamers of her copper that frayed out from her timbers, making utterly sure that she was past all hope of re-floating. When he came back on deck he was wet to the waist.

Stacked on deck near the launch's chocks was the gear to go with them: timber, sails, cordage, paint, powder, ball, canisters of grape for the swivel, muskets, spars, the carpenter's tools.

They were handling this gear, sorting it and passing it down into the launch under Doyle's supervision.

Jeremy came aft with the medicines. "Cap'n Berry says, Mr. Doyle, that this chest is to be put well up out o' the way of any water in the bilge."

Doyle turned from the rail and looked at Jeremy. Slater, about to go aft to report to Berry, stopped, looking at the chest. It was small enough, would take little enough room. But to Doyle it was the last straw. Its very smallness triggered a reaction.

"She'll be lyin' mighty low," said Doyle, meaning the launch in the water. He spoke to no one in particular, and the very generality of address caused Slater to say: "Aye, that she will."

It was agreement, the result of a comment, nothing more. There should have been an end to it, but fear—the fear that had brought this from Doyle—pushed him further. His eyes on the chest in the boy's hands, as though he were finishing what he had started out to say and with a savagery that cut across the deck and hauled up men in their work, he added: "Thanks to the murderin' tendencies of our bloody cap'n."

For a moment Slater stood, letting the words flow into him. Then he moved, swung past the carpenter and faced Doyle over the pile of gear.

As evenly as he could, Slater said: "Go aft, Mr. Doyle, will ye."

Doyle had no intention of disobeying; because it was an order and to obey is the automatic reaction of a man bred to obedience. But his vanity and the knowledge of his physical strength plucked at him and held him for a moment. It was an ugly moment. Slater knew he had committed himself deeply. The two men regarded each other steadily; work about them stopped. Finally Doyle went around the pile of gear and walked aft. Slater followed, catching him as he reached the poop companion. "In my cabin, Mister," Slater said quietly. "We can't talk here."

He had barely closed the door behind them when Doyle said: "I suppose ye've brought me here to tell me that he shouldn't have hove to; should've kep' on drivin' her like he did, though it be night and the waters as bad as they are."

"I brought ye here to tell ye that ye're a damned fool to say what ye did in front o' the men. Y'know y'duty, Doyle, as well as any officer."

"Murder, muckin' murder."

"So you say; so you said before the men. But that's only your opinion, Doyle. Persist in givin' it and I'll see ye hanged for it, as God is my judge."

"Ye seem to think he did right." Doyle leaned towards Slater, the size of him sustaining the sneer in the words. Slater watched him carefully. God, but he's big, he thought.

"I'm not prepared to discuss it, Doyle. Nor am I goin' to let ye goad me." But as he said this Slater knew he was being goaded; more, he knew the initiative was passing from him. The right in what Doyle said about heaving-to weakened Slater, for instinctively the Slaters of the world cleave to those who are right.

"An' Si James, eh?" Doyle went on, as though Slater hadn't spoken. "And Tom Davidson?"

"Well, what of 'em?"

"You ought to know. You an' Berry murdered them."

"By the livin' God, Doyle, do ye realise what ye say? We were swamped, by a sea bigger than I've ever seen. The miracle is that we all didn't go."

At that moment the brig shuddered violently, as though part of the coral on which she lay had collapsed. There was a hideous grinding and she settled deeper. Both men staggered to hold their feet and Doyle grabbed wildly for the hand-hold on the after bulkhead. Then she was still again, but Slater had seen fear in Doyle's face and it strengthened him, filled him with a curious sort of pride, and his anger went from him.

"Ye'd best get back on deck, Doyle. Christ, man," he added, almost softly, "don't be a fool. We're wrecked, never mind why; 'tis no time to go speakin' ill o' the cap'n. 'Tis remarks like yours as start mutinies."

Slater started to turn for the door but Doyle's hand shot out, grabbed him by the shoulder and spun him round. Slater was taken completely by surprise. "Are ye accusin' me o' fermentin' mutiny?" Doyle asked fiercely, eyes blazing. "Because if ye are, Mister——"

28

Slater pulled himself away, a quick, powerful movement. "I'm accusin' ye o' nothing' but a loose tongue."

"I'll not take that talk o' mutiny," Doyle said righteously, shaking his head.

"Ye don't have to," Slater said, turning for the door again. He was finished with it now, tired of it, tired of the wreck, of Doyle, of the knowledge that, so far as heaving-to went, Doyle was right. Tired of what lay ahead of them: the launch, the voyage in it, the days and the nights, months of them perhaps, which faced them.

He opened the door and stood waiting for Doyle to pass him, out of the cabin. As they stared at each other he felt a link with Doyle he had not known before, almost a feeling of affection, something quite definite, the more surprising because he had never thought there could be anything between them but the ship and her working. It was as if he had seen the humanity of Doyle for the first time. Or was it only his fear—the desire for friendship with a man who, once an enemy, would fight until he stood victorious? Then Doyle moved, went from the cabin, brushing Slater with his body as he passed through the door.

Now, as Jeremy came running back with Pain and Day, Slater could only feel that he had failed; that he'd been weak against the strength which was in Doyle.

When the report of Wilkinson's musket came from the top of the hill the *Argo* men were ready. The sun beat down and sent the sweat running on them as they crouched behind the cover on the hill. Insects whirred in the dry grass. Slater and Berry were together near the middle of the line of men stretched across the slope. Behind them were Powell and Jeremy, each with a pistol. One end of the line was held by Doyle, the other by Pepper.

"Now if it comes to shootin', lad," Slater said, turning back to Jeremy, "remember what I've taught ye—fire low, for the pistol'll kick up, an' don't pull off hard, else she'll fire to the right."

"Aye aye, Sir."

"And stick close to me, Jeremy. Unless I tell ye not to."

"I will, Sir. . . . Sir?"

"Aye, lad?"

"I'm not frightened, not really."

"O' course y'not. Why should ye be? Never fear, Jeremy, we'll lick any canoe full o' savages."

As Slater turned back Berry said: "I hope ye're right, Mister." It occurred to Slater to say that were he not they'd have Berry to thank for making him a liar. Almost the first words came into speech, but he checked himself, brought up by Berry's drawn, tense face. Instead he said: "I've been meanin' to ask ye—how's y'head, where ye cut it when we struck?"

"I'm still dazed be it, Mister. 'Twas a damned hard blow. Ah, but we were lucky. We could have lost men wi' that fallin' gear." Berry was looking down the slope to the launch. "Ye don't think Barber will fire unless he gets the order, do ye? I mean, when he sees 'em."

"Not Barber. He's among the steadiest of them. He's got Leadbeater too, another cool head."

"Ye've seen to it, Mister, that the best shots have the extra muskets?"

"I have."

"An' the rest o' the powder and shot is with Doyle?"

"Aye."

"Well, with what Barber's got of it, an' what we have here, and Doyle along there, 'tis hardly likely that we'd be without some in the event o' disaster. Is it?"

Slater said nothing, and Berry pulled out his handkerchief and mopped his face. Slater watched the launch, kedged now, riding almost abeam to the beach, the swivel gun up-pointed in its socket in the transom. Barber, huge and still, sat behind the gun, well down in the boat, eyes on the tip of land from behind which the canoe would emerge.

Slater heard Jeremy whisper something to Powell. He listened absently, then quite suddenly realised that if they were captured, if no hope remained, he would take the boy's life. He glanced back at Jeremy, who smiled at him. "Mr. Slater," the boy said quickly, "when I get back to Boston they'll not be able to say I'm not a real seaman—not after this, will they, Sir?"

"Nay, lad, nor could they now."

30

"D'ye really mean that, Mr. Slater?"

"I do."

The boy wanted to glance at Powell to make sure that he had heard, for of all the things that had ever been said to him this was the most wonderful. He wanted to stand up there on the hill and tell it to every man of them, tell it to Sam Barber out in the launch, tell it to all of Boston and Salem and Beverly and New Bedford, to tell it to all of New England, to all the world. He was a real seaman—Mr. Oliver Slater had said so.

A month before, on Jeremy's fourteenth birthday. Slater had given him a knife with a dragon carved on the handle, bought for him in Canton. Barber had made a sheath for it out of untanned pig's skin, the fat still in the leather—a sheath in which, he told Jeremy, a knife would never rust.

In some ways the lad was a misfit at sea. He was not a sturdy boy and, had he not been a distant relative of Berry's and had his father not been a partner in a firm of merchants, Jeremy would never have got to sea. This was his third voyage. Slater had seen the boy's love for the sea, his determination that frailness should not prevent him from one day being master of his own ship. This interest of Slater's kindled that of the men, and Jeremy came to be a kind of mascot, a good omen. He would go aloft, usually following Barber, and would stand with the men along the foot-rope, his thin little legs clawing at the canvas.

Best of all he loved the time he spent aloft with Slater. They would lean over the main royal yard (when the sail was furled), one on each side of the mast, feet on the top-gallant crosstrees, and they would gaze at the immensity of the ocean over which the ship found her course. Then Slater would teach Jeremy his seamanship.

One such afternoon, when they came down, Berry said to Slater: "I'll tell ye somethin', Mister, somethin' I would never have believed: I reckon now ye'll make a sailor o' the boy. He's gettin' flesh on him too, an' his bones are thickenin' out. One v'yage at the most, I says to m'self, an' we'll be glad to set him ashore again. But I was wrong, he's shapin' well and I thank ye for the trouble ye're takin' with him."

" 'Tis no trouble, Cap'n Berry. The truth o' the matter is that I've taken to him. I feel as though he were m'own."

"Aye, I've noticed it," said Berry, smiling at him. "You unmarried men are all the same—see a smart lad an' ye want one for yeselves. Maybe ye'll marry one day and get one or two. I've three, as ye know, and all fine lads they turned out too. And now the eldest is within a fraction of gettin' his first command."

Some of this came to Slater now, as he lay sweating it out on the hillside, suffering because of what he believed in his heart to be Berry's mistake.

Suddenly they saw the canoe. Every man on the hill moved behind his weapon. Thumbs went out and drew back on the knurled hammerheads, eyes screwed tighter in the glare to gaze upon the great canoe. The Americans saw the islanders catch first sight of the launch, saw their excitement, the quick pointing, the turning of every head to look into the cove at the launch riding to the long scope of its cable.

The canoe lost way and drifted. There was much movement about its deck and the sail came down. Paddles dipped, flashed up, dripping in the sunlight. On the launch, Barber began to whistle between his teeth, showing them even and white against his black beard. Slowly the canoe turned, and Barber fitted it into the slight cut in the belled rim of the gun-muzzle. "Here, Leady, Elisha," he muttered, "stick y'heads up an' take a look. 'Twould be like firin' at a haystack, so help me it would."

Chapter 4

THE size of these huge savages amazed the white men. They were all but naked, their only covering a kind of sash of brown, white or figured bark cloth passed between the legs and wound two or three times about the loins. In the stern of the canoe sat several men who were obviously chiefs, and these had several folds of this bark cloth taken up from their waists and passed over their shoulders. They all wore necklets and armlets made of sea-shells and the teeth of fish, and many had circlets of green leaves twisted about their ankles and wrists. Some had their bodies blackened, others had theirs whitened with ash and some were daubed with turmeric.

But it was the way they wore their hair that caused the white men most amazement. Few of them had the same method of dressing it. It was strong, wiry hair, more wiglike than natural, and gave the impression of having been carved out of some solid material. Some wore it black, some white, some yellow, while others combined two or more colours. Some of them were partly bald, with nothing but a high, tufted yellow top-knot showing; others looked for all the world as though they had a great black-and-white-striped ball perched between their shoulders, for the hair was combed and dressed to make it stand a good six to eight inches from the scalp. Some had the front of their heads plucked, their skulls bald and shining as far as the crowns of their heads; from there the hair reared upwards in a radiating mass of jet blackness. Others wore a weird, tonsured shape, and one appeared to have no hair at all, but a dented yellow helmet glued to his scalp.

There was a deadly determination about these men, and they were formidably armed. All about the canoe's deck were piles of weapons, most of which were clubs, huge things, carved and ornamented in rich variety. There were heaps of stones also, and bows and arrows, and long, heavy spears, hideously barbed.

In the stern of the canoe among the men of rank sat one, more richly decorated than the rest, towards whom the warriors showed great respect. One other was accorded the same respect, a younger man who stood well forward, flanked by warriors, an ornamented club clutched in his right hand.

The alert, suspicious faces of these warriors, the armament of the canoe, the canoe itself, two beautifully constructed hulls that sliced the water with barely a trace of wake—all this awed the white men. Slater could hear those about him muttering. He glanced at Berry, who seemed not to notice it.

"I think, Sir," said Slater, "ye'd better say somethin' to the men."

"Eh?" said Berry sharply, turning to him.

"Ye'd best say a word to the lads, Sir. The Indians are gettin' 'em bluffed."

But before Berry could answer, one of them—Slater thought it was Pain—said loud enough for all but those at the far end of the line to hear: " 'Tis a damn fool thing this, to be waitin' here for these savage bastards, if we want to see home again."

"Say somethin', Cap'n Berry," said Slater quietly but very earnestly. "The Indians'll have us beat afore it starts."

Berry looked back at the canoe and then along the line of men to his right. "Take heart, lads," he called, "they might look big, but a couple o' cartridges'd soon send 'em scuttling. Remember, we're Yankees, an' not such as to be frightened be a bunch o' bloody cannibals."

But Slater felt there was little spirit in the voice. It seemed that Berry had spoken a piece he didn't believe in.

The canoe ran on effortlessly, driven now by only a dozen paddles. The Fijians shot their wild, uneasy glances at the launch, pointed towards it, and chattered, their weapons swinging nervously in their hands.

"They're mighty interested in the launch, Mister," Berry murmured, moving his head to keep the canoe in sight around the roots of the screw pine behind which he and Slater lay.

"While they don't see us they'll keep interested too."

"Barber mustn't lose his head. A mistake now an' 'twould be all up with us. Mister," and Berry added this suddenly, not looking from the canoe, "do the men think we should have put straight away? That which Pain just said, do many of them think it?"

"Aye."

"Doyle too?"

"I believe so."

Berry said nothing more, and Slater felt the silence between them.

Soon the canoe was well into the cove, and once it cleared a patch of coral that all but broke the surface it steadied on a course towards the launch. Slater saw Barber stiffen; all unsuspecting, the canoe was making straight into the muzzle of the devastating little cannon.

"Hold y'fire, Barber," muttered Berry. "Hold y'fire, man."

"What's he to do?" returned Slater. "Put yeself in his place. He's steady, aye—but is he just to wait and be run down be that horde?"

"Ye remember the plan, Mister," said Berry almost petulantly. "I'm goin' down to treat with them. But I want 'em well in first. As soon as they see me they'll alter course and draw off from the boat. I'm sure of it. Ye'll be in command up here." In Berry's voice was excitement now, sending the pitch of it higher. "But for God's sake don't give the order to fire unless ye see me struck down. But when ye do, then give it quick, just as soon as ye see me go, and then shoot for y'life. I'll lead well out along the beach so as to give Barber a field o' fire clear of ye up here on the hill."

Slater looked sideways at Berry, for his speech seemed a little slurred. Then something happened which caused Slater to forget the canoe. Berry was half up, when he paused, holding to the tree. Slater saw his eyes close. He leaned heavily against the tree, as though the effort of getting to his feet had been too much for him.

"Are ye all right, Sir?" Slater spoke softly, not wanting the men around him to hear.

Berry opened his eyes. "Aye, 'tis the crack I got upon m'head. Nothin' more, Mister. I'll be all right."

"Is y'head painin' ye?"

" 'Tis bad. But 'twill pass," and he looked out through the tree down to the canoe.

"Here, Sir, ye'd best let me go down."

"Nay, nay, Mister, 'tis my place to go, and I'm goin'."

Berry stood erect now, but his head fell. He was still holding to the tree, and he let his head rest upon his arm. " 'Tis the glare, the light, Mr. Slater. 'Tis cruel sharp, an' seems on a sudden to aggravate m'head. 'Tis too bright a place."

Slater looked down the slope. The glare was no brighter than it had been.

"Sir," he said quickly, "ye'd best let me go down."

"I tell ye, nay," Berry said, raising his head and looking at

35

Slater. " 'Tis but the blow I got." His eyes were bloodshot, his face drained of colour.

" 'Tis an ache," he said, "here"—he put his hand to his forehead—"as though there was somethin' poundin' in m'brain. An' there's a sort o' strangeness all over me." There was a curiously tormented look in his face now. "Ah, ye're not to go worryin' about it, Mister, or that business of Hitchbourn Wharf. Eh?" His gaze now wandered from Slater, above him, and he shielded his eyes from the glare of the sky. "Or that of Oliver's Dock. 'Tis y'name, Mister," and now he looked down at Slater again. " 'Tis y'name, aye. An' y'know, until this I'd never connected it? On m'word I hadn't."

Hitchbourn Wharf? thought Slater. But that was Boston. . . .

"Ye'll remember Jeremiah Hodges, won't ye—him as walked down King Street an' over the end of Long Wharf? Eh? Drunk he were, an' them gettin' him out with a boat-hook a couple o' weeks later and running the spike into him and puncturin' him."

By the Holy Mary, thought Slater, looking about and trying to see if any of the men had heard. Powell and Jeremy had, and they were staring at Berry. Morgan was next closest, but he hadn't noticed; he was gazing down at the canoe, the sweat running on his face, cutting runnels in the dust that had risen from the dry hillside.

"Mister," said Berry, shaking his head, pulling himself very straight, and taking his hand from the tree, "I'm goin' down now. 'Twill be time. I see that. Now, be God, we'll soon know who was right." His voice died shakily. He screwed his eyes tight as though preparing himself for the shock of the glare and once more looked out through the sabre-like leaves to the canoe.

" 'Tis a tricky business, Mr. Slater, a bloody tricky business." He wiped his left hand over his face. "Ye realise that ye can get a threefold error in y'result. That Cap'n Bowditch—Cap'n Nat, Mister—now there's a man who can work lunars. As sweet as a young girl's breasts he can work 'em. Aye, an' I hear tell he's bringin' out a book upon the subjec'. Y'don't need a chronometer to get y'longitude, if ye can work lunars, Mister."

"For God's sake, Sir, ye've got to let me go down to meet the savages. I'm the younger man. Ye must, Sir."

"Ye forget yeself, don't ye, Mister? This o' the 'must' I got to do. I'll not have it. D'ye hear me?"

" 'Twas no offence meant, Sir."

"I should bloody well hope there was no offence meant, Mister. Ye wouldn't, be any chance, be wishin' me dead an' gone, would ye? Out o' the way, so ye could see yeself in command?"

"I'm not wishin' ye dead, Sir. 'Tis just that ye're not well. 'Tis the crack ye got."

"I was hit upon the head, Mister." Berry spoke with the exaggerated caution of a drunken man.

Then he looked out at the canoe again. It had now slackened speed, obviously afraid to close upon this strange object which floated so steadily upon the calm of the lagoon.

Suddenly Berry said: "Right . . . right, I'm goin'." But instead of starting to move out from the tree, he opened his mouth, breathed in deeply, and then swallowed hard. "Christ, Mister," he said weakly, starting to gulp on the words, "I'm . . . I'm goin' to vomit." As Slater got to him he leaned against the tree and let go. There was little enough in his stomach, but several powerful spasms worked in him.

Now the canoe began to close upon the launch. Then Slater heard movement, and over Berry's hanging head saw Doyle, crouching down as he came across the hillside, dodging from one piece of cover to the next.

"What's actin', Mister?" he said, looking queerly at Berry.

"The cap'n's ill," Slater said, and Berry straightened up, feeling for his handkerchief, looking at Doyle.

"I'm better now, thank'ee, Mister. 'Twas . . . 'twas somethin' I ate. Mr. Doyle, ye shouldn't have left y'end, should have stayed where I put ye."

"Ye look pale," Doyle said, ignoring Berry's censure.

"I'll be all right," Berry said testily, wiping his mouth with the handkerchief.

"For the last time," said Slater, "will ye let me go down to 'em, Sir?"

"Aye," put in Doyle, "or me. If ye're ill, an' ye look it, ye'd be better off up here."

"I said I'd go, and by the Christ I'm goin'." With that Berry stepped away from Slater and started to move out through the hanging leaves of the tree on to the hillside.

"Y'musket," said Doyle, picking it up and handing it to him. "Have ye seen to the primin' o' y'pistols?"

"Aye, I have," said Berry defensively.

"Then slack 'em in y'belt, Sir," said Slater. "If ye need 'em ye'll be needin' them quick."

Berry had begun to turn away when he stopped and looked back at the two men. "Now remember," he said slowly, his bloodshot eyes turning from one to the other, "don't fire. But if ye have to, wait. Wait until I get off Windmill Point." Then he started out through the tree. On his third step he slipped and crashed through the tree out into full view on the open slope. Doyle jumped to go after him, but Berry got control, and cursing to himself began to pick his way down the hill, a lean, unsteady figure, the musket hanging from his right hand.

"Windmill Point," said Doyle. "By all that's holy—Windmill Point! Don't fire until I get off Windmill Point! He's touched, Mister. The man's not right in the head."

"He hit his head on the capstan when we struck this mornin'. He's ill, but he'll get over it."

"Who says he will? I tell ye he's touched. Look at him, ye'd think a drunk were at the helm. An' makin' down to Griffin's Wharf as like as not he thinks he is. 'Tis madness—sheer, bloody madness."

The canoe was still running, but now the savages had turned from looking at the launch and were staring with even more wonder at the solitary figure picking its way out on to the beach.

"Ye'd best get back to y'place, Mister," Slater said. For a moment longer Doyle continued to watch Berry, then he cursed and went.

Berry's guess had been correct, for when the Fijians saw him on the beach they altered course for him. Slater saw the order given to the two men on the great steering oar, saw them bend to the shaft and saw the canoe go to starboard slowly as the chief pointed to Berry, now out on the stretch of blazing sand.

Slater dropped behind his musket again. "Now, lads," he called softly, "take aim, and keep it. Pick y'target bunched, then if ye miss the man ye fire for ye'll get the one abeam or astern of him."

Berry trudged on, holding his musket with both hands. He had led well along the beach, as he'd said he would, and Barber's field of fire was clear. Soon he could hear the run of the water between the canoe's twin hulls and an occasional word of the barbaric yet strangely sweet-sounding tongue. His head ached fiercely, but it was not clouded and the hideous detachment of those moments on the hill had passed. Wrong? he thought. He wasn't wrong, and he'd prove it.

Lester Light was next to Doyle, and now he started to pray out loud. Doyle turned on him, working out his frustration and spleen on the little steward. "Stow that prayin', Light, an' put up y'musket. 'Twill be more use to us than y'prayin'. Go, like I tell ye, put up y'musket, y'prayin' fool."

And Light put up his musket, pointed it with trembling hands, and prayed the harder.

As the canoe approached the beach Slater saw Berry stiffen and shift his hands on the musket. Then the men on the hill heard the smooth crunch as the canoe struck sand, and the rasping sound as it slid to a halt. The instant it touched, part of its crew slipped overboard and held it, while others went forward, and dropping into the water stood between the hulls, clustered before the leading edge of the deck platform. When these men were in position the chief moved from his place in the stern. He got to his feet slowly, moving his huge bulk easily, a train of bark cloth trailing on the deck after him. He, too, was armed with a club, an extraordinarily shaped weapon, not unlike a double-headed axe. It happened so swiftly that Slater did not see exactly how it was done, but the chief no sooner reached the edge of the platform than he was on the backs of the men gathered there and was being carried ashore. He was taken a few paces up the beach and put down carefully, facing Slater.

On the hill the sweat ran on the white men. Slater took his hand from his musket and wiped it against his shirt; then he steadied again, aiming at the chief's breast.

The Fijians leaped ashore after their chief, splashing waist-deep in the water. Twenty paces separated Berry from the chief, his warriors behind him ranged in a tight half circle. Their eyes were bright in the darkness of their faces, and when they muttered among themselves Slater could see the white flash of teeth. Immediately behind the chief and in front of the rest of the Fijians stood the younger man Slater had noticed at the head of the canoe.

Now, thought Slater, get a turn like ye did up here, Robert Berry, an' ye'll be leavin' y'bones to rot. And looking down over the musket barrel at the solitary skipper facing those barbaric men, he felt the claim of Berry's affection, knew the courage of the man. Yet there was something pathetic about Berry now—an old man trying to tread the way of the young, a man to whom fortune had come too late, a man who'd been asked to face his greatest test long past the time when he should have left adventure to others.

An' yeself, Slater—of all the damnedest fools ye're the biggest. Ye had enough, as did Berry. Ye stretched y'luck too far. 'Twas no use to fool yeself, y'luck was like an old rope, badly frayed.

Berry could feel his heart, actually feel it. The brightness seemed to strike into his brain; nausea welled up inside him.

The Fijians watched Berry, clubs half raised, arrows fitted to their bowstrings. Should this white creature be a god, they would not be surprised; should he be a devil, they might be even less so.

Berry could know nothing of their character, of their easily alarmed, suspicious natures, their unreasoning terror in the presence of anything newly glimpsed. But his native perception served him well. As the chief moved his weight from one foot to another and lifted his club, Berry took the initiative. He stepped forward quickly, disarming the Fijian by his boldness.

As Berry moved, swallowing hard, driving down the nausea in him, he took from his pocket his cigar-case—his wife's launching present for *Argo*—and, holding it out, walked to within a few paces of the chief. Fear came into the Fijian's face, his eyes rolled and his club came up quickly. But then the frailness, the pale, drawn face, the very shaking of Berry's hand calmed him. There could be little to fear from this creature; he was not even armed, except for the harmless-looking bent stick he held.

40

Yet he hesitated to take the offering. He looked from Berry to the case and then back again. Berry saw his desire for it and held it out farther, within easy reach now. Then, very slowly, the chief's hand slid out, covetousness conquering fear for the moment, and he took the case. Slater saw him bend his head to look at it, saw the sun flash on it, the reflection dance across his features as he turned it this way and that, fascinated by its brightness. When the chief looked up at Berry, he was smiling.

Without taking his eyes from Berry, he spoke to his men. For an instant they hesitated, then they surged forward, surrounding Berry, laughing, shouting, giving little coughs and hisses of glee and wonder as they touched him and fingered his clothing. Up on the hill the tension ran out of the white men; Slater found himself grinning as he eased his grip on his musket. Out in the launch, Barber stood from the swivel gun and said to Hocking and Leadbeater: "Here, ye can come up, lads, this is goin' to be a picnic, not a bloody war."

Shaking, Berry pushed through the press about him and called to Slater. Understandably there was some pride in his voice. "Bring 'em down, Mr. Slater," he called. "I believe there's naught to fear." And because he was proud of what he had done, he could not resist adding: " 'Tis as I told ye—they're easy to bluff."

Berry had not said anything about their being easy to bluff, but Slater understood why he might think he had. The mate was proud of his captain. He walked out and, crossing to Doyle, said quietly, almost, he hoped, as though it didn't matter: "We'll lead together, Mister." Doyle no more than glanced at him. Then Slater added to the men who were clustering out after him "Right, lads, we go."

They were soon surrounded as Berry had been, gazed at, touched, swivelled round, poked, even smelled. The Fijians snatched at their caps, pulled at Doyle's beard, fingered the leather in their belts, all the time shouting their discoveries to others too interested in their own to listen. Slater noticed that most of the Fijians had fingers missing, usually the little one; some had two off. There were many scars about their bodies, and a strong but not unpleasant odour which seemed familiar, but which he could not quite place. Part of it, he knew, was coconut, the oil which burnished them as they moved.

The chief could not take his eyes from the cigar-case. He sat on the sand, the better to examine it, and turned it over and over in his great hands. Slater noticed that as soon as he sat his men moved away from him, not wanting to stand in his immediate presence. Berry went and sat beside him. Between them lay his club, its handle bound with delicate black and white matting into which had been laced tiny red feathers, but what intrigued Berry most about it was that the two great curves which made its striking faces were edged with a double row of human teeth, and molars at that. He stared down at it, appalled by the thought of the many men who must have died to provide so many back teeth.

Then, in handling the case, the chief pressed the release snap and it flew open. With a shout he grabbed for his club and started to his feet. But Berry was quicker, and picking up the case made him see there was nothing to be afraid of. Grinning, the Fijian sank to the sand once more and watched in amazement as Berry took a cigar from it, closed it and returned it to the chief, and then with flint and steel, began to light the cigar.

As the first puff of smoke came from Berry's lips there was a shout and several of the warriors ran up and gazed in astonishment. By the time the cigar was drawing well Berry was hemmed about by a ring of Fijians, who sat staring into his smoke-wreathed face with such expressions of amazement that the white men could not keep themselves from laughing.

Surely, said the Fijians to themselves, these must be the gods, for who else but the gods could eat fire? An awe grew in them. But familiarity grew too, and before the first hour was out there came for the Americans the test.

It was over Jeremy that trouble developed. Jeremy had been as much an object of curiosity as any of the men. He'd been pulled at, shoved about, even lifted off his feet. He did not complain, except when three huge warriors started to take the shirt from his back. Then he called out, and Pepper, who had seen the thing begin, diverted the attention of these men by cutting off a piece of his tobacco and showing them how he chewed it. He gave some of it to one of the warriors, who, letting Jeremy go, put it in his mouth and chewed hard on it; but the tobacco bit back, and with a wry expression he spat it out, whereupon one of the others picked it up and tried it. By the time the third had tasted it Jeremy was clear, laughing at them as he tucked his shirt back into his trousers and buckled his belt again.

He was still watching them, when he felt a tug at his knife. He shouted and grabbed for the knife, but his hand closed on that of the man who wanted it. Jeremy clenched his fist and brought it down across the Fijian's forearm. His blow meant nothing to the man, but his shout brought Slater's hand to his pistol, and the Fijian, alarmed by Slater's reaction and the shouts of the white men who had seen it happen, stepped back, and in one smooth motion raised his club and swung at Jeremy.

Jeremy was part turned away from him. But he sensed the immediacy of danger and had started to move when Slater pulled him to safety. The club struck nothing but air, and the Fijian, carried forward by the swing of it, ended up crouched before Slater, looking into the muzzle of his pistol.

Berry scrambled to his feet. The man had no idea that Slater had only to squeeze a finger and his face would be blasted to pieces. He stayed crouched, staring up at Slater, a half-grin on his face. Within seconds every musket was cocked, and out in the launch Barber dropped behind the swivel gun, cursing because his target was now fouled by the crew, and if anything were to come of the incident the gun would be useless until the two sides separated.

"All right, Mister," said Berry shakily, coming to Slater, his voice high, a tormented edge in it, "the lad's not hurt, is he?"

" 'Tis but luck an' the lightness of his feet that he isn't," Slater said, not taking his eyes from the grinning islander at the end of his pistol.

Berry looked about, hesitant, afraid of taking action that might antagonise the Fijians, yet well aware of the necessity to show no weakness. He glanced at the chief; the expression he saw gave him little comfort, for it was a look of insolence—

not pride, but arrogance—and looking at the other warriors he saw it mirrored as a cocksureness, a feeling of superiority.

Berry's eyes were still on the chief when the latter turned and looked down at the canoe, his hand sliding along the shaft of his club to the grip. Now the white men felt hostility. Suddenly the chief laughed, startling Berry, frightening him, for it seemed almost a signal. Every man, brown and white, looked at the chief, then the warrior who crouched before Slater went to move and Berry shouted: "Stay where ye are."

The man could not know what Berry meant, but it was the voice of one who gave an order and the man checked his move.

"Right, men," said Berry. "No harm's been done as yet."

"A muckin' wonder," put in Pain.

"Aye, maybe. But no one's been hurt. An' just so as any won't be, I'm going to give these Indians a look at the fire they're playing with. I'm going to discharge a musket, but that don't mean I'm startin' a fight. Now don't go makin' it obvious that we're in any way nervous, lads. An', Mr. Slater, for God's sake don't shoot that devil—not yet. I think there's a way out o' this."

Berry turned back to the chief then, and holding his musket out in front of him he pointed it at himself and mimed his own death by it. He did it well enough; the Fijian saw what he was meant to see, but he was impressed only by the foolhardiness of the creature who could argue the merits of a bent stick while surrounded by clubs, spears and arrows. These white-skinned creatures could not be gods, he said to himself—unless the gods were now *lialia*. And while Berry persisted in his forlorn hope the chief got slowly to his feet. He did not wait for Berry to finish his pantomime before he turned to his men and said something. They roared with laughter, a great, instantaneous shout of mirth.

Berry stopped, staring at the chief through half-closed eyes. The chief said something else and the warrior in front of Slater thought this second remark so funny that he rolled on the sand. Slater took a step back, pushing Jeremy behind him, keeping his pistol on the man, fearing treachery, a sudden rush under cover of the wild reaction.

The chief stared about at the white men, very pleased with

44

himself, his flat, red-rimmed eyes screwed up in laughter. He moved to Berry, a slow, arrogant roll, and clasping the musket by the barrel pointed it at himself, imitating what Berry had done; then seeing the hole, the muzzle of the weapon, he put his eye to it, peered into it, talking to his men as he did so.

"Pull the trigger, Sir," growled Pain, "an' be done wi' the cocky swine."

The chief looked up, glanced at Pain, then facing Berry, again pushed the musket so hard back against him that the old man, caught off balance, nearly fell. For seconds the chief gazed into Berry's eyes; then he made another remark. The Fijians screamed with laughter, hooted with glee, slapped their thighs and rolled on the sand. But into this laughter there came an edge so dangerous that Berry realised it was now or never. All the white men felt it, and Slater heard the click of a musket being cocked.

The chief sat slowly, looking up at Berry, his face contorted with laughter. Desperately Berry looked about, searching for a target to try the musket against.

A white heron swooped low over the beach. It banked gracefully in a long, easy turn and then came to rest on a spur of rock not far from the water's edge. Slater spoke as Berry saw it. "There, Sir," he said, darting a quick look from the man who was still on the sand before him. "The seafowl."

" 'Tis a long way off, Mister," said Berry, screening his eyes to look at it. But fear prodded Berry—fear of the savages, fear of himself. Dear God, he prayed, see me through this. The bird's long neck was arching, bending.

The chief still looked at Berry, seeing the distraction in him, grinning at him. In one hand was his club, in the other the cigar-case.

Slowly Berry raised the musket. He couldn't trust himself to hold on the bird for more than a moment. He felt himself wavering. For one crazy moment he saw two birds, one sitting almost on the barrel itself. Nearly he lowered the musket in his desperation, but then he braced himself, took a deep breath, held it—and squeezed off. The powder flashed in the pan, the musket roared, jumped back against him.

45

The ball hit the stone at the bird's feet. The flaky rock shattered, and the glancing ball and splintered stone flew up and struck the bird. It was blown into the air, its head partly torn off and its white feathers strewn about the rocky outcrop. The nearly decapitated body, spurting blood, flopped to the ground, switching, flapping in a circle.

The blood had drained from the chief's face, and his mouth hung open. The cigar-case, even the club, had fallen from his hands, and he was trying to raise himself to his feet. He got up, not for a second taking his eyes from Berry, and started to back away in the direction of the canoe. It was enough for his warriors; with a wild shout they broke and ran. Some fell over, hit the beach and were on their feet in an instant, scattering the hot sand. But the man in front of Slater, a moment before among the most arrogant of them, was paralysed with fear. He crouched quaking on the sand, staring at Slater, who, as he watched, saw the stain of water run on the man's breech-cloth. Slater felt pity for him, such was the man's terror. Then from the canoe came a great wailing, a piteous sound, long drawn out. Hearing it Slater could barely suppress a shudder; it was as though the damned were wailing.

For the Fijians this was no earthly thing; the men who carried sticks which vomited such swift and awful death were no mortal men. There could be no doubt now—these were the gods; and the gods, it was plain, were above all to be respected. Who knew what other magic they possessed?

Chapter 5

SLATER was watching the Fijians running for the canoe, clambering aboard, wailing and shrieking, when Peppercorn cried: "The cap'n, Mr. Slater—he's down."

Slater whirled about. Berry had fallen with his musket under him, one side of his face pressed into the sand. Doyle and

Peppercorn were only a step behind Slater in reaching Berry. Together they turned the old man over and propped him up. His eyes were closed and sand was stuck to his sweat-wet face and neck and was clinging to his beard. His head lolled, mouth open.

"Jesus," said Peppercorn, "will ye look at his face!"

"'Tis water he needs," said Doyle, straightening up.

"Get it from the launch, Mister," said Slater. As Doyle started to move he called after him: "An' have Barber beach the boat, an' set Leadbeater and Hocking to clearin' the thwarts an' laying out the oars."

"What's wrong with his face, Sir?" asked Peppercorn as Slater turned back to Berry.

"'Tis about paralysed, if ye ask me," said Pain, who had just joined them.

"Here, back wi' ye," Slater called as the other men came crowding about. "Give him some air. An' bunch up between us and the canoe, so the Indians'll not be suspectin' anythin' has gone awry. Smart about it. Pepper, open his shirt, will ye." While Slater supported Berry, Peppercorn opened the captain's jacket. "What'd make his face go queer like that, Sir?" he said as he fumbled with the buttons of the shirt.

"The knock he got this mornin'."

"Christ!"

"He'll get over it, Pepper. 'Tis rest he needs now."

"Bloody fine time to be needin' it," said Pain.

Slater ignored the remark. "Morgan," he said quickly, "squint if ye can see what the Indians are doin'. See if ye think they've noticed the cap'n go down. Now don't all o' ye go turnin' about, let Morgan see for himself."

"I'd say, Sir," Morgan said after a moment in his slow, drawling voice, "that they was of a mind to leave, but was afeared to."

"Afeared to?"

"Looks that way to me too, Sir," put in Day.

"I didn't ask ye, Day, I asked Morgan."

"Aye," said Morgan, "that's what I'd say, Mr. Slater. Some o' them are lookin' up here, an' some at the launch. They're scared out o' their wits, Sir."

"Frightened to put out past the launch," put in Day.

"I'd say," Morgan went on, "that they was licked."

When Doyle came with a beaker of water, Slater lifted Berry until he sat almost straight up. Doyle put it to his lips. At the touch of the water, some of which ran on to his chest, Berry opened his eyes and, conscious of what he was doing, took several deep draughts. Then he moved to sit by himself.

"How d'ye feel, Sir?" asked Slater.

"I . . . I don't know quite what came over me, Mister," he said weakly.

"Just ease yeself. Ye'll be right in a minute or two."

"The Indians—are they still about?" Berry looked around as though uncertain where he might find them.

"Aye, they are. But we think they're beat."

"Where are they, Mister?"

"At their canoe."

Berry saw the canoe now. "We'd best get down to 'em," he said. "Mustn't let 'em go like that. Aye, I remember it now," he added, almost apologetically, "I fired at a bird."

Slater saw now that Berry's mouth was out of shape, the right side of it pulled back, and the bottom lid of his right eye was drawn down, showing the red of it.

"We . . . we must make the Indians see we don't mean 'em harm," Berry went on. "The musket's scared 'em, but it was all we could do. I'm afraid they're fools, which is unfortunate." With that he started to get to his feet.

Slater and Doyle helped him. "Aye, they're goats, I'm afraid, but it can't be helped. They asked for it. We'll just have to make the best o' them. No help for it. Now, Mr. Slater, what would ye say we could give them to show that we mean to be friendly?"

"Nails?"

"Aye, nails'd do."

"Could we spare some, Day?"

"We've ample. More'n we need, Sir," said Day. "When I was settin' out the gear I says to meself——"

"Fetch a few, Day," said Berry wearily.

"Big ones, Sir, or——"

"Aye, big ones. A dozen'll do."

48

Fear is an unstable base for peace, for it excludes the primary requirements of friendship. It took the next hour for the Fijians to see that these white creatures had no intention of turning their terrible fire sticks upon them. Deeply chastened, shivering with fright, they allowed themselves to be brought from the canoe. Slater himself brought the chief up and sat him on the sand next to Berry. The *Argo* men moved among them, showing them their knives, tinder-boxes, tobacco, bits of cord, coins, pipes, anything they happened to have in their pockets.

And they looked at the Fijians' weapons and marvelled at the craftsmanship. Some of the clubs were covered with fine carving, some inlaid with pearl shell. Others—*waka*, Slater thought they called them—seemed to have been partly formed while the tree was growing. The white men marvelled more when they came to a close examination of the canoe. Day said it seemed impossible that such a craft had been built without any metal tool; but the white men found no metal of any kind either in it or in the weapons. The *Argo* men would have been more amazed had they known that at its launching it had been rolled into the water over the bodies of fifty warriors, that an equal number of *vaka duri ni vana*—'raisers of the mast'—had been slaughtered and eaten when its mast was first stepped, and as many had been killed when it was lowered for the first time.

" 'Twould seem," said Pepper, "that if ye frighten 'em enough they be almost gentlemen." In a manner of speaking he was right, for no one could imagine a more courteous, willing people now than these, who little more than an hour ago had been so arrogant, overbearing and dangerous. Slater saw a lesson in it and determined not to forget it.

"Above all," said Berry, "let 'em see we mean 'em no harm; that providin' they respect us, we'll do likewise to them."

Slater reminded Berry of his burning-glass. Jeremy was sent to collect a small heap of dry grass and twigs, and the captain trained his glass on it. As the first wisp of smoke rose up, Berry blew a tiny spark to flame. The Fijians backed away. *"Isa! Isa lei!"* they cried in awe as they gazed upon the fire which gods had drawn from the sun.

Slater then asked for water by cupping his hands and pretending to drink. The Fijians brought from the canoe husked

49

drinking-nuts, which they cracked with stone axes. When the *Argo* men had drunk, the Fijians opened the nuts for them and showed them how to eat the soft white meat.

It was past the middle of the afternoon when they all set out for the island they had seen from the hill. Berry and two or three of the men, including Powell and Jeremy, went in the canoe. The launch, made lighter by the transfer, still could not keep up with the Fijian craft. On the way, Berry had to make the chief keep luffing so that the launch could follow at all closely. They sailed over patches where the bottom showed, over pale-green, dappled patches where fish swam bright and swift. They saw a pair of sharks and the rush of things so swift the eye could see only a blur. Coral waved in the depths, a fantasy of colour, and crabs and other creatures scuttled over exposed rocks. Herons, blue-black as well as white, ran over ridges of uncovered coral, shooting out their long necks and seizing prey too slow to dodge the swift lunge. And they saw birds plummeting with folded wings straight into the water, emerging with small fish in their bills.

It was not long before they were closing with the land, running into a fairly well sheltered bay ringed by a beach of bright sand. In the background the island sloped up gently, thick with vegetation, the fronds of palms shining in the sunlight. In the lee of the land the sun was hotter, the water a smooth, pale green.

"How long, Sir, would ye say we'll be here?" asked Pain. He was rowing forward. Doyle was in the bow. Slater looked from one to the other, wondering whether it was not Doyle whom Pain had addressed. Pain had been staring straight ahead at the back of Wilkinson, who pulled the oar aft of him. Doyle said nothing, did not even move, so Slater said: "Just as long as it takes to deck an' rig the launch. 'Tis up to ourselves."

It was a civil and natural enough question Pain had asked, and Slater tried to keep the edge from his voice, but as he spoke he was aware that he had failed. He could not quite put his finger on the reason, but he was afraid of Pain. Pain was a short, thick-set man with a stoop and a jutting jaw. His eyes were set in deep creases, and there was a doggedness in him that Slater realised would make him a dangerous enemy. He was not the most intelligent of them, nor yet the least—Slater held that place for Light, or possibly Morgan—but Pain was tactless, a man seemingly incapable of hiding his feelings. He was heavy of speech and, according to Barber, "the last man to go ashore alongside of, a crotchety bugger".

"I still think we're not doin' the right thing," Pain said as he finished the next stroke.

"Every man's entitled to think what he likes, Pain," returned Slater, "but that don't give him the right to go talkin' about it. Cap'n Berry has made a decision. 'Tis our place to stick by it. So far 'tis workin' out. He said he'd get the right side o' these savages, and he has. Ye can thank y'bloody stars we've got the man we have—an' not some o' the masters I've known in m'time."

"Aye," put in Barber, "and that goes for me too. He'll do for me."

A murmur came from some of the others, but none spoke out. Pain rowed on, quite unaffected by what Slater had said. For some five minutes they rowed. Then Barber stopped; he lifted his oar clear of the water, turned, and, looking out over the starboard bow, sniffed the air. Then he faced aft and bent to his oar again.

"Ye've a nose, Sam," said Slater.

"Aye, Sir, that I have. An' 'tis like the rest o' me—'tis a big 'un and smells well."

"Was ye thinkin' o' the meal the savages'll be makin' of it, Mr. Slater?" asked Morgan.

Barber answered: "Nay, Johnny, he weren't. He were thinkin' of the smell of the land, same as I were. Weren't ye, Sir?"

"Aye, Barber, I was."

" 'Tis a rare smell o' dampness I'm smellin'," said Morgan.

"That's what we said when we saw the island from the top o' the hill, wasn't it, Mr. Slater?" said Wilkinson quickly. "We said it looked damp. Boggy, I mind the cap'n said."

"We did, Wilky," said Slater, "and I don't think we were far wrong."

"I never struck a damp place without there was fever," said Pain, pulling and looking over his shoulder at the land. "An'

51

another thing, wetness breeds gnats and flies. I know it does. There'll be mosquitoes here."

"Or worse," added Barber. And at that moment Doyle called from forward: "Starboard y'helm, Mister. Coral ahead. Steady . . . steady as she goes."

Nothing more was said. Doyle conned the launch until they neared the yellow sand at the water's edge. Then Slater gave the order, and with half a dozen quick strokes they drove the bow of the launch up on the beach, a hundred yards to port of where the canoe was beached. Slater took in the rudder and then looked for Berry. He was still on the canoe, standing, about to follow the chief along the deck. The moment before he moved he glanced at the launch. It was an instant's glimpse, but it startled Slater, for not only was it the drawn face of a man who is suffering, it was the face of one who in a few hours had aged years.

Chapter 6

It was a fantastic scene; to the Americans it seemed the island spewed its every human being on to that beach. Old men, women and children came shouting down the sand, pointing at the launch and the white men, calling out, waving their arms. Some of them got no farther than a quarter of the way down when, overcome by fear, they stopped in full rush, turned and ran back as fast as they had come; others got half-way and stopped there, muttering to themselves and to one another; but a few, far braver, came on closer, calling to their men at the canoe, and getting for answer that these were gods.

"*Sobosobo!*" came the cry, a long hiss of wonder and mingled pleasure and fear. Out into the confusion strode the chief, arms upraised, shouting to the people to be silent. Then he told them that the gods meant them no harm, though they came armed with the thunder itself, thunder which killed with a flash of fire, instantly and from a great distance.

Now the white men saw women for the first time, and men not of the warrior class, old men, and children. All but a few of the women wore a short skirt made of grass and hibiscus bark. A kind of cincture, the band beautifully woven and variegated, carried a fringe from three to ten inches deep. Hanging from its centre, below the navel, was a long tuft of fibre which fell, on some of them, below the knees. Some skirts were almost white, others a tan colour, and some jet-black—these, Slater noticed, being made of a different kind of material. Many of the women had their hair dressed in the same fantastic shapes as the men, but some of them had hair of a different type altogether, hair without any kink in it, long tresses such as any European woman might have. These also, Slater noticed, were lighter of skin than the others, less negroid in character.

The bodies of many of them were daubed with various colours, turmeric predominating, and all of them wore ornaments made of sea-shells or fish-teeth or bone. Armlets and breastplates were common, the breastplates made of pearl shells, some of them as large as a dessert plate—beautiful iridescent shells which glistened as they moved. Some of the women had pierced ears, and they wore shells—mostly cowrie—tied up against the lobes with pieces of sennit; a number of them had the lobes stretched so wide that they were able to accommodate cowrie shells of the largest size in the perforations.

Some of the older women had scars cut in concentric circles on their backs and barbed lines tattooed on their hands and fingers; most of these women were tattooed blue about the mouth also, and, as with the men, Slater noticed that nearly all had at least one finger missing. The children, boys and girls, up to the age of ten or eleven, were quite naked.

Now it was the turn of the white men to be astonished. They stood in a close bunch, midway between the launch and the canoe, staring at this display of savagery, these naked, painted bodies, and it was some moments before any of them spoke.

Wilkinson was the first to comment. "There's some queer-lookin' folk I know," he said, the wonder sounding clear in his voice, "but if ye'd tol' me—an' I'd not seen it—I'd never had believed there was them as queer as some o' these."

"Aye," said Hocking, "though mixed up with them there be some fine-lookin' women——"

"Belay there, Elisha," said Barber, grinning, not looking at Hocking. "Them as are, aren't for the likes o' ye."

"An' what's the matter with me?" asked Hocking, rising, as he invariably did, to Barber's bait. "They'd have a damn sight less to fear from me than from some I know."

"Then which one strikes y'fancy, Elisha? That little bit near the end down here?" Barber pointed to a pretty girl who stood with her mouth open and her eyes staring out of her head in amazement.

"She'd do for me," said Morgan, gazing back with fully as much wonder as that in the face of the girl, "or the one behind her. I'd say them two was as pretty as ye'd sail on anywhere."

"What about the one in front?" asked Day. "There's a wench as can share my bed any time she likes. Juicy, I'd call that one, like a cherry for the pluckin'."

"Aye, lads, 'tis a sailor's dream come true," said Barber, shaking his head as if he found it impossible to believe his eyes. "I ask ye—did ye ever expect ye'd be thrown among such a collection o' bare-skinned beauties? Wherever ye look there's somethin' either pointin' or waggin' at ye."

"'Tis the pointers rather than the waggers as tickle my fancy," said Wilkinson.

"Aye," said Pain.

Barber turned upon Pain. "I thought, Jeb, ye wasn't in favour of us landin' here, was keen to get away to sea again?"

Pain scowled, but did not speak, and Wilkinson said: "I wonder does the paint rub off?"

"We'll bloody soon know, Wilky," said Day. "A look at ye tomorrow mornin' an' we'll have the answer to that one."

"I still say 'tis the pointers, painted or not, as tickle my fancy," went on Wilkinson, ignoring Day.

"Aye," said Morgan, "the upward pointers. What say ye, Pepper?"

Peppercorn grinned back at him. "I'm a bit old, Johnny, for

54

the delights ye lads be thinkin' on, but I must say there's some trim little craft among 'em."

"What would y'old lady say now, Johnny," said Day to Morgan, "if she saw ye oglin' these bare-skinned wenches. Eh?"

Morgan turned on Day quickly, grinning sheepishly. Barber saw it and said: "What, Johnny Morgan, has Jo Day caught ye thinkin' ye was in among 'em? Which one is it, Johnny?"

"'Tis the old duchess right in front," said Wilkinson, pointing to an incredibly old hag with great pendulous breasts, an extraordinary mop of hair which stood out like a golliwog's, and not a tooth in her head.

"Nay," said Barber emphatically. " 'Twon't do, Wilky. She's reserved, that one is—for Light. As soon as I clapped eyes on her I says to meself, well, come what may, Les is fixed. What say ye, Les?"

Slater, standing beside Berry, listened to the remarks of the men and smiled to himself. Curious, he thought, 'twas something that living in a clothes-covered world ye weren't so conscious of, but 'twas fantastic when you put a few hundred women together, near as naked as the day they were born, just what a marvellous variety of shape the human body could assume. Especially did this seem the case with their breasts, for no other part of the body seemed capable of such variation. The young people, he noticed, seemed to outnumber the old, though they who were old—the women particularly—appeared extremely so. Some were so thin as to be almost skin and bone, others flabby and worn-out-looking, as if all the juices in them had dried up, leaving but desiccated pockets of skin-covered flesh; yet others again were fat, one with breasts of such size Slater could only conclude she was deformed by growth of disease. But these were the exceptions; for the most part they were a good-looking, healthy people.

So the *Argo* men gazed. Much of their preoccupation with the women, while natural enough, was due to a certain nervousness they felt at the strangeness of their surroundings. Also, they were a little apprehensive; they had caught a glimpse of another side of these people. For all his breadth of travel a seaman is by nature among the most conservative of men; lose him his ship, and his simplicity and inability to adapt himself are often the most obvious things about him.

But whatever their individual feelings as they stood there, whatever their private fears and hopes, they felt one thing in common—a predominant sense of being alive. For all their remarks about the women, this consciousness of survival filled them almost to the exclusion of all else, the more so as they had not felt it on the islet. There they had come to grips with nothing. Here it was different; they had won the first round, tested the first of the hazards they would meet on the way to Port Jackson and had found themselves not wanting. For the present it was enough that they lived. But it was a transitory state, and a state which often precedes an awful awakening to the truths life has to offer. As he stood there listening to the men, Slater caught a glimpse of something of this. He glanced at Pain, then at Doyle, then at Morgan and wondered how soon it would be before this novelty—and that, he decided, was all this nakedness of the women was to them—would pass and their minds would turn again to their survival, the launch and the work on her, and the voyage.

How much of it Berry felt, Slater did not know; but the captain too must have glimpsed it, for he soon turned to Slater and said quietly: "The lads seem happy enough, Mister. I hope to God it holds."

"It had better," Slater said.

"Aye. Yet, y'know, I'm a bit afeared o' these women. Some o' them are mighty handsome. An' no doubt willin' enough."

"There's one way out o' that difficulty—tell the lads they're to have naught to do with them."

"I been thinkin' on those lines. At any rate, we'll see. I'll turn it over some more afore I make up m'mind. Ye'll notice, Mister," said Berry then, "that some o' these people are fairer than others an' have straight hair. 'Twould almost seem to be another race."

"I noticed that."

"Nothin' of the negro in 'em at all. Cast y'eyes now at this girl with the old man over here. They're a fine-lookin' pair, particularly so, and surprisin' light o' skin."

Slater looked to where Berry pointed. The man he took in at

56

a glance, a tall, dignified figure, middle-aged, wearing a pearl-shell breastplate like the chief, but the woman held him, fixing his attention. She was slightly taller than most of the women, and her body seemed to glow under its coating of oil. Her skin was a pale nut-brown, almost a dark peach, and her breasts were full and tight, nearly perfect in their roundness. Her eyes were set wide apart. Her mouth was well shaped, and her even teeth showed brilliant against the dark redness of her slightly parted lips. Luxuriant, shining black hair cascaded down over her shoulders. No ornament or dressing adorned it except a flower inserted on one side above the ear. A few errant strands fell forward from her left shoulder and gently screened the dark nipple of her breast.

Her *liku* fell to her knees, the strands of it straw-yellow, spaced about an inch apart along the lower edge of the beautifully woven band, in the pattern of which were worked small red seeds. The tassel which fell down in front of her, between her legs, was silky-soft, moving in the breeze of the beach, brushing against the inside of her thighs.

Slater gazed at her, fascinated. He had known women as lovely—a Chinese girl, and a New Englander, who were, feature for feature, perhaps more exquisitely formed—but, in a way he could not describe, this girl was instantly set apart from any other he had known.

There were others about her as perfectly formed, some of them as fair of skin, as lustrous of hair, but this he saw was different about her—she bore herself with a grace not apparent in the other women, as though she was aware of being in some way superior to them. Yet, curiously, she deepened the chasm that lay between his former world and this fantastic one. Seemingly less of a savage than the others, she yet increased his wariness rather than diminished it. This puzzled him, for he felt it should not be, and he caught for an instant a glimpse of something which, he sensed, could grow until it would consume him. Suddenly the idea of rescue, Port Jackson, the launch, Berry—even Jeremy—seemed so very far away.

Then, while sunk in this abstraction, he saw her look at him; and it was only when their eyes met that he realised the intensity with which he had been staring at her. He felt his skin grow hot with embarrassment, as if she had discovered him peeping at her as she exposed herself, believing herself unseen. He turned from her, and sweat prickled his skin.

It was her nakedness, he thought; none of them seemed as bare as she. Yet she wore no less than the others; nor was she wantonly posing to attract.

He wondered what she would make of his gaze. Would she take it that he wanted to lie with her? What were their customs? Was she a virgin? Who was this man who stood near her, what was his relation to her? He was older—was he her father? Would she take his stare to mean (according to some custom which might be theirs) that he had put his mark on her?

Nay, he thought, 'twas not so. Nor did he want it so, for if it was that way, then other men could have seen her loveliness, her tight breasts, her silk-smooth thighs and claimed her as theirs. He wanted not to believe that, and he was surprised to feel the hurt that the idea brought. Yet could such a woman be unmated? Or mated, could she shed the bond? be his? or any other man's?

Berry's voice came from somewhere far away, and Slater heard only the sound of it, not what the words meant. Then followed Doyle's voice. The captain was plucking at his sleeve and speaking to him. Slater faced about, carrying in his mind a last glimpse of her against the yellow sand as she turned to walk back up the beach, the clean line of her thighs and buttocks showing between the strands of her skirt.

". . . wool-gatherin', Mister."

"What's that, Sir?"

"I say ye're wool-gatherin'. I was telling ye that I figure the chief here wants us to go with him."

"What about the launch?" said Doyle. With his thumb stuck in his belt, Doyle was facing Berry and completely ignoring Slater.

Slater glanced at Doyle and then at Berry. He was conscious of being left out of some decision that was being made and wanted desperately now to learn what had been said. "Where does he figure on takin' us?" he asked.

"How the hell would I know? If ye'd been listenin' instead o' gazin' about . . ." Berry didn't finish the sentence. Instead he turned to Doyle and said: "I don't suppose we should leave the launch unguarded, Mister. I take it that's what ye was meanin'?"

"It was."

"Aye. Well, we'll leave a couple o' the lads on her. Here, Elisha, an' you, Wilky, stay with the boat. Now, should anythin' happen, though I don't figure it will, fire a musket in the air an' we'll be right down."

"Would ye mind, Sir," said Powell, "if I was to stay here too? I've no heart for walkin', unless ye thought 'twas necessary."

"Nay, Powell, stay be all means."

"Now all together, an' keep together," said Berry. "I want none o' ye wandering off be yeselves." He started off up the beach, the chief smiling at him, walking a step ahead, leading him. After Berry and the chief went Slater. Jeremy, slipping between the men, came forward to walk beside him. Then came Doyle, walking alone, and after him the other men in a tight bunch. A little distance back followed some of the Fijians, elders and petty chiefs, led by the young chief.

Slater felt the girl had made a fool of him and wondered at the way she had so quickly affected him. Though Berry had given little enough sign of it, Slater knew he had been annoyed. And Doyle, he thought suddenly—had Doyle seen it, and known it was preoccupation with a woman?

"Where are they takin' us, Mr. Slater?" Jeremy asked as they reached the top of the beach.

"I can't tell ye, lad."

"Perhaps to some house, some place where we're to stay."

"Aye, very probably."

" 'Tis awfully queer, isn't it, Sir? I mean all these people with no clothes on. But I don't think they'll eat us, do ye? They really do eat people, don't they, Sir?"

"So I believe, Jeremy."

"A lot of people?"

"They're said to be among the worst of all the savages in this ocean."

And as he finished saying this there came to him a thought which filled him with horror. He saw himself with the girl he'd seen on the beach, making love to her, locked to her—making love to a woman who ate human flesh, who had felt on her lips, between her teeth, the meat of an arm, the fat of a cheek—saw himself feeling for those lips with his own. Instantly he was repelled.

Then Jeremy was speaking again. "That musket the cap'n fired, Sir—that fixed 'em, I reckon. 'Tis a good thing he's such a smart shot, isn't it? Though I'll tell ye something. Would ye like me to?" His bright eyes gazed up at Slater.

"Aye, lad, tell me."

"Well, this is what I think." Jeremy's voice fell to a whisper, and Slater had to bend his head to hear. "I think, Sir, that they took a good look at us, pinched us between their fingers—an' they did, y'know, or they did me—pinched us, I say, Sir, between their fingers, and said we'd be too tough."

At the top of the beach the chief led them to a path which ran through dense, jungly growth, under trees draped with creepers and with hanging vines. Fungus, startling in its colour, grew on rotting tree trunks, and orchids bore bright flowers on dull grey-green stems. They saw no birds and only one butterfly, chopping at the air on jewelled wings.

They came upon the house suddenly, a long building that stood in a clearing, the grass about it close-cropped, bright green against the darkness of the bush and jungle surrounding it. The walls of the house were of reed, and the steeply pitched roof was thatched with pandanus. This was the *bure ni vulagi*—the receiving-house for strangers. It was a pleasant-looking building, made for the reception of many more men than *Argo* had brought. In fact, the crews of half a dozen ships of *Argo*'s tonnage could have been accommodated in it comfortably.

Berry was very pleased with it and said so to Slater. "Aye," replied Slater, "an' she's well situated too, Sir."

"No more than—what, ten–twelve minutes' walk to the beach? Close to our work."

"I was thinkin' rather of the village. This seems well away from it."

"Ye feel that's to the good, eh?"

"I do."

"An' ye might have somethin' too, be thunder. I'd not

60

thought o' that side of it, but it could be to our good in the event o' trouble. Ah, but I hardly think 'twill come to trouble, Mister. Just see how pleased they are to help us."

"What do ye think of it, lads?" asked Berry as the last of the men stepped inside. "Ye couldn't ask for much more could ye?"

"We're to doss here, Sir?" asked Day, looking about.

"So I take it," said Berry. "Eh, Mr. Slater?"

" 'Twould seem so."

" 'Twill do me," said Day. "Don't say as I'd rather it than me berth in *Argo*, but I've heard o' them as was shipwrecked findin' it worse."

"So have I," put in Barber. " 'Tis a home away from home, so help me if it isn't."

Then Berry turned to Doyle. "What think ye of it, Mister?" Berry was smiling, and the twist to his face was not now quite as apparent as it had been.

" 'Twill do," said Doyle quietly. "We shouldn't be in it long."

Slater saw the disappointment pass on Berry's face, felt the hurt in him. Berry was not a particularly sensitive man, but his delight in finding them with such comfortable quarters was so plain that Doyle's surly admission of their good fortune was a blow to him.

As each man spoke, or moved, looked about him, touching the textured walls, the chief's eyes jumped to him. He was smiling, trying desperately to know what they thought of it, determined above all to please these visitors from the clouds.

There was much to intrigue the white men, for the house was like none they had ever seen before. Its main framework was attached to heavy posts, stripped of their bark and polished, sunk in the ground. The walls were faced with reed lashed together with sennit, which, being dyed several different colours, formed a pattern, so that the walls gave the effect of being covered with a continuous strip of finely woven carpet, yet a carpet which was at the same time part of the structure. At places the pattern was continued away from the walls, on to the posts, and even across the heavy beams of timber that ran across the building at the level of the top plate and tied the

61

whole structure together. The floor was everywhere spread about with mats woven from coconut or pandanus leaves. At both ends of the building were raised platforms which, Slater presumed, were for sleeping upon. There was a fireplace in the centre of the house, a shallow pit framed by heavy, squared logs. With no chimney, no opening at all in the roof, the rafters and the thatch were blackened by smoke.

Behind the house, where the white men had not seen it as they approached, was another, smaller house; this was for cooking in. At one end was a great fireplace sunk into the ground, with racks above for storing utensils and for keeping food warm. On the racks were some dozen or more huge earthenware pots, many bowls of hardwood, some oval in shape, some round, and a few having small legs carved out of their bottoms. At the opposite end were low benches upon which food could be prepared.

Berry did his best to make the chief see they were satisfied. The Fijian returned Berry's head-nodding vigorously and then, beckoning them to follow, led the way out of the cooking-house and across the clearing to a path which wound its way farther inland. Berry seemed to Slater to be preoccupied; he walked with his head down, looking to neither right nor left of him.

They had gone some four or five hundred yards when they came to another house, set, as was the first one, in a well-kept clearing. This house was smaller, more finely built, more carefully thatched and walled. The ridge-pole of the roof projected for a yard or more at each end. It was blackened and was adzed to curve out to a funnel-like shape. Its extremities were decorated with white shells. The first house had been raised only a few inches from the ground, but this stood at least three feet off it. The chief walked to the door and then, turning, indicated that of the white men only Berry and Slater were to enter with him. One other man went in—the young chief.

Berry and Slater could see immediately that this was a house reserved for men of rank. Its posts were more highly polished than those in the other house, and the woven work was far finer in texture. The floor mats, some six to eight deep, were made from thinner, more supple strands and were bordered with a black pattern which fitted gracefully on to their creamy whiteness. The structural members of the sleeping-platform at the far end of the house were completely covered with sennit binding in the same pattern as that of the bands on the four main corner posts. The effect of the house was one of dignity, beauty and coolness.

Here, the chief indicated, Berry and Slater were to live.

"D'ye think 'tis wise, Mister?" asked Berry, once they had understood this.

"Ye mean, for us to be separated from the men?"

"Aye."

"I can see no harm in it," Slater said slowly. "I'd say we should try to make it a rule to do what they want, whenever we can. They've we two marked down as chiefs evidently."

" 'Tis smart o' them, how they've separated us so quickly," said Berry as he gazed about at the beautifully-patterned lacing, feeling in his nostrils the tangy smell of old smoke and the sweetness of pandanus. "Ye're right, they regard us as the chiefs. Then that means," he went on slowly, as though he spoke to himself, "that Doyle'll be in command down at the other house."

The remark took Slater by surprise. On its face it was nothing more than a simple statement of fact, yet Slater felt that with it Berry had lowered a barrier, had revealed a fear, or a germ of distrust, in his thinking about Doyle. Berry continued to gaze at the house for a moment or two, then suddenly he looked at the chief and, gesturing towards him, said: "I suppose ye can't guess what his name is, Mister? Might be of some help if we knew."

"Nay, Sir, I can't. But I've the feelin' that if ye could spell it, it'd begin with the letter A."

"Well, I'm damned. How did ye find that out?"

"I don't say I have. 'Tis more probable that I'm wrong than right, but I've heard several of those men outside address him and I'd say his name were something like Abeela."

With a quickness of perception that astonished Berry and Slater, the Fijian, hearing something which sounded like his name, and divining that they were talking about him, gave a little shout and said, pointing to himself and nodding his head several times in rapid succession: "*Io*. Awila."

63

Berry looked to Slater. "Ye're right, Mister. Or near enough. Well, I'm damned."

"A-wila," said Slater.

The Fijian nodded again and repeated his name.

Slater pointed to himself and said both his first name and his surname. The chief made a try at it, but it was obviously beyond him.

"Try just y'first," said Berry. " 'Tis too much, both at once."

After several tries Awila came close to it, though he made it a softer, thicker sound, as if it were spelled O-l-i-v-a.

" 'Tis near enough." Berry smiled and nodded at Awila, who, proud of his accomplishment, turned to the young chief. They discovered then that the young man's name was Duadua. Both chiefs were delighted, Awila particularly so, and he repeated Slater's name over and over, smiling broadly. Then he taught Slater their title, Ratu. "Ratu Awila," he said as he pointed to himself, "Ratu Duadua," as he pointed to the younger man.

"Now what's the *Io*, Mister?"

"I'd guess it was 'Yes', Sir."

"Ye'll be right too. Lord, ye'll soon be masterin' the lingo. See if ye can find out the name they have for the island."

By pointing first to the ground and then all around him, Slater learned that the island's name was Oneata. He then tried to teach them Berry's name, but they were not interested. Berry was the *turagu levu*, the big chief, and they were content to call him that.

Looking at Awila and seeing the pleasure in his face, Slater came near to believing in Berry's plan. There was still an instinctive rejection of it left somewhere in his mind, but it seemed impossible, at that moment, for any conflict to come between them and Awila and his people. In Berry's face he saw a contentment he had not seen since before the wreck. The captain looked drawn and was obviously suffering, but, aged or not, his was the face of a man who is seeing what he hoped to see. The distracted look which had been in his face on the little island was gone; his mouth was still partly out of shape, and his speech was somewhat slurred, but there was now little left to remind one of the beaten man who had spoken of Windmill Point as he went down that sun-baked hill.

64

Awila, Slater judged, was well into middle age. His face was flat, the nose broad and the lips full. There was nothing in him of the fair-skinned, straight-haired people of the island. The breastplate which hung from his neck on a sennit cord was made from a gold-lipped pearl shell; there was no carving on it, but about its edge were a number of holes. Above his right elbow was an armlet of small, oval, pearly-yellow shells, and similar shells in the necklet of the young chief.

"We'd best be gettin' out to the lads, Mister," said Berry.

"How do ye feel now?" asked Slater.

" 'Tis m'head. What I need, Mister, is to lie down a while—here, on these soft mats—an' just close m'eyes and shut out the light. The light is bad, Oliver."

"Why not do it? I can handle the rest of this. Give me your orders and I'll see they're carried out."

"I know it. But, not yet. Soon I'll be able to get m'head down and sleep."

"Would ye take some laudanum? It's in the chest——"

"After, Mister—when we've seen to it all. Then I will. Now come on, an' we'll tell the men of the arrangement."

"I'd not meant we'd be separated, lads, but it can't be helped," Berry said when they were outside. "Now, I've a word o' warnin' for ye. We'll not be here any longer than we can help. Once the launch is ready we'll make away, and we'll be aimin' for Port Jackson. But while we're here we want no trouble with the natives. We can't afford to have any. Ye must all see to that. True, we've the muskets and they're mighty scared o' them, but we're outnumbered and in no position to be on anythin' but our best behaviour. Which means—an' I'm puttin' it to ye straight—ye're to keep away from the women.

"Ye'll say 'twill be hard," he went on. "So it might be, but we've too much at stake to go gettin' into trouble over them."

"An' what, Sir, if they wasn't to regard it as trouble?" put in Pain, a smirk on his face.

"I'm not sayin' they would, Pain"—Berry looked at him—"but their men might. As a matter o' fact from the bit I seen this afternoon I'd say there'd be plenty who'd be pleased to give ye all ye might want. But 'twould lead to trouble. We're not in *Argo*, we're shipwrecked, come ashore to deck and rig a

65

launch, an' we're goin' to keep our noses clean. Mr. Doyle, ye'll be in command down at the other house. I want ye to report at once any man who even as much as thinks about breakin' out. Ye got that?"

"Aye," said Doyle gruffly.

"I've only one other thing to add. I don't like the mention of it, but ye'd better know. I intend a floggin' for the man who goes foolin' with the women."

Several of the crew looked sideways at one another. Barber grinned; seldom did Barber fail to see the bizarre or humorous side of a thing. Slater wondered whether Barber was grinning because he thought the pleasure would be worth the flogging.

"We'll be needin' an anchor watch for the launch, Mr. Doyle. Ye'll exclude yeself, the boy, an' Powell, as well as Mr. Slater and me. 'Twill only be needed at nights; four hours'll be the length of it and two men company for one another. An' o' course 'twill be an armed watch. All hands now'll set to unloadin' the launch. Have all the gear brought up to that house o' yours, Mr. Doyle."

Doyle nodded.

"Tomorrow, I mind, lads, is the Sabbath. We'll lie easy, as though we were at sea. We can't afford to, I suppose, but we've been through somethin' and earned a rest. And another thing— it might be the last easy Sabbath we'll be gettin' for some time to come."

He dismissed the men and they went off under Doyle. It was clear that some resented the prohibition Berry had put upon intercourse with the women. There was a sullenness, even in the way some of them walked. "They don't like what I said about the women, Mister. But I'm determined. We know naught o' the customs of these Indians and the risk of giving offence that might end in massacre is too great."

Even as Berry was saying this, Awila was pulling gently at his arm.

Slater fell in beside Duadua and they followed Berry and Awila out of the clearing, along the path over which they had come. Awila led them left on to a track Slater remembered having passed on the way in. They were being taken to the village, a scatter of houses stretching along the curve of the bay.

66

The size of the settlement surprised Berry and Slater, for they had seen just a part of it from the beach. Though the village was narrow, it occupied a large section of the crescent-shaped shore line. They were conscious of many eyes on them, peeping from doorways, from behind trees, from around the corners of houses; children ran screaming, tumbling over in their fright, were snatched up, gagged with a hand over the mouth, and hurried out of sight lest they be spirited away by these creatures who could take the shape of men.

They marched past cooking-places, fires smouldering and giving off strange odours; past coconut meat set out in the sun to drip its oil into earthenware pots; past new houses, old houses, houses being built, or repaired—and almost everywhere the activities were abandoned, the startled men and women having fled as they caught sight of the gods approaching. The visitors saw other houses mouldering away, roofs and walls falling in, rotting, their posts grey with weathering, waiting for a time when heirs would grow to manhood and build once more.

About half-way through the village they came to an open square; this was the *rara*, and from it they caught their first sight of the temple—the *bure kalou*, or 'house of the gods'—its steeply pitched roof standing above the buildings about it. Crossing the *rara* they soon reached the temple. It stood upon a mound some fifteen feet high, faced with a rubble-work of dry-bedded stone. The stairway up to it was a log into which steps had been notched. At the base of this log were several sacred stones. One of these was ornamented with a *liku* made from hibiscus fibre, its tassel touching the ground; the other stone had no skirt but was decorated with a series of concentric circles painted upon it. There was only one door into the temple, but there were windows in every wall, all these openings framed with closely bound sennit. The amount of sennit in the house amazed Slater, for loops of it hung from the eaves, and the timbers were covered with it. From the ends of the projecting ridge-poles some forty feet from the ground hung more sennit, into which were knotted white cowrie shells.

The white men stood in awe before this building. It rose towards the sky like some monstrous, decorated phallus, and

67

Slater barely repressed a shudder, for it indicated too clearly the savage mysteries it ministered to. And he thought of the sailors' stories he had heard—of cannibalism, of insensate cruelty, of sexual liberties, of dark practices, of evil of all kinds, of crimes that the imagination boggled at. How much of this, he wondered, applied to these people?

He glanced at Awila, but there was no clue to be gained there; Awila was looking at Berry and smiling with pride at Berry's amazement. About the temple's base were small *mavunitoga* trees, with crimson fruit the size of an apricot; the visitors were not told that the gum of this tree was a poison in which the Fijians dipped their spear and arrow points.

Not far past the *bure kalou* they crossed a stream, little more than a trickle, sweet and cold, wandering on a sandy flat before it reached the lagoon. Drawn up above the beach at this place were a number of canoes under palm-leaf shelters.

All about the village were trees: *ivi*, or Tahitian chestnut trees; *baka* trees, from which trailed a thousand aerial roots; breadfruit trees, the fruit hanging green and yellow-green among their dark-shadowed leaves; and coconut palms. Over the ground, in and out of the shadow patterns, trailed vines and creepers with vividly coloured flowers. And they passed some pigs, curious creatures with long snouts.

They were now drawing near to Awila's house. They entered a grove of *nokonoko*, or casuarina trees, singing softly in the wind, which carried to the island the distant thunder of the great sea reef.

Awila's house astonished them almost as much as the *bure kalou* had. In style it was not unlike the other houses of the village, but its roof was steeper, though not so steep as that of the temple. Its walls were of reed, more than three feet thick, and the thatching leaves were thin and closely packed, even thicker than the walls.

Awila led the way in. After the heat and the brightness of the day outside, the coolness of the house was dramatic in its suddenness. Ten great posts carried the main structure, bound with red and black sennit, a pattern which was repeated in the lacing of the reeds in the walls. The floor mats, of extremely fine weave, with patterned borders, were deep enough to cushion the feet as though they fell upon cool moss. The timbering of the roof was dark with age and smoke. Hanging from a twisted grass cable which was wound under the ridge were more shells and tassels of sennit. Nowhere was there a misplaced knot, or a careless execution of the complicated patterns; mystery was there, even savagery, but with them were the majesty and the quiet of a cathedral.

Awila took them to the end farthest from the door where they had entered and sat himself between them, an expression of deep satisfaction on his face. And why not? Why conceal it? What other man had been so favoured as to be visited by the gods?

Several warriors then entered the house carrying between them a wooden bowl about three feet across, which they set down some distance in front of Awila and the white men. The construction of this bowl intrigued Slater, for though it was supported on many short legs which grew out immediately below its thin, curved rim, it had been carved from one piece of wood, a section cut from the trunk of what must have been a very big tree. This was the *tanoa*, or *yaqona* bowl.

Soon the house began to fill with warriors, unarmed but dressed and painted as though for war. As they entered the house they dropped to their knees and moved on them, not daring to stand in the presence of Awila. Slater counted about fifty of them. By far the majority sat themselves well back from the *tanoa* and to one side of it. The rest clustered close in a half-circle behind it, their faces to Awila and the white men.

One of them crawled forward and put before Awila and Berry and Slater cups made from half sections of inner coconut shell. Their exteriors were polished a dark brown, almost black, and their inner surfaces were mottled with a purple-grey glaze, similar to that on the inside of the great bowl.

Six young women entered the house and crossing quickly to the *tanoa* sat with lowered heads at the left side of it.

"By the Lord, Mister," said Berry, staring at them, "there's a sight for ye. Why, 'tis one to stir even my old blood." Unlike the rest of the women Slater had seen, these wore skirts of green pandanus leaves and about their ankles and wrists were circlets of freshly plucked fern. Their skins were the colour of dark honey, and their oiled shoulders, arms, bellies and tight girls' breasts glistened. And once again Slater smelled the sweet, pungent smell he had noticed on the warriors on the islet.

As each girl sat she was handed a bundle of freshly dug roots. These she proceeded to chew, biting off a portion and chewing it thoroughly, spewing out the root in fibrous balls and placing them in the bowl. They set these balls systematically about the sides of the *tanoa*, and after placing one the girl would rinse her mouth with water from a bamboo cup handed her from behind. Once Slater had tasted the drink he realised that such rinsing was necessary to alleviate the sting of the peppery root.

"We're to drink what they make from this chewed root, Mister?" asked Berry, making a wry face.

" 'Twould seem so, Sir." Slater smiled at Berry, but the idea was just as distasteful to him. And the thought brought back his revulsion at the mental image of the girl on the beach eating human flesh. He saw her again, feeding, eating meat identifiable as human—a leg, part of the foot hanging from it; and he realised now that this idea of cannibalism was beginning to colour all his thinking about these people. There was danger in this, he knew, and he would have to watch himself, for if it became an obsession it could well prevent him from reasoning soundly about them. All the same, as he looked at the men and women out in front of him he couldn't help wondering whether they had tasted human flesh. Watching the hands of the girls as they moulded the little balls, the light moving on their oiled fingers, he saw in his mind the hands of the girl on the beach; her fingers too were shining, but it was not oil which made them glisten.

The requisite number of balls was now in the *tanoa* and the warrior nearest to it shuffled forward on his buttocks until he sat all but touching the bowl. This was the *yaqona* maker. He placed both his hands on the *tanoa*'s rim and for some moments sat quite still. Then he bent forward, gathered up the little spheres and rolled them into one large ball.

As he did this, an elder sitting some distance from the bowl called out softly, and a man came into the house carrying a piece of bamboo about six feet long, a wide pipe of wood with a tampon of green grass stuffed into its upper end. Crouched, he carried it to the *tanoa*'s edge and tilting it let water run from it into the bowl. The water gurgled as it ran through the grass stopper and as it moved in the bamboo it made a sound that at first Slater and Berry thought was the beat of far-off drums. But for this, utter silence reigned in the house. Now it was taboo for any noise to enter.

Slater felt a beginning of tension as he realised that he was a participant in a solemn ceremony, almost a rite, which might even have religious significance. But no, he thought, for if it were a religious affair the temple would have been its setting. He glanced at Berry, who seemed also conscious of the moment, for he was staring steadily at the *yaqona* maker, his lips slightly parted and a beading of sweat forming on his forehead.

Then from the warriors who sat back from the *tanoa* there came a gentle clapping of hands, a rhythmic beating which grew quickly until with startling suddenness one of them began to chant, a deep, round sound, and the others made gestures with their fingers, hands, arms and heads. This was a choir, accompanying the ritual at the bowl. Soon every man but those close about the bowl was chanting. Then a strainer made of teased-out hibiscus bark was drawn slowly through the bowl by the *yaqona* maker. As he lifted it, yellow in his hands, he twisted it, wringing it out, and without taking his eyes from the bowl passed it back to another, who shook from it the particles of chewed root. Then came the cup-bearer. Quickly, almost arrogantly, he entered the house, showing no subservience in the presence of Awila. A huge man, he was more elaborately dressed than the others. Like the women he wore a skirt of green pandanus leaves, but over it were yards of tapa cloth, dark, heavily patterned stuff, dyed red and brown. Garlands of leaves and flowers circled his head and wrists and ankles, and his body was daubed with black paint. He came to the *tanoa* proudly, bearing before him a cup like those set before Awila and the white men. Slowly he knelt by the side of the bowl and held the cup out over it while the *yaqona* maker lifted the strainer and let some of the drink run from it into the cup.

This cup, the *bilo*, filled, he held it out at arm's length and turned slowly to face Awila. Now the song of the warriors

71

quickened, the sound thick on the air and with it a rapid, heavily accentuated hand-clapping. Then—still with the *bilo* out before him—he began to dance, first on one leg and then on the other. Linked with the rising rhythm of the chant he approached Awila, then retreated, skirt swaying, skin glistening, beads of sweat standing out on his oiled skin. As the chant reached a coda, he began to lower himself to the mats until he was squatting on his haunches. Then he rose and kneeling before Berry offered him the cup.

Berry was nonplussed. Obviously he was meant to take the drink; but what of the cup before him? Awila saw his confusion and leaning forward picked up his own *bilo* and held it out towards the cup-bearer, indicating that Berry should do likewise. Slowly the bearer poured the drink into Berry's cup. Berry put it to his lips and drank. As he did, the bearer sat, put his own *bilo* on the floor and clapped his hands three times.

As suddenly as it had begun the chant ended. As Berry drained the last of the peppery fluid a shout broke from the warriors, followed by more rhythmic hand-clapping. Then it was Awila's turn and then Slater's.

Slater found the drink tingled his tongue, but it had a tangy, refreshing bite to it and, once he had overcome the initial revulsion from taking into his mouth something which had been in another's, he found he liked it—more so than Berry. However, determined to do nothing which might offend them, the captain gave no indication of his distaste. His head still troubled him, his eyes ached, and the muscles of his face still twisted his expression. He longed for rest more than ever—to close his eyes and shut out the light which so tormented him.

72

Chapter 7

THE Sabbath dawned cool and sweet. The trade wind came softly out of the south-east, curling over the island, dispersing the early-morning smoke that climbed blue from the thatches.

Slater woke at the first lightening of the day. For some moments he was unable to orient himself; the darkened house, shuttered against the mosquitoes, the faint smell of the slow fire the Fijians had showed them how to set the night before, and that curious indescribable softness which surrounds one in a grass house numbed him.

Then he remembered. He glanced across at Berry, lying on the sleeping-platform. He was breathing heavily, on his back. Several times in the night Berry had cried out, turning restlessly on the mats, but when Slater had gone to him and called to him, he had not answered. Slater got up and taking down one of the window shutters went to Berry and looked at him more closely in the light which now came into the room, remembering that at one time during the night it had seemed to him that Berry lay more in coma than in normal sleep. He decided against waking him and went outside, leaving the other shutters in place.

The sun was not yet up and light was coming from the whole of the sky, already blue but tinted yellow-red in the east. The air was like some cool liquid flowing about him, and from the jungle which surrounded the clearing came the call of birds. In the shadowless light a solitary orchid hanging from a tree blazed like a blob of dull fire.

He walked slowly down to the men's house. All except Powell were up, and several had gone to the beach to bathe. Powell said he felt better this morning. "How's the cap'n, Sir?" he asked.

"Still asleep."

"A sick man gets to know the worth o' sleep, Sir. 'Tis balm, providin' ye don't dream. Then 'tis hell."

Slater gave Powell a draught of medicine, which was mostly brandy, and then, asking him to have Jeremy sent up as soon as he returned from the beach, he went back to the house. Berry was awake now, his face pale, little less drawn than it had been the day before.

"Ye've been to the men, Mister," he said as Slater came into the house.

"I have, Sir, an' all is well. They're at the beach, bathing themselves."

"An' Powell?"

"I'd say he's more rested. I've given him his physic. But yeself—how is y'head this morning?"

"Still aching, Mister. Damn it. I could be better. The sleep don't seem to have done me the good I thought it would."

"Ye need more of it."

"Did I cry out at all?"

"Once or twice ye did, Sir."

"And broke y'rest, I guess. I'm sorry. Now, Mister, 'tis the Sabbath, I know, but had ye any plans for it?"

"What would ye say to me getting to know something of the island? I'm not saying we'll have trouble with the Indians, but if we did, a knowledge of the place might stand us in good stead."

" 'Tis a right good notion. Though I'd rather ye counted me out."

"I was thinkin' of going myself and takin' the boy."

"I'll give m'blessin' to it, Oliver. Ye can start as soon as ye like."

This was only the second time Berry had called him by his first name, and for the moment it embarrassed him; but he felt the warmth of it, as though by it Berry had transferred to him a greater trust.

Then Jeremy was there, standing in the doorway. "Mr. Doyle says, Sir, to tell ye that the Indians have sent us enough food to victual a whaler for a three-year v'yage."

"What sort o' food?" asked Berry, smiling back at him.

"There's vegetables, Sir, all wrapped up in leaves. An' fish, an' a pig."

"Oliver," said Berry, "what did I tell ye? The gods are

74

lookin' after us. Here, without us even mentioning it, the Indians have sent us food." Slater smiled at him. As with the business of the Indians being easily bluffed, Berry had predicted nothing about the gods looking after them. It was new in Berry, this ex-post-facto claim to successful prophecy.

"Great news, boy, great news. Nay, Mr. Slater, the more I see of it the more I believe we did the right thing be not makin' away."

"Aye. Now, Jeremy," said Slater, "you an' me are going to take a look about the island. I want ye to go down to the men's house an' ask Mr. Doyle for some salt meat an' biscuit for the two of us, enough for a couple o' meals. Have ye still the pistol I gave ye on the other island?"

"Mr. Doyle's got it, Sir."

"Then ask him for it, an' for some bullets. Ye needn't bring a powder flask, for I've enough cartridges made up. And ask him when the food is sorted to have some sent up here for the cap'n."

There was a path at the back of the house. Unlike that which led up from the men's house, it appeared not much used and somewhat overgrown, but it led inland, and Slater decided to take it. He went in front, pistols in his belt, carrying the food that Jeremy brought, wrapped in a bandana and slipped inside his shirt.

It was not long before they had left the dense bush of the coast and were on high land, bare of almost any growth but coconuts and screw pines and grass. The character of the island differed widely from place to place. Some parts were damp, others were dry. From high land they looked down to where grass grew rank and trees and ferns thrust up through a carpet of creeper and vine, and the stench of bog crept up to them. Yet much of the island was firm, good ground, where the islanders had their gardens and where some fine trees grew. For an hour they walked and then, on a rise from which much of the western end of the island could be seen, Slater called a halt. The sun was now high, already starting to get hot, and they sat in the shade of a tree to eat.

They ate in silence, looking out towards the reef—a thread

of silver, dividing the green of the lagoon from the blue of the ocean. Below them lay a stretch of beach, and before long Jeremy pointed to it. "That would be a good place to swim, Sir."

"Did ye enjoy the water this morning?"

" 'Twas better than I ever thought water could be, Sir. 'Twas cool an' as smooth as glass. Ye should have come, Sir."

Up the wind to them came mosquitoes. Slater killed one or two and asked Jeremy whether the insects had bothered them in the men's house during the night.

"For a while they did, Sir."

"Did not the Indians come and show ye how to put a smoky fire, and how to use the bamboo mats for stoppin' the windows?"

"Aye, but the men scattered the fire, Sir, an' took down the bamboos."

"The hell they did! The bloody fools. Who put 'em up to that?"

"Mr. Doyle really, Sir. While the Indians was doing it he said he didn't hold with it. And when it started to get a bit hot in the house, what with the top part bein' full of smoke and the openings closed up, some of the men started complaining, and Mr. Doyle got up and Jeb Pain after him, and they scattered the fire and took down the bamboos."

"And they were left down?"

"Nay, Sir. It wasn't long before we were all scratching, and Barber said he couldn't get to sleep for the humming in his ears. He got angry and started swearing and got up and lit one of the lanterns. Mr. Doyle said he was wasting oil and Barber said there'd be no need to waste oil if people wasn't such fools as to try and know better than the Indians how was the best way to catch sleep. I think, Sir, Mr. Doyle would have ordered them to do nothing, but old Pepper said he'd had enough too, and started in helping Sam. Then Elisha and Wilky got up, and they soon had the fire going and the windows blocked again."

Slater sat eating, wondering why Doyle would act that way. Doyle was not a fool; he must have realised that if the natives

76

had learned that this was the way to sleep, then to attempt otherwise was folly.

"Jeremy, while Mr. Doyle was being angry, did he say anything about the captain, or about me?"

"He mentioned Cap'n Berry." Jeremy went to say more, then looked away from Slater.

"I want to know, Jeremy."

" 'Tis just that it seems like tellin' tales, Sir."

"Look here, lad. Ye must learn the difference between tellin' tales and reportin' what 'tis y'duty to. There are times when if a man doesn't speak he's guilty of a far more serious breach o' good behaviour than any tellin' o' tales. Now, what did he say?"

" 'Twas o' something called barratry."

"Barratry?" said Slater quickly.

"What is barratry, Sir?"

" 'Tis a crime, Jeremy. What did Mr. Doyle say?"

"He said Cap'n Berry was guilty of barratry. He said if we was ever to get out of this, he was going to make sure that the cap'n was brought to trial for castin' away his ship. That couldn't be so, could it, Mr. Slater?"

"Nay, lad, it couldn't. If Mr. Doyle isn't careful 'twill be himself he'll be findin' on trial—for incitin' men to mutiny, and the penalty for mutiny, Jeremy, is hangin'. Now was there anythin' else?"

"This mornin', Sir, there was something, when I went down to get the pistol and the food."

Jeremy told how he had gone to the house and found Doyle there, and how he had asked for the pistol and the meat and biscuit. . . .

"I thought we was goin' to try and save the sea stores?" Doyle said, glaring at him.

"I'm only askin' for what I was told to," Jeremy said.

"What do ye want the sea stores for? Where are ye goin'?"

"I don't know, Sir."

At first Jeremy thought Doyle was not going to let him have the food. Doyle looked angrily at him and then told him to go and get it while he went to a chest and took out the pistol and a bullet-pouch. Jeremy wrapped the food in a clean bandana, and as soon as Doyle gave him the pistol he stepped outside, glad to be quit of the place and Doyle's unconcealed anger.

He was almost to the corner of the house when Pain came from behind it, nearly running into him. He saw the pistol and the bundle and said: "Where the hell do ye think y'goin' with that pistol, Jeremy? Does Mr. Doyle know ye have it? And what have ye in the cloth?"

"Meat and biscuit," said the boy, irritated by Pain's suddenly arrogant attitude. "O' course Mr. Doyle knows."

"Just a minute." Pain took Jeremy by the arm and pulled him back towards the door of the house.

Jeremy struggled to get free. "Let me alone, Jeb," he said angrily, but Pain ignored him and called: "Here, Mr. Doyle, is this true what the boy says—that ye know he's takin' a pistol an' such?"

Doyle came to the door and looked from Jeremy to Pain. "Aye, Jeb, 'tis right," he said slowly.

Pain still held Jeremy tightly. " 'Tis a muckin' waste o' stores," he said after a moment.

"I told him that," said Doyle.

"Leave me be, d'ye hear," Jeremy was shouting now, "or— or, by Lord, I'll strike ye." He raised the hand which held the pistol.

Pain saw that the boy meant it and clenched his fist. "By God, Jeb, let me go or I'll shoot ye—so help me I will," said the boy cocking the weapon.

Jeremy did not know whether the charge had been withdrawn since he had given the pistol to Doyle, or whether the powder in the pan was dry or not, but neither did Pain know these things. For an instant longer he held Jeremy, then he cursed and let go. Jeremy, shaking with anger, and distressed that he had been forced to threaten Pain in such a manner, stepped away from him.

Suddenly Doyle leaped from the doorway and grabbed Pain by the shoulder. He swung him round, throwing him against one of the doorposts with sickening force. Doyle was furious, terrifying. Pain cowered before him, his lips trembling.

"By the Jesus, Pain," said Doyle, "you hurt a hair o' that

78

lad's head an' I'll flay ye. Do ye hear? I'll strip the hide off y'worthless carcass."

"I—I on'y was askin' about the pistol. I thought . . ." His voice died; he stared at Doyle. Jeremy gazed in fascination at the terror in his face.

"What did ye think?" said Doyle levelly.

"I thought ye meant what ye said about the weapons——"

Doyle struck Pain with the back of his right hand. Pain's head snapped back against the post. He did not fall, but was off balance, his hands clutching at the wall behind him, a trickle of blood starting from the corner of his mouth.

Doyle turned to Jeremy. "Go on, off wi' ye, lad. Tell the cap'n I'll send up his food."

Jeremy had reached the corner of the house and was about to turn it when he heard Doyle say: "Do ye want us undone, ye loud-mouthed bastard?"

"The boy won't split. What could he make of it?"

"A bloody sight more than what ye think he might. *Christ*, I've a good mind to let ye stew in it."

"And that was all, Mr. Slater," said Jeremy. "What do ye think they meant by it, Sir?"

"Who among the lads saw this, Jeremy?"

"I couldn't tell ye. Most of 'em were lookin' at the food or not yet returned from the beach. And the food was in the cooking-house. Some of the Indians were still there with the lads, I think. I'd say none of 'em saw it, Sir. Except Duke Powell, who was in the house."

What did Doyle mean by leaving Pain to 'stew in it'? Did that mean Pain alone, or did it include others? Did it mean he was threatening to withdraw, say, his leadership? Doyle had seen Berry take that turn on the islet. Suppose he'd seen enough then to make up his mind about taking command? That might be the reason for his talk of barratry—a plan to justify mutiny on the strength of what he claimed was a criminal act of Berry's. When would he be ready? And how many of the men did he have? Only Pain, by the look of it. But there might be more. Then who?

He wasn't even going to guess at it. It was too dangerous a game to guess; nor was he going to let himself see, in any of the men, differences which he might imagine as a change of heart. That way you could end up suspecting the lot.

"Jeremy," he said suddenly, "I wouldn't go thinkin' on this too much. There's probably nothing in it."

"What about Pain, Sir? He might have it in for me?"

"I don't think he will. Ye saw what Mr. Doyle said about him hurtin' ye. He'll not let ye come to harm. Whoever else he might dislike, he's fond of ye. Isn't he?"

"He is, Sir. He's never spoke even gruffly to me."

"Not like I have at times, eh?" said Slater, smiling at him.

"Ah, but that's different, Sir. Ye're just like m'father. Fathers are allowed to be hard."

Slater laughed and got to his feet. "Come on, lad. We'll never be findin' out about this island just be sitting here."

Keeping to high ground they bore south to pass the badly drained land that seemed to occupy most of the centre of the island. They spoke little. Slater was intent upon fixing in his mind details of the land. He told Jeremy to do the same.

Jeremy saw it before Slater. "Sir, 'tis the canoe that brought us from the little island," he cried excitedly. It was a double canoe, travelling quickly, inside the lagoon, running over the shallows which lay off the south-western point of the island. But it was not the vessel which had brought them.

"I've no spy-glass, but I'd say this was bigger."

"Then is she one of Awila's, Sir?"

"Hard to say. He may have more than one. But we didn't see another yesterday when Cap'n Berry an' me went through the village. We saw smaller craft, but none bigger. Somehow I had it in m'head that they had but one large craft of this kind."

"Then this must be from some other island, Sir—from perhaps far away."

Slater said nothing to that, but he did not discount the possibility, for it looked like a craft quite capable of ocean voyaging. They watched it out of sight, close in behind coconut trees on rising land, and then Slater decided they would cut down to the beach they'd seen, making west. The going was heavy, the sun was hot, and more than once Jeremy mentioned the idea of swimming.

Some thirty minutes later they crossed a small stretch of

swampy ground and came to a well-marked track, which Slater took to be the main way along this part of the coast. They followed it for some distance, and quite suddenly came out on to the beach. It was bright and wide and sloped down to water, which glittered in the sunlight. Jeremy could hardly restrain himself.

They undressed, leaving their clothes up off the beach, not far from the path, their pistols and ammunition sitting on the top of them. Jeremy dived down the coral faces, seeing fish such as he had never imagined existed. Then he joined Slater and they waded up to their waists in the water, peering at the fish that swam about them, at bright-blue starfish, at deep-purple anemones. One pair of fish that played about a coral face, orange and scarlet, were so bright they seemed afire, and another pair, which persisted in making short, swooping rushes at Jeremy, nipped him. The boy, half laughing, half scared, lifted his hand from the water and showed Slater two tiny pricks, beads of blood, where one of these fish had sent its tiny teeth into him.

Jeremy saw a coral snake, banded yellow and brown, that foraged, head under the sand and twisting deep in a gutter in the reef. A shark, inexpressibly graceful, fascinated him until fear prompted him to swim back to shallower water and tell Slater what he had seen.

They went up the beach side by side, Jeremy telling him how he had seen first the shadow of the shark, then its whole pointed bulk.

Scattered about the beach both above and below the tide line were shells, many of them broken, but many intact. Jeremy found part of a white cowrie.

Slater walked on slowly, thinking about Doyle, while Jeremy fell behind, working his way farther up the beach, hunting for a whole cowrie. Slater reached the place where they had left their clothes. He turned when Jeremy called and watched the boy come along the top of the beach. Jeremy had no shell, but his right hand was clenched, and he held it out before him as though there was something in it.

"What have ye there, lad?"

"I don't know, Sir. 'Tis a sort o' wood dust, and it's under

81

a tree along there, just in off the beach." He showed Slater a little powdered wood mixed with sand and earth.

Slater looked, then bent and smelled it. "Where did ye get this?" he asked quickly.

It was not a big tree, and it had small leaves; where the bark had been scraped away the wood showed a pale brown. Slater went on his knees, and taking up a little of the dust rubbed it between his thumb and forefinger. Heated by this gentle friction, the dust produced a pungent, sweet perfume.

"What is it, Sir?" Jeremy asked, kneeling down beside Slater. "It's sawdust, I know, but what sort?"

Slater got to his feet, looking at the tree as though it were the first he'd ever seen. "As ye say, 'tis sawdust, but with this difference—'tis the richest kind of sawdust God ever made. 'Tis sandalwood, Jeremy." He stepped up to it again and bent to it, sniffing at a bare patch on one of the branches.

"Sandalwood! By the Lord Harry, Jeremy, we're made! D'ye hear, lad?—we're made. 'Tis a fortune." Throwing his hands in the air he gave a shout and started to dance round the tree, plucking at its leaves, shouting at the top of his voice. Jeremy watched him, amazement and then laughter in his face, until he, too, caught it and went round after Slater, laughing until the tears came into his eyes.

It took Slater a half-hour to get dressed. He pulled on his trousers and went back to the tree, sniffing it, rubbing it where it had been scraped at, fingering at the small light-green leaves, making little nicks in the tree with his knife, smelling them, rubbing slivers of the wood between his palms to heat them and bring out the perfume. Slater knew now that this was the perfume he had smelled on the Fijians, and he told Jeremy.

Within the first hour Slater began to consider ways of getting the wood, of searching for it among the islands to the west. But it was out of these thoughts that a sudden, overwhelming despair was born, for he saw with terrible clarity that to take this wealth they needed first to survive, and this now struck him as so improbable that he could only wonder why it had escaped him until that moment. The irony of it filled him—he had it, yet he would never be able to use it. Something of life went from him and he fell prey to doubt and fear such as he hadn't felt before.

First there were the five hundred leagues to Port Jackson, the launch, Doyle, Pain, Berry, all of them. Then there would be the finding of a ship to return with; and the caution, scheming and care which would be necessary if they were not to lose their secret and see it enrich only men who had stolen it from them. It seemed too much to surmount. But the secret was not entirely his or Jeremy's—it was Berry's, really, because it was Berry's ship that had brought them here.

"Jeremy, ye're to keep this to yeself. I'll tell Cap'n Berry, for we're in his service an' 'tis his right to know, but ye must say nothing to the crew."

"Aye aye, Sir."

They left then. It was nearly mid-afternoon, and the sun was hot in a cloudless sky, but the path was well shaded and the wind which blew in from the sea was cool. They had been walking for some time and Slater was beginning to wonder when the path would turn inland, or they might come to a branch which would lead to higher ground, when from somewhere ahead there came a shout. They stopped instantly. It was not a loud shout, nor was it far away.

"Sounded like a woman, Sir," whispered Jeremy.

Slater put out his hand, signalling Jeremy to be quiet, and for several seconds stood still, listening intently. Then he moved and said: "Aye, lad, it could have been." But at that moment, as though a shutter had been opened, letting out the sound, there came a scream, followed by the noise of violent movement through the undergrowth.

Slater drew his pistol and looked about for a place of concealment. Ahead of them the track turned sharply. Calling to Jeremy, he ran on to this turn, where he found the path went straight again for about a hundred feet. The growth here was heavy; vines and creepers looped across the path. Pressing Jeremy ahead of him he pushed in off the track and crouched behind a fallen log. Drawing his other pistol, he cocked it and laid it ready at hand beside him. Then, pistol in his right hand out before him covering the track, he waited.

This was the densest part of the coastal strip. The air lay

heavy, smelling of earth, and from stagnant pools mosquitoes rose up and settled over them. Though they were close to the sea, the thick jungle shut out even the sound of the reef.

There came a crash of mouldering branches, a rustling of creepers pushed at and torn aside, and then, startling in its nearness, the unmistakable shriek of a woman.

A moment later the wall of jungle at the far end of the path opened and a girl burst from it. She hit the straight path, sobbing, half tripping, running with the fear of death in her. On her neck and shoulder was blood and her left breast was splashed with it. Slater recognised her as the girl on the beach.

Behind her was more movement.

Slater's pistol went up and he fired. Slater saw the missile club thrown as he pulled the trigger. In the moment it took the powder to burn in the pan, the man saw Slater, and Slater saw his terror. An infinitesimal instant later, the man had taken the ball just over the bridge of the nose.

The girl screamed and pitched forward, but Slater did not see her fall, for he had taken up his second pistol and was aiming it at another man who now appeared out behind the first. This second man Slater shot as he stood, mouth open, rooted to the path. Another, who burst through as the second fell, gave a shriek, turned and crashed through the jungle, throwing himself at the matted tangle in a frenzied rush to get away.

Slater, dropping his second pistol, swung on Jeremy. "Quick, lad, give me y'pistol. An' reload mine." As he spoke he grabbed Jeremy's weapon and ran out on to the path.

"Mr. Slater! Sir!" cried Jeremy, remembering that he had not looked to his pistol since he'd threatened Pain with it early that morning. But Slater didn't hear; he was running, past the girl and on into the opening from which the natives had burst.

Jeremy took up the first of Slater's pistols and reloaded it. Then he ran after Slater with it. He reached him as he came from the jungle.

"Where's the other?" asked Slater, taking the pistol. "I told ye to do both."

"Aye, Sir, but I don't know whether mine'll fire. Could be 'tis damp."

84

Slater looked down at the weapon and smiled wryly. " 'Twas as well I didn't need it. All right, lad, get ye back an' load the other an' draw the charge in this, just to be sure. Load 'em carefully, but be quick, we don't know how many of these savages are about."

The girl was lying on her side. High on her left shoulder was a lump, the skin over it broken. Near her was the club that that brought her down. Gently Slater turned her over. The blood came from a wound at the base of her neck; it was little more than a long, fairly deep cut and looked like a spear or arrow graze. Otherwise she was uninjured, for the club had but winded her.

He got up and went back to the warriors. The second one had taken the ball in the chest. The other was a hideous sight —the ball had broken the whole of the top of his face and head. Grotesquely, he still twitched.

Slater left them and returned to stand looking down at the girl, marvelling that of all the women on the island she was the one he was to rescue. Then he knelt beside her and she stirred and opened her eyes. For a second or two she seemed to see nothing; then she saw him.

She drew in her breath and screamed.

As she made to rise, he held her, saying the first thing that came into his head, trying to pacify her, to make her see that she had nothing more to fear. Once she nearly got to her feet, but he bore down on her. Then it occurred to Slater to show her the men he had killed. Holding her with one hand he pointed to them, and then to himself. She turned her frightened eyes about, saw the bodies and gasped. Then she looked back to Slater, who pointed to himself again. She understood, and he felt her body go limp. He got up, smiling. Then he helped her to her feet.

Slater took the club and the spears from the dead men and then he, Jeremy and the girl set off for the village. Jeremy went in front, the girl between them. She walked stiffly, and Slater had to call to Jeremy to make the pace a slower one.

Slater wondered what Berry would make of it all—the sandalwood, and who these Indians he had killed might have been.

Were they connected with the canoe they had seen? He supposed so. Then where were they from? And—even more important—did they often raid the island? He must try to discover that, for if such attacks occurred often, it was possible they might interrupt the work on the launch. All of this would have to be put to Berry.

As they drew near the village, the girl turned and looked at him. She smiled. Her lips did not part, but a barely perceptible tremor passed over them. Then she faced ahead to the path again.

He walked mechanically, not looking at the path, but watching the blackness of her hair, and the curves of her body, and feeling an urge to touch her. He could smell her on his hands. He found himself trembling, and he stumbled. His eyes were dimming; he raised his hand and wiped the back of it across them, cursing himself silently for a fool.

Chapter 8

"SANDALWOOD is worth what, Mister—seventy pounds a ton?"

"Nearer eighty when we cleared Canton, and as high or higher in Calcutta."

"And ye found but one tree?"

"But the lad says he saw another on the way back, bigger than what I saw."

It was now dusk and they were talking in their house. Berry had accompanied Jeremy and Slater to Awila's with the girl. They had arrived there surrounded by a great number of people. Every house they passed had added its tenants to the shouting, gesticulating crowd. The girl had walked proudly, looking neither to right nor to left of her.

"Ye mentioned, Oliver, that ye thought ye knew where that canoe came from?"

"I wondered could it have been from the Friendly Islands.

86

The island of Tongatabu, as mentioned by Captain Cook, can't be too far east o' here. And the men I killed were fair o' skin, as fair as the girl."

" 'Twould account for the general fairness of some of these people if 'twas so, Oliver. Ye saw the craft but once?"

"Aye."

Berry was lying on the sleeping-platform and now he put his head back and closed his eyes. He was wearing only trousers, and his feet were bare.

"Ye rested well today?" Slater asked after a moment.

"Nay," said Berry, opening his eyes. "To tell ye the truth, Oliver, I fretted much wi' ye away. I'm right glad to see ye back. The lads swum some, or most o' them did. An' they brought me m'victuals at noon. Doyle himself come up. Y'know, Oliver, he's a surly devil, but I'm glad he's with us. He's got the men right where they should be. I don't think we'll be having our troubles on that account."

Slater felt uneasy at this mention of Doyle. There was much he could say to Berry then; the opening was there; but, looking at Berry's drawn face and the hollows under his eyes, he hesitated.

"Changin' the subject, Oliver, I'll admit 'tis no good thing to kill, but this business today hasn't done us any harm."

"With Awila, ye mean?"

"With the lot o' them. The girl is obviously not just the ordinary run o' the mill. Nay, I'd stake *Argo*—if I still had her —that ye've done us a power o' good with these people. Well, ye must've seen how pleased they were, an' how intrigued with the weapons ye captured. Ah, but, Oliver, 'twas damned ill luck to lose *Argo* as we did. I been lyin' here today thinkin' on it. Damned ill luck. Tell me, are the men sayin' anything?"

Should he answer with the truth? What was Berry expecting? Had he heard something? Was he testing him to see if he too knew? Knew what?

Aye, the men were saying something. The incident Jeremy had told him of was "saying something". But what had Doyle said to Berry when he came up to the house? Slater felt his uncertainty when he thought of what Doyle might have said— not because he feared the truth, but because Doyle might have been trying to undermine Berry's confidence in him. There was a look of pain, even of despair, in the captain's face as he lay there, his eyes closed and a vein pulsing visibly on his temple.

Then Slater thought of the girl, who now entered all his thinking. He felt her so positively, he felt the touch of her skin again, the nipple which had brushed him, her smoothness —and he felt a deep yearning for her. He looked away out of the door, where the grass in the dusk was like a dark sea which spread to a cliff-bound coast that was the jungle surrounding them.

"They can't be very happy, Mister," Berry said, opening his eyes. "The men, I mean. They can't be, can they?" It was a senseless thing a man could say of a shipwrecked crew.

Slater felt the island about him like a trap into which he had fallen; he heard the distant growl of the reef, and the night noises beginning, the mounting whine of the mosquitoes, the chatter of nesting birds.

"Um. . . ?" said Berry.

"Nay, they're not."

"Yet I've heard none o' them complainin', Mister." There was in the voice a sound of wonder and of pride, as though of all the crews of all the ships which had ever been, his was one to suffer without complaint.

Jeremy brought their food, and they lit their lantern (they had taken two from the brig, and one was with the men). Then they spread the food on the banana leaves the Fijians had taught them to wrap it in and serve it on. Light had sent up a fish, baked whole, the skin peeling in places and showing the succulent white meat. With it were boiled bananas still in their skins, yam and arrowroot, small prawns, and a gluey mess of fermented breadfruit which, Jeremy told them, Light described as "Indian bread".

They sat on the floor, the food spread between them, eating with their fingers and using their sheath knives to cut the food into manageable portions.

They were well into the meal, eating in silence, when they heard the sound of voices. Slater got up and went to the door; taking down the shutter, he saw the blaze of torches between the trees.

" 'Tis people from the village," he said back over his shoulder. Berry joined him and together they went outside. "Now what the hell would they be wantin' at this hour?" asked Berry.

" 'Tis Duadua, Sir."

"Aye, an' half of Awila's guard with him, be the looks of it. There's a good thirty of them, Oliver."

As they entered the clearing, the torch-bearers moved out on both flanks. Slater saw that Duadua carried in his arms a parcel wrapped in banana leaves, the green of them bright against the darkness of his body. As he came up to Slater and Berry, the warriors dropped to the grass and sat motionless, looking more like oiled bronzes than men.

Duadua began to speak, quietly at first, looking not at Berry, but at Slater. Gradually his voice rose as greater feeling entered it. They soon realised that he was thanking Slater for rescuing the girl and the leaf-wrapped bundle was a gift for Slater, and one, they judged, of considerable value. Several times Slater caught the mention of his own name—Oliva—and always after he said it Duadua paused and from the warriors came a long aspirate sound of appreciation and agreement.

When he finished speaking he held out the parcel to Slater, who took it. "Say somethin', Mister," said Berry. " 'Tis respect they're showin' ye. Speak to 'em."

The Fijians understood Slater's words as little as he had understood theirs, but they saw his sincerity, and Berry's. When Slater had finished, Duadua turned away. His men formed two lines for him to go between. Then, with torch-bearers out ahead and in the rear, the party made off, the torchlight casting eerie shadows among the trees.

Turning from them Berry looked at the parcel. "Now what the hell d'ye say it is, Oliver? Probably the club ye captured, a trophy of war. Bring it in be the lantern and we'll open it up."

As Slater followed Berry through the door he said: " 'Tis not the club, Sir. 'Tis soft. Probably something to eat."

"Then 'tis a fish. 'Tis the long shape o' one, and as like as not a special sort, to be eaten only be chiefs and those favoured be the gods. I tell ye, Oliver, this business o' the girl today has done us a power of good with these Indians."

Berry picked up the lantern and held it while Slater squatted with the parcel near their partly eaten food. Holding the gift across his left hand he took his knife and cut the pandanus string with which the leaves were bound. The string fell to the floor and the top leaf sprang open. Berry held the lantern high, leaning forward in his eagerness to see the gift uncovered. Slater unrolled this leaf and beneath was another, more tightly wrapped.

" 'Tis warm," he said, glancing up at Berry.

"Warm?"

"Aye." Now he began to unroll the second leaf.

" 'Tis a fish, I tell ye, Mister."

"Of a fair size. 'Tis quite heavy." Slater took off the next leaf, letting it fall to the mat with the others. Underneath was another.

Suddenly he gasped in horror and dropped the bundle and threw himself backward—in one violent emotion.

"What the hell's the matter with ye?" shouted Berry, leaping out of Slater's way. The latter was up now and lunging towards the door, his hand clapped over his mouth.

It was a man's right arm and it had been baked. Where it had burned a little it was black, two heat splits showing the flesh beneath; and where it had been taken from the shoulder it was a watery, half-cooked pink, bright in the lantern light. The hand was clenched and the nails curled away from the tips of the fingers. The top part of the arm, above the muscle and about the hacked-off bone that protruded, bore quite plainly the marks of teeth.

Slater, behind the house, was violently sick. Berry was not long in joining him.

As soon as he had recovered, Slater took the lantern and went down to the men's house. From the carpenter he borrowed an adze, the nearest thing to a digging tool they had. Day and Jeremy returned with him and, with Berry's help, Slater and Day re-wrapped the grisly fragment and went into the jungle to bury it.

When they came back into the house and saw the food, neither Berry nor Slater could touch it. "Nor would I, be God," said Day. "I seen some things in me time—but a cooked arm—God, Cap'n Berry, I never figured I'd see that."

Sleep came slowly to Slater that night. He lay in the hot, shuttered house, sweating, seeing the man with no top to his face and the ghastly arm with the hideous heat splits, and smelling the odour of the partly cooked meat. He wondered which of them the arm had belonged to. And the girl! She—with him —was the cause of it. Had she taken part in the feast? For it was a feast; until far into the night the seamen heard the sounds of revelry coming from the village, saw the glow of fire, the sparks climbing bright in the columns of smoke.

Then, well after midnight, he fell asleep and dreamed. He dreamed he saw himself, Oliver Slater, quite alive, being devoured by the girl, a painless transubstantiation into her flawless body. She ate, yet her lips didn't move. And as she ate, she looked at him. He saw himself as though he stood apart, as if his eye remained the one organ undevoured by her. She was smiling; it was the smile she had given him as they had breasted the hill and started down into the village.

He awoke, trembling, and for an instant the dream carried a ghastly reality. He lay drenched with sweat, his skin burning, and until he moved, crying out in his terror, it was as though he lay in a fluid in which he was beginning to macerate.

He stood in the thick darkness of the house, leaning against one of the posts. Then, as quickly as he could, he took the shutter from the door and went outside. It was not much before dawn, and on the air was the smell of burning and once a shout, sharp and clear.

He went down past the men's house, silent and dark, reached the beach and stood there, looking out to sea, while the new day climbed over the island and touched with its light the water and the reef ahead of him.

If the events of that Sunday served to enhance the stature of the white men in the eyes of the Fijians, in the eyes of the white men the Fijians lost all claim to respect and trust. Slater was still on the beach when the crew came to start work on the launch. All that day a grim determination drove them, harder than any exhortation Berry or Slater might have made. Day's tale of what he had seen had lost nothing in the telling. The men worked silently, adzed and bored and sawed and chiselled, pestered the carpenter and sailmaker for orders, worked so that the launch might be finished and they might leave Oneata and its man-eating inhabitants.

There were too many of them to go in the launch to allow room for more than a small half-cabin immediately abaft the mainmast. But this could be large enough to allow about half of them—the watch below—to rest under cover. It would also form a screen in heavy weather for the watch on deck. Once the placing of the masts had been decided upon, John Morgan, who was sailmaker, set about cutting and making up the canvas they had brought from the brig. They had cloth for two suits of sails and a square sail that Slater said might be useful on the course they would be making. They also had canvas enough for a mizzen staysail suggested by Morgan and some heavier stuff for a spitfire jib and a storm mizzen.

Yet for Slater, despite the work which was done, it was a disturbing day. Berry was unusually quiet, speaking no more than a dozen words all morning, agreeing without comment to Slater's and Day's suggestions for the launch. This puzzled Slater, for he would have said that Berry, even in sickness, was not a man to stand by and watch his launch converted to a half-cabin ketch without comment. Slater felt an uneasiness in Berry, as though the captain was privy to some glimpse of the future —no vague, partly realised fear, but something so certain as to exclude room for hope. He lacked interest and watched them as he might watch strangers working.

Was it his injury? Slater wondered. Some secondary stage commencing, wherein Berry would no longer consider himself a part of them, but see their endeavours merely as some curious activity outside of himself? Slater had heard of such things happening to men. Or was it merely that awful business of the arm? That was enough to slow a man down, especially a sick one—and one who, in a way, had brought it about. Was Berry now beginning to question his own decision to land on the island or, worse, to see downright folly in it?

Slater's speculations on Berry irritated him, shortened his temper and made him wonder just how deeply he himself had been touched by the wreck, by the killing and by the girl. Her image swam into his consciousness repeatedly, sexually provoking him as no other woman ever had; yet it was an image fouled with the all but certain knowledge that she was an eater of human flesh. Once, when he bent over the gunwale of the launch to examine an overside repair, Slater remembered his dream and saw a hideous picture of the girl holding that arm; nausea rose in him and he gulped and very nearly vomited.

An incident that occurred in the middle of the afternoon showed Slater how seriously disturbed Berry had become. Towards noon, Day had requested the assignment of a couple of men to look for some curved branches for knees and breast-hooks. Slater had put the proposal to Berry, who nodded his approval. "But don't make it too late," Slater told Day. "They might have a way to go, and darkness falls rapidly in these latitudes."

Immediately after they had eaten, Day came to Slater and said he wanted to send off Wilkinson and Peppercorn.

"I'll mention it to the cap'n, Day, an' let ye know," said Slater, and he walked up to the spar trestles, where Berry was watching Doyle supervising Hocking and Leadbeater.

"The carpenter, Sir," he said, "wants permission to send out Pepper and Wilky for those timbers I told ye of this morning."

Slater thought that Berry, who continued to watch the men, hadn't heard him or hadn't realised that he was being addressed. Doyle looked at Berry, then at Slater, who after a moment's pause began to repeat: "The carpenter, Sir, would like permission to send out for those timbers——"

He got no further; the captain turned and said sharply: "What timbers, Mr. Slater?"

"The knees and the breasthooks."

Berry frowned, looked back at the trestles. Slater felt Doyle's eyes on him, and the men slowed up their work to listen.

"He can do what he bloody well likes," said the captain suddenly. " 'Tis his look-out." He glared at Slater as if he was expecting the mate to argue the point. A reply was on the tip of Slater's tongue, but he held it back, and went down the beach to Day.

Yet, whatever was working in Berry seemed to pass. An hour

93

later he came down to the launch, and when Pepper and Wilky returned with several crooks he looked at them carefully. "As ye said, Jonas, 'tis a hard enough wood. Aye, I agree with ye, she'll be a better boat with them in her. What say ye, Mr. Slater?"

It was nearly dark when the men finished and left the beach. Slater and Berry treated Powell and went on up to their house. As they walked, Slater began to wonder just how much of the incident Berry remembered, for as they reached the house the captain said: "That was a good idea to get them timbers, Oliver. Who thought of it?"

"The carpenter, Sir."

"Ah. And where did he get them?"

"I'm not too sure just where, but not far in, I believe."

"He wasn't gone long."

"Day didn't go himself, Sir——"

"He didn't? Then who went?"

"Pepper an' Wilky."

"Aahh, that explains it. A right good idea."

But if this puzzled Slater, there was worse to come. That evening, after Jeremy had taken away the remains of their food, Berry revealed a side of his thinking that was entirely unexpected, and one which, Slater realised, could have only the gravest consequences for him if it were to become fixed in his mind.

Hurricanes were mentioned—afterwards Slater did not remember by which one of them—and Berry said: " 'Tis the curse o' these waters at this time o' the year. The worst possible time to be sailin' about in a little cockleshell like our ketch'll be. Ye don't think, do ye, seein' as how well we're gettin' on with the Indians, that it might be wise to wait for the winter to set in afore we make off? The longer we wait the less chance there'll be o' findin' bad weather."

To Slater the idea was so fantastic and came so unexpectedly that before he could check himself he said: "Ye're serious, Sir, I take it?" No sooner was it out than he knew it had been a foolish thing to say.

The captain was not a man to indulge in frivolous speculation, and nothing could have been further from his intention.

"O' course I'm serious. What the hell do ye think I'd mention it for?" he said angrily.

"I didn't mean to irritate ye, Sir," Slater said quickly, uncertain how to handle the old man, "but the idea surprised me."

"Ah," said Berry softly, accepting the explanation, "I suppose it was a bit sudden to spring it on ye like that. I'm sorry if I was short wi' ye, Oliver. But now what do ye think of it?"

"What ye say about the weather improving is right, but the longer we wait the less chance we'll have of keeping friendly with these savages. Didn't ye notice the crew today? I'm not saying they're hostile to the Indians yet; but that o' the arm last night hasn't made them any easier to love."

"Aye, I noticed that."

"I'd say we should stick to our original intention to make away as soon as possible. 'Tis the difference between the devil we know and the devil we don't. We might strike a hurricane. I say we might, but we might not. Please God we don't. But many a little ship has fared better in a blow than a big 'un. Besides, if we stay and a hurricane hit here, who's to say it wouldn't tear up that beach, pick up our ketch and smash it to pieces?"

Berry said nothing, sat hunched, staring at the lantern. "We'd have to wait all o' three or four months," Slater went on, encouraged by the captain's silence, "to be sure o' missing a blow. 'Tis a damn long time. What o' the men, Sir? Would ye be surprised if they got out o' hand—wantin' to go and knowin' they had a seaworthy little craft all ready for sea? I wouldn't be, and what's more I wouldn't blame 'em. I don't say I'd be with them, but I'd understand their reason for it. There'd be trouble, bound to be. Nay, Sir, let's make it the devil we know—the sea. And as soon as possible."

Berry got to his feet slowly, took a few steps towards the door, then stopped and looked back. "I wonder, Oliver, would ye mind fetchin' the medicine chest from the other house. I've a mind to take a little laudanum for this headache o' mine."

" 'Tis still troublin' ye?"

"Aye, it is," he said queerly, as though he had been hurt by Slater's question. "You don't mind fetchin' it, do ye?"

"Nay, Sir. I'll go now."

But as Slater reached the door, Berry called after him: "If 'tis any trouble to ye, Mister, I can do without it." There was an old-man, cantankerous edge in his voice.

Slater did not answer, hoping to give the impression he had not heard. He had no wish to be rude to the captain, but he wanted to get away from the house, wanted time to think; for the impression was beginning to take root in him that Berry was losing his mind.

Chapter 9

THREE days later, Slater got a warning, a glimpse of danger ahead, and it came from the girl.

Her father—the man Slater had seen standing with her that day they landed—was a chief, now past his fighting days, but a man held in high esteem by those about Awila. Since many of these came to the old man's house and talked freely about developments within their official councils, the girl came to know two things—and also became the first person on the island to see the connection between them.

On this fourth working day it rained and thundered in the afternoon, but the men kept at their work and by evening were further on than Slater had dared to hope. The Fijians, standing off up near the top of the beach or sitting on the sand nearby, watched them closely and spoke with one another about what they saw. They were fascinated by the tools and coveted them. Truly were these the tools of gods, for their edges were bright and they sliced hard wood as a shell might cut a soft, cooked yam; with tools like these, men could build houses and canoes such as only the gods might build better.

Berry now seemed, to Slater, to be improving in health. He still complained of headaches and took laudanum, but he was now more interested in the work, more a part of it, and he had admitted to Slater the day before that he saw the sense of making away as soon as possible: " 'Twas folly, that idea o' mine, Mister, that waitin' for the hurricane season to pass. 'Twould never have worked, I see that now, not with the men as keen on gettin' away as they are. Just as soon as she's finished, we'll make sail."

Powell was lower, but still tenaciously clinging to life. Now the captain added laudanum to Powell's mixture and, if it did nothing else, it soothed him. Light asked Berry for the loan of his prayer-book and several times throughout that wet and humid day came from his cooking-pots and read to Powell. The earthy colour in Powell's skin now seemed fixed.

That evening Slater didn't stay with Berry to treat Powell. The carpenter wanted the dimensions of the compass so he might make a box for it, and since all the instruments had been stored with Berry's personal belongings Slater went to get the compass for Day. It was still full daylight when he reached the house, and as he was about to enter he heard a sound like that of a bird. He stopped, for he had never heard that call before. Then it came again, part whistle, part cry. He stood for a moment listening to it, and then, stooping under the low thatch over the doorway, went inside. When he had the compass un-wrapped from its sailcloth, he heard the cry once more; he stopped what he was doing and listened more carefully. Over and over it came, persisting. He re-wrapped the compass, put it back in the chest with the other instruments, and went out-side.

The sound came from the path that led from the back of the house. He thought of calling, but then, realising the futility of it, he entered the path. He had gone some distance along it and had passed two bends before he realised he was unarmed. He slowed down, debating whether to return for his pistols, but the call was so close now that he decided to chance it; he slid the sheath of his knife to a handier position and went on.

He came upon her suddenly; she stood about sixty feet in front of him. As their eyes met, as she saw him recognise her, she turned and passed out of sight round the next bend. She made no signal but her every movement seemed to beckon. He looked behind him and saw no one, heard nothing, and followed after her.

He had gone a hundred yards before he caught sight of her again. The bush was thinner here and she was waiting, looking back over her left shoulder, and the instant she saw him she stepped off the track. He ran to the place, a willowy branch was still moving where she'd brushed past it, and he followed down a grassy slope to an open sandy patch, surrounded by trees and well hidden from the path above. Draped about the trees on one side of it was a vine with bright-yellow flowers.

He stepped out into the clearing, feeling the sand soft under his feet. She stood at the far end, her body tense, ready to fly; in her right hand she held a twig.

He moved towards her, her closeness exciting him, rising over any repulsion he may have known. His eyes fed on her—her parted lips which showed the even row of her teeth, the proud set of her head, and the wide-apart, almost almond-shaped, eyes. There came from her the slightest perfume of sandalwood.

They stood regarding one another and he said his name as Awila had said it, pointing to himself. She tilted her head as a young bird might and he moved closer, saying his name once more. The third time he said it her eyes filled with understanding and pointing to herself she said her own name, almost a whisper: "Seyawa."

"Seyawa?" he asked.

"*Io*. Adi Seyawa."

"Seyawa." He could say no more than this and his inability nettled him. She saw his frustration and smiled. It was almost the same smile she had given him on the way down into the village after he had rescued her; and, as a distinctive odour will call out of the past a sensation, so now did this smile bring back his dream, and his abhorrence came welling back into him, together with the desire to possess her. To be torn between his loathing for the cannibal image of her and his burning physical urge for her voluptuous presence; to want so ardently an object that so repelled him—the conflict set his brain spinning as if he were being sucked into some whirling sea of insanity.

But who was she to know the mind of a god? Yet she had

seen men look at her as this creature did. She had flown from what they would do with her and had moved swiftly through the lonely places of the island that she might evade them, for she was not free to give herself. She had been promised to the son of a chief; the first of the *tabuas* had been presented.

But this creature from the clouds looked at her as if he would possess her, made her feel her spirit turn within her and a weakness come in her. Yet she was not afraid—had he not taken her from death? So now, perhaps, she in her turn might stand in the way of his destruction. She moved and, as a woman might beckon a child, she led him to a patch of sand, grassless and smooth. Kneeling at the edge of it, she gestured to him to do likewise, opposite her.

He squatted where she pointed, an arm's length from her. She sat back on her buttocks, regarding him, her eyes steady and glistening. The perfume of sandalwood inflamed his senses. The tips of his fingers tingled as he fought the desire to move towards her.

She patted flat an area of sand and began to draw with the twig. She made a set of straight lines, a few inches long, and connected them so that they formed a human shape, rudimentary but easily enough identifiable. Then she looked up at him for a sign that he understood. He nodded and she bent again, and upon what stood for the head she drew the shape of Slater's straw hat.

She glanced at him and seeing he understood drew again, but this time a reclining figure. Slater looked at it, puzzled; he thought it was sleep she was trying to describe, but she leaned forward half closing her eyes, breathing in and out slowly, her breasts rising and falling; then, dropping the twig, she put both hands over her abdomen and moaned softly, feigning pain.

Then he saw it—she meant Powell.

She picked up the twig and drew again, but this time a foot or more away from the other figures. On this one she put no hat, and from the way she drew the hair he took it to represent her. He pointed to the drawing and then to her but she shook her head vigorously, and then—in the manner of a Cro-Magnon artist—she added the symbol which made the masculinity of the figure unmistakable. She then drew another figure beside this and added two circles, side by side, a little way under the square she had made to stand for the head. When she had done this she looked up at him and pointed to her breasts, then back to the two circles on the drawing. She told him the words these symbols stood for and in his way he learned the words for man and woman, and for sick and healthy.

Next she pointed to Powell and drew among the second group of figures—which he now saw stood for her own people—a man lying as Powell was shown. It took him little time to see she was trying to speak of one of the islanders as being ill, but he understood no more than that. But, touching him with the twig, she pointed once more to Powell and then back to the Fijian. After which she drew another and yet another islander, all men, all lying down, and she linked each of them with the figure that stood for Powell.

Suddenly she started to her feet. He too had heard a noise, but, absorbed in his deciphering of the drawings, had taken little notice of it. She looked about her, eyes wide, like an animal sensing danger. Seeing her fear he moved up to her. He was too late; his fingers slid on her oiled skin and she was gone, a solitary yellow flower falling after her. For moments he stood listening; then, realising the futility of following her, turned to the drawings once more. By now, daylight was fading. He knelt down beside the figures and pored. Suddenly, as he moved to wipe them from the sand, it all became clear. His hand stopped in mid-air. Shaking, he got to his feet and went back to the path.

The captain was outside the house, waiting for him. "Where the hell have ye been, Mister? I was about to fetch the men an' send 'em out to search for ye. What's the matter? Ye look as if ye'd seen a ghost."

"I have," Slater said grimly, "as like as not the ghost of every one of us. Come into the house and I'll tell ye."

Berry's first reaction was that the Fijians had become ill after eating the bodies. "That is, Mister, if her story's true. After all, ye don't know for sure, do ye? Ye might well have misunderstood her——"

"Damn it, Sir, I'm not a fool!"

"I'm not sayin' ye are. But ye can't speak the lingo, an' ye might well have been mistaken."

"She put it too clear for that, Sir."

"Then 'tis the result of eatin' those bodies."

"I'll not have that. These people are cannibals. They're used to human flesh; 'twould take more than just a couple of bodies to get so many of them ill. I tell ye, Sir, the girl is certain the disease is Powell's."

"But she hasn't seen Powell—not to know he's ill."

"The men have, Duadua and Awila."

"Listen, Mister, it don't make sense. If 'twas a plague o' some sort, why haven't we all got it? Eh, can ye tell me that?"

"I'm not pretendin' to be able to understand it, nor can I explain it, but the fact remains that there are people ill in the village."

"An' have there not been people ill there before? God damn it, are ye tryin' to make me believe this is the first time any of these Indians has been ailin'?"

"All I'm sayin'," Slater said slowly, "is that whoever is ill there now has Powell's sickness—the dysentery, if 'tis that which ails him."

"But who the bloody hell says they're ill with the dysentery?"

"The girl."

"God, Mister, belay there about that bleedin' woman."

"Then I take it ye intend to disregard the warnin'?"

"I won't have it that it is a warnin'. For all we know they're often ill. With the habits they've got I'd not be surprised to hear they was ailin' regularly. Nay, Mister, ye won't have a chit of a girl frightenin' me with some yarn of Powell's sickness appearin' among them. We've been alongside Powell a damn sight longer than they have. Nay"—and he shook his head stubbornly—"ye can't answer that one, Oliver. Because there is no answer. Any rate, supposin' it was what ailed Powell, there's naught we can do about it, is there?"

"We could make away."

"Ye mean now?" Berry's face twisted into an incredulous mask. "Afore we finish work on the launch?"

"If there's danger for us in stayin', yes."

"Listen, Mr. Slater. Get this—we'll not be leavin' this island until the boat is ready."

Berry spoke slowly, but his calmness was gone, driven from him by anger, which grabbed at his words and set a vein on his forehead throbbing. The pitch of his voice had risen so that he all but screamed: "An' I'll not be tellin' ye that again. D'ye hear me? Of all the whore-struck bastards I've known in me time at sea ye take the ribbon."

His rage overpowered him. He swayed, his face contorted, livid. "D'ye hear me, Slater?" he screamed. "Now get out! Or by the livin' Christ I'll have ye clapped in irons. Get out!" The last word rose to an insane shriek.

Blinded by his own anger and hurt, astonished at the suddenness of the change in Berry, Slater made for the door. He was at it when a choking cry came from the old man. "Mister——" he gasped out. Slater stopped short and turned round.

"Ye understand?" The question was anti-climactic, the voice thin and reedy, all the passion gone from it as warm blood washed from a cloth. Berry was holding himself upright by one of the posts, and his gaze was directed unsteadily towards Slater.

"Understand what?"

"That we'll not be goin'."

"An' if the girl is right?"

Berry seemed unable to comprehend the question. "What d'ye say?" he asked. His tormented mind, unwilling to face the possibility, clutched at delay as though it were the stuff of survival.

"I said, what if the girl is right?"

"If the girl is right?"

"Aye."

"Then . . . then God help us, Mister. God help us." He put his hands to his face and sliding to the floor wept the tears of a broken man.

It was dark when Slater had finished calming the old man. He lit the lantern, put him on the sleeping-platform, eased the buckle of his belt and gave him a strong tot of brandy. Berry's manner puzzled Slater; for while he was conscious enough of his surroundings, he seemed detached from them, remembering, evidently, only certain things and completely forgetting others. As he sat and sipped the spirit he looked upon Slater with such warmth and friendship that Slater found it hard to believe this was the man who, only minutes ago, had reviled him as no other man ever had, and escaped. Finally he gave him laudanum. He waited until he slept and then went down to the men's house to treat Powell.

Jeremy was asleep near Powell; there was no one else in the house. Barber and Pepper were outside, talking; Doyle and the rest of them were on the beach with the watch, enjoying the cool of the evening after the heat of the day.

When Slater came out, Barber asked him what he thought about Powell.

"Failing, Sam—though 'tis hard to admit it."

"Aye. Like Pepper an' me was sayin' as ye went in to him." Then, after a moment's pause, he added: "Queer about the Indians comin' like that, weren't it, Sir?"

"The Indians?"

"Aye."

"How d'ye mean, Barber?"

"Comin' to look at Powell the way they did."

"I know naught of it," said Slater, and Pepper looked at him quickly.

"Didn't Cap'n Berry tell ye?" asked Barber.

"Nay. What happened?"

"Well, I'll be damned," Barber said quietly, puzzled by Slater's answer. "What d'ye know about that, Pepper? Ye was there, wasn't ye?"

"Aye," Peppercorn said, not looking at Slater now but at the weave of the mat beneath him.

"Tell me, Barber."

"Aye, I will. 'Twas this evenin', when ye was up getting the measurements of the compass for the carpenter. Cap'n Berry were down here. Well, the Indians come with the food, like they do every evenin', only there was more of 'em tonight. They took it into the cookin'-house and I heard 'em tryin' to tell Light somethin', God knows what. After a bit they come out and a few more arrive—some old men, one or two important-lookin'. Well, then, without as much as a kiss-my-backside or a by-y'-leave they walk straight up to the house, go in, and start lookin' at Powell. Cap'n Berry got quite a start, seein' 'em go in like that, and he follows 'em. They didn't stay long, but they had a bloody good look at him afore they come out. Then they sails off back to the village."

If Slater wanted confirmation of the girl's story he had it now. And Berry had had it and had chosen to ignore it. Then had Berry realised, when the Indians were there looking at Powell, what their interest meant? It would almost seem like it. And what had Doyle made of it? What was Doyle thinking now on the beach?

Chapter 10

THE captain appeared almost entirely recovered next morning. He had slept well and looked refreshed, and Slater noticed that though there was still a slight slur in his words the facial paralysis was gone. As they ate breakfast and discussed the work to be done that day, Slater came to realise that Berry's instability was connected with stress; so long as there was no strain he would behave normally. Then the captain must be kept from strain; Slater would try to be at Berry's side continually.

They finished breakfast. Jeremy had not yet come to clear away the meal when Berry, who was standing outside, called to Slater that the young chief was coming. Before Slater even saw Duadua he knew there was trouble.

All but three of the men with Duadua waited at the edge of the clearing. Duadua was polite, but frigidly so. He stood off from Berry and Slater, pointed to the village and mentioned Awila's name. It was clear he had been sent to bring Berry and Slater back with him.

Awila greeted them civilly enough, but there was no mistaking his coolness. He did not invite them to sit; in fact, they

were no sooner shown into his presence than he led them outside again to a house which stood on the edge of the *rara*.
Duadua and several other chiefs followed them. They went in
silence, a deadly earnest procession. The captain walked with
his head up and looked straight before him. Slater could not
help feeling they were walking to an execution. The pistols,
inside his shirt, lay heavy against his skin, cold and reassuring.

It was a large house before which Awila stopped. The finish
of it denoted the owner as a man of rank. He paused at the
door, called out and then entered, beckoning Berry and Slater
in after him. Then came Duadua. The others remained outside, talking quietly among themselves.

In the dusk of the house the white men took a few moments
to make out the figure to which Awila pointed. An old man
lay on a pile of mats against the wall. Awila crossed to him and
spoke softly. The man listened and then looked past Awila to
Berry and on to Slater, his old eyes unnaturally bright. There
was a dank, unpleasant smell in the house. Awila turned and
motioned Berry forward; Slater went behind him and stood
while Berry lowered himself to one knee by the side of the
old man.

Looking at him there, Slater had not the slightest doubt that
the invalid had Powell's disease. By nature a thin old man, he
now seemed wasted, his eyes sunk in and his skin dry and
tight over the bones of his face. He was feverish, and there
were traces of vomit about the edge of the mat on which he
lay. His abdomen was distended, curiously boat-shaped, his lips
dry and beginning to peel. He stared above him and soon began
to mutter to himself, as if in delirium.

Berry turned to look up at Slater. "We can't ask him a bloody
thing. What do ye make of it?"

Slater refrained from saying what he thought. He bit his lip.

"I'll tell ye what I think," said Berry, looking back to the old
man. "I think the poor devil's got what ails Powell. That's
what I think." He got to his feet and looked about the room.

"Or a disease similar to it," he added.

"'Twould seem like it," Slater said, astonished by Berry's
acceptance of the fact.

"I don't mean to say he's *caught* it from Powell. But 'tis their variation o' the same sort o' dysentery. Maybe it come from them in the first place. We'll dose him. I've not much faith in the medicine, but ye never know. 'Tis deception, in a way, but we've got to do somethin'. Ye seem to have a bit of an ear for the lingo, Oliver. Try tellin' Awila that we'll bring physic to cure the old man."

With the few words he had learned from Seyawa, Slater tried to make Awila understand that they would be back. Then they left the house. The Fijians stared at them levelly.

Slater's fears for Berry were not realised. Without any assistance from Slater, Berry found his own composure—by telling himself that, while it was Powell's disease, it had not been Powell who had brought it to the island.

" 'Tis a coincidence, ye know, Oliver," he said, almost light-heartedly. "I wouldn't mind bettin' that as this ocean is laid open we'll find more and more of our diseases among the Indians. Mayhap even find cures they've discovered, for they're not without intelligence."

Slater rejected the argument; for, had the islanders known the disease, they would have a treatment for it. He had looked for signs of medication but had seen nothing, had seen only the faces of people who saw something new and feared it.

Within an hour they were back. Now there were women with the old man; they sat at the far end of the house, impassive and suspicious, watching while they dosed him. The invalid appeared to relish the mixture and smiled weakly at Berry. When Berry and Slater went outside, Duadua was waiting for them and led them to another house. Here were two sick men. Slater recognised one as the man who had tried to take Jeremy's knife on the islet. About the house was the odour of fæces and vomit. In deadly silence they dosed these men. When Slater handed the draught to the warrior he had nearly shot, the man's hand shook with fear and he could scarcely raise it to his lips. Slater helped him, holding his head with one hand while he steadied the cup with the other.

In all they treated ten men that morning.

The swift spreading of the disease appalled the white men. It swept from house to house, ravaging the island. It demoralised the people so that those who were not ill sat and waited for it to engulf them. Soon the food gardens were neglected, and the fish-traps remained unemptied. Taboos which had prevented indiscriminate defecation lapsed. Flies crawled on the house mats. Then the people began dying, lying in their own filth in the reeking houses or wandering out, wasted and weak, collapsing, putrefying where they lay.

Slater found his sleep tormented by the sight of them. He saw their haggard, muddy faces, their eyes red-rimmed and purulent, for an infection of the eyes accompanied the disease in many cases. Some victims found their last days tormented by a stiffening of their joints, and once they began to hiccup, in ghastly spasms that set their whole bodies jerking, the end was usually but hours away. Slater could understand little of what was said, but much of it was the raving of the delirious.

Much of the Fijian character emerged to startle the white men, particularly Slater, who, with Berry, saw more of the village than any of them. Slater saw an old man spitting into another's food-bowl that he too might become diseased—*vaka sabiri*; he saw the sick driven from houses that they might not, for the same reason, mix their excreta with the food of others; he saw the hairs of the healthy done up in little bundles with leaves and tied to trees in the forest that the evil spirits might strike at these who were well—*vaka draunikau taka*; the custom of *nocaca*, which purported to infect the end of the waist-cloth of a man or the fringe of a woman's *liku* with a spell that would surely kill unless a counter-spell were worked.

They saw men dying in ghastly fear because they had not yet killed another, and therefore their lot in *Bulu*—the spirit-land—would be to beat a pile of fæces for eternity. Thus, men with strength enough started up, staggered to a sick child or an old woman, and strangled or clubbed the life out of the victim, thereby escaping this ignominy, the brand of *datuvu*, 'coward'.

The children not old enough to forage for themselves in the bush lay and starved to death. Women gave birth to dead children, or bore them alive but did not feed them, not even the first bitter juice of the leaves of the candlenut—*sova dadogo*—the meal which the Fijians believe causes the child to vomit the food it has eaten in its mother's womb. The infants were left to whimper until they were quiet. Slater saw several being eaten by the pigs.

Women collected the drugs called *wai ni vakalutu*—leaves, bark and roots of trees and shrubs which they hoped would make them drop their unborn children. They searched the swamps for the spiky-flowered *kalakalauwisoni*, plucked its leaves and squeezed the juice from them. They chewed the leaves of the *losilosi* bush and the *drala* shrub, and the wood of the *boi boi da* tree they shaved from the trunk and steeped in water and drank it. They ate the fruit of the *siti* tree, normally but the food of the bats.

And when these methods failed they lost their children by other means—*sau gone*.

One morning Slater woke well before dawn. It was hot in the house and he turned restlessly on his mat, again realising that by holding the *Argo* men on the island Berry would destroy them.

He got up, took his pistols and left the house. At the top of the beach he could see the vague shapes of the two men on watch at the launch. On earlier occasions when he could not sleep he had walked down and talked to them, but this morning he made his way along the top of the beach, back under the coconuts, making no noise, just able to see his way. All the stillness, the coolness of an island dawn was about him, refreshing him.

He had walked some distance, travelling away from the village, when he heard voices ahead. He went on cautiously and came to an indentation in the line of the beach, where the water was very shallow and spread in a little cove.

Now the sound of voices was louder. They were women's voices and a large number of them, their sharp, feminine intonations bright in the stillness. Yet they were voices held in check, as if they spoke of secret, hidden things. Making no noise at all on the sand under the trees, he went forward. Now the day was beginning to touch the island and first the trees and then the land began to emerge from the darkness. Before he reached the cove he crouched down, then wriggling eased himself forward until, on a slight rise, he looked out over it.

He saw a number of women, maybe thirty, merging fuzzily in the half-light, silent now, clustered about two older women, one a veritable hag from whose skinny body hung the two flattened tubes of her hanging breasts. In her hand she held something, but he could not see what. They stood in water ankle-deep.

The hag was looking eastward into the sky, and as the light grew Slater made out the features of her wrinkled face. She was toothless, and her lower jaw worked unceasingly against her upper. She spoke. He could just hear the sound of her voice, surprisingly youthful. As she talked she moved out into deeper water, followed by the other old woman. When the water was above their knees—grey and cold it looked in the dawn light—they turned and faced back towards the other women.

Now in the growing light Slater could see that the women in the shallow water were young; and all seemed a few months pregnant. They looked at one another and spoke among themselves. The older women waited.

The girl who walked out first was tall and well developed, with long thighs and a straight back. She was not wearing a *liku* but a breech-cloth such as the men of the island wore. The others watched her, drawing closer together now, as if seeking solace in the touch of their bodies. Reaching the old women she put her hands to the knot of her cloth and twisting quickly let it fall away between her legs. As it touched the water they drew it from her, the last turn clinging to her thighs.

She stood naked, then flexing her legs she squatted slowly, until the water reached her navel. As she moved she looked steadily at the old hag, who, Slater now saw, held in her hand a thin stick. When the girl was down, the old woman knelt in front of her, first on one knee and then on both, a movement stiff with age, the tips of her breasts just submerged. She said something to the girl and put her hands out towards her under the water. The girl tensed, her shoulders straightening and fists clenched before her.

Then Slater knew. It seemed to take an age. Only once did the girl cry out, her mouth an open dark hole in her face. The old woman moved her shoulders, and her arms pressed at the water, rippling it. Once, when she cried out, the woman who held her cloth murmured something, her head moving in the grey light which the water reflected.

Then it was done. The old woman stood up, the stick in her right hand hanging by her side. The girl moved up, looking down at herself. The woman held out her cloth; she took it and as she made back to the beach it dragged after her, floating under her hand. The others watched her; she reached them and passed on. Slater moved to a half-crouch, sick within himself.

As he left the place another girl detached herself from the group and started out towards the old woman, who stood waiting with the stick of *losilosi* wood in her hand.

It rained again that day and as they worked in the dripping heat Slater felt the island closing in on them. He wondered if Doyle, if any of them, felt as he did. There was virtually no conversation; what had to be said for the sake of the work was said, but that was all. Water ran on the men—and sweat and rain. Tempers were high, and more than once Slater found himself hating Berry, found himself near to losing his control. They had the boat, yet he would not use it—to leave an island they had polluted, to escape from people who were about to destroy them for what they had done.

In the morning Doyle struck Wilkinson because he broke an auger; looking at Doyle as he cursed Wilkinson, Slater saw a rage such as all but withered his fears, made all else of no account.

Then after they had eaten at noon Doyle went to Wilkinson, his face sombre and dark.

"I hit ye," he said quietly.

Doyle had made a cut about an inch long over Wilkinson's left eye. Now terror was in Wilkinson's face. Slater saw it, and he saw the emotion that worked in Doyle, knew he regretted having struck the man, yet knew, or thought he knew, that Doyle would be unable to say that. Then it burst from Doyle: "God damn it, 'tis this cursed island."

The evening was hot, but the rain had stopped. Slater had spoken to Berry about setting sentries on the houses and that night they were to be placed. Slater found it hard to return to the house, and to Berry. He walked slowly, hearing the dripping of the jungle, smelling the earthy smell the rain had brought, his heart despairing. Now he was becoming aware of a change in himself, seeing himself as less and less linked with Berry, more and more with . . . with Doyle? Could it be? he wondered. With the men, then, with—God, with anyone but Berry—even with Light, who gibbered his prayers to Powell. And Powell? Powell who was teetering now at the very edge of death; whose desperate, tortured mind had lost all contact with reality; whose breath smelled like the stench that blew from the village; whom he had found that day, crawling to the door, a trail of liquid after him. . . .

Die, Powell, ye poor, helpless bastard. Die! Dear Christ, hear me; hear me, and if Ye wish us to live, then shift us from this place. He prayed, as he had not since he was a child.

"Mister!"

He was clear of the path and Berry stood before the house, tall against the low doorway. There, Oliver Slater, is the cause of it—not Powell.

"There's a cry comin' from the path. 'Tis the girl, I'd say. Listen!"

Now there was a greater urgency in Seyawa. He followed her down into the clearing, catching her as she reached the sandy patch where they had 'talked' before.

He moved close to her, putting out his arms. They stood with their bodies almost touching. Then he drew her to him, knowing no revulsion, only desire. Her head fell on his chest and he felt her body pressing against him, her heart throbbing, her firm breasts through the thin stuff of his shirt. What she said he could not understand, but she murmured, a tiny chatter of words running from her as the purring of some young animal. Slowly he lifted her head, brought her face to his, seeking her lips.

But she drew her face away, pushing him back gently. Then her hands fell to her side, and she slipped from his grasp to the sand. For a moment they stood thus—he looking down, she looking up at him. Then she beckoned him to her.

Side by side they knelt in the last of the day, struggling to speak with each other, drawing, scratching out, marking symbols, seeking desperately to understand, for now he had sensed her deadly earnestness.

He came to see she was trying to convey the idea of a god or a god-head. She drew what he took to be people humbling themselves before something. He saw that a priest was involved and she taught him the name for a priest. She looked to the sky and when the first star came she pointed to it and drew a star with five points, to which she added a long streak. He gazed at it and saw the streak as a tail; she was trying to describe a comet. But they'd seen no comet. He had not, and if any of the men had seen one, surely he would have been told?

But it was a comet she meant, for when he took the stick and drew his own version of one she nodded her head, eyes bright as she saw him understand. Then she went back to the symbol and the word she had taught him for priest.

Then she put both hands about her throat and clasping it tight opened her mouth and rolled her eyes, as if she were choking. It was clear to Slater that she was describing a death by strangling. As soon as she saw that he understood she got to her feet. He rose up after her and put out his hands for her, but she slipped away, ran to the path and out of the clearing, and was gone.

"All I can say, Mr. Slater," said the captain, "is if it be a comet—which I very much doubt—it hasn't been visible for long. Otherwise some of us would have seen it. Ye say 'tis in the southern sky?"

" 'Twas south she kept pointin'."

"Then why haven't the watch spied it? Eh?"

"God knows. Asleep maybe. But 'tis not the main thing. The main thing is this of the priest we've to fear; the *bete* she calls him. She's still drawing sick people and they connect this sickness with us. The comet puts the lid on it. 'Tis the sign to do away with us afore we make any more mischief."

"Ah, Mister, ye must be daft to believe such stuff." Berry gave a curious, mirthless giggle. "So help me I'd never have said a mate o' mine'd come to believin' such bilge water. God damn me if I would have. Ye must be takin' leave o' y'senses,

Mr. Slater, if ye believe a comet could be tellin' them to up and do away with us."

Slater saw that it was hopeless to argue. Berry had made up his mind not to take the warning but to refute the evidence of danger by ridiculing it.

The night was well advanced before they saw the comet. It rode high, climbing past the stars until it dominated the southern sky. Slater watched it and then went to his mat. He could not sleep. On his skin and on his shirt were the scent of the girl and the perfume of sandalwood, and they tormented him.

Chapter 11

IF Berry had spent that night quietly loading the launch; if he had shifted his men on to the beach and, just before dawn, had slid the boat into the water, and at first light had stood out through the lagoon to the sea, covered astern by the swivel and the muskets and the pistols, and had faced the hazards of the sea; if he had made away to another island and there finished the work on the boat; or even if he had given up all hope of fully converting it and had set sail westward in it as it was—he would have had a seaman's chance of surviving. But he did none of these things. Stubbornly he clung to his idea of leaving the island in a completed craft and, clinging to that, told Slater next day that they would wait for three more days, when, he said, the mizzen should be stepped (the main-mast was ready for stepping) and the decking caulked.

Again the day dawned hot and thundery, a day of piled masses of cloud and little wind, a humidity-saturated atmosphere in which the slightest effort brought the sweat running.

Now the village seemed used to its character of death, used to its stench. A darkness lay over the place, filled the air of the houses so that it clung to the bodies of any who entered. When Berry and Slater returned from their visits to dose the people, the men would stand off from the sweet sickliness of the smell they carried on them until they had washed themselves in the sea.

That morning, as Berry and Slater entered one of the larger houses, there rose from the gloom a weird, half-smothered cry. It came from a young woman. She was lying on her back, and at her head knelt a man, holding her shoulders; another was straddling her, face to face. She was not more than twenty-five and rather plump. She appeared to be quite healthy. Her legs were bent, knees up behind the buttocks of the man who was over her. She looked at Berry and Slater as they drew near, but she gave no sign of wanting aid. The men looked too, until the one across her turned back and said something, whereupon the other behind her head pressed down upon her shoulders, his arms straightening as he exerted force. The man straddling leaned farther over her, his forearms pushing into her fat breasts, and pressed his hands around her throat.

Berry gasped and cried out: "Dear Jesus, Oliver, they're strangling her!"

The girl's lips began to swell about her open mouth, and her tongue protruded. Her eyes bulged. She made a bubbling sound. Berry turned, pushed past Slater and rushed from the house.

When she stopped jerking, the man straddling her relaxed, and as he got up from her he took a sennit string from a groove in her neck. He grinned at Slater, half fearfully, half arrogantly. The white man seemed displeased, but what of it. The strangler had performed an honourable task. For this was one of the twenty-seven wives of the chief who had died. Nine of them had pre-deceased him; the other eighteen were dispatched to comfort him in *Bulu*.

Outside, Slater saw that Berry was badly shaken. He stood staring about him, muttering to himself, a wild look in his eye.

"Ah, Oliver, they're damned, if ever a people were. Aye, hell is too good for them. An' they'll be givin' it to us next. Watch out if they don't. Powell, now—he's ill and ye'll mind a sick

114

man catches things easily. Watch Powell, Mister, for any sign o' this disease. I wouldn't put it past them to try it on him."

Berry raved on about *Argo*, his beautiful ship, and how they would sail away in her. But Slater wasn't listening. He had missed the way and had come too far along the inland side of the village.

They soon reached the edge of the village and turned seaward. Berry was silent now, walking with his head down, as though preoccupied. There was noise coming from somewhere ahead, to their right, and as they neared the place Slater saw a young man run out from between the houses some fifty or sixty yards in front of them and disappear into the bush. They heard screams, among them a woman's voice, followed by the steadier note of male voices.

But it was the stench that stopped them. Berry threw up his head, snapped from his half-real world into one of ghastly reality. Slater swallowed hard, fighting the desire to retch. Looking to the right between the trees Slater saw people moving, but what they were doing was not clear, for they were partly obscured. Then there came more screaming and a shouted, pitiful protest.

"What is it, Mister?" asked Berry, his voice almost a whine.

"Stay here, Sir, I'm goin' to take a look."

"Nay, nay, Oliver, leave 'em to their depravity." But Slater had already started to move forward.

The people were struggling round a pit. Most of them were men; only six or seven were women. Not far from the edge of the pit three men held a middle-aged woman, dragging and pushing her to it. She was screaming and with feet and hands was scrabbling at the earth. One of the men was pushing her with his foot against her buttocks. As Slater drew near, from over the edge of the hole crawled a girl, little more than a child. Quite naked, she got her head above the rim of earth, then half her body. For a moment she gazed about her, then, chattering with terror, got out on to the edge of the hole and squatted there, too weak to go farther.

The stench came from the hole—an open grave.

Berry shouted something and stumbled forward, muttering incoherently. The man pushing at the woman saw him and called out. The others turned to look, and the woman, murmuring a single phrase, over and over, saw him too, and finding herself free started to crawl towards him. But one of the men grabbed her again, and as Berry still tottered on ahead this man shouted and, thrusting the others aside, lifted the woman and hurled her, screaming, towards the hole. She struck the mound and lay there, dazed. He followed, and shoving hard with his foot sent her tumbling into the grave. Then he jumped in on top of her and stayed on her, looking up over the rim at Berry and Slater.

With this, the little girl squatting on the edge began to move and another of the men went for her, but as he did Slater rushed forward. Reaching the warrior, he swung him from the child. For a moment they teetered on the edge of the grave, then Slater found his balance and, pressing back the man's head, chopped down across his throat with the side of his hand. The Fijian let go his furious grip and turned away, eyes wide with fright, and as he did Slater drew his pistol and clubbed him with the butt. He fell into the grave and Slater turned on another, and then another, laying into them with the butt of the heavy weapon.

Berry, meanwhile, had drawn and fired, and now with a mechanical chopping action was hitting at the Fijians with his pistol as they ran, yelping with fright.

In moments the place was cleared, except for an old woman who lay on the other side of the grave with her ankles tied. Slater dropped to her and cut the vines that bound her. She could not stand, but she could crawl, and without any sound at all she started off, on hands and knees, thin breasts hanging, her thigh bones showing as they worked under her skin.

Slater went up to the edge of the grave and looked in. It was some fifteen or more feet long, not quite that in width, nor was it as deep. Putrefying bodies half filled it. At the other end of the pit was the man Slater had struck. He was on his face and he was dead. Berry tottered up to Slater and fell heavily forward on to him.

Slater got Berry to the path and was some way along it when Light and Wilkinson came running. Wilkinson, Light and Jeremy had been at the house and had heard the report of

Berry's pistol shot. They had sent Jeremy to the beach for Doyle and the rest of the men and, arming themselves, had come running.

They helped Slater get Berry to the men's house. Slater made much of the fight Berry had been in, telling how, only after a tremendous effort, the captain had mastered the warrior who had attacked him. With this lie he explained Berry's fainting condition. The men expressed their praise of the old man for his courage, but as Slater told the story he felt Doyle's eyes steady on him and wondered if he, too, believed.

That night Powell slid in and out of delirium, babbling about the sea, about his father, and about the syphilitic judge who had condemned him to death by transporting him to New South Wales. In Doyle was a brooding, dangerous savagery and the men kept clear of him. Berry, though able to get about, seemed half dazed, and once the issue of spirit had been made Slater took him up to their house.

They were soon finished with the meal and the captain got up on to the sleeping-platform. As Slater was about to give him some laudanum, Peppercorn came running and calling to Berry. Slater met him at the door. Pepper was carrying a musket and after him came Leadbeater, whose turn it was for sentry duty at the house.

" 'Tis Light, Sir," Peppercorn cried. "He's not come back."

"What's this? Eh? Who is it, Mister?" called Berry, sitting up.

"Tom Pepper, Sir," Slater said over his shoulder. "He says the steward's not come back."

"How do ye mean he's not come back? Where the hell did he go?" Berry got down and went to the door.

"He took the food to them, did he, Pepper?" asked Slater.

"Aye, Sir, to the watch at the launch, like he always does. But he didn't come back, an' when Mr. Doyle sends down to see what might be keepin' him, Hockin' an' Pain say they haven't set eyes on him."

As they proceeded to the men's house, Slater had little hope that they would find Light alive. But search for him they must, and therein lay more cause for fear. If Berry should undertake to lead the search his mind might snap under the strain and perhaps Doyle might seize the opportunity to strike. God knew, thought Slater, Doyle had some reason to revolt. And if the men were ever to be in a mood to follow him, surely now would be the time, with the islanders beginning to attack, and with the launch all but ready for sea.

Doyle spoke, while they were still approaching. "The swine have him, nothin' surer."

"Who did ye send to the beach lookin' for him, Mister?" asked Berry.

"Wilkinson."

"He kep' a sharp look-out there an' back?"

"I had no lantern, Sir," said Wilkinson, stepping from behind Doyle.

"If ye ask me, he's gone," said Day.

"I didn't ask ye, Day," said Berry slowly, with not a little dignity. For a moment Berry kept his eyes on Day and then he turned to Slater. "We'll look for him, Mister. An' somethin' else—we'll abandon that house of ours. Mr. Doyle, take a couple of the men to the other house and bring all our gear down here and put it in with yours."

Slater watched Berry, marvelling at him; the captain seemed more self-possessed than he had for days. It puzzled Slater, and gave him little comfort—it seemed too good to be true.

"Very well, let's go, Mr. Slater. Pepper, give me the lantern. An', Morgan, ye'll come with us too."

They soon found the spot where Light had been ambushed. A few pieces of tapioca lay on the edge of the path about midway between the house and the launch. The grass about was pressed flat and several small, broken branches hung from a tree on the village side.

"There's no blood," said Peppercorn.

" 'Twould be hard to see in the lantern-light," said Berry, "but it don't look like there's any."

" 'Tis easy to see which way they went with him," said Morgan, "be the broken branches."

"Aye," put in Peppercorn, "an' 'twould look like there was a fair crowd of 'em."

"Now follow close up, lads." And, holding the lantern out ahead of him, Berry stepped off the path.

They had not gone far when Berry tripped on a root and fell, sending the lantern flying. It crashed into a bush and went out. Slater leaped forward, and taking Berry under the arms lifted him to his feet.

"God damn an' curse it," muttered Berry, rubbing his shin, "the light had me blinded."

"Are ye hurt?" asked Slater, still holding him.

"Nay, except for m'leg."

"Pepper," said Slater, "go and see if ye can find the lantern."

"I was a fool to have the bloody thing alight, Mister. Now I suppose 'tis smashed."

But it had not been broken. A moment later Pepper found it. "Cracked, that's all, an' some o' the oil run out," he said as he picked it up.

As they went on, Slater saw that Berry was limping.

The village looked almost deserted. There were lights in only a few of the houses and an eerie stillness enfolded it. "Somethin' afoot here," muttered Morgan.

Berry stopped, uncertain which way to go. "What would ye say, Mister? Would they have him at Awila's?"

"Maybe the temple?"

"The temple?"

"If a priest is involved they might." Slater didn't care to remind Berry of his conversation with Seyawa.

"We should bear to port, Sir, then we'll pass the temple on the way to Awila's."

"Which way, Mister?"

"Port, Sir," whispered Slater.

"Mister, ye seem to remember the course through the village better than me. Would—would ye like to lead?" There was something pathetic in the old man's voice.

The moon was rising and the stars were bright in a cloudless sky. With Slater a few feet in front they slipped silently between the houses. Slater was making for the *rara*, where he would be able to see the *bure kalou* and get his bearings for Awila's house. Well into the village it seemed even quieter, more sinister. They stopped often, muskets at the ready, alert for the slightest sound. From a few of the houses came low mutterings, most of which Slater felt sure were the rambling of

119

the delirious. The stench of the village appalled Peppercorn and Morgan.

Now they were nearing the *rara*, and could see its open space between the houses. Slater stopped, considering whether to work around its left side, or bear to the right and pass along the sea side. Suddenly, from a house directly in front of them, about a hundred feet away, came a noise. It sounded like someone falling, and an instant later there came another, louder, sound, followed by a voice, an urgent, too-loud, whispered order, or exclamation. All the white men heard it, and at Slater's command they fell flat upon the turf.

Berry wriggled up level with him. "What d'ye make of it, Oliver?" he whispered hoarsely. "D'ye think they have Light in there?"

"I don't know." Slater found it hard to keep the note of impatience out of his voice. "If it's Light, there's others with him —an' they'll be armed, ye can bet on that. We'd best concentrate our fire on the ends of the house."

"Ye mean *shoot*, Oliver?"

"If we have to. We've been seen. Nothin' surer."

"Then"—Berry leaned his head until his mouth was almost touching Slater's ear—"we go back, Oliver. Aye, we go back to the men."

God in heaven, thought Slater, why should he have been plagued with this? He lay there feeling Berry's breath on his neck. He glanced past the captain, at Morgan and Peppercorn. They were looking straight ahead at the house and sighting their muskets.

Slater was listening to the noise from behind the house and tried not to hear Berry's rambling. From somewhere beyond the house, from over the *rara*, there came a scream. It was not very loud and not very long; it ended abruptly.

Peppercorn shouted and dropped his head to his musket. Berry's head snapped up, and he leaped to his feet. An instant later Peppercorn fired.

The air was suddenly filled with wild war-cries as a leaping, howling throng burst from around both sides of the house. Big fighting men they were, painted for war. Slater, cursing, taken completely by surprise, swung about, his pistols jumping in his hands, the balls thudding into the human press.

The muskets of Morgan and Peppercorn soon turned the worst of it; the forward advance stopped. Berry still remained upon his feet, in a daze; Slater pulled him down just as the air suddenly sang with the flight of arrows.

"The cap'n's pistols, Mister," called Peppercorn, ramming his musket. Slater rolled Berry over and pulled one of them from him. As Slater got up, cocking it, he saw Pepper get off another shot. But he fired at a retreating target. The Fijians had stood all they could; throwing down their weapons they were running, howling, out across the *rara*.

Slater steadied for his shot, and as there came a flare of light from an opened door across the green he fired. A fluke, the shot hit the target. A man staggered, appeared to recover, then swung into profile against the light, a grotesque figure, screaming, clawing at his back.

The immediate danger was past. Pepper was reloading, sliding in the ball. Morgan was sitting up, his mouth open, gasping. He stared at Berry, as if he would speak. Then he groaned and fell sideways, against Berry; and from his mouth came a rush of blood, black in the starlight, drenching his beard, flowing dark on to the captain's sleeve and on to the grass. Berry shrieked and Slater steadied him while Peppercorn eased Morgan away. From the wounded man's throat protruded the feathered shaft of an arrow. Peppercorn laid Morgan gently back upon the grass and Slater pulled the captain to his feet. "He's one of us as'll not be seein' Port Jackson," said Peppercorn softly, looking at Morgan.

Berry, oblivious of what was going on, suddenly dropped to his knees and began frantically feeling about in the blood-wet grass. "M'pistol, Mister," he complained, " 'Tis gone. They've took it. They've took m'pistol."

"I've got it," Slater said sharply, and he handed it to Berry, who stared at it dully.

Peppercorn looked at Slater. "That were Light?" he asked quietly.

"Ye mean the scream just afore they attacked?"

"Aye. Who else could it be? 'Twas no Indian sound."

Berry sat with his pistols in his hands, pointed down into the ground. Slater looked at him, wondering whether to go on, on the chance that they were mistaken about the scream, or to go back. There were now virtually but two of them—he and Pepper; against how many? But that wasn't all; for if they went to Awila's, what would they do with Berry? He couldn't be left there with poor Morgan and trusted to wait for them to return. It was out of the question to bring him with them. Suddenly Pepper tapped Slater's arm.

"I've been watchin' the house, Sir. There's someone in it. Can ye hear?"

Slater stood listening. "One o' the wounded Indians," he said.

"Nay, Sir," returned Peppercorn. " 'Tis more like someone knockin'. There it is. 'Tis a knockin' against the reeds o' the walls. It couldn't be Light, could it?"

"Hardly."

"But if we've been mistook about the scream?" Peppercorn paused, then added: "Any rate, 'tis worth a look, be Jesus. I'd like to get even with a few o' the swine."

The idea of vengeance did not move Slater, but it just might be that Light was in there. They had evidently surprised a guard of some sort.

"I'll go, Sir," said Peppercorn, cocking his musket.

"Nay, we'll both go."

"What about Cap'n Berry?"

"We'll leave him here." As Slater spoke he turned about— and looked into the muzzle of the pistol Berry had pointed at him.

Chapter 12

WHEN Lester Light died there went with him the islanders' fear of the white men as gods. They were not gods if they died like men, and as the Fijians shed their fear, the white men lost their greatest strength.

Light was unarmed. He had passed the half-way mark to the beach when the Fijians took him. He had reached a straight part of the track and was humming a hymn to himself, the handle of the bucket in the crook of his left arm. He was well into this straight stretch when he looked up and saw a warrior planted on the path ahead of him, not sixty feet away. His body was painted and he was swinging a club.

Light's fright killed him. Had he been Barber, or Peppercorn, Doyle or Slater, even perhaps Jeremy, he might have won through by bluffing the man from the track. With the heavy bucket as his weapon, he might have rushed the Fijian and driven him from the path. For, if Light was frightened, the Fijian was terrified. It was not his wish that set him there, holding the path against this creature who could have come from nowhere but the clouds. It was the wish of the *bete*, the product of his desperation, for the islanders had reached the stage when their priest must deliver them from those who tormented them—or die and make way for another. The *bete* was not without rivals, men prepared to stake all on a desperate gamble.

But Light stopped and stared at the Fijian, who, encouraged by Light's fear, took a step towards him. Light spun round, to run back to the house. But behind him stood another islander. If Light had not panicked then, there might still have been a chance for him; if he had used the next moment to shout, Pain and Hocking might have heard him, or Doyle and the men at the house. But he made no noise at all; his mind, his voice, were paralysed by fright.

He turned to go forward again, then swung to go back, and as they reached him he dropped the bucket. The first man to touch him came from behind, then they came at him from the bush on either side. He was thrown to the ground and a huge hand closed over his mouth. He tried to bite—his one show of fight—but the spread of the hand clamped his jaws together. He was lashed with vine and about his mouth was bound a piece of tapa, pulled tight and wound several times about the lower part of his face. He was quite conscious and recognised Duadua as the leader of the party.

Awila, the *bete*, the elders, lesser chiefs and priests were waiting for him at Awila's house. It was lighted by a score of candle-nut lamps. The *buli* shells which hung from the roof were globules of white against the darkness of the timbering above them. Of the *Argo* men only Berry and Slater had seen inside this house. Now its majesty and savagery pressed relentlessly down on the little man. He cowered, and the silent, sweating faces in the corners of the house watched with rapt attention.

Light was pushed forward until he stood half a dozen paces from Awila. The tapa over his mouth was now beginning to spread an ache through the lower part of his face, distorting his vision by its upward press against his cheeks. Awila watched through red-rimmed eyes, his heavy body hunched forward, frantically thinking only of his own survival. Awila's life had reached a turning-point; whether Light be god or devil or a being like themselves. Awila knew that the pattern of his life would be altered from this night on.

In Awila, Light saw the shape of retribution, the face of evil personified, the heathen, the anti-Christ. He prayed, but, pathetically, he only half believed his prayer would be heard. The words of the prayer, the idea of prayer, jabbered in his skull, the phrases tumbling over and over, automatically, unheard by him so that he did not know they were there, knew only that in prayer was the hope of his salvation. And the harder he threw his appeal to his God the harder seemed the loss of his life.

Awila moved, and his red-rimmed eyes rolled, and he looked at an old man who stood alone against a stretch of wall. This was the *bete*.

For the space of carefully measured seconds he was motionless. Then he stepped out towards Light. Sweat stood on the knobby, blackened walnut of his skull. Over all his skin was a greyish scale and his eyes were sunk behind bright rims, redder than those of any man Light had ever seen. The sweat trickled down, ran from under his armpits and soaked the stained strip of tapa that hung from his scrawny hips.

He started to speak, and Light saw the creased leather of his face opening and shutting, the yellow teeth stuck in gums as bright as the lids of his eyes.

"Here is the white-skin, the *kai vavalagi*," he said, "he who comes as a god but brings that which is evil, who turns our bowels to water, who rots our bodies, makes of us a place for maggots; who plants in us the seeds of death which spread in us and befoul us.

"They are not the gods, these who bring to us this death, and the tailed star, the *kalokalo vakabuina*, tells us so. They are those who would steal our lives as Daucina would steal our women; Ravuravu they put to shame; they eat at our bodies as Batimona would our brains.

"I say to you, the fruit is rotten. They are as a *bu* that rattled will not give the sound of sweet water, that opened is green with decay. Their blood—for I say there is blood in them—is black with desires they do not understand and fears they are terrified lest we see.

"I am the instrument of the gods, the gods that *are*. Listen well to what I say, and do as I say, and we shall rid ourselves of this filth which streams into us and kills us as we would our enemies."

The priest paused, looking at Light, and gaining courage from the terror he saw. Then he turned back to Awila.

"And there is she who was once one of us; she into whom has been injected the sperm which will grow until a demon crawls from her who will—in his turn—inject his kind into other of our women, so that, unknowing, we will nurture that which we should destroy.

"But first"—and he faced slowly about to Light, pointing his long arm at him—"there is this of them who stands now among us. You will see"—and he let his hand sink down as he turned to Awila again—"this devil is destructible."

As he said this, and closed his mouth, fear ran through the house. Light felt it and looked about him wildly. The *bete* watched him, his eyes like two stones in his face.

"Now," he said quietly, lowering his head, "let me pause.

"Lord, I would speak with you; consult you who are my familiar and seek to guide your hand that you may sweep clear this evil which besmirches us, that shall be remembered and spoken of among us for a thousand moons. That would destroy us, were we weak, wrench from us our beliefs, trample the places of our gods, split us with their devil's thunder and twist our children and our children's children from the ways of our living."

He finished and, lifting an arm upon which the flesh clung thin and flabby, pointed up to the great roof. His body began to stiffen. Silence filled the room, even breathing seemed suspended. Stiffer grew his body, seeming to stretch out along its pointed, wizened length, and a trembling entered him, as though a breeze were rippling him.

"Aaaiii."

The scream shredded the silence, made those who watched tremble, paled their faces, grabbed at Light, hounded his spirit, and wrenched from him a hideous groan; and he fell, sobbing his fear into the mats.

The priest swung his arm down and pointed to the floor. He stood, perfectly still; then, taking up his arm as though it had been no connected part of him, he faced a man who crouched by the door through which Light had come. This man now slid forward, shuffling on hands, buttocks and heels, rolling ahead of him a large, green drinking nut.

The priest waited until the nut was at his feet. Then he picked it up and held it out to Awila, who looked at it and then at Light. The *bete* moved slowly until he stood over Light, then with a dreadful shout he raised the nut and hurled it to the floor. The nut hit the mat a foot from Light's head and went rolling away. The priest's eyes never left it and the instant it stopped he bounded after it, his skinny legs a twinkle of movement. He grabbed it and held it close to his eyes, turning it this way and that, his fingers trembling and searching its surface, seeking a sign.

Suddenly he cast it from him.

Light felt arms under him, lifting him to his feet; he felt hope start in him as the gag was ripped from his mouth, snapping his head about; but when he saw the eyes of the man who had wrenched it from him, he quailed. And as the words of his prayer chattered about the spaces of his mind there came the pitiful notion that this *couldn't* be he, that soon it would cease, and he would walk again, unfettered, and kneel and give thanks for his deliverance and read to poor, half-dead Powell.

Stumbling on his feet he faced about to Awila.

Had he not said to Powell that God was the All Merciful? That what tormented Powell would pass, was but part of the Way, that God was at the end of it, was the beginning, the middle, the All.

He saw the club, with its great double head and its rows of teeth. He saw it start the swing, saw the sweat glisten on the underside of Awila's arm, saw the heavy-lidded eyes. . . .

He had no idea he was screaming.

The *bete* waited until Light's body stopped jerking. Then he moved out to it with an easy, arrogant motion. Awila stepped back, the club swinging in his shaking hand, his eyes fixed on the body. The priest bent and his fingers felt into the mess that had been the seaman's head and came up bloody. It could have been a smile that lay on his face for that second. Then it vanished and his fingers probed deeper, past the pieces of bone, and came out flecked with grey. This, he said, was not the head of a god.

Chapter 13

"Ye'll be leavin' me nowhere, Mister," said Berry quietly, the pistol steady in his hand and pointed at Slater.

Slater heard Peppercorn's breath whistle between his teeth in a long sigh. Curiously, he did not immediately think of himself but of Pepper, who was so close to him that if Berry shot he could not fail to hit one of them.

One of Berry's pistols had been fired. Was it the one he now aimed at them, or the other? The weapon was cocked; Slater could see that. He could see also, out of the corner of his eye, the muzzle of Peppercorn's musket; and he knew that was loaded, for he had seen Pepper ramming the charge.

"Where were ye aimin' to go, Mister?" Berry's voice was lower than usual, and this, more than the sight of the levelled pistol, was to Slater the measure of the old man's distress.

Slater's voice nearly broke as he answered: "There's someone, we think, in this house yonder."

"Well?"

"It could be Light."

"Light?"

"Aye."

"Where is Light?"

"I can't tell ye for sure, but he could be in this house. That might have been his guard we surprised."

The captain looked from Slater to Peppercorn. He seemed undecided what to do next, as if he had gone as far as his mind would carry him. Slater wondered whether he could just walk up to him, lean down, and take the pistol. It seemed so simple. Yet Berry might fire, for in his present mood he could not be trusted.

At this moment the noise came from the house once more, louder now, more insistent and longer. Berry heard it and warily turned his head to look at the house, but he kept the pistol pointed at Slater. Yet this seemed Slater's chance. He started forward and Peppercorn lifted his musket. Quickly Berry turned back to face them. But he did not pull the trigger. Instead he went limp and, like a frightened child, allowed Slater to take the pistol from him. Slater put the muzzle to his nose and smelled it. It was the loaded weapon.

"Give me y'other pistol, too," he said. "Pepper'll load it for ye," he added soothingly. Berry handed it over.

A moment later the captain stood up and, as if he were resuming an ordinary conversation, said: "Who did ye say was in the house yonder?"

"I can't be sure, Sir, but I think it might be Light."

"Light?"

"Aye, Sir. Y'steward."

"Ah. An' ye'll take a look, will ye?"

"I think 'twould be best, Sir."

"I agree wi' ye, Oliver. Light has no business to be there at all. Will ye go alone?"

"Nay, Peppercorn will come with me, and perhaps ye'd best come too, Sir."

Peppercorn had reloaded the pistol, and now he gave it to Slater, who hesitated a moment and then returned it to Berry, together with the other one. For, if Berry was to go with them, he could not go unarmed. He sent Berry and Peppercorn to opposite sides of the house; he made for the entrance. The doorway was sealed with a bamboo matting. He put his shoulder to it and the matting fell back; then, pistol out before him, he kicked the matting flat and moved in over it.

As he stepped inside the bamboo cracked under his feet. The air was foul and the darkness was intense. He stood just beyond the threshold and peered about, but the inky blackness revealed nothing. He heard a noise to his right and swung to face it, but realised as he did that it was outside the house, at Berry's end. God alone knew what Berry was doing!

Slater called the steward's name softly, uncertain whether to call at all; it seemed now so senseless to hope that Light would be here. He must have been mad even to have thought it.

"Are ye there, Light?" he called again. And for answer came a mumbling sentence from Berry, through the reed wall.

He wanted to go, but there was someone there. He froze, for from the blackness there came a sound of movement, a stirring, and then, startlingly loud and near, that noise of rapping against the wall that he and Pepper and Berry had heard.

Outside, Pepper started and gripped his musket tight, for the noise came from his end of the house, from so close that he felt the wall shiver. He pointed his musket at the place and stood ready, wondering what Slater was doing.

"Light, are ye there?" he called quietly. "If ye are, kick at the wall."

The bamboo mat upon which Slater stood sloped up, as if it lay upon a mound of some kind. It was firm under his feet, and to his left, towards Pepper's side of the house, whence the sound had come, it sloped up more sharply. Slowly, feeling out each step, Slater shuffled over the bamboo. Then he crouched down and with his left hand felt the way ahead of him. A few steps forward he reached the end of the mat and his feet came in touch with earth. It seemed smooth enough, still a rising slope, and he went on.

Suddenly the sandy soil crumbled under him, and he felt himself falling. Somehow he managed to straighten himself. He thought it was a trap that he had fallen into; and in that trap he felt the touch of another human being. Recoiling, he jerked his right hand down and fired.

The jet of flame which burst from his pistol was illumination enough to reveal the inert body of a man sprawled across the bottom of the pit, face upward, legs twisted back under him. Crazily, it seemed to Slater that the native was grinning at the joke he had played on the white man. Crazily, too, it seemed to Slater that he had seen, above the farther edge of the pit, a bundled figure.

Pepper was now at the door, with his musket at the ready, and he called Slater's name. Berry was right behind him. Slater answered, cautioning them to halt, and with trembling hands he felt about the earth beyond the hole. Then he touched cloth and, through it, the firm shape of a human being. From it rose the fragrance of sandalwood perfume.

"Come, Pepper," he cried. "Circle round, and mind the hole, 'tis a grave." He leaped up out of the pit and with his hands explored the bundle, which vibrated with movement against the tight confinement of the cloth. He tore at the tightened vines and bands he found; in a moment the figure was released and its limbs stretched free.

"What is it, Sir?" said Pepper as he got to Slater's side. "Is it Light?" he added.

"Nay," said Slater, without concealing the excitement that he felt. "But 'tis a friend I've found, I think. Now lead the way out slowly, and we'll follow you."

Outside, on her feet, Seyawa breathed deep and stumbled. Had Slater not held her she would have fallen, for her legs were cramped from the ties that had bound her, and the blood rushing in them caused her to cry out with pain. She half fell against him and rested there.

When they got back to Morgan, Peppercorn, with a sudden curse, turned and ran back to the house. "What the hell—"

began Berry. "Here, Pepper, come back wi' ye." But Peppercorn was gone. A moment later from behind the house there came the report of a musket. Slater started, wondering.

"There was one o' them behind the house," Berry explained. "His leg were broke be a musket ball."

Pepper returned, bringing with him a faint smell of fired powder. He stood over Morgan's body. For a few seconds no one spoke. Then Berry said softly: "Of all of us, Tom Pepper, I'd have said ye'd have been the last to do that."

"Ye'll argue I shouldn't have done it, Cap'n," Peppercorn said fiercely, looking up at him. "Ye'll say 'twas un-Christian, but they done for two good men tonight—God rest their souls. If that's murder," he added, more quietly, "then I'll burn for it."

"We'd best be gettin' back, Sir," said Slater.

"Aye. And away, Oliver."

"Ye mean the launch—we make away?"

"I do. We'll bury poor Morgan and just as soon as 'tis light enough we'll start gettin' the gear down from the house."

Berry went ahead, followed by Seyawa. Slater and Peppercorn carried Morgan. When they reached the house, Doyle and the men, using the adze and several pieces of planking, dug a hole and they buried him as deep as they could. By the light of the lantern Berry read the service. Slater only half listened. Merged with his sorrow over Morgan's death was almost a hatred for Berry, whose futility, stubbornness, madness, had done this to them.

Chapter 14

THE attack upon the *Argo* men came an hour after midnight.

The first warning came just after they had buried Morgan. Day called out, trying to keep the fear out of his voice: "Mr. Slater, there's people in the bush."

Slater had expected it. "Get back to the house," he said to some of the men, who had stopped and were looking back at Day. "I'll see to this. Lively, lads, for God's sake." Then he went to where Day was standing, near the grave mound.

"There, Sir," said Day, pointing, "in the shadow under the big tree, this side o' where the path comes from your place."

And no sooner had he said this than Wilkinson, from near the door of the house, cried out in panic: "Aye, an' over here there's more o' the swine. We're surrounded, be Jesus."

"Enough o' that, Wilkinson," called Slater. "Now, all o' ye, inside, behind cover." And as some started to run, he added: "Take y'time. We're not afraid o' them." Slater was last in, Seyawa waiting for him. Gently he pushed her ahead.

The lantern stood on the floor, in the middle of the room; ranged behind it were the men, a single line of them, nervous, strained. From outside came the snapping of a branch and Wilkinson cursed and several of the men looked anxiously from Slater to Berry. Berry stared at Slater, and Doyle went to the window opposite the door and peered out.

"What do we do, Oliver?" said Berry quickly. "Fight for the house, eh?"

"The house?"

"Aye, the house." There was a petulant, cranky tone in his voice.

" 'Tis not the house we want—'tis the boat."

"Eh?"

"I say 'tis not this house we've to fight for, 'tis the boat."

"The boat's all right, Mister," said Berry, shaking his head. "Two men to guard her, well armed with a swivel, grape an' plenty o' powder. They'll never get the boat."

Slater stepped up to Berry. "Look, Sir, we leave here now."

"Ye mean *here*? The house?"

"Aye."

"But, God in heaven, Mister, we're surrounded."

"We don't know we are for sure. Any rate, we can fight our way out."

"But what o' the gear?" Berry looked hopelessly about him. "What o' that? There's a bloody lot of it."

" 'Tis not so much that we can't get it down in one trip. Or the best part of it. Much o' the really important stuff is there already. Nay, we can do it."

Powell lay under his window, looking about, spun half out of his shadow world. Seyawa stood just behind Slater, the lantern brushing her fine body with light. Some of the men were looking at her.

"But, Oliver"—and now a whine began to enter Berry's voice —"we'd . . . we'd be in the open down there."

"We'd be where we should be. 'Tis the launch will take us away, not this damned house."

"Nay, nay, Oliver," said Berry, shaking his head, "not in the open. Too easy a target. Ye must see that, man." He looked at Slater as though he had said the most obvious thing in all the world. But all Slater saw was his stupidity.

Now for the first time, Slater felt Seyawa as a person—not any longer merely a desirable woman who had been faithful to them and had done what she believed would help them, but someone who was now part of them. She was his responsibility. The beginning of this realisation had come to him when he brought her into the house, but now the rest of the pattern was clear. Being one of them, she must go with them. And this idea rose for that moment above even the thought of Berry's futility or the presence of the savages around the house. She was committed to his care.

Yet, there still was Berry and the greater issue of whether they were to leave at all.

"Sir, 'tis not so dark a night as we couldn't push the boat out a way. We've the swivel; we'd make bloody short work of any canoe they might send against us——"

"I'm damned if I can see the sense in leavin' the house, Oliver. 'Tis us they're after, not the launch. Nay, we stay till dawn. When there's light enough we'll make off."

Powell now began to babble about the launch, and Jeremy went softly across to him, the only one to move. Doyle was holding a pistol.

"Look here, Mr. Slater," cried Wilkinson suddenly. "Ye can see the swine dodgin' about out there." Slater merely glanced at Wilkinson, but Doyle went and stood beside him. "There, Sir, see 'em? Christ in heaven!"

Wilkinson's nervousness spread, and the men looked at one another, at Berry, at Slater and at Doyle. But Berry said nothing, nor did he shift his eyes from Slater. And Powell's voice came again, and in its babbling, it seemed to Slater, was all their hopelessness.

At that moment, Slater knew he had to take command.

"Mr. Doyle," he said, turning from Berry, "one seaman an' set about gettin' the bamboo mats from the windows." Doyle did not move. His face was calm, the pistol pointing at the mats. Now that he had taken command Slater felt all his doubts slide from him; he was surprised at the clarity with which he saw everything—his own position, Berry's incompetence, Doyle's surliness—and, above all, at the naturalness with which he found himself linked with Seyawa. He realised that Doyle, too, would see what he had discovered in himself. He called Jeremy. Doyle moved, tapped Leadbeater on the back and started to take down the bamboos.

"Pepper," said Slater as Jeremy came up to him, "the lad to help ye an' the extra muskets and cartridges, the powder, wad and ball here in the centre of the house. Now, Jeremy, if the savages attack ye'll be a key man, for ye're to reload for us. Don't lose y'head, whatever happens. Load as fast as ye can, but as carefully as ye can. Misfires might cost us dear. Go to it, lad. Wilkinson, away from the door and see to it the fire's out, properly out."

"Christ," said Wilkinson, starting towards the fire, "how the hell will I see to that?"

"Piss on it, if ye like, I don't care how it's done, but I want it done. Barber——"

"Sir?"

"With Day, see to gettin' the gear stacked up where it won't be in our way at the windows. The walls, lads"—and Slater raised his voice to include all of them—"won't give us a great deal o' protection, but they'll be better than nothin'. And remember that we don't know how accurate these Indians are, so don't go showing yeselves unnecessarily. And a ball that don't feel flesh don't do much good."

"Easier said than done," said Leadbeater.

"Maybe so," returned Slater, "but if ye want to see Boston again, ye'd best be tryin'."

Slater almost found himself enjoying this. He looked at Seyawa and smiled, and very nearly coaxed an answering smile from her. He crossed to her and taking her by the hand led her to Powell, indicating that she should remain by him. Powell started to babble again.

"The chests near the post, Sam," Slater called to Barber, "put 'em alongside Powell. They'll give him some protection."

Berry stood with his head bent, a queer, twisted expression in his face.

"Directly opposite, Mr. Slater," said Day from the doorway. "One, might even been two o' them." He tried to make his voice seem almost casual, in order to keep his fright from showing. Then he added, still looking out: "Ye'd best see for y'self, Sir. Aye, there's another. And another, Sir."

The lantern was still near Berry. Slater went over, took it up and blew out the light. Now only the moon lighted the house.

"There's a good half-dozen, Sir."

"Ye're sure?"

"I'm sure all right. God damn 'em."

Then Slater saw two of them, slipping between the trees on the very edge of the clearing. He got up and went back to Berry.

"Ye heard what the carpenter said, Sir?" he asked.

"Aye, I did."

"I've seen them too."

The old man seemed to have difficulty in forcing the words from him. "What . . . what would ye suggest, Oliver?" he asked quietly.

"That we give it to 'em."

"As you wish. Aye, as ye say. Give it to 'em." He turned, went a few paces and stopped with the moon full on him, turning his hair into a fuzz of tiny, bright wires.

Slater waited a second, looking at him. Then he said: "Right, lads. To the openings. And keep y'eyes peeled."

"An' if we see anythin'?" asked Barber.

"Shoot."

135

Berry went to Jeremy and, taking the musket the boy held out to him, went to a window in the western wall.

Expected, yet unexpected, a musket's roar shattered the silence in the house, and for a tiny fraction of a second Barber's window opening lit red in the powder flame. Immediately following the report came a long scream. "Ye got the swine," said Doyle.

Then Day fired, and as he drew back for another musket from Jeremy, Wilkinson shouted: "We're surrounded. I said we were." Then he, too, fired.

Every man stood tense, peering into the jungle that ringed them. Wilkinson got another musket and returned to his place. Berry fired and there came another scream, and the noise of a branch breaking. Doyle, half turning from his window, said to Barber, loud enough for all to hear: "I wish 'twas our muckin' cap'n screamin'. I'd like to be there, be Jesus, when they cut him——"

As Doyle spoke, Barber turned from the window. "Devil take ye, Doyle," he said quietly, but venomously, "for a mutinous swine." Slater heard, as every man did, and slowly moved towards Doyle, to settle—if now it had to be—what had waited until this of all moments to be settled. Doyle's musket fell against the wall and he waited for Slater, who was advancing with arms out by his side. Jeremy scrabbled at a line of muskets to shift them from Slater's path.

At that moment the Fijians attacked.

The initial advantage was theirs. They gave no warning. As the *Argo* men watched and waited for the life-or-death struggle between Doyle and Slater that would decide who would be their leader, their ears were assailed by a fiendish yelling and the walls of the house began to shake as arrows and heavy stones rained against them.

"*Fire!*" shouted Slater, diving for a musket. Within seconds the house was wreathed in smoke and reeking with the smell of burnt powder, and the air was jumping with the banging of muskets and pistols. Soon the advantage turned as the attacked recovered from their surprise and sent a withering volley of musket and pistol shot into the vanguard of the attackers. From outside came the shrieking of those hit, the yelling of men driven back.

As fast as the *Argo* men fired they reloaded or got from the boy another musket and fired again. Some of the balls fell harmlessly into the jungle, but many more found their marks. Solidly, relentlessly, the muskets spoke, jets of flame through the smoke. The smoke rolled from the house, drifted off among the trees and caught the throats of the islanders with its acrid, unknown odour.

Seyawa cowered against the floor, eyes and ears assailed by this devil's thunder; the powder smoke set her coughing. Powell, roused by the firing, eyes burning with fever and the thrill of battle, grabbed at her and tried to hold himself up against her. When Slater saw her thus and their eyes met, he smiled at her, feeling her fear and her suffering.

The fire held the Fijians and turned their courage so that they dared not take the one chance—a sudden rush at the house —that would have overwhelmed the white men. Ignorance and timidity conquered them as Slater knew it would as long as the fire could be kept up.

Slater saw the first of the fire arrows, saw, clear in the blaze of the shredded coconut fibre, the arrow nocked to the string. burning on the ground beside him. Two more fire arrows fell, not to be fired, for the men behind the arrows stood bright as targets. One fell, shot twice, and rolled on to his arrow; the tapa about his waist ignited and burned up bright between his legs.

Then once more it was the white men's turn to suffer. Day was hit by an arrow that entered under his right ear. He made no noise in dying, but fell against Slater, who cursed, pulled the dead man back, laid him down upon the floor and returned to the firing line.

A stone struck Barber a glancing blow along the side of his head, mashing his ear. He fell back, half stunned, still holding his musket. For a moment he sat shaking his great head, rubbing at his bloodied ear, and then, getting to his feet, went back to his place and shot again.

A hoarse cry came from Peppercorn, who was at Berry's end.

"Mr. Slater! Quick, Sir, the cookin'-house's been fired." Slater ran to Pepper's window. At first all he saw was the bulk of the cooking-house looming in the moonlight. Then he saw chinks of orange light dancing on the wall nearest them and heard a crackling, roaring sound.

Shouting to the men to keep shooting—for the ruddy glow that bathed the house, the whole clearing, had distracted them —Slater watched for the first sign of a spark shower that might set their big house aflame. But there was no wind, the column of smoke and the great, licking flames roared straight up into the night. Whether the Fijians had fired it intentionally or not Slater could not know, but some of their men had been trapped in it. As part of the roof collapsed in a great eruption of flame, several screaming figures ran from the building; one man with his head alight, shrieking and clawing at his oiled hair, pulled it from his scalp in flaming handfuls, another with his breech-cloth afire, and one who was caught in part of a thatch panel and was enveloped by the flames.

In a few minutes the fire had consumed the building, the posts standing eerily, tongues of flame running along their blackened surfaces. And now on the other side of the cooking-house could be seen a line of Fijians, staring at the smoking ruins. "By the livin'——" broke from Pepper, and he fired at them. Berry too got off a shot before the Fijians realised they were exposed and ran back into the jungle.

The burning of the cooking-house marked a stage in the battle. Perhaps the Fijians had hoped it would fire the big house; had there been a wind, any wind, Slater knew nothing would have saved them, and he shuddered at the thought of such a death.

A final volley cut a hole in the night. It was a blast of sound that wrenched from the Fijians the last vestiges of their daring. The *Argo* men heard a shouted command repeated by several voices. As soon as she heard it, Sewaya scrambled to her feet, ran to Slater, and pulled at him. He swung about, angry at her intrusion. Then he understood. It was a signal they had heard and only she knew what it meant. Doyle was still firing his pistols, but the Fijians already had fled and were crashing through the jungle, leaving their wounded to drag themselves after.

The white men had won a battle.

Chapter 15

EXCEPT for the loss of Jonas Day their injuries were slight enough. Berry's right eye was swollen; part of the wall, driven in by a stone, had swung back into it. Barber's ear was cut; Doyle had a long scratch on his right arm, probably from an arrow; and Wilkinson a bruised leg, hit on the knee by a stone.

Day was lying in the doorway. Slater went to move him and was bending over him when Doyle, holding a handkerchief to his arm, went to pass outside. Slater looked up quickly and his eyes met Doyle's. For a long second the two men gazed at one another. The battle and the death of the carpenter had shaken Slater, but he still retained some of the elation he had felt when he took command. He was still ready for the show-down, more than ready, even though he realised that in a hand-to-hand encounter the odds were all in favour of the huge and savage Doyle. They watched each other, the eyes of the men steady on them. Very quietly Slater said: "Help me with him, will ye? We'll get him outside." For an instant Doyle hesitated, then wrapping his handkerchief about his arm he bent and took Day by the shoulders. Slater took his legs and they carried him out.

Seyawa sat by Powell; Jeremy had reloaded the weapons and had stacked them in the centre of the room. Slater came back into the house to light the lantern and as he did Jeremy went over and sat near Powell and the girl, and he looked at her with a shy, wondering gaze. He was embarrassed by her nakedness, yet he saw the softness of the look she returned him and felt her desire for friendship; but he felt also a tiny stir of jealousy, because now, he sensed, there was someone else with whom he must share his beloved Slater.

Berry watched Slater light the lantern, saw the light climb against his face and flood yellow over the inside of the house.

"Ye'll say I was wrong, Mr. Slater," he said quietly. "Ye'll say I've been a fool. As like as not, ye'll say I've thrown away a chance, and killed Jonas Day."

"Nay, Sir, I'll not," said Slater.

"Then the others will, be Jesus." The old man looked out through the doorway. The crew stood about in silence. In the jungle a man sobbed.

"Then 'tis the launch now, Sir," Slater said softly. It was not a question. Nor did Berry take it as one.

"Aye," the captain murmured. "Ye'd best go yeself and ready the men there. An', Barber, ask Mr. Doyle to step in here a moment. . . . Come in, Mister," he said softly as Doyle came to the door and looked in. Doyle ducked under the low eave and stood inside the doorway. "We're makin' away. Mr. Slater's goin' to the launch now. Ye'd best take a man with ye, Mister," he added, turning back to Slater; then to Doyle again: "Get the men started on readyin' the gear, Mister."

"What about the carpenter?" said Doyle.

Berry looked past him, out of the doorway. "We'll bury him at sea."

"We'd need weights for that, Sir," said Slater.

"Weights?" asked Berry, looking at Slater.

"For a sea-buryin'."

"Ah. Aye, I was forgettin' that. Then we'll bury him afore we go. Mr. Slater, get to the launch, will ye please. Take Barber with ye. Tell Hockin' and Wilkinson——"

"Pain's with Hocking, Sir."

"Eh?"

"Pain and Hocking are the watch."

"Well, tell 'em to start rolling up the logs for gettin' her in." Berry watched Slater put the lantern on the floor. Slater looked at Seyawa, who sensed he was leaving. She moved to come with him, her eyes begging.

"Right," Slater said as he got to his feet. Berry took the word as addressed to him, but it was spoken to Jeremy, who knew

140

it. As Slater took one last look back at her and went out through the door, Barber following him, he saw that Jeremy was sitting near her and there was a pistol in his lap.

Slater led Barber cautiously. As they came from the path and reached the slight rise over which lay the beach, Slater put his hand on Barber's arm and whispered: "Now easy does it, Sam. They'll have heard the firin' an'll have mighty itchy fingers. We don't want to be mistaken for somethin' else and get in the way of a charge o' grape."

"Call to 'em," Barber whispered back at him.

"Aye, but we wriggle out to the top o' the beach first. That way." He pointed to a few screw pines which grew to their right, on the sand's edge. "Under the shadow, Sam."

Slater called softly, but there was no answer. He felt a chill pass over him, and he heard Barber curse under his breath and say: "Bit louder, Sir."

Slater called again; he called Pain's name and then Hocking's. But no cry came in answer. On the beach sand, all about the launch and the trees that stood over it, the moonlight lay bright. "Cock y'musket, Sam, an' we'll rush it."

The launch had been destroyed, stove in. Gunwales gaped, her decking had been torn from her, her planks sprung out from her frames. She was past repair, the result of a frenzied smashing and tearing, and over what was left of her forward decking was blood, already congealing, black against her unpainted wood. Only the transom was untouched. It lay canted, still locked to keel and deadwood. The swivel, loaded and shotted, pointed impotently up through the shadow to the moon.

Curiously, the Fijians had not taken the tools; most of them lay, as the men had left them, in their sailcloth rolls under the boat.

Slater turned away and looked at the water lying so softly ridged and silver-barred under the moon. Neither he nor Barber spoke; it seemed too big a thing to speak about. This, Slater knew, was the end of them. Now there could be no escape, unless, perhaps, they could build a boat, start from scratch, cut trees, shape them. Desolation filled him, a frightening, icy hand seemed to grip his heart. Barber broke the silence.

"The tools," he said quietly, clearing his throat. "We'll take 'em up?"

"Aye."

"Would it be worth a look be the masts, Sir?" he added, after he had collected the tools.

"Aye. Aye, it might be," said Slater as he led off up to the left. Fifty feet from the trestles they heard a moan. The pistol in Slater's right hand rose and, stopping, he drew his other weapon. "Stay here," he whispered back to Barber, "an' keep me covered."

He went on slowly, and near the edge of the shadow he stopped, searching the darkness of the patch ahead of him. The moan came again, quieter now, and he thought he heard the noises of something moving on the sand. He stepped forward and, as he did, knew what Peppercorn had felt when he'd gone behind the house. He was well into the shadow, casting about him, trying to find where the sounds were coming from, when something moved. He lifted his pistols. Fire the right first, he thought. Steady, ready for the jump when it fires. Then if there's more than one o' the swine give 'em the left an' hope Barber doesn't miss with the musket. There! He was on it, and it was rising up at him. His fingers tightened on the trigger when he heard what sounded like an oath.

"Who's there?" he asked, and his throat tightened as he spoke. Was it an oath? Or was it some wounded savage, mumbling in his own language? Then it came again—unmistakably an oath. Slipping his pistols back into his belt he ran forward, calling to Barber.

It was Jeb Pain.

Between them, Barber and Slater half carried him, half walked him, back to the house. There the men propped him up against a corner post. There was blood, crinkled and dried, around his left eye, and powder smoke blackened his cheeks and forehead.

As the wounded man relaxed, Slater repeated the story the half-stunned Pain had told on the way back to the house: how Pain had been up the beach relieving himself, when the Fijians came from the water at the back of the launch; how Hocking hardly knew what struck him; how Pain had taken several of

142

the Fijians (he was sure of that); how a stone or missile club must have grazed his head, stunning him, knocking him down; and how he had then known no more.

Slater finished, and in the silence Powell rose out of his delirium, struggled to sit, and grabbed at the girl for support. His eyes were wide, like bright marbles in his face, and a trickle of saliva ran from each corner of his papery lips. His voice was strangely, startlingly strong.

"Now, lads. Ye'll not be seein' Port Jackson nor nowhere else but this, this island, these eaters o' men. Not nohow will ye, an' ye have m'word on it." As if there could be nothing more to say he fell backward, his eyes wide open, staring without sight towards the high, dark roof. Then, thrusting out his stick of an arm, he clutched at Seyawa for water. It was the last thing he did. Half-way out his arm fell; his eyes rolled towards Berry in a hideous appeal, and he fell back against the mats.

Seyawa got to her feet, trembling, her eyes darting from one man to the other, as if she feared that they would hold her responsible for this death. Slater moved and picked up the lantern, and she ran to him.

Chapter 16

SLATER suggested that they bury Powell and Day under the floor-mats. It took them an hour before the earth went in again and the mats were back. Only Seyawa saw nothing strange in it, for to be buried under one's own house was the custom for those of her people fortunate enough to die among friends.

Berry was still holding the prayer-book when he ordered an issue of spirits. Doyle measured it out, each man stepping up for his ration. Then men moved mechanically, silently. Slater watched them, looking for the first sign that would mean they were breaking; he watched Doyle, who was doling out the spirits, saying nothing, passing out the mug, waiting until the man had drunk and handed it back, filling it for the next man. Berry, still grasping the prayer-book as if it was some talisman, began to speak.

"Then we've lost the launch," he started in his high-pitched voice, as though carrying on from some other interrupted conversation. "An' it was, ye'll say, about the last thing we could afford to lose. But it don't mean, lads, that we're done. We've still a good chance. We've the tools, an' though we mightn't have our carpenter any more—God rest his soul—we can build a boat. An', an', we're good seamen. We know that. An' we know God's with us." He paused, glancing down at the prayer-book, and added: "We know that, lads."

Berry's voice was the sound of defeat itself. Words that spoke of hope, had the sound of hope, but not the heart of hope in them. The men shifted uneasily.

"There's the brig, don't ye forget, lads," continued Berry. "There's old *Argo*." Dear Christ, thought Slater, moving as if to ease the weight of his exasperation, but still keeping his eye on Doyle and making sure of the pistol-ball path clear between them.

"I'm not a-sayin', lads," Berry stumbled on, "that she'll be of any use. Not any more. But the longboat—we left that in her, an' not too bad damaged. A day or two'd see her seaworthy again. Nay, lads, we've hope, even though it seems the Indians might have us cornered f'a bit." Still speaking, Berry had turned about and was pointing at Seyawa. Slater tensed, and for a moment his eyes left Doyle.

"We've got the girl," Berry went on. "She, she can guide us across the island." His voice was rising now as if to conceal the wave of despair that belied his words. "We can find some place to lie up in, lads. She can show us that"—he still gazed at her —"an' we can make some sort of a raft to get back to *Argo*. We can do that. We can build a raft. We can get across the island. We, we've got instruments, an' we can sail clear to Port Jackson in the longboat."

Doyle took a quick pace forward, but Slater was ready, and stepping out into the middle of the group he cut in on the old man's squeaky rambling. "Cap'n Berry, 'twill soon enough be dawn and if we're to cross the island we'd best do it afore daylight."

Berry looked at him, water from his injured eye running on his cheek. "Aye, Mister, ye're right. The longboat, eh? Aye, we get to the brig, like I said."

But Slater had begun to move before Berry finished speaking, and once again he took command. "Mr. Doyle," he said, "see to gettin' the gear outside, will ye?"

The men moved willingly enough, each turning to the chest or bundle nearest him. But Slater waited, for he sensed Doyle's rebellion and he knew again, intermingled with his fear, that link with Doyle that he had felt in his cabin when *Argo* lay upon the reef. Now, as he looked at him, seeing the handsome, dark-bearded face, the eyes as tired as his own, he thought of the big man's worth as a seaman, of what he had done in the hurricane, and of his love for Jeremy. Slater wanted to strengthen that link with Doyle and to break the barrier that Doyle had put up between them.

It wasn't long before the gear was packed, the loads were distributed, and they were on their way. Seyawa led them quickly and Slater had to check her, for along the valley beds, where the moonlight did not penetrate, a step from the path meant a stumble on the tangled creeper and vine or a headlong plunge into a stinking bog or stagnant pool. The mosquitoes rose up about them and stuck to them. Seyawa kept them off the high ridges, for the moon, though not yet full, was bright; she led them along the shoulders of the hills and down the easier slopes. Slater twice called a halt in the scrub on the windward slopes. No one spoke except to curse, but as they drew farther from the village they began to hope again.

When they reached the coast the comet no longer streamed across the sky, and the stars—even the moon—were growing dim. She led them down an open slope where there was no trail and brought them to a thinly wooded place, level and grassy, perched between a barren hill above and a slope which ran down to the sand and the sea below. Here they put down their loads and rested.

As the first light of the day touched the hill behind them, Seyawa came to Slater and beckoned him, drawing him away.

She took him out to the edge of the trees, where he felt the stirring of the sea wind on his face and heard the thunder of the reefs and saw them, grey in the half-light. Then the waves, whitening, grew out of the dawn and soon all the sea was before him.

But of the brig there was nothing to be seen.

Chapter 17

No one said anything when Slater came back with Seyawa and told them there was nothing to be seen of the brig. No matter now what Berry had rambled about, no matter what any of them might have felt as they came through the darkness to that place upon the hill, they knew now that *Argo* was gone and they felt her dragging themselves after her. They would never reach Port Jackson, would never even escape from the island.

Doyle began to get to his feet, his eyes cold and steady. Slater spread his legs a little, preparing himself. Yet there was still time. There must be. Or did Doyle see otherwise? Did Doyle see only that now it must be settled, one way or the other? Strangely, the thought of Berry did not enter Slater's mind at all. Berry was of the past, that which had led them thus far; this now was for the future.

Slater saw again his first meeting with Doyle. . . .

Doyle had brought his chest aboard one night in Boston as *Argo* lay at the Old Wharf, near the South Battery. It was a wet, cold night. Slater had seen Doyle to his tiny cabin and then had gone to his own, to be awakened an hour later by the watch, who spoke of a woman.

He went on deck and saw her, a big, dark woman, standing in the rain, the wharf planks cracked and splintered about her. She did not see Slater. " 'Tis the new mate, the Second, she's after," said Pearce, the man on watch, a small, rabbity man with huge hands, who was to disappear at Whampoa a voyage later.

"What's she want?" asked Slater.

"How the hell do I know?" growled Pearce, looking down at her. "If they don't get paid first, they'll never get it." But the woman did not look like a whore.

"Don't let her aboard," Slater muttered and turned to go below.

"Is that all?" Pearce called after him.

"Nay, I'll be back," said Slater. He found Doyle in his cabin unpacking a brace of pistols. Doyle looked round, one of the weapons in his hand.

"It's a woman?" he asked quietly.

"Aye," answered Slater.

"Do ye mind tellin' her I'm not aboard?"

"Nay, I don't suppose I do," Slater said, and he was about to turn for the door. "She's not a harlot," Doyle said, as if it was an afterthought, some curiously inverted justification, and as he said it a flash of anger passed over his face.

"I didn't say she was," Slater said, and going from the cabin he made his way to the deck. "Listen, ye've not told her he's aboard?" he asked Pearce.

"I've told her nothin'."

"Then tell her that ye've sent a man to look, and he's not here."

Slater slipped back to the poop and through the mizzen shrouds watched the woman as she came close in under the lantern that was hung over the gangway. He saw that she was a remarkably good-looking woman, big and handsome rather than beautiful, with large dark eyes. She was wet to the skin, her clothing stuck to her, and the outline of her full breasts showed under the sodden shawl she pulled tight about her. In her face was a look of despair.

Argo sailed at dawn; there was no sign of the woman among the little crowd that saw them leave. Doyle said nothing, but Slater found himself thinking much of her, wondering why Doyle had cast her off. Then, on the fourth night out as he took over the watch, Doyle called Slater over to the poop rail

147

where they would not be overheard by the helmsman, and with a half-embarrassed, half-aggressive look he told him the woman was his wife. Nothing more, only ten or eleven words. Then he stood regarding Slater truculently, waiting for him to comment.

"I'm sorry," Slater said. "She's a fine-lookin' woman." He may have wanted to say more, know more, but Doyle's aggressiveness discouraged inquiry and prevented any confidence between them. Slater did not mean to censure Doyle or to cut him for deserting the woman, but as he went below he wondered whether he had given Doyle that impression. He found it hard to shake from his mind the sight of the woman's face and her look of inexpressible despair when she was turned away.

Doyle never mentioned her again.

Argo returned to Boston only once thereafter, but it was then that Slater learned that the woman was dead; she had been found, the day after their sailing, over a cross-piece under the *Argo*'s wharf. Pearce too was dead by then. Slater had never reported her visit that night. It was his secret—and Doyle's—but Doyle never thawed. During the time they lay in Boston, Slater often wondered whether Doyle knew she was dead and whether he knew that Slater knew.

Now as he watched Doyle rise to his feet with exaggerated slowness, as though he too feared, yet was incapable of stopping himself. God, the size of him! thought Slater. Doyle was a man who could fight; and he was fast and intelligent. If only Slater could make him a part of their survival.

"What's on y'mind, Mr. Doyle?" Slater asked quietly.

"You ought to know, *Mister* Slater—you, an' that murderin' swine of a cap'n."

At Doyle's first words, even before Slater had finished asking his question, the men were moving to their feet, spreading out to watch. And, as they moved, Slater wanted to look at them, to see how each one reacted and whose side each one took. Berry, sitting a little way off, behind where Slater stood, didn't seem to hear what was said, either by Slater or by Doyle. He sat with bent head, overwhelmed by the enormity of this final calamity.

148

"Ye'd best take that back, Mr. Doyle," Slater said. "Ye can't mean it——"

"Can't I? Nay, I'll take nothin' back. Why should I? Berry run us on this reef, threw away his ship, an' well ye know it. He knew land was near—we all did—an' he knew if he kep' on like a madman he'd have us ashore."

Slater felt the strength in Doyle's argument and it hampered him. But stronger now than anything else was his sense of duty; he saw nothing else but his duty and set himself against anything that was not in line with it; it pushed from his mind the possibility of peace with Doyle. This now was mutiny, and, like most officers, Slater had not known its like before.

"I'll warn ye once, Doyle," he said, still speaking quietly enough, still in control of himself against the mounting rage in Doyle. "Ye're layin' yeself open to a serious charge. Take back what ye've said against the captain an' ye can remain with us. I'll see ye disranked, but ye can stay."

"Ye'll warn me o' nothin', Slater. I'll not be needin', or takin' it from the likes o' ye an' Berry."

"Ye've one chance, Doyle. Take back what ye said an' obey orders. Or take the consequences."

"Obey *your* orders?" Doyle snarled. "I'd eat muck first. An' that goes for the swine who put us here."

Doyle, pointing to Berry, turned towards the men. "Look at him, lads," he cried. "Have ever ye seen a guiltier-lookin' man? Nay, an' ye won't—not this side o' hell! An' he's cap'n. Unless"—Doyle turned back to Slater—"he's made ye cap'n, *Mister* Slater. Or the——" He checked himself after a half-glance at Jeremy. "Nay, leave the boy out of it," he added, as though to himself.

Slater wanted to cry to Doyle to stop, to see the senselessness of abusing each other, of digging deeper the gulf which lay between them. He wanted to speak but Doyle gave him no chance.

"Ye think y'clever, don't ye, Slater, makin' Berry order us to have naught to do with the women, then pickin' yeself a nice little bitch an' askin' us to believe she was givin' ye messages about what the cannibals was doin'? I hope she's given ye such a dose o' the pox that ye'll rot, that ye'll stink to high heaven as ye rot. I know what he wants, lads," he went on, turning back to the men again, shaking in his rage and driven by his fury to say what he didn't believe. "He wants us all out o' the way, an' then when we're gone like Powell an' Day and Johnny Morgan, he an' that brown whore'll go back to these devils an' live among 'em. That's it, lads."

Jeremy cried out, a sudden shout of dismay; Slater thought he was going to rush Doyle. "Out o' this, Jeremy," he cried. "Back with ye. Barber, fetch the boy."

Doyle muttered, "Aye, 'tis none o' his doin'." Then, after a pause: "I didn't mean to include ye, lad."

Then Berry moved; it was as if Berry had heard nothing until that instant, as if at last the thing had penetrated him. "What's this?" he said. "What's this ye're sayin', Mr. Doyle?"

"I'm sayin'," said Doyle, "that ye're a bloody murderer. That's what I'm sayin'. Ye, an' that cannibal-lovin' whore-monger of a mate."

Berry's mouth fell open, then he shut it, then it opened again, but no words came. Clenching and unclenching his hands, he started to move uncertainly towards Doyle. It was a threatening move and Doyle contemptuously, defiantly, stood with his hands hanging ready at his sides, waiting for the old man.

But Berry never reached him. Slater put out his arm and barred his passing. Doyle sneered at him. "Gutless, eh, Berry?" The old man shook as the words hit him, and Doyle went on: "Ye gutless, maggot-faced swine. Castin' honest seamen away——" As Doyle spoke, he crouched slightly, hunching his shoulders, and his right hand moved towards his pistol. "Ye'll be doin' no more murder, Berry," he said quickly, his face draining of blood. "I'll see to that, be Christ." As he spoke he drew.

He had made up his mind. He had to kill Berry; there was no turning back. But he gave an instant's warning, and Slater saw it and shot first.

The powder flashed in the pan of Doyle's pistol and the weapon flew from his hand, struck by Slater's bullet. Doyle staggered, then recovered and leaped to a position behind the girl, where he drew his other pistol. Slater was moving to pass round her when Doyle fired. Slater saw the fire burst out at him, and he felt a searing pain along the right side of his face. Seyawa screamed and rushed to him.

Doyle's ball had grazed Slater's temple and blood began to trickle down his cheek. But Slater still had not fired his second pistol. It was now in his right hand, and Doyle was before him, kneeling on one leg, in the position from which he had shot.

Shoot. Shoot, was the thought in Slater's mind. Settle it. 'Tis mutiny. Doyle saw it in the pistol's rise, in Slater's grim face. To shoot? Aye, but to shoot when the moment's gone? To aim into a man who looks at ye unarmed? Your first ball, thought Slater, shouldn't have gone wide. That was the ball for the killing.

Doyle's right hand lay across his right knee, bloodied. In his left hand was the exploded pistol, its muzzle on the ground. His body was pressing forward towards Slater, his eyes, expressionless, on him.

"Get up," Slater said. Doyle didn't move. He breathed a little quicker but no other movement came, and now for the first time Slater felt anger. He stepped towards Doyle, knowing he could shoot.

"I'll kill ye if ye don't," he said.

For a second Doyle's eyes rested on the muzzle of the pistol, then he got to his feet, his right hand hanging and blood dripping from two fingers. From his other hand hung the useless weapon.

"Drop the pistol."

Doyle opened his hand and the heavy weapon made a thudding noise as it fell on to the grass. Now, thought Slater, it was Berry who must decide, or at any rate be given the chance to decide. Without taking his eyes from Doyle he said to Berry: " 'Tis for ye to say now, Sir."

Berry stood looking at Doyle, his eyes wide open. He heard Slater, knew he was being spoken to, but to decide Doyle's fate seemed too much for him. Even to answer was an effort. His words came suddenly. "Do as ye think fit, Mister." He made as if to add something, but instead he turned away, the wind stirring his thin hair.

"Ye're goin', Doyle," Slater said.

Doyle's voice was almost a croak. "What do ye mean?"

"What I say. Ye're goin'."

"Mister." Berry clutched at Slater's sleeve. Slater angrily drew his arm away.

"I'm not goin' to kill him," said Slater, free of Berry. "But he's goin'. He's no longer part of us."

"Do I get arms?" Doyle asked.

"Aye. Throw y'powder-flask, not y'bullet-pouch, in front of ye. Well out in front." Doyle did that.

Slater hesitated, then called, "Barber?" The seaman let Jeremy go and stepped forward.

"Search Mr. Doyle. But mind, Barber, no tricks. And that goes for ye, too, Doyle. See if he has any more powder about him, Barber." Barber went to move across the front of Doyle.

"Behind him, Barber, behind him," Slater barked. Barber went through Doyle's pockets, felt inside his shirt but found no powder, only ball.

"Step away, Barber. Now, Doyle, I'm goin' to give ye a share of the food, y'musket an' pistols. I'm also goin' to give ye more ball, but no powder."

"That's murder," Doyle began, taking a step towards Slater.

"Let me finish," said Slater, matching Doyle's step forward with one backward. "But no powder, I said. When we have left this place ye can return here and I give ye my word there'll be powder for ye, buried under that tree astern o' ye. Take a look at the tree, so ye'll be makin' no mistakes."

Now came the moment Slater had dreaded more than any— the moment which would decide how right, or how wrong, he had been. "Now," he asked, "does any among ye men want to go with him?"

The moments dripped by. Two of the men shuffled (Slater heard them move) but none stepped out. Pain was nearest Doyle, and for an instant Slater risked looking at him. But Pain was not among the men who had even as much as shuffled; he was looking at the ground, his left eye almost closed.

Slater looked back at Doyle before he spoke again. "Ye'll get arms. And there'll be powder for ye—with Doyle's."

Dear God, prayed Slater, let them be honest; if any man is coming let him come, or let him not waver after this.

"Then ye go alone, Doyle." As Slater said this he felt pity for the man; it seemed so terrible a fate; alone on this—what had he called it?—devil's island. "Barber, pick up his pistols."

The one Doyle had dropped Barber took in his left hand; the other he picked up in his right.

"Did it fire, Barber?" Slater asked, for all he knew was that he had knocked it from Doyle's hand by some lucky chance.

Barber smelled it. "Nay, Sir. But it flashed."

"Withdraw the charge."

" 'Twould be easier to fire it, Sir."

Slater did not expect that Barber would double-cross him; nevertheless the pistol rose a little in his hand, an involuntary movement. Barber saw it move, then glanced to the weapon in his own right hand. "Very well, Barber," said Slater. "Peppercorn, bring him priming for it." Pepper came out and while Barber held the weapon up he primed it. "Stand back," said Slater to Peppercorn when he had done. "Now, Barber, into the ground."

The pistol jumped in Barber's hand and the ball made a tiny crater in the earth at his feet.

"Now the musket. Is that it against the tree behind ye, Doyle?"

Doyle turned only his head and when he faced about again he nodded. "Go to it, Barber."

Barber was about to fire the musket when he checked himself. He looked quickly at Slater, who saw the look and shifted his pistol slightly, not trusting Barber, trusting none of them, feeling desperately alone.

"Sir——" said Barber.

"Fire that musket."

"Sir. 'Tis a waste o' powder, to fire into the ground. Let me plant the ball in that bugger." He raised the musket so that it was in line with Doyle. The latter, feeling the threat and the dead earnestness in the words, swung towards Barber, then looked back at Slater.

Nay, it wasn't the way of it, Slater told himself. "Barber, shoot it into the earth." Barber cursed, not looking at Doyle, lowered the musket and pulled the trigger; it missed fire. He cocked it again and the second time it went off. Slater told him

153

to put it and the pistols in front of Doyle. Then he called out Jeremy and had him set aside a liberal share of the pork and biscuit for Doyle.

"Now, pick up y'gear and go. And if ye value y'life, keep as far away from us as ye can." Slater paused; then, because he could not help himself, he added quietly, "Good luck."

It was sincerely meant, but a second later he regretted having said it. Doyle looked past him at Berry. "Ye'll live to regret this," he said, sweeping Berry with a look of intense hatred. "Ye'll die here, Berry; ye'll rot here as we all will. But, alone of us, ye deserve it, ye prawn-gutted bastard of a cap'n——"

"Get out! Get out," Slater shouted, near now than ever to killing Doyle, "or, by the livin' God, I'll shoot ye now, an' rid the world o' ye." He was shaking with anger, and the hurt of it was the deeper because in some way he felt he was partly responsible for Doyle's defection; felt it had been his fault that Doyle had been driven from them. Doyle didn't look at the men. He bent, took up his food and weapons, and went.

Chapter 18

FIRST, Slater organised the place on the hill as a camp. There were two ways into it, one over the hill—the way Seyawa had led him—and the other up the slope from the beach. He found two positions from which anyone approaching the camp would be detected. He sent Barber to the one above and Leadbeater to that below. The other men he put to stretching a sail to shelter their gear, stacked upon stones off the ground in case of rain. Then he took Jeremy and Seyawa to search the shore for anything of the brig that might have been washed up. It was just conceivable that the whaleboat, even though damaged, might have come ashore.

They searched until well into the morning but found only a

few staves from the barrels of salt meat, a length of broken spar and a piece of planking. By noon he knew they would find nothing of any use to them and despair filled him. If, he thought, they still had the boat. Or if the island were uninhabited so that they could wander all over it unmolested, cut the trees they would need and quietly set about the building of a boat. They had feed, tools and some nails; they could make tree-nails. They had her sails; poor Morgan had all but finished sewing them.

Would it be possible to build a boat? They would need some fortified place. Could they fortify themselves so well that the savages would keep clear of them and let them take the trees they needed? He'd passed a place that morning, fit for such an undertaking. With an earthwork thrown up around it and the muskets laid out ready, the men could leave their work at a moment's notice and throw themselves down and fight. Aye, a little fort.

But, better than that, might it not be possible to get to another island?

A canoe! Aye, o' course, an' what a fool he'd been not to think of it before. A canoe. There was danger in going after it, but the opportunity for the canoe was there.

"Seyawa," he called, for she and Jeremy had gone some way ahead. He saw Jeremy touch her shyly and she turned. "Bring her back, Jeremy. I've thought o' somethin'." She soon understood what he wanted. As well as he could, he drew in the sand an outrigger canoe he'd seen in the village. Some twenty-five or thirty feet long, it had looked seaworthy enough, but whether it would carry them and their gear he was not sure. He said the word Seyawa had taught him for man, and for each of them he made a stroke on the drawing. Nodding her head, she added what he took to represent their gear. Then she pointed away to the west, indicating the direction in which they should sail.

They hurried back to the camp. The guard had now been changed, Wilkinson replacing Leadbeater on the beach side and Jeb Pain, who said he was fit enough to take a watch, Sam Barber on the other. There had been no sign of Fijians, nor of Doyle, Barber told him as he came into the camp. "The bastard's bit off a mite more than he can chew this time," said Barber. "I reckon that's the last we'll be seein' o' Mr. Bloody Doyle."

Peppercorn heard this and, when Slater went on to look for Berry, he crossed over to Barber and said quietly: "I wouldn't go bein' too sure o' that, Sam. That Doyle, he's got brains; he could be a nasty customer."

"What think ye o' the girl bein' with us?" asked Barber suddenly.

" 'Tis none o' my business."

"She's helped us."

"Aye, I'll allow that."

"Don't ye approve?"

"I say 'tis none o' my concern."

"That don't mean ye can't have an opinion."

Peppercorn watched Barber a moment and then said: "Well, I'll tell ye this much. The mate's shot on her, and seein' as he is, 'tis a bloody good thing Doyle's gone. He were always one for a woman. The mate had better watch out for her."

"Who d'ye think might have a go at her?"

"I tell ye, Doyle."

"Ye mean now?"

"Aye, I do."

Barber shook his head and drew breath in through his teeth. "He should've shot the swine—or let me do it. Sol Doyle's dangerous all right. Jeb were minded to listen to him."

"He stuck," said Pepper.

"Aye, he did. An' to his good name. But he were minded not to once, as ye know. Queer, that." Barber paused; then he looked about him, saw no one was near, and leaning closer to Peppercorn added: "Ye noticed how keen Pain were to take that watch from me. Or didn't ye see?"

"Nay, I saw."

"Now why?"

"I suppose he wanted to do his bit."

"Nay, I'm thinking somethin' else."

"What?"

"Supposin' Pain was bein' crafty, what'd be easier now'n for him out there to slip Doyle some powder?"

"Nothin'. But would he?"

"Pepper, me lad, that's the question. Would he?"

Slater found Berry sitting against a tree, head down, shoulders bent, hands in his lap. His trousers were caked with mud, his shirt was open down the front, his jacket off and lying beside him. He was defeat, a man who had given up.

He lifted his head slowly. "Ye found sign of her, Oliver?" he asked.

"Aye," said Slater as he dropped down beside him, "but that were all."

"I thought as much. We're done, Oliver."

"Nay, Sir, an' don't ye think it. There's hope yet."

"Hope?" said Berry, feeling for his handkerchief and putting it to his inflamed eye. "Hope? I've forgot the meanin' of the word." He took the handkerchief down and looked at Slater with his watering, bloodshot eye. "Nay, there's no hope. 'Tis the coral. 'Tis cruel to a ship unhappy enough to touch upon it. And there's the break ye see, 'tis heavy at the edge o' the reef."

"Aye, but have ye thought of a canoe?"

"A canoe?"

"Aye."

"Ye're not goin' to suggest, are ye, that we make for Port Jackson in a damned canoe?"

"Nay, Sir."

" 'Tis all o' five hundred leagues. An' a damned tricky thing to sail in a lagoon, let alone across an ocean, an' us not havin' the hang o' the thing——"

"Sir, if ye'll but hear me out——"

"I'll hear ye out. Get on wi' it."

"First, I don't mean that big craft, and second, I mean a canoe to take us to another island——"

"Out o' the fryin'-pan into the fire——"

"God Jesus, Cap'n Berry, let me finish." In his exasperation Slater spoke loud enough for two men in the camp to hear him. They looked at him, then at Berry, who let his head fall once more. But this time, Slater saw, the captain was going to listen. "I mean, Sir, a canoe to take us to an island where there'd be timber so we could build a boat." He paused a moment, trying to gauge Berry's reaction, but the old man sat unmoving, the expression on his face unchanged. "I've in mind a craft I saw the day we went first to Awila's," he added.

"Sailin'?"

"Aye, though her sail were furled when I saw her."

"The girl knows what's on y'mind?"

"She does."

"Who'd ye take with ye?"

"I'd want to get the lie o' the land first. I'd want to see the craft again, and the place where they keep it, and plan how to manage it. For a start I'd take the girl, to guide, and Jeremy."

"The girl, I see the reason for her, but the boy? He's only a lad, Oliver."

"He's fast an' lively, and if it comes to a fight he's as handy as any of us with a pistol." It was the truth Slater spoke, but even had it not been, he was determined Jeremy should go with him, for he had decided that from now on neither Jeremy nor Seyawa would be far from him.

"Do as ye see fit, then, Oliver?" Berry said after a moment.

"When'll ye leave?"

"Tomorrow's dawn."

Half an hour to the dawn he rose and woke Jeremy and Seyawa. They ate some biscuits and some pork, and packed some more, dividing it between Slater and Jeremy in handkerchiefs inside their shirts. As the first of the day reddened the east they took their weapons and slipped out of the camp.

Chapter 19

THE day was partly overcast, and there was little wind. In the valleys there was no breeze at all. In the first few hours Slater twice called a halt, and they rested in shade, facing the sea and the breeze that came off it. On the move, the sun burned down upon them; flying insects flew about them and crawled on their sweating skins; in the low-lying parts the mosquitoes stung them. On the open hillsides the grass was dry and the earth hard, and dust rose about them as they slithered and climbed. On one steep descent Slater fell and a stone cut his elbow to the bone. He wrapped his handkerchief about it, but within the hour his arm was swollen and it hurt when he bent it.

He wanted to get as near to the village as he could safely go and then to lie up in some hidden place until dusk, when they could reach the hill from which he hoped to be able to see the canoe. But before they were half-way to the village they came upon Fijians.

They had been moving under coconut trees, skirting the edge of a food garden, and came to a slope where arrowroot had been harvested sometime before. Above the long grass on the slope there still stood a few of the star-shaped heads of the plant. Seyawa was leading and suddenly—with no more warning than a gasp of surprise—she dropped flat. Slater followed, whispering to Jeremy to do the same. Slater had not seen the islanders. He drew his pistols and set them in the grass before him.

It seemed an age before Slate saw Seyawa rise in the waist-high grass, turn and beckon him. There was no question of going on; she led them back a short distance to a grove of breadfruit and candle-nut trees. Here in the deep shade, she made it clear, they would have to spend the remainder of the day.

Seyawa gestured to Slater and Jeremy to sit and wait for her and slipped away, to return with green drinking-nuts, from which they drank as they ate some of their food. The mosquitoes whined about them, but there were no flies, and in the shade it was cool.

Now, under those wide-leaved trees, Slater came closer to Seyawa, to knowing and understanding her. And Jeremy helped him, for in some inverted fashion his shyness in Seyawa's presence and his regard and affection for her seemed to provide a bridge between them.

Slater and Seyawa were 'talking' by drawing on a piece of ground under one of the breadfruits. Slater was trying to make certain she understood his wish to be on the hill above the village while there was still light left to see down on to the beach. He drew and scratched out, as well as he could, a moon, a setting sun, a canoe, a man looking. In his frustration he swore and Jeremy, watching all this, started to laugh.

"What's so funny?"

"It is funny, Sir. Ye're a proper artist."

"I can't see anything funny about it." And there was a trace of annoyance in his voice.

"But Seyawa understands ye, Sir. I'll tell ye somethin'," he said, leaning towards Slater. "She *knows*."

"Knows?"

"Of course she does. An', Sir, if she'd not the manners she has, she'd be laughin' at ye too."

Slater looked at her. She was half smiling at him. "Do ye know what I'm drivin' at, lass?" he said with mock seriousness. She looked from Slater to Jeremy and back again.

"I tell ye, Sir, she's far ahead o' ye," Jeremy said.

Then, as if she were agreeing with Jeremy, she spoke the longest sentence Slater had heard from her.

Slater smiled at them. "I think ye're both makin' fun o' me, that's what I think. I've a great mind to clap ye both in irons."

"Ye'd best not put her in, Sir. Otherwise ye'll never get to that bloody hill."

"What sort of a hill, Jeremy?"

"That blo—that very good hill near the village, Sir."

Slater watched them as they ate. They were poles apart. Yet, for all their differences, he saw there was understanding between them. He watched them as, sitting opposite each other, they cut and divided the nuts, working as though they had done it together a hundred times before. It pleased him and showed him another side of Seyawa. She was older than Jeremy, and in the work they were doing she was the leader, and Jeremy accepted that, except when it came to her first trying to use his knife. Then he took it from her and showed her how it should be handled. She accepted that, looking at him with that shy, wild look, the faintest of smiles about her soft red mouth, which so fascinated Slater.

When the sun had all but dropped out of sight they left. They went quickly and Slater was soon picking up marks he knew, ground he and Jeremy had passed over the day they rescued Seyawa. They saw sandalwood trees which had been cut and scraped by the people for the wood with which to perfume their oil. That afternoon Slater learned from Seyawa the name by which the Fijians knew the wood—*yasi*, she called it.

They crossed a shallow valley where the mosquitoes descended upon them in a cloud. Slater felt his ankles and wrists swelling and Jeremy's eyes were soon puffed, their lids red. The sun had burned Jeremy's skin in several places; now when he exerted himself it felt tight and cold. In the dusk of the valley they stumbled and fell. Once, before she realised it, Seyawa had led them into boggy ground, and they had to retrace their steps, above their knees in stagnant water, feet sucked at by ooze that stank and legs entangled in the plant that spread its trap over the place.

They came to the hill in the last of the day's light, and Slater urged her forward. She took them to a ridge of the hill, below which jutted a tree-covered shoulder. She pointed to this and he nodded, hurrying her down under the screw pines, to the coconuts, the *ivi* trees and the few *baka* trees that grew on the shoulder. He told Jeremy to wait with Seyawa; then he went on out alone. He dropped flat, for near the edge there was little enough cover, and wriggled over the grass until he saw below him the pale curve of the beach that marked the edge of the village. Lights winked up at him and the smell of fire drifted in the air; he could see four fires, the smoke of them new, yellow-white columns above the dancing flames at their feet.

Eagerly he looked for the canoe, straining his eyes in the dying light. And when he saw it he doubted it, for it was longer than he had remembered. It was a narrow vessel, the framework of its outrigger platform frail-looking in the dusk, and the float barely more than a loosely connected log lying parallel to it. On the platform were stacked the mast and the rolled-up sail; in the hull were the paddles, and lines made from plaited sennit and vine. All in all it was better than he had imagined. With luck—the luck they had not had up to now—another island was possible.

He wriggled back and called softly to Jeremy, who left Seyawa and came out to him cautiously. "Down, lad. While

161

there's still light, come an' see for y'self." The boy came smiling. "There, Jeremy, see?" Slater watched him through eyes as bright and expectant as if he were watching the boy accept a gift.

"There's three o' them, Sir," said Jeremy eagerly. "Which is ours?"

"The biggest. The middle one."

"Do we get it tonight? You an' me an' Seyawa?"

"Nay. Though I'd like to. But we must plan this well. There must be no hitch. She'll be a heavy thing to shift into the water."

"An' 'tis quite a way from where she lies too, Sir. How will we get her down?"

"Ye see the logs afore her? With them." Slater was thinking aloud now. "We'll need three or four men to do it quietly, with m'self and ve and Sevawa. Then we've to get her around to the camp. And all must be ready there, everythin' to go stacked waiting on the beach. Not a hitch anywhere. Aye, Jeremy, we'll do it. We've got to. Right, lad, we go back."

Jeremy started to move, then stopped. "Back to the camp, sir?" he asked, still whispering.

"Nay, we'll lie up under the trees for the night and when first light comes we'll start back. Jeremy, slide in an' call Seyawa, will ye? 'Twill be as well for her to take a look. Just call her and beckon. I'll wait here."

As Jeremy left him, away at the far end of the village a drumbeat started, a measured, heavy sound, beaten out by cudgels on a hollowed log. Two herons lifted from the beach and flew along it, grey-white in the vanishing day. Slater watched them until they disappeared climbing to pass over the hill that ran down to the lagoon at the other end of the bay. Then he looked at the canoe again, searching the darkening places around it and the ground over which they would have to pass to take it. Things seemed to shift in the dusk as he peered at them. He looked along the beach, trying to make out the place where the launch had stood. And he wondered whether Hocking and Light had been eaten yet; whether the Fijians had found the bodies behind the house, under the floor-mats.

He heard movement behind him and half turned. "Seyawa," he called softly.

" 'Tis not Seyawa, Sir. 'Tis me, Jeremy. She . . . she's not there, Mister Slater. I've looked and called her and everything, Sir, but she's gone."

Chapter 20

"Gone?"

"Aye, Sir. I've cast about everywhere an' I can't find her."

"Are the muskets still there?"

"Right where we left them."

Slater said nothing more but wriggled back until he could stand safely, then went quickly to where he had left her, Jeremy close at his heels. The drumbeat came up unceasing, hammering at the air.

"Jeremy, ye're sure ye didn't see anythin' as ye came back?"

"Nay, Sir."

"This was where ye sat all the time I was out there?"

"Aye, Sir. An' Seyawa just there. An' when I came back I thought she'd be there, but she wasn't. So I looked about a bit an' called her an' . . . an' then I thought, Sir, maybe she might be wantin' to do something for herself. So I waited a minute or two, and then I called again, but when she didn't come I went out to ye."

"When ye were here alone with her, did she seem anxious, or excited, in any way nervous?"

"Once or twice she smiled at me, Sir, and I smiled back too."

Slowly Slater let himself down to the ground. This he had not expected. Then he had been deceived, he thought. These people were cleverer than he had given them credit for; she had been placed to watch them, and now the Indians knew exactly where they were camped and what their plan was.

163

Still the drumbeat, and between the trees the starlight, not yet the moon or the comet.

Suddenly he got to his feet and went for the muskets. "Right, lad. We go back," he said.

"To the camp, Sir?"

"Aye. Come on."

"But what about Seyawa, Sir?"

"She's gone, lad."

"But she'll be back, Mr. Slater. It'd be desertin' her, just to leave like this."

"I said we're goin'."

"Please, Sir. We can't leave her. They'll kill her. Ye know they will." He ran to Slater and stood before him, blocking his way. "She'll be back, Sir, I know she will, and she'll find us gone and somethin' terrible might happen. Don't leave, Mr. Slater. Please."

But Jeremy's words only hardened him. He picked up the muskets, slinging one across his back. "I'll carry these," he said quietly. "Take the rest o' the meat an' biscuit." Waiting barely long enough for the boy to pick up the food, he set off out of the wooded slope on to the open hill, Jeremy stumbling after him.

An hour later they saw the comet. They rested then, and the boy sat quiet, exhausted. "Will ye eat a little, Jeremy?" Slater asked, seeing his tiredness and unhappiness.

"Nay, thank'ee, Sir."

Slater realised now that he had driven the boy too hard. Without any justification but his own anguish, fear and desire to return to the camp, he had driven Jeremy as he would have driven a man. He wanted to say something, but could not bring himself to it.

Within a half-hour they came to the hill over which lay the camp. From the top they saw the sea; the silvered reef was brilliant and its thunder strong on the air. A little way down, Slater slowed, for he picked up the mark near where the sentry should be. But he was mistaken; though he himself had selected the position, the approach from outside the camp had confused him, and it was not until he came to a large, twisted tree that he saw his mistake and realised that something must have been wrong for him to have got this far in without being stopped.

Then from dead ahead came a voice, almost a hiss; a hard, nervous challenge.

"Who's there? Don't move." Then before he could answer, "Is that ye, Mr. Slater?"

He recognised Barber's voice. "Aye," he said, "an' the boy. That's ye, Sam?"

"By Christ, Sir! Thank God ye've come." Jeremy, a step or so behind Slater, gave a gasp of surprise as he saw Barber. The big seaman had a handkerchief wrapped about his head and the top of his face was blackened with powder smoke. He walked with a lumbering gait, as though carrying a burden.

"What's happened, Barber?"

"We were raided. This afternoon——"

"Raided?"

"Aye."

"An' the lads?"

"Done for, Sir."

"All o' them?"

"Aye. So far as I know, only Cap'n Berry an' me got clear away." He wore a pistol; he carried one musket in the crook of his arm and another slung across his back.

"Where's the cap'n now?"

"God knows, Sir. I don't."

"But ye say he escaped?"

"When I last seen him he was goin' for his life. The Indians didn't see him or me properly—though they felt us, be Jesus," he added, savagely, spitting to one side of him.

"God Almighty!" Slater felt sick in his stomach. "What time was it, Barber?"

" 'Bout three o'clock. They come from all sides—rushed us. I was with the cap'n. We was buryin' the gear. 'Twas Cap'n Berry's idea, but we didn't get it done an' the Indians got some of it. They got the navigatin' instruments, God damn 'em. Pepper had 'em. Christ knows what they'll do with them, except smash 'em. I found one o' the timekeepers, or what was left of it. The devils must have taken a club to it."

"What have we left, Barber?" Slater felt a hollowness in him.

"The powder and the tools an' some o' the meat and biscuit. An' the muskets. They didn't touch them—frightened to, I suppose. I come out here because I figured ye'd return this way. An' 'tis not the place that devil Doyle knew."

"Doyle's been back?"

Barber nodded, put up his hand and tugged at his beard. "Did ye see him?"

"Nay, or one of us'd be dead be this. Ah, Mr. Slater, ye should have shot the bugger while ye had the chance."

Jeremy stepped up beside Slater, touching him. Slater put out his hand and rested it on the boy's shoulder. Barber looked down at Jeremy, then past him, along the dapple of moonlight and shadow to the fuzziness of the open hill behind. "Where's the lass?" he asked quietly.

"I don't know," Slater said.

"They didn't get her too, did they?"

"I tell ye, I don't know." And the sound of defeat showed in Slater's voice. Now he began to see something of what had happened to Berry's mind and know some of the hopelessness that Berry had felt. Jeremy pressed closer to him, and as a sob broke from him Slater put his hand on the boy's head, his fingers working in his hair. Slater spoke, looking past Barber. "Aye, Jeremy. 'Tis hard, damned hard, but ye've to put a brave face on it."

The sobs came freely then, the dry sobbing of an exhausted child. "He's about done," said Barber. " 'Tis no life for a boy, or them as is not much more." Then after a moment, still looking at Jeremy, he added: "We'd better be gettin' in. No use waitin' here any longer." Slater followed Barber in to where he had left Berry sleeping that morning.

"Now set ye down, lad, and get some sleep," Slater said, taking Jeremy under one of the largest trees. "Keep y'pistol ready by ye. Sam an' me'll be close. but if we call ye, cock y'pistol an' come as quiet as ye can. Right, lad?"

Sobbing, Jeremy nodded, and drawing his pistol laid it beside him. Then he looked up. "Mr. Slater?" he said quietly.

"Aye, lad?"

" 'Tis not, Sir, that I want to cry. 'Tis just that I can't help it. Ye'll not think the worse o' me for it, will ye?"

"Nay, Jeremy, I'd think it queer if ye didn't. 'Tis no seaman worthy o' the name that doesn't grieve for his shipmates."

Barber was standing a few paces off, watching them. "Aye," he growled, "if they be worthy o' the name o' shipmates. There's some as aren't."

Jeremy fell asleep almost immediately. Then men waited until he was breathing deeply; then, crossing to more shadow, they set themselves down.

"Tell me, Barber, did ye see them go, see what happened?"

" 'Twould be best, Sir, for me to begin at the beginnin'."

Chapter 21

SOMETHING like panic seized Berry when he awoke and found Slater gone. At first, remembering nothing of Slater's plan, he got to his feet and walked about the camp with a hurt and puzzled look on his face. Then it came to him—from a shred a conversation he overheard between Barber and Peppercorn. He looked from Barber, who had made the remark, to Pepper, and then back to Barber, mumbled something which neither of them understood and went off. Barber, watching him go, had the feeling that the captain did not trust them.

As the morning wore on, the air still and heavy and the men sweating as they lay about the camp or kept watch, Berry became more and more distrustful of them. He sat with his back against his tree, pistols eased in his belt and musket near at hand, looking at them and saying nothing. It affected Barber deeply, for several times he caught Berry's grey-flecked eyes upon him. Barber wanted to get away from the camp, but hesitated to leave, for such intense suspicion oozed from Berry that he feared that even a walk as far as the beach below might precipitate something.

Then Berry spoke—to Wilkinson, of all *Argo*'s people one of the least likely to initiate anything; he was a timid man, a follower of the herd, a good enough seaman, unimaginative except where fear and his timidity touched him. It was mid-morning and Wilkinson had just been relieved of his watch. He came back into the camp and sat not far from Berry, opposite him. Insensitive to Berry's steady gaze, he saw nothing but Berry's depression. Barber sensed Wilkinson's obliviousness of the captain's abnormal state of mind. He thought of drawing Wilkinson away, yet he was afraid to for fear that it might bring about some reaction in Berry.

Suddenly Berry shifted, drew a pistol from his belt, rested it on his lap, and looked at Wilkinson. "I'm watchin' ye," he said.

"What's that, Sir?" asked Wilkinson respectfully.

"I say I'm watchin' ye." Berry continued to stare at Wilkinson, who glanced about him quickly, looking to one of the other men to help him out of his puzzlement.

"An' I'll let ye know somethin' else, Wilkinson," Berry went on in the same deliberate tone. "I'm ready for the next one o' ye as turns out to be a mutinous dog." After staring at Wilkinson for a long, tense moment he put up his pistol, took his musket, got to his feet and walked off, muttering.

Somewhere about noon, after the men had eaten, Berry, sitting beneath his tree, called Barber to him. As the seaman approached, Berry's hand closed about the butt of his pistol, the muzzle lifting slightly from his lap. Barber saw it and thought the old man was going to shoot. He stopped and watched carefully.

"What do ye want, Barber?" asked Berry.

"Nothin', Sir. But ye called, so I thought. Is there anythin' I might be doin' for ye?"

"Aye, there is." Berry sat up straight and cocked his head. "Where's Peppercorn?"

"I could get him for ye."

"Get him."

Barber brought Peppercorn back, warning him to expect the worst. Berry watched them come, his eyes partly closed. He waited until they stood before him, and then said: "Right, we're goin' to bury the powder. Barber, get the adze for diggin' the hole."

Barber got the adze and Berry made them wrap the cask of powder in sailcloth. Berry inspected the wrapping carefully and then led them down the hill, Barber carrying the powder, Pepper the adze. About half-way down there was a level stretch where a few scraggy screw pines grew in dry and pebbly soil. Here, Berry said, they would bury the powder.

Barber did most of the digging, but he hadn't finished the hole when Berry, who had stood silently watching them, said: "I been thinkin'. We'll make the hole bigger an' include the tools an' what we got left o' the medicines as well. Pepper, up an' fetch them while Barber digs some more. An' we'll put the ball in too. But get the tools first. Then Barber'll help ye down with the ball."

It was an hour before the powder, tools and ball, together with an iron cooking-pot and some other articles, were in the hole. Peppercorn stood up out of it and Barber was about to start filling it in when he remembered the instruments. He wondered whether to mention them or not, then decided he would, if only to prevent Berry thinking of them later and making him open the hole to include them. Neither he nor Peppercorn had any idea why Berry was doing this; for all they knew, it was part of a plan Berry had discussed with Slater before he had gone to see about the canoe.

"Good idea, Barber," said Berry. "Pepper, fetch them, will ye. Ye'll find 'em with the chart roll in a chest near the tree I been restin' under."

Peppercorn turned and went up the hill.

Barber retained only a confused impression of what happened next. He got down into the hole again and began throwing up some of the earth which had slid down its sides. Peppercorn had been gone some time when there was a shout—Barber thought it was Homer Wilkinson, but couldn't be certain— and then a shot. He scrambled from the hole and looked up the hill, but could see nothing unusual. He heard Berry curse and then there came an awful howling followed by a ragged volley of musket fire. Barber grabbed for his musket, Berry drew both pistols, and with a cry they started running up the hill. Barber had not gone far when he looked up and saw Leadbeater facing back into the trees with his musket to his shoulder. Barber didn't hear the shots, although there were several fired at the moment, above the blood-curdling howls and screams of the Fijians. When he looked up again, Leadbeater was gone.

Suddenly Berry, ahead of Barber, slowed to a stop and called back to him: "Stop there, Barber. Cover the hole." Barber stopped and Berry started off again, brandishing his pistols above his head. Berry was almost at the top when out of the timber burst a number of Fijians, howling and waving clubs. Berry did not hesitate; he raised his right pistol and fired while still moving. The ball struck one of the savages in the chest and he pitched forward with a look of astonishment on his painted face. The man immediately behind him screamed and turned to run back, but Barber's ball broke his back. Then Berry fired again, into a bunch of Fijians who stood hesitating, transfixed for the instant. Berry's second ball took one low and he fell forward grabbing at his abdomen.

Barber, who had nothing but a musket, dropped to reload while Berry went on. Barber finished loading, slid back the ramrod, and as he got to his feet saw Berry coming back down the hill, scattering the pebbly earth, running with the fear of death in him. Still yards away, Berry started shouting: "Run, Barber. Run for ye life, there's a hundred o' the swine. Run! We're done."

Before he reached Barber he made to his left, his pistols still in his hands, musket across his back, an eerie, ragged figure, leaping on long legs over the roughness of the barren hillside. That was the last Barber saw of him, a dipping, bobbing head, an up-raised pistol and a scatter of pebbles and soil.

Barber stopped speaking. Slater stared at the ground, seeing nothing.

"After the cap'n was out o' sight," Barber added, "I went back down to the hole and sat guard over it. I must've waited 'bout half an hour, I suppose, then the noise stopped and I came back here. I picked up the muskets, they was lyin' about all over the place, and I brought them down to the hole and put

170

them in with the rest of the gear, all but one, which I kep' out as extra to m'own. Then I filled the hole in."

"They took the bodies?"

"Aye. They did. But 'twasn't all their way. There was a lot o' blood about up here, more than just our lads could have lost."

"Barber, I took it out there"—Slater pointed towards the way they had come into the camp—"that ye meant Doyle returned. Was that before or after this?"

" 'Twas before."

"An' he come here?"

"Aye, be Jesus."

"What happened?"

" 'Tis about Jeb Pain," he said slowly.

"He went with Doyle?"

"Nay, not that. Jeb were loyal in the end. Nay, 'tis not that. 'Tis that the bastard killed him."

"Killed Pain?"

"Nobody else did. Had it been the savages they'd not have touched the muskets. Jeb had two o' them. They were gone when Pepper found him."

"I wondered what ye meant out there when ye spoke about us bein' a target for Doyle," Slater said slowly. "What happened?"

" 'Tis guessin' mostly, except that the muskets and powder an' ball was gone. Pain's neck were broke. Pepper discovered it when he brought up some hard tack at noon. Pain was right where he should have been, only he was dead. It must've been Doyle. The Indians wouldn't have left his body, would they? They'd have taken him to eat and they'd have left the muskets. He must've come up to Jeb with some yarn or another—got close to him, see—an' then put it on him for some powder. Jeb stuck it out, 'tis my guessin', probably told him to get the hell away from the place. God knows what happened, but Doyle got the powder. Did ye see the canoe?"

Slater looked up. "Aye," he said, as though he didn't care now whether he had seen it or not.

"Can we get her?"

"I suppose so," he said softly. " 'Tis somehow different now."

171

"We got ourselves to think on, Mr. Slater; there's the boy, don't ye be forgettin'."

"I'm not forgettin'. God, Barber, no matter what we do we seem to lose."

"Ye mean we shouldn't go after the canoe?"

"I'm damned if I know what I mean. 'Tis not only the canoe. There's the reef too."

"The reef?"

"Aye, the way out o' the lagoon. 'Twould be madness to hope to get out except at this end o' the island, even at night. I was expectin' we'd have the girl for that part of it."

Barber felt the effort it took him to speak about her. "Ye've no idea what happened to her?" he asked.

"Nay." Slater shook his head.

"Was she took?"

Again Slater shook his head. "I think," he said in the same quiet voice, "she just slipped away from us."

Barber grunted, then after a moment or two he said: " 'Twould be hard leavin' here not knowin' for sure whether the cap'n had been caught or not."

For a few moments Slater stared at nothing at all. It all seemed impossible: the men dead, probably eaten, Berry gone, God knew where, Seyawa . . . But Slater's mind would carry him no further. He said: "Sam, I'm going to rest two hours, but no more than two hours. Ye can judge the time well enough. Wake me then."

"Aye."

"Then you take two hours and I watch. When day comes we'll try to find the cap'n."

"Ye're not forgettin' Doyle, are ye? He's armed."

" 'Tis a risk we must take."

"I'd say he'd send a ball into your gut as quick as look at ye. An' mine too, for that matter."

"Aye," said Slater. Nothing seemed real to him now. God, but he was tired. His body ached. He turned and, one hand flung out near his pistol, fell asleep.

More than half of Slater's time to rest had gone.

Suddenly Barber shifted, head up, alert. He turned, listening.

It was no sound he knew, a wailing thing that hung in the air, rising and falling. It came from in front of him, and he moved behind a fallen tree-trunk and rested his musket across it, making sure that no moonlight fell either on it or on him. He glanced quickly at Slater and Jeremy, both asleep. His right hand went out and the hammer came back, its sharp click the only sound he made.

Then he saw something move and he shifted, sighting on it, praying it might be Doyle. It was quite still, but then he saw it was not Doyle, though it was something to be killed, for a beam of moonlight fell on flesh, shining with what he knew was oil. He squeezed on the trigger, feeling its first movement under his finger. Then the sound came again and the trigger went another fraction. He remembered this musket was light on the sear and he held there, ready now.

Should he call Slater? Or should he wait? If they were surrounded he would get this one and the shot would wake Slater and the boy. He heard his own breathing, and there was more movement; he looked past the fore-sight, staring into the darkness and the dappled moonlight, and he held tight, ready for the kick of the musket.

Then out stood the girl, clear in a shaft of light. For another moment he held on her, then his finger eased the pressure off the trigger and his left hand came back and the muzzle went up. She was carrying something; a cord was over one shoulder and down between her breasts, pressing a deep ridge in one of them. He glimpsed the criss-cross weave of a green frond basket. His eyes searched past, out on each side of her, but there was no other movement. She called again, and he stood and stepped out of the shadow. She started, her breath caught.

Barber hesitated, making up his mind. Then, turning to where Slater lay, he gestured with his musket. She, too, hesitated, but he pointed again and she came forward. She passed him, and going into the shadow went to Slater and bent, listening to him. She took the basket from her shoulder and lowered it to the ground, all the time watching the slow rise and fall of his body as he breathed.

Feeling her, Slater started up alarmed and grabbed for a pistol, but she held him back and calmed him. He felt her softness and smelled her sandalwood fragrance. Then she had not betrayed them. He clutched out at her, the bitter, dry hurt running from him. All his doubts of her vanished.

She whispered his name and pressed him back to the ground. He could hear the catch of her heart in her breath sweet as milk against him. Fatigue sharpened his longing, his desire. As she whispered her shy, wild protest he sought her lips, fondling her.

Before Barber returned to wake him she stirred; a band of moonlight lay across them; she was naked, except for the necklet of sharks' teeth which glowed hard, white and triangular against the softness of her skin.

Chapter 22

JEREMY could not restrain his pleasure at the sight of her next morning. When he awoke she was still sleeping; it was light and Slater was on watch. He ran to him, calling over and over again that Seyawa had returned to them.

"She's not short on courage, that one," said Barber with admiration. "To get these victuals she must have stuck her head in the lion's mouth." When the four of them ate some of the food—yam, and *roro* and a piece of fish apiece—the yam was still faintly warm. There was enough food left over for about four days if they rationed it; Seyawa wrapped it in banana leaves and returned it to the basket.

"Ye seem happy, Sam," Slater said as Barber stood up and wiped his mouth with his handkerchief.

"Aye, I am that. We'll lick 'em now. I can feel it in m'bones, God help me I can."

While Barber and Jeremy went about clearing the camp and making sure their cache of arms and tools was still well concealed, Slater sat with Seyawa and questioned her about the tide in the lagoon and its effect on their getting the canoe round.

He drew an elongated shape for the island and marked on it the places of the village and their camp. Then he asked her to show him the course they would have to take through the lagoon with the canoe. She showed him where the pass lay. It was north-west of them and was little used because it was dangerous and narrow, but she thought the canoe could make it. She described the reach of the tides; even at low tide, she told him, there would be enough water to get the canoe, close in under the shore, to the beach below the camp. By using that passage they could pick up the gear from the beach and be well away from the island by daylight.

It was still early when they set out to look for Berry. Hot and sticky with sweat, weapons at the ready, they went carefully, knowing that Doyle was near and was armed to strike. Slater had no doubt that the man would attack—hadn't he killed Pain?—and without warning. They spoke little.

By noon they had covered a good portion of the western end of the island, but they had found no trace of Berry. Soon after, there was a sudden drenching rain. Grey sheets of water streamed between the trees and sent brown runnels rushing down the sides of the hills. The sky was split with tremendous streaks of lightning, and thunderclaps shook the earth.

When the storm passed and the rumble of the thunder rolled out over the sea, the sun shone out in dazzling white rays and vapour rose from the warmed earth. The trees dripped silently, leaves trembling with the fall of the water drops, the pools disappeared and the birds returned to the air.

On into the afternoon they went, hope fading as they explored valley after valley, bay after bay, without finding any trace of the captain. Finally, well past the middle of the afternoon, Slater concluded that Berry must have been taken.

"Aye, 'twould seem like it," Barber said. "But then we've not had sight of Doyle either, an' I doubt whether he's been taken."

"True enough, Barber, but Doyle might be anywhere on the island. He's no coward; could be he's deliberately hid himself up the other end, it bein', he might figure, an unlikely place for the savages to go huntin' us. Berry, now, so I'd a thought, would have made for this end."

175

"Mr. Slater," said Barber quietly, "I don't wish to speak disrespectful o' the cap'n, but ye'll mind he was ill and his sickness were queerness; his mind were such that he'd be likely to do anything. He might even have walked into the village an' give himself up to the swine." It was a fantastic idea, but Slater had to admit that Berry was ill enough to do anything. More important than any speculation, however, were the facts that they had seen no sign of Berry and that they had to get along. Slater gave the order to turn back.

"Ye never know," Barber said when they had gone a little way, "he might even be back at the camp, waitin' for us." But Berry was not waiting for them at the camp, nor was there sign that anyone had visited it in their absence. Without resting, they set out for the village.

The rain had aggravated every difficult feature of the journey. The mosquitoes and flies were worse now. Where the high ground had been hard and dry, now it was muddy and treacherous; the sodden jungle steamed, and rotting dampness surrounded them. Slater estimated there was less than an hour of daylight left when they reached the hill from which he had looked down upon the canoes. He ordered Jeremy to wait with Seyawa while he took Barber forward.

The beach was clear enough in the beginning dusk; they could see the houses in from the edge of the sand, the coconuts and Tahitian chestnuts, the breadfruits (black now in the shadow), the candle-nuts, the fires and the lights starting to wink up at them. But the canoes were no longer there.

Barber was first to speak. "They're gone?" he asked.

"Aye. . . . Aye, be Jesus, they're gone."

"Where were they?"

"Right below. 'Bout four-five fathoms inboard o' the logs. Barber, stay here an' keep an eye out. I'm goin' back to the girl. There's somethin' queer, something I don't understand."

"Ye mean with her? Because I noticed that——"

"What did ye notice?" Slater asked quickly.

"Like as though she were frightened."

"That's it. But I put it down to what we were goin' to do. Mayhap there's more in it than that?"

"God knows, but I see somethin' about her."

Seyawa was not surprised. Before he had finished trying to tell her, she was nodding her understanding. He was puzzled by her reaction and irritated by his inability to talk to her. She pulled a blade of grass and began to tease it between her fingers. It was darker back here under the trees. Wood smoke filtered through from the village, and when she smelled it she stiffened, eyes suddenly wide with fear.

"Jeremy," said Slater suddenly, "go out to Barber."

If only he could speak to her, he thought. Not only were all the canoes missing, but it seemed that there was an unusually great number of people about the village, and that there was a strange excitement in the sounds which drifted up from it. Seyawa sat with her head down, still shredding the grass blade with her thumb-nail.

My God, he thought, I see it. Aye, I see it. Without stopping to reason, and shaking with sudden rage, he reached out, grabbed Seyawa by the chin and swivelled her face up to him.

"Aye," he said, not caring whether she understood him or not. "I'll tell ye why the canoes are gone, ye black bitch. They're gone because ye've told 'em in the village that we would be takin' one. They've been hidden. That's why they're gone." And taking his hand from her chin, he struck her. She gave a little shriek of astonishment, but made no attempt to protect herself.

"Aye, be God! An' to think I didn't see it! Didn't see why ye went as ye did, an' come back, after tellin' 'em what we planned to do. And bringin' us food—no wonder ye were brave, ye could afford to be, y'spyin' slut." He struck her again, harder this time, a double blow, slapping with the palm of his hand and chopping with the back of it so that her head shook violently. But she made no sound; the grass stem was wrapped still about her fingers.

He drew a pistol and got to his feet. His hand trembled, but his rage had gone. The pistol felt heavy, his skin thick. His forefinger wrapped itself about the trigger. Seyawa saw the move, but made no effort to escape. She sat looking up at him and her lips parted slowly.

He wondered how he would tell Barber and Jeremy. They would come when they heard the shot. He would just say he had killed her because she had betrayed them; that was why the canoe wasn't there.

She had now stopped turning the piece of grass. Her eyes were incredibly quiet, no expression in them at all. She looked not at him but at the pistol.

"Sir. . . . Sir, Mr. Slater, Sir." Jeremy's voice sounded very far away.

God, the boy mustn't see! Do it. Then turn and send him back, tell him to make Barber come.

"Mr. Slater, Sir, Barber says will ye——Mr. Slater!" Jeremy's shriek hit him as he turned to order him back.

"Mr. Slater, what are ye doin' wi' the pistol? 'Tis Seyawa, Sir!" Jeremy threw himself upon Slater, pulling down the arm that held the pistol. Slater, cursing, struggled with the boy and at the same time desperately tried to uncock the weapon, afraid it might fire.

"Away wi' ye, lad. Out of it!" Regaining his balance, he threw Jeremy from him so that the boy fell partly over Seyawa, who cried out and got to her feet. Jeremy was up and at Slater again, hammering at him and shouting: "Sam! Sam! Quick, Sa-a-am!" As the high, broken cry echoed about the place, Barber rushed to the scene. Jeremy was still hanging on to Slater; the pistol, uncocked now, had fallen to the ground.

Gently Barber pulled Jeremy away. Slater did not move. Still holding Jeremy, Barber turned, looking for Seyawa, but she was nowhere to be seen.

Chapter 23

WHEN Berry escaped after the attack on the camp he had no doubt that the Fijians had taken Slater, Jeremy and Seyawa and had killed Barber. He was certain that he alone survived. In his mind, Doyle had ceased to exist from the moment Slater drove him from the camp; to the old man, even Pain's strange death was an unrelated incident signifying nothing. Doyle was gone as utterly as Powell, or Light, or Morgan, or any of them. It was as if, not being able to see them, his mind could not comprehend their living. He, Robert Berry, alone had survived.

At first this pleased him. He found himself gratified that he, the eldest of them, had lived where younger men had perished. Well away from the camp and keeping off the beach, he came to a small gully, where he sat down in the shade. There he began a loud harangue.

"Aye, the last o' them. And not only was I alone, ye'll mind, gentlemen, but I was alone on a savage island, inhabited by demons got up to represent blacks. Aye, demons, I say, not men, for God never made such monsters. They were spawned be Lucifer himself, gentlemen, damn me if they were not. Aye, an' a diseased an' sickly race into the bargain, wi' habits ye'd think twice about afore ye told of. . . ."

But as he felt the effects of his exertion and the frightful excitement of the fight, he stopped speaking and relaxed with his back resting against a tree-trunk. In that position he fell asleep. Unseen by him the evening gathered, the wind off the sea ceased to blow and the temperature fell. He stirred and woke, and got wearily to his feet, calling for Slater. Several times he called, then muttering of the drubbing he would give someone for not sending a boat for him he made his way to the top of the beach, and standing there called out loud for a boat-man.

It was dark before some shred of sanity returned. Then, momentarily, he caught a glimpse of his predicament—alone, without food or water, without ship or crew—without anything but his musket, his pistols, his knife and the clothes he was wearing.

He struck off west, back into the scrubby bush above the sand, stumbling in the dark and cursing to himself. In one spot he tripped and fell so heavily that he lay dazed for a few moments. When he got up, somewhat sobered by the fall, he looked about and found a grass-covered clearing, where he fell asleep. He did not wake until dawn.

Cut and bruised, and raving with thirst, he staggered inland and by chance came upon a pool. He lowered himself over the water and drank some of it. Vaguely he realised there was danger in drinking it, but he kept on, drawing it into his mouth and filling his belly, while over and over in his mind went the story he was telling in Boston—how he was forced to drink his own urine, gentlemen; how all about the island was as dry as a lump o' coral.

When he left the pool, without knowing it he headed back in the direction of the camp. He was tired now and moved slowly, stopping often. He looked straight ahead, his eyes narrowed in the glare of the blazing sun. After a while, feeling the water heavy on his stomach, he stopped on a small rise. Two *ivi* trees shaded this mound and he lay down, head towards the sea. He could not see the beach in this position, but he could see a tide-exposed flat a cable's length from the water's edge. He had been there about a half-hour when a small bird alighted on the flat and began to feed, darting its long, curved beak into the sand.

He was still looking at the bird a few minutes later when it rose into the air and flew out over the lagoon. Berry let his head fall, for the flight of the bird was of no importance to him. Had it been, had he wriggled forward to seek the reason for its flight, he would have seen Slater, Barber, Jeremy and Seyawa as they went along the beach in search of him.

When he went on, it was nearly noon. He kept in the shade well off the beach, for the sun was now beginning to torment him. As he passed below the camp his eye fell on the clump of screw pines near which they had buried the gear. But though his eye saw them his brain did not fully comprehend; he stopped, looked up at them for a moment or two and stumbled on.

Then it rained. When it had ceased he was wet through. He went on, slipping several times on the wet earth. The sun was out full and strong when he found *Argo*'s longboat.

Following the coast he was well out along a promontory, walking on creeper-covered, sandy soil under scraggy trees when he caught sight of what he took to be a house—a rudely built shelter of fronds supported on six uprights made from drift and green wood. Inexplicably the sight of the little structure filled him with rage. Muttering something about routing the last remaining opposition, he raised his musket ponderously and pulled the trigger. But the weapon wouldn't fire. He dropped it and drew one of his pistols, which sent a ball clipping through the fronds that overhung the edges of the roof. Then, leaving the musket, he stumbled up to the place, raving about an attack on a heavily fortified village.

He showed no elation when he saw the boat. He brushed through the hanging fronds and stood looking at it. He was still holding the pistol. Now he remembered it and sat down to load it again. Then he walked about, examining the boat carefully. The bow, fore-quarters and midship sections were intact, though scored in places where she had scraped against the coral. The stern was badly damaged, but her ribs, stringers and most of her planking were sound enough. She was a boat that a carpenter or a few good seamen could soon have seaworthy.

He looked at it as if he had never doubted he would find it. "Aaahhh, Oliver," he said, shaking his head, "ye didn't believe, and so y'lost y'chance, for y'see, ye never found the longboat. But 'twere there, all the time, put there be God, who hadn't forgotten me." Then slipping back to the dream of Boston again, he went on: "Aye, gentlemen, 'twas an act o' Providence. I see that now. God sent the boat, an' erected a shelter over it so's to keep it from the rain and the sun until He should lead me to it. Aye, 'twas the gettin' of the whaler that done it. So I fetched her ashore, rebuilt her from the keel up, masted and rigged her."

Wearily he climbed in over the broken stern, and stepping forward sat on a thwart. The Fijians had not chocked the boat securely, and it shook as he moved. The thwart he sat on was cracked, at one end all but torn from its fixing. The thwart shifted and he stood, seeing the boat pulled by an imaginary crew.

"Pull, lads," he called. "Aye, pull away for home an' mother. Pull . . . pull . . . pull, me hearties." Calling the stroke, he flexed his body backwards and forwards as though he, too, held an oar. "Pull . . . pull . . . pull . . . pull, me hearties. . . ."

But his movement set the longboat rocking, and as he struggled to recover his balance the chocks on the starboard side of the boat gave way. She held a moment and then toppled. Berry, arms flailing, fell backwards, crashed against the broken thwart and rolled out on to the ground.

Chapter 24

"THE girl's gone," said Barber, turning back to Slater. "What happened?"

"I tried to kill her," said Slater.

"Ye tried to kill her?"

"Aye, I was goin' to, but the boy stopped me."

"But, in God's name, why?"

"I thought she had betrayed us. I was mad, mad, I tell ye. I thought the canoes weren't there because she'd told 'em, and they'd hidden them."

"The canoes are there."

Slater looked up quickly. "They're there," Barber went on. "Or one o' them is, and there's another makin' in now. I sent the boy to tell ye. Didn't he?"

"I had no time to," said Jeremy.

"'Tis true," said Slater. "But he come in the nick o' time. Dear God! I tell ye, Sam, I was mad."

"We must find her, Sam," said Jeremy earnestly. "We must look for her. They'll eat her if we don't. I know they will."

"'Tis a hell of a time to go lookin'," Barber said, "with the canoe waitin' for us. 'Twas a sailing canoe ye was thinkin' of, wasn't it?"

"Aye."

"She's comin' now," said Barber. "A fair lump of a thing, narrow-gutted, but she'd be fast. There's another thing we need the girl for, the workin' of the canoe. 'Tis a queer rig."

Now a drumbeat hammered on the air. Slater felt his skin cold and damp.

"Barber," he said suddenly, "this is it: ye an' Jeremy take the canoe and get to the camp. I'll help ye launch it and then I'll look for her. If we're at the camp be daylight, well an' good; if not, ye're to make away, with Jeremy."

"Nay, I won't do it."

"'Tis an order, Barber."

"It might be, but I'm not takin' it. Call it mutiny if ye like, but I'll not do it. If we go, we go together."

"Barber!"

"I'll not do it," said Barber grimly. "Use y'head, Mr. Slater. To split us now is to weaken us the more. Any rate, where do I go with him?"

"Ye can get him off this island."

"An' what o' the girl?"

"God damn it, how do I know? She's gone."

For a minute none of them spoke. Then Slater said: "Nay, Barber, I'm goin' to find her."

"Then we'd better be started," said Barber.

Barber saw her, a fleeting glimpse of her running, and he moved, quickly for a man his size. Coming level with Slater, he took his arm and turned him about. "Stay here," he said.

"What is it?"

"'Tis the girl."

"Where?"

"On the hill yonder," said Barber, pointing left of him.

"Quick——"

"Nay, ye stay here. I'm goin' alone."

"But, Barber——"

"I said I was goin' alone, an' I mean to." There was no doubt of the menace in Barber's voice. "Ye may do as ye like about it, after I'm back." Barber's voice dropped, the threat in it more positive. "But if ye follow, I'll kill ye, Mr. Slater, so help me." He made off down the slope and disappeared in the dusk. Fifteen minutes later he returned with her. When they started off she went in front, a step or two before Slater.

Not a word was said until Barber and Slater lay looking down at the village once more. Now there were four canoes on the beach; the one they wanted was second from the near end. One of them had just been beached and there were people about it, some of them holding coconut frond torches; others were coming down the beach to it.

"They got fish," said Barber.

"Aye."

"An' d'ye notice that they seem different somehow, more excited? And there's more fires. See the big pit there."

"Aye, 'tis a feastin' oven. They don't cook there every day. Mostly they cook in their houses, an' there's them other cookin' places somewhere underneath us."

Now the smell of wood smoke came up strong, and in the gathering darkness the fires cast an eerie light. The wind had fallen and the smoke climbed straight in the air. In his absorption with the scene Slater didn't hear Jeremy come up behind him.

" 'Tis the boy," said Barber. "He wants ye." Slater turned.

"I think, Sir," said Jeremy, "Seyawa'd like ye to come back."

He went slowly, dreading being alone with her, yet wanting to cry for forgiveness. She watched him come, a wary, frightened look in her eye. Slowly, looking at her, he sat himself down opposite her and she pointed to a canoe she had drawn. He could just see it, and beside it she had drawn a fish. Then she drew what he took to be a fire and, scraping out a little trough in the earth, pointed to the fish and then to the fire. He saw the trough as the underground oven, the fish to be cooked in it. But he saw it only vaguely, for he seemed incapable of passing from the horrified contemplation of his own act to query her. She sat unmoving, looking at the trough, her statement incomplete. He saw there was more, but it didn't seem to matter to him. She was still staring at the ground when he left her and went back.

"What she want?" asked Barber.

"I don't know." There was desperation in Slater's voice. "I don't know."

"I figure I do, be Jesus. She wanted to ask ye somethin' or tell ye somethin'?"

"Tell me, I think. She told me they'd be cookin' fish."

"They'll be cookin' more than fish. See the big fire, the pit there, an' the mats an' bowls and things spread about? And notice the swine, comin' from everywhere. Remember the two savages ye killed? And how that night we heard these devils shoutin', and saw the smoke, and smelled cookin'?"

Above the oven pit the sparks climbed and the light of the flames spread out and touched the houses and the people, who were squatting or moving about, cutting and carrying food for the oven. The women, breasts swinging, came up from the canoe with more fish and dropped them on to the mats. The red-and-yellow light or torches gleamed on oiled skin, and above all this there arose a din of voices that had about it the accents of intoxication. Then, in time with the drumbeat, came a chanting.

"May God have mercy on 'em," said Barber. "But that's it. They're goin' to eat them."

Then Slater said to himself, this was what she was trying to describe, but she was afraid to draw the figure of a man lying in the little trough.

They had no difficulty in recognising the first of the bodies. " 'Tis Pepper," said Barber.

"Lad, go back an' stay with Seyawa, will ye," Slater said to Jeremy.

Peppercorn's body had been stripped, all but the sea boots had been taken from it. Already it was swelling, the belly bigger than it had been in life. The Fijians moved about it, expectation in their walk. Awila was seated to windward of the ovens. Behind him loomed the *bure kalou*, its great phallic shape outlined by the flickering light of the fire and the torches. On the mats before him were many kinds of food in pots and wooden bowls. About Awila sat other chiefs, and immediately behind him the priest.

Pepper's face had been daubed with turmeric. Four men who had brought the body out, one at each leg and arm, carried it along the side of the fire pit and set it down a few yards in front of Awila. As they did, more logs, torch butts and nut husks were thrown on to the fire, the yellow flame and sparks climbing high in the columns of smoke.

Then the *yaqona* bowl was brought and the root was chewed by the women. As the drink was being mixed, men went round the oven pit with long poles, pushing the flaming wood to one side and patting flat a glowing bed of embers.

Now the men who had carried Pepper began to truss him with strips of tapa. They drew his thighs upwards, pulled his arms forward and bound his hands over his knees. They then sat him up and stood back, pointing and shouting, laughing at him—a pathetic, grotesque figure with his painted face and bloated body. But he fell rolling on to his right side and they hooted with laughter, crying to one another, to Awila and the other chiefs. Another man ran from the pit with a burning stick and stuck the unlighted end into the ground. The other men sat Pepper up and pressed him back against it, propping him. The man who had set the stick up stood above it, inhaling the odour of burning flesh, rolling his eyes and grinning exaggeratedly.

There was a shout as the men drew away from him, and a tall, thin woman with tube-like legs, incredibly supple, danced from behind the pit, her body twisting sinuously, until she stood facing Peppercorn. A dozen other women, one a hag and another little more than a child, writhed out after her and executed an obscene dance of mockery before him. They twisted and turned, exposed parts of their anatomy to him, fondled themselves, and made lewd gestures with hands and bodies. They began to sing, matching their words to the rhythm of the chant which overhung the place. About them the excitement of the men mounted in a rising pitch of licentiousness. Brands were snatched from the fire and waved about as if they were phalli, their burning tips rubbed over the seaman's face while the women writhed about him.

Then all but the woman who had led the dance drew back. She stopped before him, swaying slightly, lips and chin bright with saliva. Hers was the privilege of making the supreme gesture of ridicule. Hands lifting her breasts out towards him, she moved until she was over him and performed the final obscenity.

Slater saw that the face of the man who was about to cut off Pepper's head also was daubed with turmeric. The knife was made from a piece of clam-shell. First he cut all around; then dropping the knife he got above Pepper's head, and gripping it over the temples twisted it until it came free. He held it up and was greeted by a shout. Another raced in and snatched it and held it up by the greying hair. Many of the Fijians pulled at their own faces, mimicking the ghastly expression on Pepper's. Then the man holding the head put it to his mouth, as though he would bite it. No sooner did his lips touch the face than Awila shouted and pointed to the fire pit, and the man lowered the head instantly and went with it to the fire. He leaned over and dropped it on to the coals. A mask of flame grew on it, then died. The man poked at it with a long stick for a minute or two, then he edged it from the fire.

Now it looked like a caricature of Peppercorn. The man who had put it into the fire then prised open the mouth and inserting the knife well back carried the head that way to Awila. Before the chief was a long wooden trough; the trough had no feet, and when the man dropped the head into it it wobbled.

Then they cut the tapa trussing and started to dismember the body. Three men, all with clam-shell knives.

"Holy Mother!" said Barber. "Look at the devils. Look what they got now. Dear Jesus, Sir, these ain't men."

"Come away," said Slater. Turning, they wriggled back until it was safe to stand and walk to where Jeremy and the girl waited for them under the trees.

Barber asked Slater when they would go down for the canoe. "Near about midnight," said Slater. "When it's at full pitch'll be the best time for us."

Chapter 25

"It must be near midnight," said Barber. "Ye don't think we should wait a bit, until it gets quieter?"

" 'Tis the start with the canoe I'm thinkin' of. We should be well off the island by daylight. An' we've to get the gear, an' wait as long as possible for the cap'n." Slater got to his feet.

"Jeremy, there's naught to be afraid of, lad. Either we do it, or we don't. If we don't, at least we'll go knowin' we made a man's stab at it. Barber, take the rear. Then'll come Jeremy, then me. Seyawa will lead. Unless we're attacked be numbers, Barber—which'll be the end of us—'tis the knife. 'Tis quieter."

Off the hill Seyawa bore left until she found a path that brought them to the stream. They didn't cross but turned left along its bank. Soon they smelled the sea and heard the sound of a wave, a solitary splash on the sand. She slowed and a moment later they saw the first wink of a light through the trees.

She stopped, looked back at Slater, and pointing to the light tried to tell him something. He stepped up level with her, inclining his head towards her and struggling to understand. He made out only the word for house. Then she slipped away from him without any more sound than the faint rustle of her *liku*.

"What's actin', Mr. Slater?" Barber asked in a hoarse whisper.

"I think she's gone to have a look."

"God, how long'll that take?"

For about ten minutes they waited, eaten at by mosquitoes. When she returned Seyawa indicated they were to approach the beach by way of the cooking places in the base of the hill.

"There's no more direct way?" Barber asked.

"Doesn't seem to be," Slater answered.

Very soon they were within sight of two or three houses. To their left loomed the hill through the thinning trees. Then they saw more houses, squat and dark, and behind them, silhouetting them, the glow of the fires and torches at the ovens. From the village came a snatch of shouted conversation, the occasional cry of a tired child, and the chanting, still the chanting and the drumbeat.

They came in under the hill, and when they saw the first of the cooking-houses Seyawa stopped. There were six of them, spaced about a hundred feet apart, a thatched porch framing each entrance. Out in front of them no grass grew. The houses that ran in a ragged line in front of them appeared deserted. Barber whispered to Slater that he could see a light coming from one of the cooking places.

"Aye, a fire, I'd say," Slater answered. "Like as not they keep one goin' for a coal."

He was on the point of whispering the order to go when Seyawa's hand shot out and closed about his wrist. Something had moved under the porch of the third house from them. Then from it came a laugh, low and voluptuous. Slater tensed and Barber swore to himself, easing his knife in its sheath, for now there was more movement and a girl came from the house.

She was naked, wide-hipped. She stood full in the open where the light of the moon rested on her head and shoulders and breasts. For a moment she faced them, and Slater thought they had been seen; then she turned back to the house and stooped, partly under the shadow of the thatch. As she stood full in the light again, a breech-cloth was in her hand, white against the darkness behind her. She looked into the house and spoke softly, passing the end of the cloth about her waist as she did so. Then she bent again, from the hips, slowly passed the free end of the tapa forward between her legs, drew the cloth tight and, standing straight again, folded the end in at her waist with an easy automatic motion. All the time, curiosity showing in the tilt of her head, she kept looking into the house.

She spoke once more and laughed, the same laugh, almost a chuckle. Seyawa grunted, startling Slater. Then a man came out. The girl watched him come into the light, then she turned and left him. As she walked away, with an easy rhythmic roll to her hips, he watched her. Then he moved off after her.

They gave the man and the woman time to be well clear and then went on, keeping close to the scrubby brush that grew about the base of the hill. When they reached the first of the places Seyawa led them inside. Motioning them behind her, she stood against the wall at the opening and looked out towards the beach. About the place was the smell of cold ashes, dampness and old smoke.

She glanced at Slater, who nodded, and they followed her. Outside they ran hugging the shadow until they came to the next one. Inside it the noises of the village were louder and more penetrating. Slater stood with her, looking from the opening. Next was the one with the fire, the earth about its mouth dusted with a ruddy glow. As they watched, the fire shifted,

189

and for a moment the glow of it flared yellow as far as the wall of a house opposite, nearly a hundred feet away. Seyawa pointed there and shook her head.

"We miss the next one," Slater said to Barber in the darkness behind him. " 'Tis the one with the fire. Ready, Jeremy?"

"Aye, Sir." Jeremy was just behind Slater, who put his hand out and felt the boy shivering.

"Are ye all right, lad?" he said softly, bending his head to the boy.

"Aye, Sir. I'm not really frightened, just—just a bit shivery, Sir."

"Ye're doin' all right," muttered Barber. " 'Twouldn't be natural if ye weren't shivery. I am."

They were running under the cliff when they saw a Fijian. He came from between two houses, a big man. Slater and Seyawa saw him at the same instant. There was no help for it but to enter the house with the fire. Slater was next in after Seyawa, cursing their luck; Jeremy a yard or two behind him and then came Barber. "The game's up," he said, breathing quickly from excitement and the exertion of running.

"Ye're sure he saw us?" whispered Slater.

"Aye. Saw him stop. Looked fair at me."

Slater peered from the opening. There could be no doubt that the Fijian had seen them, for he took a few steps towards them, then stopped as if uncertain what to make of it.

"Barber," whispered Slater, not looking from the Fijian, "you stay that side. Jeremy, get behind me."

Then he drew right back. "He's coming all right. Y'ready, Sam?"

"Aye." Barber moved, his knife gleaming. Seyawa slipped past Jeremy and, taking a piece of wood from a heap against the wall, scattered the fire; there was a sudden hissing, a warm steamy smell.

"If he gets level with the openin', Barber, he'll see us. It'll have to be quick—before he can shout. Ye'll get sight of him on your side before me."

Slater half crouched, watching Barber for sign that he had seen the Fijian. A little smoke and steam curled from under the roof, filtered through the panels of broken thatch over the opening. The smell of food was in the place. Under his left hand, back against the wall, Slater felt a dried fish scale stuck on the blackened timber. From somewhere at the back there came the round, plunking drip of water into water.

Barber tensed as he saw the man. He was coming slowly but steadily towards them, head slightly on one side.

As he came opposite them, Slater heard Jeremy's breath hiss in. Slater swore to himself; the man was too far out, much too far. But they would have to take him there. Slater glanced at Barber; he was ready, muscles taut for the leap, when from the back of the house came Seyawa's voice. Slater froze. He couldn't follow what she said, but he heard her say her name and her title, and he saw the astonishment in the man's face. "Adi Seyawa?" he asked.

Her answer came softly, almost a whisper. It was an invitation.

He was a heavy-browed man, young and powerful. He stepped forward and, the instant before he saw Barber, Slater jumped. He had begun a cry when Slater's arm closed about his neck, drew back his head and shut off his air. The man's full strength was just beginning to draw Slater's feet from the ground when Barber struck. Slater felt the thud as the knife struck home. The Fijian made no noise in dying; there was a gasp and Slater let him fall.

With Slater in front they raced on, close together, and reaching the top of the beach fell flat, searching the sand for sign of anyone. Then Slater was up, and they followed him down a long diagonal to the canoe, which was just aground.

Barber, Jeremy and the girl pushed it out, while Slater waded ahead, feeling along the vine that ran to its anchor, which he put aboard. They turned the canoe (an unnecessary manœuvre which confused Seyawa) and pushed it until there was a foot of water under it.

"Jeremy," Slater whispered, "in wi' ye, lad. Quick! Up, Seyawa."

The canoe was now well afloat; Jeremy's hands were on the gunwale. The outrigger lifted and fell back with a sharp smack on the top of the water. "Try again, lad. Now! Jump!"

Jeremy went up, then Seyawa and Barber. Slater clambered aboard as the shove he gave the craft shot it out, and they were away. The four paddles struck together, and along the outrigger a twisting ribbon of light cut through the water.

Chapter 26

BARBER was bow, Slater stern—the steering paddle. Both men struck to port, the side of the outrigger, Jeremy and Seyawa to starboard. Over the spars between the hull and the float was a deck of split bamboo, lashed in place with sennit. Across this lay the mast, the rolled sail, the vine rigging and a long vine cable. The anchor, a piece of sandstone with a hole through it, lay on top of this gear. The hull of the canoe was a single hollowed log, its sides built up by planks laced together; in fact the whole craft was laced together; there was not a solid fixing anywhere. She leaked a little, and there were a few inches of water in her. At Jeremy's feet, just floating, was a baler, a wooden scoop.

Barber was stroke, and as his paddle dipped and drove astern Slater could hear the breath leave his body; Barber's was a powerful stroke, deep and long. The four paddles struck as one and the canoe rode from the stroke in a clean, swift run.

Out of arrow-shot of the beach they bore to port and made for the easternmost tip of the island, where they could turn and make west for the camp. Several times Slater glanced astern.

"I think, Barber," he said between strokes, "we've got away with it."

"Nothin' followin'?"

"Nay."

"Ah," grunted Barber, but no more than that; and soon the first of the points they had to round began to show ahead. As they neared it they felt the current set harder against them. Now the canoe fell away faster after the stroke and the stern settled deeper.

The course ran in and out as Seyawa directed the way. It took Slater a few minutes to get the knack of changing course, but between changes he found it surprisingly easy to hold a steady heading. Seyawa led them into a channel; on their starboard side were several sandstone islets, against which the water pushed, silver-ridged and silent in the bright light of the moon and the stars and the high streaming comet.

When Seyawa pointed one change of course, Barber asked: "What's she usin' for marks?"

"Hard to be certain," Slater answered, "but I'd say 'twas the shape o' the land against the sky."

"We round yet?"

"Almost, a cable or two an' we'll be safe—from the village at any rate."

"Thank God for the girl. We'd have come to grief on our own." Barber was right, for the course twisted and turned, very often skirting coral heads that were invisible until they were only a few yards away—dark, menacing clumps of growth only a few inches under water.

When they had rounded the point Slater called a stop and they took in their paddles and rested. Ahead of them now was the northernmost tip of the island; once clear of that, they would be well on their way to the camp.

"Jeremy," said Slater, "ye'd best bale a bit." The boy was still at it when Slater took up his paddle and called to them to go on. Now the girl led them out towards the reef, the thunder of it loud in their ears. Then in again she piloted them and they passed a limestone spit, running close under it. They almost touched once when a heavy swell carried them down towards the streaming ledge exposed by the backwash. Slater cried out for the stroke and the canoe slid past, only a foot or two between their frail outrigger and the coral.

The worst of the journey was over; they were soon rounding the northern point, well out in deep water. Long rollers were running in under them, the canoe rising and falling as the rowers drove it along the coast. Now for the first time they felt the motion of the canoe in a seaway. She seemed stable enough, but her movement was strange to Barber and Slater. "She can be cranky," growled Barber.

And Jeremy answered, pleasure and hope rising in him: "What say ye we make for Port Jackson in her, Sam?"

"Might as well make for the moon, lad. But, aye, on second thought I'd have a go at it if ye'd be cabin-boy."

"I would, Sam." Turning to Slater, he asked: "Will ye be skipper, Sir?"

"Aye, lad, that I will," Slater answered, catching the boy's happiness and seeing an end to the hurt which had come between them. Seyawa caught it too and smiled, but no one saw it.

When the sweep of beach below their camp came in sight, Barber said: "D'ye reckon, Sir, the cabin-boy should look to the primin' of our muskets?"

"Aye," Slater said. "See to 'em, Jeremy. Ye'd best prime all round, just in case."

Jeremy put up his paddle, took the muskets from the outrigger platform and set to work. When he had done he said: "I've pushed yours as far for'ard as I can, Mr. Barber!"

"Eh!"

"I've pushed yours as far for'ard——"

"Aye, I got that," said Barber, "but what's the Mister?"

"I've promoted ye, Sam. Didn't ye know? Ye're mate o' this here hooker. From now on ye're Mister."

"Well, I'll be damned!" said Barber.

As Slater swung the craft to go in, he said: "When I give the word, lads, up paddles, and when I call for 'em again, go for y'lives."

As they turned the canoe it took water, starboard gunwale under, outrigger high. "I said she could be cranky," said Barber, throwing his weight to port. But they made it safely, three paddles up while Slater leaned on his and lined the craft for the run in. Then he called for the stroke and they sent her leaping in over the little surf that broke on the shore. Barber's paddle came down with a thump on the outrigger deck and he crouched, hands on the gunwales.

"Out, Barber," cried Slater. Barber jumped into the water and an instant later Jeremy went over with Seyawa. Then Slater followed and they stood in the thigh-deep water holding the canoe. Slater laid his pistols on the deck, took the anchor and, wading out, dropped it. Moored, the canoe lay just clear of the sand.

Slater left Jeremy and Seyawa at the canoe. "If y'see or hear anythin' suspicious, lad, fire in the air," he said; then he and Barber went up through the narrow belt of scrubby brush and creeper that stood above the sand. They came to the screw pines where the gear lay buried; the ground was undisturbed.

"Let's go up to the camp," Slater said, "before we start loadin' the canoe."

Near the top, Barber said: " 'Tis unearthly quiet." As they drew their pistols, he added: " 'Twas somewhere about here the cap'n got the savage. Fell like a clown, he did."

"Easy, Barber. Quiet does it."

But there was no one at the camp. They went through it, but all was as they had left it. They returned to the cache, dejected, for they had hoped to find the captain waiting. It took several trips to load the canoe. They climbed and slid, loaded to the limit of what they could carry on the slope. Each time down Slater told Jeremy how to distribute and lash the gear to the outrigger deck. The heavy ball they stowed as near to the centre line as they could.

Finally it was done; Barber went over Jeremy's work and found it good. Then over all they placed a sail and lashed it down, leaving a long flapped pocket under which they put, to be ready at hand, the muskets, powder flasks, ball pouches, some pork and biscuit, the small water-cask and the girl's basket of food. On top they tied the mast and its sail.

"We'll be needin' some luck in that pass through the reef, I'm thinkin'," Barber said. "She'll be mighty low."

"We can do naught but try. Whichever way it goes, 'twill not be the Indians who'll be eatin' us—once we get as far as the pass."

"Then we go?"

"We've a good two hours to daylight," Slater said slowly. "Maybe more. Nay, we'll wait a bit. God, Barber, he still might come." He paused for a moment. "We'll wait at the camp. An' I'd like to go right through on to the hill at the back."

"The tide's fallin', Mr. Slater. What o' the canoe? The lad can't manage it alone. Even with the girl 'twould be too much. An' loaded as she is, we don't want her left high and dry."

"Then I'll go on m'own."

"Take the boy for company."

"Nay, he'd better remain. I'd like to see the muskets we brought down reloaded."

As Slater climbed his fatigue pressed heavily upon him. Part way up the hill, just below where the cache had been, he stopped and looked back. The lagoon was a lake, startlingly light against the sea beyond it. Standing there on the hill, Slater felt his fears deepen. He thought of Berry, by some chance alive, seeing them leave the island, perhaps running on the beach and screaming to them as he saw them disappearing in the dawn. He passed the hole under the screw pines and came to the edge of the trees. Then he drew his pistol, cocked it and went into the shadow.

He was still thinking of Berry when he heard the voice of Doyle.

Slater was clear in a patch of moonlight. Instantly he knew he had but one chance, and he swung about, searching the shadow. The hammer fell and the spark was bright, but the powder in the pan was damp. It was the sound of death itself to Slater. Just the snap, and then nothing.

Doyle stepped out of the shadow. His face was ash-grey, a savage smile on it.

"Y'powder's wet," he said as he came towards Slater. "But ye're fast, I'll give ye that—bloody fast." It was an honest statement, the admiration given ungrudgingly. He came close to Slater. There was no doubt in Slater's mind that Doyle would kill him.

"Y'got the canoe," said Doyle. "I saw ye come. 'Tis clear from up here. Besides, I knew ye was gone for it. Jeb told me. Was it hard to get?"

Fantastically, this seemed to Slater like some idle conversation at sea, something to break the monotony of a watch. "Nay," he said, "not hard." On the word 'hard' his voice all but broke with the strain.

" 'Twas a good idea. 'Tis a pity ye won't be usin' it."

"Do you want it?"

"In exchange for y'life. Nay, Slater, not that. I've got it—ye got it for me. But I don't want the canoe. I've got somethin' better."

"Then what do ye want?"

"Mostly to kill ye, but I'd like ye to know about the longboat." He paused, watching for Slater's reaction.

"What about it?" To Slater this was meaningless. The boat was gone with *Argo*.

"I've got it."

"The longboat?"

Doyle nodded his head, his eyes steady on Slater. He was enjoying this.

"Ye're mad, Doyle. The longboat's gone."

"So you think. But y'thinkin' is wrong, Slater."

"Then where is it?" Slater asked, curiosity for the moment running higher than anything else in him.

Doyle laughed, a sudden, deep chuckle. "Nay, Slater, I'll not be tellin' ye that, not yet. But I will, when I've a ball in ye. Afore I go down to settle with the others."

Slater noticed now that Doyle had four muskets slung across his back, two on each side. Four? he thought. There was his own, that which he went with; there was Pain's pair. That made three. But he had four—where had that extra one come from? Four muskets, four pistols, counting his own. Aye, he was well prepared to settle with the others. But there was a weakness showing. He was not speaking the whole truth, for he wouldn't kill Jeremy.

"Doyle?"

"Aye."

"Ye're lyin'."

"Nay." He shook his head.

"Ye won't kill the boy."

"Leave the boy out of it." Doyle's quick response and the twist in his voice told Slater that he had scored a hit.

"Doyle"—the words tumbled from him, driven out by his concern for the boy—"put up the weapon an' let's talk of it."

"Talk of it? Nay, I've got ye an' I'm goin' to kill ye."

"But, the boy——"

"Ye should've thought o' that when ye sent me out, Slater. Nay, I'll not be puttin' up the pistol until 'tis over. M'mind's made up," Doyle went on more quietly, almost matter-of-factly. "I'll gut-shoot ye, an' strip ye so the flies and these damned midges can have a good go at ye afore ye die. Your mistake, Slater, was to count me out. Ye shouldn't have."

"Ye got yeself out."

"I was kicked out be ye, Slater. Tipped out without a grain o' powder to fend for m'self among these devils, but I got it, didn't I?"

"Aye, ye did, be murder——"

Slater wasn't quick enough. Doyle was close and his reach was long. He struck out with his left hand, catching Slater across the face. It was a vicious, stinging blow and Slater reeled from it, his ear singing, the inside of his cheek torn against his teeth.

"Just mind what ye say," said Doyle, breathing quickly, "an' who ye accuse o' murder."

Slater saw his lower lip trembling. It was more than anger. Slater had reminded him of that which he wanted to forget. He, Solomon Doyle, could mention Pain. But no other man might, if it was to speak of murder, the killing of a shipmate.

Doyle wanted to kill Slater. Or rather he wanted him dead. But he knew that by killing him and then the others he would leave himself the last of his kind. This fact held him. With them dispatched he would have won a victory, but he also would be alone and easier prey for the Fijians.

However, he had the longboat. His head was slightly tilted, the right side heavy with shadow, the forehead, shoulders, wrist and pistol clear in the light. Slater wondered how much closer he needed to be to strike at him. To come out alive one needed a lot of luck.

"Slater, that was clever o' ye to be away from here when they raided it. Did y'cannibal whore tip ye off?"

Then it came to this, thought Slater—either he attempted the strike or he waited for the bullet.

"Eh? I asked ye, Slater, did the bitch tip ye off?" Doyle took a step closer, and Slater thought he was going to hit him again. "Be the God, Slater, ye'll talk when I stick a ball in ye. Ye'll scream for me to follow it with another, to get ye out of y'misery."

From the beach came a shot, a puff of sound. Slater started, turned his head towards it. "Listen," he said.

" 'Twas a shot. But ye don't get me that way," said Doyle. Yet despite his words his curiosity showed.

It was the signal, thought Slater. But why? Was it that they had found Berry? Aye, that could be. Then, when he didn't come down, Barber would come up, Doyle would be distracted, and in that instant Slater would lunge. Or Barber would shoot. Time, then, that was it. Talk, Doyle, talk and talk, and Barber would come.

"She's a pretty little bitch, Slater. I'll not kill her, not straight away. I might even bring her with me, for a time."

Keep on, Doyle. And Doyle went on, because he was afraid to make the decision to kill. The words clattered about Slater but didn't touch him; he was waiting for Barber.

Then a second shot came from the beach, and with it the instant realisation that it was no signal. Slater started to move.

Doyle jumped at him and thrust his pistol in Slater's ribs. "Stay where ye are," he ordered.

"For God's sake, Doyle, let me go. There's the boy, an' Barber, an' the girl. Somethin's gone wrong."

"I'll not let ye go, Slater."

"I'll come back, I give ye m'word on that. There's no need for us all to die. Or come with me." But Doyle was caught in the trap of his indecision and fear. Now was the time to kill Slater, then go to the beach and become the master there. But he could not; he could not free his mind for the decisive act.

Slater saw Doyle's distraction. He saw a man who was less alert than himself and saw that this was an instant to be seized —or for ever lost.

He jumped. Doyle's shot passed under Slater's right arm and Doyle twisted, grabbing for his other weapon; it was in his hand when Slater's crashed against his head. Doyle groaned and his knees buckled. Slater's left hand shot out and closed about the big man's shoulder, holding him, and Slater struck again with his pistol, this time down across his face. He saw the blood start, saw Doyle's eyes roll, and he ran from the place.

Out of the shadow and on to the hill slope he raced, down past the hole under the screw pines, slipping, pitching forward and grasping at the few bushes. He crashed into the line of scrub above the beach and his face was whipped by the branches. He tripped on a twisted root and fell, winded. Back on his feet, he was unsteady but he staggered on, to the top of the beach, where he grasped a tree and clung to it for support. He felt his head thudding with pain. Then when his breath came easier he went out on to the sand.

He was well down the beach before he remembered his pistol wouldn't fire, and he cursed himself for not taking Doyle's loaded one. And suddenly he saw ahead of him a body, sprawled. He had no doubt that it was dead.

Chapter 27

WHEN Slater left the beach to go up the hill Barber helped Jeremy to take the muskets from the canoe. Barber then put his pistols on the sail over the gear on the outrigger deck and waded in, feeling the vine that ran to the anchor. He hauled the canoe a fathom or so farther off the beach, paying out about five fathoms of the cable which ran from the inboard end of the forward outrigger strut. Then satisfied that the canoe was safe he stuck his pistols back into his belt and went from the water.

Jeremy was not far up the beach. Seyawa, mortally afraid of the weapons, stayed at the edge of the dry sand. As Barber passed her he smiled; she returned the smile shyly. Jeremy was unscrewing the cap from a powder-flask.

"Ye all right, lad?" Barber asked looking down at him.

"Aye, Sam."

"I'll leave ye to it then." He went on up the beach, bearing to his right. More than half-way up he sat. He knew now that their chances of survival were high. He had confidence in

Slater, faith in himself; none of the fears which had worked in Berry—and to a lesser extent in Slater—had touched him yet. They had the canoe to take them to an island; he knew they could build a boat because they had tools, sails, cordage. And they could sail it; Jeremy could stand a watch; maybe the girl could be taught, too. To Barber, what had been done before could be done again. Navigating the boat he didn't think of. That was for Slater.

He thought of Slater wanting to kill the girl. He could understand that; for when he went with Slater and the canoe wasn't there, he too felt she had betrayed them. He remembered that he'd wanted to kill Doyle, still wanted to, always would want to. Aye, he could understand Slater; Slater said he'd been mad. Berry was mad, or near enough to it. Poor Pepper, Leady, Wilkinson! Wilky were a scared 'un; a good 'un, but a scared 'un; Wilky could have just about died o' fright. He wondered how he did die. Perhaps, after all, poor bloody Powell had the best of it; at least he'd died naturally.

When Barber heard a twig snap at the top of the beach he turned about, thinking that Slater must have changed his mind, because the two hours were nowhere near gone. But he couldn't see him; he saw nothing but the darkness of the brush above the sand. He leaned forward, peering.

He looked down at the canoe. Jeremy was there, ramming charge or wad or ball into a musket. And so was the girl there, standing now.

Puzzled, Barber faced back quickly and saw someone moving stealthily down towards them. He drew his legs under him, feeling for his pistol. Somehow it didn't seem like an Indian. It wasn't Slater; he wouldn't come that way. It was not big enough for Doyle; God, if it had been, what a chance! But nay, Doyle wouldn't come that way either.

Barber scrambled to his feet. There was something familiar about it. Aye, be thunder, could it be Berry? He peered into the shadow, but he could not be sure.

"Who goes?" Barber cried suddenly. "Is that ye, Cap'n Berry? 'Tis Barber here, Sir." Uncertain, he drew his pistol and stood leaning forward with the weapon hanging by his side. There was no answer, nor any movement. "Here," he said, "if that's ye, Cap'n Berry, ye'd best speak up, if ye don't want a ball in ye."

Now there was a grunt, almost a chuckle, and the figure started down towards Barber once more. By the sound and by the walk, Barber knew it was Berry. In each hand he held a pistol. The captain's face was a long, bony mask, cut and bruised and sunburned. His shirt was in tatters and his torn trousers fluttered about his skinny legs. It was an animated skeleton of a man. He laughed, still moving down but weaving from side to side and starting to chatter, still with the pistols up-raised, and peering at Barber as though never in his life had he seen another man. Barber stared back, horrified at the sight of him and struck with pity for him.

Barber was hurrying to him when Berry stopped weaving and fired. Barber had virtually no warning; he threw himself forward and was moving when the ball thudded into his left shoulder, spinning him about. He went down. There was no pain, just the numbing impact and a feeling of helplessness in his arm. He felt sand against his face, in his mouth and between his fingers as he pulled himself up. He had his pistol cocked; Berry was clear against the star-studded sky, filling the space over and beyond the pistol when he pulled the trigger. It did not fire.

Jeremy hadn't heard Barber's call to Berry. When the shot sounded he jumped to his feet and looked up the beach, but he could see nothing. Alarmed, he picked up one of the loaded muskets. Then he saw that Seyawa was not where she had been; at the sound of the shot, she had run to the canoe and now stood by it, in the water to her thighs. Jeremy, thinking of the safety of the canoe, ran towards it, almost reaching it before he saw her and saw she was pointing back up the beach. Suddenly fear for Barber gripped him. As fast as he could he started up the beach again. "Sam," he called. "Sam, where are ye?"

Berry heard him and turned from Barber; he saw Jeremy clearly silhouetted against the silvery sea. Barber raised himself partly and forced himself about, feeling pain now and a wetness of blood down his side. "Back, lad!" he shouted. "Back wi' ye, Jeremy. To the canoe!"

Jeremy must have heard part of what Barber said and, hearing it, may have slowed, making himself a better target; but the last of Barber's cry was drowned by the crash of Berry's other pistol. The ball struck the boy in the chest. He pitched forward over his musket, arms flailing, legs moving.

With a terrible cry Barber staggered to his feet and with all his strength hurled his pistol; it hit Berry in the face. There was no pain in Barber now; frenzied, sobbing in his rage, he clawed out at Berry, who fell back, dropping his pistols. Barber reached him and struck, his blow snapping back the old man's head. Blood sticky under his arm, Barber drove his fist hard into Berry's abdomen; a sound, half groan and half shriek, broke from the captain and he fell forward on to Barber, who with terrible deliberation set him up, waited for the precise instant and struck again. He felt the old face smash under his hand. But his frenzy was not yet spent; he grabbed, held him and struck again. As Berry fell away there was death in the wide, staring eyes and the grotesque, hanging, broken jaw.

Staggering from the fallen man, Barber dropped to his knees beside Jeremy and saw the boy was dead. For minutes he knelt there, holding the boy and looking incredulously into the pale face. Then, letting him down, he went back to Berry and rolling him over put his ear to his chest. He heard nothing.

He stood, his fingers feeling at the wound in his shoulder. He pulled at his shirt and a piece of it came out of the wound. His arm was numb and he could feel blood down his side as far as his wrist. There stole into him an overwhelming longing for Slater; loneliness enveloped him. Wrung with anguish he looked from the body of the boy to the body of the man. Then he had survived for this—to lose the boy and kill his captain? A moment longer he stood, then bending, muttering to himself, he picked Berry up as gently as he could and started down to the canoe with him, his shoulder thudding with pain.

He had almost reached it when he stopped, realising he had heard a shot. He turned and looked back up the hill, as if expecting to see something; then he went on and reaching the water waded out to the canoe. Seyawa, terrified at the sight of the bloodied, open face of the captain, watched Barber put Berry on the sail, face down, spreading the arms and legs so that the body would not roll off. He started back for Jeremy's body, but before he had gone a canoe's length he slowed and stood, looking up the hill.

It was not something reasoned; it was an instinctive reaction. Barber stopped because he realised the canoe was their link with life. It must be protected. He turned and made his way back to it. He was in the water before he remembered the muskets; they were almost as much a part of the pattern as the canoe. He went up to them and bundling them in his arms, his shoulder stabbing with pain, brought them to the canoe and put them near Berry. As he turned to Seyawa, she guessed his intention and went to slip past him. He grabbed her. "Back wi' ye!" he barked, and he pointed up the hill, trying to make her see that Slater would come. All she saw was his tormented face, his wild eyes and tousled hair and drooping, bleeding shoulder. But she felt his strength and feared it, and as he gazed at her, gripping her arm in his good hand, she somehow realised that he was not abandoning Slater.

She nodded. For a moment he continued to hold her, then he let his hand fall and waded forward, feeling out along the cable for the anchor stone. He got it, the water drenching him to the neck, and lifted it into the canoe. Then, working aft, he stood at the after outrigger strut and called to her.

Luck was with Barber; he should not have got the canoe out, but he did. One sea, that might have turned it beam on, flattened and ran under, lifting it high and drenching them, but somehow they held it. Then came their moment, a sweep of clear water and the returning surge of the wave which had passed under them. He shouted; she saw his meaning and rolled in over the gunwale. She grabbed for a paddle and as the canoe went from him Barber swung his body up.

They were clear, the broken water astern of them. Three cables out he turned the canoe and they sat, watching the shore. Barber cursed the pain in his shoulder and realised that the ball must still be in him.

Chapter 28

As Slater looked up from Jeremy's body and stood gazing along the beach, seeing the canoe gone from it, a cloud, long and thin, like the hull of a twisted canoe, slid across the disc of the moon. That Barber was no longer there meant nothing; he saw clearly only the death of Jeremy, an envelopment of his world. Some part of him died.

He dropped to the boy's side again, lifted his head and saw that a spatter of sand was stuck on one of the eyes. Cupping the head in his left hand, he closed the eyes with his right, holding his thumb and forefinger on the eyelids. He looked at Jeremy's breast; the bleeding had been violent and sudden, the heart had been penetrated and the sand about was marked with much blood. He clutched the boy to him and pressed his face up against his own. A tiny last rush of air came from Jeremy's mouth, startling Slater.

He laid him back on the sand and felt under him for the boy's knife. It was still there and he undid the belt gently and slid off the sheath. Then he buckled the belt and slipped the knife inside his shirt. Barely conscious of what he was doing he walked away from the body and by accident came to the place where Barber and Berry had fought. He saw more blood and followed the footprints, and they brought him back to Jeremy.

From the lagoon came the report of a musket. Slater turned towards it, went down the beach and stood at the water's edge. Barber saw him and called. Slater did not answer, but Barber murmured to the girl and together they paddled the canoe in. Slater helped them beach it and Barber waded out on to the beach, his shoulder sagging and the water streaming from his legs.

"Ye saw the boy?"

"Aye." Slater answered. Then he saw the body of the captain on the canoe.

"He did it," said Barber. "The boy went tryin' to help me. If ye'd seen him"—he nodded his head in the direction of Berry—"ye'd have known he were mad. I had to kill him. God forgive me, but I had to."

Slater went into the water and looked at Berry. This was a different grief, a softer thing; carrying over into his loss of Jeremy it somehow calmed him rather than added to his distraction. Vaguely he felt the desire to know how it had happened, but it did not last and he turned back, on to the beach. Barber waded in and lifted Berry, Slater took up Jeremy, and they carried the bodies into the scrub.

They dug a hole with their hands; it was a shallow grave but wide enough to lay them side by side. Barber had sent the first scatter of sand down over them when Slater said: "Wait a moment, Barber."

"The prayer?" asked Barber, looking up.

"Do ye remember any of it?"

"A word here an' there, no more."

"Then say 'em, for we'll not go for the book."

Barber bowed his head. Slater listened to the mumbled words. Barber said the Lord's Prayer, and Slater joined him.

Then Slater felt for his knife and drew it from its sheath, remembering how Jeremy had loved to sharpen it.

"I'll swap wi' ye, Jeremy," he said softly, and he knelt, reached into the hole and laid the knife on Jeremy's bloodied chest. Then he took Jeremy's knife from his shirt, drew it from its sheath and slipped it into his own. The sheath he held in his hand. "Ye made this?" he said, looking at Barber.

"Aye, I did. Give it me." Barber got down and put it on Berry's breast.

Slater said: "We'll fill it in," and they worked quickly, setting the thinly grassed turves back on the top, leaving a mound which would settle.

As they came down the beach the moon slid from behind a cloud. Slater looked up. " 'Twill be clear for the pass," said Barber as he waded in to feel out along the anchor cable.

They reached the pass in the first light of the day. The pass was narrow, as Seyawa had said it would be, and the seas that thundered about it were steep, grey-white in the early light. It was a frightening thing to see: the heaping of the water and the swirling currents.

Slater was cold now, dry-cold, deep inside; and he was oppressed by hunger and exhaustion—hunger for what he had lost, exhaustion of the spirit, of the heart as well as the body. As the canoe met the first seas it quivered like a live thing and came to a momentary, sickening halt before plunging down and on. Slater was stern and as he dug his paddle into the water, as the bow of the canoe went to sheer away, as he realised the effort it would take, his spirit quailed; he saw in one awful glimpse all that lay ahead, all that had been and all that was gone. His paddle came up and stayed there. He saw Barber's paddle dig again, and Seyawa's, saw them as if from a distance and with a disinterested awareness of something which no longer touched him.

He missed four of those desperate strokes. He saw the wonder in the girl, saw it in her wild yet powerful stroking, saw it in the further hunching of her body. Barber stroked on, magnificently unaware of Slater's withdrawal; but Slater realised that Seyawa knew, that she, with the feel of the canoe as part of her body, knew he was not paddling.

Pride rose above his defeat and despair; he shouted, saw Barber half turn, dig deep with his paddle into the crested grey water. The stern of the canoe settled and when it rose again they were committed. Now there could be no turning back; it was through the pass or perish in it. The outrigger buried itself all but to the deck above it. The noise of the water and the rush of the wind filled their ears.

Then Seyawa stopped paddling and went for the baler. Barber's shoulder beat with the pain; the wound worked and blood ran from it. Slater heard him groan and curse. Half-way through, Barber missed a stroke and for a terrible moment the canoe began to slew, until Barber's paddle plucked the bow about and it ran straight again.

For five cable lengths they drove the canoe before they rested, rising and falling upon the seas sweeping to the pass. Then Seyawa lifted her paddle and pointed out over Barber's head.

"West nor'west," said Slater, just loud enough for Barber to hear. Barber grunted, his paddle went over and Slater and the girl took the stroke from him.

Chapter 29

THERE was no wind at first. At the sky's edge, where it rested on the sea, was the great bank of pale-grey cloud. Above this was a sky of incredible blue, touched here and there by a trace of cloud, rose-coloured and tawny. In the east, almost over the place where the limb of the sun would soon show through, was a star glowing yellow-red. Even the moon, nearly full and almost overhead, was only half as bright as the star.

Now that they were away from the island, the canoe seemed smaller than it had in the lagoon, and closer to the water, so close that as the seas ran by them sometimes the lower hand on the paddle shaft was in the water. Seyawa baled, but still there was water running fore and aft about their feet with the movement of the canoe. Slater saw the struts of the outrigger working as the canoe weaved, saw the pieces that would rub under their hibiscus bindings and chafe at them. Once, soon after they made away, Barber looked back at the sail-covered deck and at the stain where Berry had lain. Slater watched him and saw the haggard face, eyes screwed tight against the beginning glare that came from the sky and against the heaving sea.

Slowly the island began to lose detail. About two hours out, Slater called a rest and they turned and looked at the island; it was still green, but distance was beginning to give it the blue that would turn to grey-blue before it vanished among the horizontal clouds.

Before they started again Barber put his paddle down between his legs and pulled his shirt over his head. He sat looking at it, his great shoulders curved. Slater saw a bruise which spread below his shoulder, and under the arm dry blood. Barber turned the shirt in his hands, drew his knife (a little rust on it now) and cut out a piece of the tail. After trailing it in the water, he swabbed his wound with it. Next, he filled the baler over the side and poured sea water over the wound. Then he got back into his shirt, took his paddle and started again.

It was nearly half-way through the morning before the wind came. As soon as she felt it, Seyawa looked back to Slater and pointed to the sail. He nodded and she put down her paddle and began to disentangle the rigging. Strange to Slater and Barber, the rig of the canoe confused them at first, and had they attempted to make sail themselves they might have lost the craft. But once set and drawing, it drove them far faster than they could paddle. Now there was but steering and seeing to the set of the sail. Slater steered and Seyawa watched the sheet.

When they stopped paddling the sun seemed even hotter. But the wind was south-easterly—the trade wind of these islands—and the canoe went well before it. Slater knew the craft could not be tacked, for to tack they would have to wear the canoe around; but with the course they would be making if the wind continued to blow from its usual quarter little manœuvring would be necessary. To Slater and Barber the canoe had seemed unstable and for those first hours they felt her every roll, every deep dipping of the outrigger. But gradually they grew confident as they became used to her motion: the water creaming to the deck above the float and then the canoe steadying, the tip of her long, decked stern under water and the steering paddle buried to the thin of the shank, her lift and roll to leeward, the water swirling and bubbling along the gunwale's edge, her bow dipping again and the stern rising to carry Slater high above Barber's hunched shoulders.

It was not easy to steer her under sail; Slater found that save for what leverage he got with the paddle shaft on the gunwale his arms must do all the work. Soon his hands ached with the twisting motion of the paddle, his arms with the slicing effect of the blade. He thought of binding the paddle in some way, but there was nothing on the canoe to which he could lash the shaft. He must bear it.

And as he worked, riding the craft from his hips, the desire to know how Jeremy, and Berry, had died returned to him, stronger now. "Barber," he said suddenly, almost unconsciously, "how did the boy go?"

Resting the weight of his left arm in his right hand and staring ahead, Barber told him.

". . . I called to him, Sir, shouted to him to go back, but Berry had seen him. An' he were a good shot wi' a pistol, too good a shot."

And after minutes the question came from Barber: "Ye believe me?" But Slater did not answer.

"She might o' seen it. Or some of it," Barber added.

"Aye, but I can't ask her."

"Nay, ye can't. But that were the way of it."

"Barber?"

"Aye?"

" 'Tis in m'heart to doubt ye."

"Ye doubted the girl." Then after a pause. "Ye could doubt me too. I've thought of it."

"What have ye thought?"

"This—that if ye do, ye've to out wi' it, an' let me leave ye."

"Leave?"

"Aye. 'Twould be best, for if ye doubt 'twill grow to belief. 'Twill end in a killin'."

It was now late in the afternoon and Seyawa, who had been staring out over the starboard bow, glanced round at Slater and pointed. He looked, and saw land, and leaning on the paddle started to bear towards it. She waited until she saw it was no yaw of the craft that had altered its heading and then, swivelling about, spoke to him, shaking her head. Barber turned and watched, his eyes dead-looking in his great head, his beard pressed back against his throat by the wind.

Barber saw what she meant, and Slater even understood some of the words she used. There were no people on the island, but it would be the place Awila would search first. She called the island Aiwa.

As Slater steadied on the old course, Barber said: "Aye, best leave her to do the thinkin'." Slater said nothing, curiously disinterested in their fate, where they landed or what happened to them. But Barber felt an equally curious confidence of success, though his wound throbbed steadily and he could not shake from his mind the sight of Jeremy and Berry lying in the grave.

They saw Aiwa as two islands, thrusting up out of reef, a gloomy place of cliffs and bluffs that dropped into a lagoon. There were no beaches, nor any trees that they could see, just low scrub. Seafowl hunted the shallows and dived at the water. They saw herons too, slowly flapping over the lagoon. And as this first day ended they saw another, larger island, which no sooner loomed out of the dusk than it vanished and night was upon them. Seyawa pointed another course now and they sailed north-west.

With the darkness the wind fell. They took down the sail and as the cool of the night touched them they knew what the sun had done to them. Their skin felt as though it would crack, and the cuts and insect stings from Oneata opened. Barber's wound had stiffened and when he came to paddle again it bled and a faintness overcame him. Every stroke of the paddle now was a conscious stepping over the threshold of pain. He caught himself groaning and coughed, attempting to conceal his suffering, afraid that Slater might hear. He paddled, fought the weakness, and kept his agony from Slater.

With the coolness of the evening, so came the desire to relieve themselves. Barber stopped paddling and looked aft to Slater and spoke of his wish. Slater glanced at Seyawa and seated between them she looked from one to the other.

"If she'd turn away, Sir," said Barber quietly.

"I can't tell her. I know but few words, Barber."

But she saw their need and with the faintest of smiles, with a motion that was scarcely felt in the movement of the canoe she slipped overboard.

"Ahhh," grunted Barber approvingly, and turned forward once again.

It was nearly fifteen minutes before she returned to the canoe. By this time it was fully dark. It was harder for her to regain the craft than it had been to leave it, but both men helped her and as Barber leaned back Slater saw that the wound in his shoulder was running blood down his shirt.

"The ball's still in ye, Barber?" Slater said when Seyawa was aboard and they were paddling again.

"It is."

" 'Twill have to come out."

"Aye, when we get ashore somewhere."

For much of that night they paddled; several times they rested and sipped water. Slater kept his course by the stars, and when the first of the day came it brought wind which drove them steadily. Seyawa tried to tell them of the island they had seen at dusk and which now lay grey and faint astern of them, set against the eastern limits of their world. It was the island of Lakeba, bigger than either Oneata or Aiwa, and there were many people on it. It was the home of the Tui Nayau, the great chief of all these small islands. Seyawa blessed the wind that drove them from it; several times she looked astern, searching for sign of a sail, for she knew what their fate would be once one of the swift raiding canoes of the Tui Nayau sighted them.

That day Slater and Barber realised that Seyawa's skills in handling and piloting the canoe were no ordinary ones. They did not know that hers was a heritage of the sea and its vessels rather than of the land; that she came from a canoe-building tribe and had grown up listening to tales of canoes and their voyages, had travelled much with her father and his brothers and others of her *mataqali* to islands where trees grew clean and high, ready for the adzes and the hollowing fires. They could not know this, but, seamen themselves, they could recognise the art in another; twice that day she saw before either of them the sign that a breeze was coming and had the sail hoisted, and once lowered when neither Barber nor Slater had seen the shape of a wind which might have knocked them down, undercrewed and weakened as they were.

They ate three times that day—first a few mouthfuls of the pork and biscuit, at midday some of the food Seyawa had brought, then as the wind fell at dusk some more of the ship's stores. The sun scorched them, for the shelter from the sail was negligible. Their feet, continually wet, began to soften and

Slater noticed that the skin between his toes and fingers was flaking away and wet, and that the cuts and scratches about his ankles were beginning to fester. Just before dark they ran upon a coconut. Seyawa grabbed it and opened it with Barber's knife. They had plenty of water aboard, but it was warm and flat-tasting; that of the nut was sweet and cool.

It was while they were drinking this water that Barber thought he saw land, a faint mass, bearing north by west. He turned aft, pointing to it. Seyawa nodded her head and stood, clearly not surprised; Slater bore more west to clear it; the wind held and they sailed through a beam sea which wore at them, slopping water over the gunwale, necessitating almost continuous baling.

There was still a full hour to midnight, the canoe was going well through the water under a cloudy sky, when they saw a budding of orange fires ahead of them, as though they had been suddenly uncovered by some neck of land. Barber called out and Seyawa, full of fear, stood, riding the pitch and roll of the canoe easily.

" 'Tis a current," said Slater, "settin' us in to that island." Barber and Seyawa saw that he was making no attempt to alter course. Seyawa turned about to him pointing away from the island. He did not understand all of what she said but her meaning was clear enough.

"She's tryin' to warn us," said Barber. " 'Tis dangerous." Then a little later he added: "There's people. Eh?" and he looked aft, puzzled why Slater should continue on the course. "I'd make away, Sir. We'd best paddle, help ye get around." As he said this he moved for his paddle.

"Leave it, Barber," Slater said quickly, a grimness in his voice that startled Barber and which did not pass unobserved by Seyawa. "We'll go in."

"Ye mean land there?" Barber asked. "Touch upon the place?" He could not keep the astonishment from his voice.

But Slater did not answer him; for a moment longer Barber looked at him crouched over the steering paddle, then turned forward again, puzzled and distressed. Seyawa saw what she took to be anger in Slater and feared it even more than she did the island he had decided to land upon.

Yet had he tried to explain why he wanted to go in he would not have been able to, except for this—all but unrecognised by him, his doubts of Barber had grown. Why land? How could that help? He did not know, nor was it clear to him yet what he should do there; but this he knew: he was going in.

He felt the cracks in his skin run blood and was aware of a confusion in his vision and an aching of his body. He leaned forward, keeping his eye on those tiny blossoms of fire, seeing them double, struggling to find the wells of strength into which he could dip to keep the canoe sliding across the current. After an hour he felt the tide slacking and eased a little on the helm. The wind held well and the moon remained clouded. The canoe ran on and the fires grew bigger. And as his desire to touch the island deepened so did that of Barber and Seyawa diminish.

Barber sat feeling his shoulder tight and thudding with pain as the canoe rolled. This, he knew, was madness. They would die. An explosion of surf, of twisting, wrenched-apart canoe, and they would be in the water, sucked at by the rolling waves and hurled against the reef. Barber felt his spirit falling. This was the end, the deliberate throwing-away of their lives against the outliers of this looming steep-to land. Soon there was light enough from the stars and the moon to see the island of precipitous cliffs, table-topped, high and lonely, except where the beads of fire strung a tiny necklace against its sombre darkness. Almost directly above it streamed the comet.

To Barber and Seyawa, it almost seemed that Slater knew the way into the island. As they came under its lee the sea fell, so that they no longer had to bale, yet still they kept enough wind to make paddling unnecessary. Sheer good fortune pointed the way. Barber sat, prepared for his end, and watched the canoe head into water which led to reef flats and then, miraculously, to a pass. In the pass there was little more than a short, sloppy sea, and into it Slater put the canoe, as some pilot might who knew every fathom of the water. Barber cursed silently in his amazement; it was as though the devil himself were at the helm. To Seyawa it was another sign that these were more than men, that part of them were of the gods. When the wind fell off she tumbled the sail, mast and all, on to the canvas-covered heap of gear on the outrigger platform and they began to paddle.

Only then did Slater look at her. Leaning forward he touched her; she saw the query in his face and pointed to port. As far out from the shore as possible she guided the canoe. Soon the fires were lost to sight round the curve of land, and they put in to a shallow beach under beetling cliffs. Nearly sobbing with the pain in his shoulder Barber pulled the head of the canoe about and they ran over eerie starlit shadows, between coral heads which glowed with dark fire.

Barber took the anchor stone up the beach, dropped it and turned to watch Slater and Seyawa as they left the water. To Seyawa this was the rankest folly; great was the distance they must travel before they would be safe from Awila's reach. All Barber could think was that Slater had put in here to take the ball from his shoulder. Walking up the beach Slater stumbled; he did not see Barber against the darkness of the cliff. Barber called; slowly Slater came up to him.

"We'll go along a bit, Barber," Slater said.

Barber's face was heavy in shadow and his huge bulk leaned as he held his left arm; his eyes and mouth were twisted by the pain that racked him as he moved.

When they were out of sight of the girl Slater stopped. Barber looked at him, waiting for him to speak. But Slater said nothing. "Aye, Mr. Slater, what was it ye be wantin'?" Barber said, his mouth barely moving in the bush of his beard.

To Slater, Barber seemed to sway. "Don't go, Barber."

Barber had made no move. "I'll not, Sir," he returned softly. His shoulder throbbed and he lifted his arm, trying to ease it.

"Barber, ye killed the boy, didn't ye?"

There, thought Slater, it was out; he'd said what he hadn't even faced thinking. He looked at Barber steadily.

"Nay, Sir. I killed Cap'n Berry because he were mad—God forgive me—but not the boy."

"I said I could doubt ye, Barber."

"Aye, an' I said if ye did ye was to out wi' it, and I'd leave ye."

Slater felt a detachment, as though his brain was floating

about in his skull. Somewhere it touched Doyle, something Doyle had said. He looked from Barber, trying to remember.

"Ye'd best leave me here," Barber was saying. But Slater wasn't listening because he was remembering what it was Doyle had told him.

"Barber, did ye know Doyle found the longboat?"

Barber wondered whether Slater's mind was wandering.

"He found the longboat?" he said after a moment.

"Aye. An' somethin' else: how many muskets should he have had?"

"There were his own," said Barber slowly, "what he went with, an' the two he got from Jeb. Aye, that were all, three, an' a pair o' pistols."

"He had four."

"Then," said Barber suddenly, "he had the cap'n's musket. Must have. The cap'n had but pistols when—when he come on to the beach. That also I'd swear to. How come he got the boat?"

"I don't know."

Barber paused, wondering what to make of it all. "Ye've not told me what happened on the hill," he said. "I heard a shot. I take it then ye ran into Doyle an' killed him."

"Nay. I ran into him, but I didn't kill him."

"An' he told ye he had the boat?"

"He did."

"Did it seem like he was tellin' the truth?"

"It did."

"Ye're sure ye didn't kill Doyle?"

" 'Twas not me who fired. 'Twas him, at me. The ball went under m'arm."

"Ye can thank God it did," said Barber bitterly. "I wish to Christ Berry's had gone under my arm. Or," he added more quietly, "been a bit more where it was meant an' killed me clean, as clean as the next one did the boy."

Slater threw himself at Barber. Grasping him by the shoulders he held him, staring up into his face as Barber, taken utterly by surprise, kicked back. But Slater held him, sending waves of pain through his shoulder. "Barber"—he was all but shrieking—"tell me, did ye kill the boy?"

"Nay, I didn't. On m'oath, I didn't."

"God, Barber, if I thought ye'd killed him——"

"Ye'd kill me. I know it. But I didn't. I killed Berry. Aye, but not the boy. Jesus, Mr. Slater, ye remember Berry were always one with a pistol, or a musket. Ye saw him hit that bird on the little island? Ye know how he could shoot. I seen him take two Indians, one with each pistol, an' one o' them fourteen, fifteen fathoms off, maybe more."

"Ye can shoot too, Barber."

"Aye, so I can. But m'pistols were damp. Wet as a bilge. I told ye how I killed Berry, wi' m'hands."

Barber did not flinch under Slater's steady gaze, though in his anguish Slater was pulling hard at his shoulder, which began now to bleed so that he felt the blood warm down his side once more. He saw Slater's grief, but Slater did not have a monopoly of grief. He had seen the boy die: he had been there and hadn't prevented it; and had killed his captain. He, too, had his share of grief, and remorse.

Slater let his hands fall by his side. He felt his legs trembling, his body weakened, but he was calmer, purged of his frenzy, as though it had been some cathartic.

As they reached the canoe Seyawa came running, in her arms a bundle of leaves. Dropping them into the canoe, she pointed back up the cliffs, calling to Slater something about men. That she had run some distance was obvious, for the words jumped from her and her breasts heaved.

"We've been seen," said Slater. "Come on." He turned to the anchor vine, following it up the beach.

Barber did not move, but watched him, and when Slater came down with the anchor Seyawa was starting to push the canoe out over the coral flats.

Barber was not a profound man, nor was he used to thinking long about anything. Watching them, he soon made up his mind. He would see them out until the canoe was afloat, then take a pair of muskets (he had his pistols), a powder flask and some bullets, and when Slater got aboard push the canoe clear and go back. It was not a matter of sulking; but Slater had doubted him, he would do as he'd said and leave them.

"For God's sake, Barber, hurry," Slater growled. "We've been seen."

Barber waded in and put his weight behind the outrigger strut.

The flats over which they pushed the canoe were creased with gutters and pools of deeper water. Behind and beside the canoe they picked their way through the shallows, avoiding the deeper places, some of which Seyawa knew would be over her head. They were within a canoe's length of where they would be able to climb aboard when Slater fell.

Several times both he and Barber had felt loose coral crunch under their feet; once Barber went through as far as his ankle, and the sharp coral sliced at his sea boots. Slater was to starboard of the canoe and got some warning that he was on soft ground. On his immediate right was a deep pool, and he stopped to let the canoe pass him before he sought the harder surface over which its hull and outrigger were passing. He did not know he was on a ledge.

His right foot went suddenly, tearing through the coral. He gave a shout and grabbed wildly for the gunwale of the canoe, but missed it. He saw moonlit water streak before his eyes and then felt it close over his head, filling his mouth and nostrils. He kicked out and felt the sandy bottom of the pool, then pain ripped into his leg and thigh as a hideous, muscular, twisting body slid against him, rolled him over and thrust him down against the bottom.

He felt Barber pulling at him, hauling him into the air and setting him against the canoe while Seyawa held it, and manœuvring him into it. He was conscious of coughing and then vomiting water and of the dry saltiness in his throat as he gasped for air. He saw Barber, pressed back against the canoe, waist-deep in the water, and heard him shout something about an eel. It was as thick through as a man's thigh and six feet long; it slithered, sinuously twisting, up into the shallows, made its way partly out of water to another pool, and disappeared with a rolling of the water and a streaking of light as fish shot away from it.

Barber looked at Slater's leg. The trouser leg was shredded; under the cloth were strips of flesh hanging, almost detached.

"Up, girl," he growled. She understood, and while he held the canoe she went forward and climbed in. For a second he hesitated, looking at Slater slumped over the starboard gunwale; then, cursing the pain in his shoulder, he hauled himself up into Slater's place in the stern.

Chapter 30

IT was long after midnight when Barber ordered Seyawa to drop the sail. He helped her, leaning forward over Slater. The moon was setting, but the sky was nearly cloudless. The canoe rode easily on a long swell from the east.

By chance Barber had placed Slater facing aft. Slater was conscious enough but badly shocked, and he had lost a lot of blood. Gently Barber examined him. The eel had struck more than once, its long teeth puncturing and lacerating the flesh rather than removing it, as a shark would have done. Seyawa's distress at his injury was acute; several times she said the name she knew the creature by—*dabea*, she called it.

The leaves she had brought were for Barber's wound. She showed him this by pointing to them, then to his shoulder. In the same way she indicated that they should dress Slater's leg with some of them.

The movement of getting the leaves roused Slater and he asked Barber why the canoe was stopped. " 'Tis to see to y'leg," Barber told him. " 'Tis bleedin' still, an' ye'll be weakened bad if ye lose much more blood."

Carefully Barber slit the trouser leg while Seyawa plucked the leaves from the branches and, crushing them between her hands, kneaded them into a thick wad. Barber then poured water from the baler over the wound and packed the leaves against it. For a bandage he cut a strip of sailcloth from the pocket they'd worked in the sail.

When Seyawa wanted to treat his shoulder in the same way he would not let her, for he was afraid of encouraging any healing while the ball was in him. Until it had been removed he knew his chances of recovery were slight. He now began to notice a different character in the pain; now it was more of a throb, and he knew that if he was to recover the ball must be taken from him soon. He wondered, could Seyawa do it? Could he get the forceps and show her how they could grasp an object, show her a musket ball—aye, that'd be clear enough—and ask her to probe for it? But she was forward of Slater; too far forward. Could she move aft? Could Slater be shifted forward and she take his place? Nay, too risky, with the swell that was on. It'd have to wait for Slater.

Once or twice Slater opened his eyes, saw the curve of the matting sail above him and then lapsed back, feeling the sides of the canoe confining him, pressing his arms against him. He heard Barber's voice, saying something to himself about a star.

Barber talking to himself, looking for a star, cursing quietly . . .

"Barber"—he struggled up, gripping the gunwales each side of him, trying to rid himself of the coffin-like hull that was wrapped about him—"Barber. Say it, man, ye didn't kill the boy, did ye?" His eyes were pleading with Barber to say he had not.

"Nay, I killed the cap'n."

"He were mad, ye say?"

"He were. I had to. 'Fore God, I did."

"He shot the boy?"

"When the boy come to help me. By the Christ, Sir, can't ye see I'm tellin' ye the truth?"

"Aye, I believe ye. 'Tis gone from me now." His leg hurt, and his blistered skin where it had rubbed against the wood of the canoe, but his mind was clear now and he knew again that up-surge of life.

"Ye'll mind y'leg. 'Twas an eel that bit ye."

"Aye, I mind it all now. An' ye talkin'."

Barber grinned. "I was lookin' for a star, the star ye've been usin'."

"Mostly, Sam, I went be the wind, where there was any."

"Ah, she be a witch to steer."

"Aye, but ye'll get used to it."

"Out to port here, there's the Southern Cross," said Barber, pointing with his head. "She's got a name for it."

Slater looked at Seyawa. *Kalokalo* he knew was the word for star, and he said it, pointing to the constellation.

"*Io,*" she said, seeing his meaning. "*Na ga.*"

"That's it," put in Barber, "*na ga.*"

"*Ga,*" said Slater, "is, I think, a bird of some sort."

"Could be," said Barber. "I suppose it does look at bit like a bird, with its wings stretched out."

"'Tis good, eh?"

"Very good."

When dawn came Slater saw that Barber's condition was much worse. Barber had fallen asleep, and when Slater woke and saw his hanging head, his tangled hair and beard, the great circles under his eyes, he cursed himself for not having taken the ball from him sooner. He would have to do it now, in the canoe. While Barber slept he eased himself around until he could loosen some of the forward lashings and get at the little chest in which were packed the few surgical instruments they had and the last of the drugs. He took a probe and the forceps and the flask of brandy; then, when turning back, had to rest, for the stiffness and pain in his leg nearly overcame him. Seyawa watched him, suffering with him, and she helped him, holding his shoulders and trying to keep the weight from bearing on his injured leg.

"Sam," he called, gently plucking at Barber's good arm.

Barber stirred, opened his eyes and saw him. "Aye," he grunted, and he hauled himself straight and went automatically for the paddle, murmuring something about being forgiven for falling asleep.

"Nay, 'tis not that, lad. Stay where ye are. But I'm goin' to have a go at y'shoulder."

"Ah. 'Tis the very devil. The girl's got leaves," he added weakly, closing his eyes.

"Take a swig o' this," said Slater, holding the flask out to him.

Barber opened his eyes. "What is it?"

"Never mind what it is, just drink it. Ye'll know soon enough, ye lucky bugger." Slater grinned a little and got in return the faintest smile.

Barber took the flask. " 'Tis the brandy," he said.

"Aye."

"I'll not take it."

"The hell ye won't. If I say so 'tis an order."

" 'Tis all we got, Sir. Nay, we may be needin' it worse later on. An' what about yeself?"

"Barber, ye've to drink it, a good slug."

"But, Sir——"

"D'ye realise, man, how 'twill hurt, diggin' for that pistol ball?"

"More than it did goin' in, I'll be bound."

"Then drink it an' let me get on wi' it. Otherwise Seyawa here'll think ye be funkin' it." Barber growled, and putting up the flask drank a few mouthfuls. "More, Sam. Down wi' it, a good swill." Then he took the probe. Barber watched it come, sweat beginning to form on his forehead, about his temple. "Put y'head back, Sam, lay it on y'other shoulder."

Hard enough to accomplish on land, it was much more difficult in the canoe. And the ball was deeper than either of them had thought it would be. He had to pick about for it, Barber clutching the strut before him, the sweat running on his haggard, sunburned face and seeping into his eyes and his beard. His lips were pale and drawn into a thin line.

"God, Barber, but I'm sorry to have to do this to ye."

"Keep goin'. Ye've touched it yet?"

"Nay." Slater felt deeper. The wound was festering now, and thin pus ran from it. He located the ball and, taking up the forceps, reached in for it; he got the forceps open over the ball, but when he tried to withdraw it he lost it. He opened them over it three times before he got it. He held the ball up for Barber to see, then dropped it down between his legs to the bottom of the canoe and felt into the wound again. He found a piece of Barber's shirt and some of the wadding.

He gave him some more of the brandy and Seyawa kneaded the leaves as she had done for Slater. They were the leaves of

222

the *meme* shrub, she told him, and with much nodding of her head she assured him they would heal their wounds. He did not understand all of what she said, but noticed that he was more quickly getting the sense of her sentences.

"Ye feelin' any better, Sam?"

"Aye, Sir, I am that, though I'd not go through it again, not for a pipe o' brandy would I."

"But 'tis easier?"

"Aye, thankee kindly, Sir."

"Thank me for nothin', Barber. Ye should be cursin' me for not doin' it for ye sooner. 'Twas me duty to."

That day, the fourth since leaving the island, the wind was not strong, but it drove them steadily under an azure-blue sky until about midday, when it fell and then shifted to a new quarter. Once again, had Seyawa not been with them, they would have lost the canoe. Neither Slater nor Barber had realised before this how important it was to keep the outrigger to windward. But once Seyawa saw the change in the wind she lost no time preparing to make the canoe ready for it.

The white men had seen the way sail was hoisted and the sheet held by a couple of turns about one of the deck beams, but what they did not fully understand was that the helm was used at either end of the canoe. Now Seyawa called to Barber to put the tiller up. He looked to Slater, for though by pointing she made it clear which way it should go, he could not but believe she must have meant to put it down. But she was adamant and made Slater see that this was done to keep the outrigger to windward.

The wind then was brought aft and Slater saw that Seyawa would now be helm. So the tack was passed from Barber to Seyawa; bow became stern, and the mast was slacked back to suit this alteration. Now Slater was sheet-holder and Seyawa did her best to explain to him that should a gust of wind come he must slack away promptly, otherwise the *cama*, the outrigger, would be lifted from the water and the canoe would turn turtle.

The wind held from this quarter until night fell with its welcome shade. To paddle now was beyond them; Seyawa was bearing it much better than the men, but to expect that she should paddle alone was out of the question. They ate some of the meat and biscuit, washing it down with water. Then, propping themselves as best they could to alleviate the strain and the rubbing of their bodies as the canoe rolled, they prepared to get what rest they could.

But when the morning of the fifth day dawned Slater knew they were well started on the way to death; he saw it in Barber's bloodied shirt, in his salt-encrusted beard and bright, red-rimmed eyes; he knew it in the pain and burning in his own eyes and the effort it took to do anything requiring any strength; he felt it in the rawness where his body chafed against the canoe and in the stings and cuts from Oneata that had grown to salt-encrusted sores. He knew it in the stiffness that was now beginning to claim his wounded leg, in the faint reek that came from under the bandage, in the monotonous scooping of the baler; he knew it every time the canoe drove deep into a swell and the seam of the top strake spurted water, and saw it in other seams that wept their silent trickle into the hollowed log that was bilge and keel.

They were making west-north-west now, with the wind steady from the south-east and sometimes freshening so that they had to drop sail and lie baling. On the night of the sixth day the wind did not die and they sailed on, getting some refreshment from the coolness and the fact that they were making knots towards land. What that land was, and whether they might ever find it, Slater had no idea. But that they were making for some definite place seemed evident by Seyawa's incessant attention to their course; she was continually alert, watching the stars, feeling the wind, seeing the sun go down and rise; even the shape of the waves seemed to tell her something, and more than once at the sight of a sea bird she stood and watched it, shading her eyes with her hand until it was out of sight.

When the next night came the wind still blew, but after they had eaten and had relieved themselves, Seyawa leaving the canoe as usual for some ten or fifteen minutes, they sat slumped in their places, fighting for rest and for the energy they would need with the day. Now Slater found himself wondering about their sail and rigging; in parts it was chafing badly. Each dawn now was a torment and they found themselves dreading it, sitting as defiant as they could to face the wearing hours which would follow it. No cloud gave them shelter from the sun, yet the horizon was ever clouded, a bank of shade which they sailed towards but never reached, which seemed to shift ever away from them.

The seventh morning was clouded and soon rain fell. At first it was welcome and they stripped and washed the salt from their skins, but heavier and heavier the rain fell until it came to pound on them, sloughing the crusts from the sores that had grown from their sun blisters. Water filled the canoe so that it lay lower, and in the flat grey sea of that day Slater saw that several of the lashings were strained and no longer held properly. All that day the rain hammered at them. They uttered barely a dozen words, for speech now was agony between lips that cracked and bled when they moved. Their wounds throbbed, the leaves over them were rotting and the sailcloth bandages were sodden. This was nightmare, and the plainest thing they saw was the certainty of death, almost with a longing for it.

Yet Seyawa continued to stand it well enough. For one thing, her pigmented skin was better able to bear the sun, even though she had no coconut oil to insulate her skin, nor any of the lotions her people made for use against the weathering of the open sea. Hers was as much an escape as Barber's or Slater's, but she had begun the voyage in better condition; she had no wound, nor any sores, her mosquito bites not having become infected as had the men's.

Daily Slater's love for her grew. More and more his hopes of rescue and return to the world he came from predicated Seyawa's being with him, so that he knew that if she was not to survive then he would not want life. And Barber saw her strength and her steadfastness, and saw that her love for Slater was deeper than mere physical desire.

Then out of the dawn of the eighth day came land.

The wind had blown steadily all through that night and they had kept on sailing. It was not part of a plan, but simply that when night fell and the wind continued it seemer easier to sail

225

on with it than to lower and stow the sail and rigging. Astern of them a long, phosphorescent wake trailed on the water; above were the comet and a brilliant scatter of stars; the sea was smooth and patchy with glowing mists that moved in the depths below the surface. That night there was not even the very limited oblivion they knew as sleep. The sea was so smooth, the wind so steady, the canoe went so well through the water that one by one they began to doubt. Suppose, said Slater to himself, that now they sailed not towards some island but, driven by this wind of the darkness, far beyond it. The canoe, Slater knew, would take them to nothing but their death if they missed the islands.

Barber, too, had these fears, and sat, hesitating to speak, staring ahead and wondering was there land astern of them. But came the first dawning of the day and hope flared anew in Barber. He turned to Slater and spoke of land and pointed over the starboard bow. When the day came clear it was land all right, an island misted in the early light.

This was more than island; it was high, beetling cliffs, tall trees, grassy slopes and the birds of land, a place of ferns and rain and streams, shade and shelter from the burning sun. They found a cove, a lonely place, save for the birds that cried above it, and there they beached the canoe. To stagger from it to the shade of a great *baka* tree was all they had strength for.

Chapter 31

THE island was Koro, and by good fortune they had come to one of its loneliest parts. They might have been less lucky. For Koro was densely populated—on its western side by native Fijians, and on its eastern by Tongan invaders. The two peoples were at war and bitter, bloody encounters were common, but the canoe had hit upon the lonely southern tip of the no-man's-land that ran north and south along the island.

They let themselves sink on to the soft grass. Automatically Seyawa set herself down near Slater. They looked at each other and she smiled. Above them the aerial roots of the tree waved gently. He felt a detached, floating sensation, and he fell asleep.

When he awoke Barber and Seyawa had gone. He stood, looking about, for a wild moment of panic, until he saw them at the canoe; they were hauling it higher up the beach. He limped down to them. There was a rocky cleft not far from where they had landed, and he suggested that they float the canoe into it; the tide was high enough. Then they gathered fronds to cover it, to hide it from the eyes of any craft that might pass along the shore.

They brought some of the gear up and made camp in the valley that stood behind the big *baka* tree. In the next valley, beyond a wooded rise, there was a stream which ran clear and cold. Seyawa went to it and brought back water in *Argo*'s iron pot and Slater lit a fire by emptying a little gunpowder on to the ground and igniting it with his flint and steel. While Seyawa gathered sticks for the fire, Barber got out some of the salt meat and biscuit, put it in the pot and made a sort of stew. Before noon they ate, sitting in the shade under the trees.

For the rest of that day, Slater said, they must sleep. Their sleep carried on into the night and through it. When the men woke at dawn next morning Seyawa had already gone out in search of leaves for their wounds. That morning they stripped their bandages and bathed their wounds in warm salt water. Slater was astonished at the healing that was taking place in Barber's shoulder.

While they rested, Seyawa collected coconuts and set the meat in the sun to dry, so that she would be able to extract the oil, which she made them understand would be good for their skins.

The next day they were surprised at the strength they found in themselves. She showed them how to catch prawns in the stream; fine, fat creatures they were, and she cooked them in *lolo*, the thick cream she squeezed from coconut meat.

They saw no man-made thing. In the forests the ground beneath them was firm, the trees high-standing giants of the sweet, strong earth. About them flew and piped the *gigi*, the bird said by the people of the island to have loved this land so dearly that many, many moons ago, when all but the island's highest peak had sunk beneath the water, the little *gigi* would fly to this peak and alight on it and weep over the flooded land for what lay lost under the blue ocean. Parrots flashed past the shafts of light between the trees or went chattering to themselves and walking upside down along the branches. Butterflies like large, flat jewels chopped at the air, or stuck, trembling, on the smooth green leaves. With the night would come a cool dusk and a breeze that filled the valley, sliding from slopes nearly two thousand feet above the valley's bed, coming from the clouds.

Slater found Seyawa occupying more and more of his thoughts. Usually she went from the camp soon after dawn, to the stream for water, or to the hills for leaves for their wounds or for wild yam and plantain or for young nuts for drinking; and though he knew she would soon return, if he woke and found her gone he would be angry even with her because she had not been there when he woke. Then she would come swinging down the valley smiling her shy smile, holding up what she had for them and flushing at the love and desire she saw in his face as his eyes fell on her rounded thighs, tight breasts and full, dark lips.

Early in the morning of their fifth day on Koro they began to work on the canoe. They re-lashed many of its joints, drove copper nails into some of them (not clinching the nails, so that they could use them again) and re-threaded and re-caulked many of the 'stitch' holes and the gunwale plank with a putty-like substance which Seyawa made from breadfruit gum and coconut juice. They also had a little pitch, which they melted and ran into two cracks that were beginning to show on the port side. They enjoyed the work, but when noon and the full heat of the day descended upon them Slater called a halt. They returned to the camp and ate a meal of wild plantain—*vudi*, Seyawa called it—which she had boiled in *lolo* and had set to cool. This was fast becoming Barber's favourite dish, and he ate more of it than Slater and Seyawa together.

Slater could not say exactly why he felt as he did then. Perhaps, he thought, it was because they had done some work; or it was Barber's delight in the *vudi*, and the pleasure which showed on Seyawa's face as she saw him relish it; or it was that their wounds and cuts and blisters were healing rapidly in the peace and security of this lovely island. Whatever it was, that day he knew a happiness that he had not known for a long time, a fullness of living he had almost come to believe had passed him by.

Yet his happiness was not great enough to drive the thought of Jeremy from him; rather, it increased his sense of loss. He found himself fitting Jeremy into almost everything they did, seeing him so clearly that when Barber was eating the *vudi* he thought for one fantastic moment that he heard the boy laughing and beginning a joke with Barber because he ate so much.

After the meal they stretched on the grass and slept. Barber was the first to wake. Quietly he got up and making down to the canoe did a little more caulking and then started off along the coast, feeling, like Slater, a satisfaction with life which was new and exciting.

When Slater woke, Seyawa had gone to the stream; her prawning-net was no longer spread over the bush where she dried it. This net she had made from the bark of a vine she called *yaka*. She collected many yards of this vine, cut them into pieces about nine inches in length and boiled them in the iron pot for more than an hour. Thus softened, the bark could be split from the wood with a thumb-nail, and the furry epidermis could be scraped from the bark, to leave only the bast or fibre. The men, with much interest, had watched her do this, and when it came to the making of the cord from this fibre and they saw she did it exactly as a cobbler might, by rolling it with the open hand against the thigh, after moistening it with saliva, they joined in; and soon there was enough fine, strong line to weave two or three prawning-nets. The needle, she explained, should have been made from the wing bone of a fruit bat; this she did not have, so she cut a needle from the piece of bamboo out of which she shaped the gauge that determined the size of the mesh.

The first day she went to use the net Slater saw her go and called to her, wishing her good luck. Immediately her face fell, for to be called after on the way to fish is to have bad luck. She then had to wait until the next day to try it. And that evening when Barber asked why there were no prawns, she guessed what he had said and pointing to Slater said that if they wished to eat *ura* again Oliva must mind his own business and not interfere in arts about which he knew nothing at all. Slater understood the gist of what she said, as did Barber, who pretended not to follow at all and to be very angry. As Slater watched her, he felt his love for her so strong that it hurt.

Waking then, he saw her net was no longer on the bush, and he imagined her as she had gone off that first day on the beach at Oneata, her short *liku* swinging and revealing the smooth tan of the skin of her thighs and buttocks. Desire flooded him, and he started off up the little rise which stood between their camp and the stream. Above him towered the mountains, the ever shifting clouds about their peaks, and under the clouds the frigate birds soaring.

The stream cascaded from pool into pool, running over rapids and foaming about smooth boulders. The trees that bordered it rose straight up for forty, fifty, sixty feet before sending their branches into the sunlit air, and from these branches hung vines and creepers as thick as a man's arm.

She was in the water, a beam of sunlight splashing down on to her. The prawns she had caught were wrapped in a huge *via mila* leaf tied with hibiscus bark and lay on a rock near her. She was motionless, turned partly away from him and bending as she held out her net over the pool's pebbly floor. On the stream bank was her *liku*, its strands spread yellow over a patch of grass.

She heard him and looked round: then, feeling her utter nakedness and smiling self-consciously, she dropped slowly down into the pool, the triangles of her shark-tooth necklet glistening under the water.

He felt the coolness of the water rise about him; a bird called insistently from some high tree far up the mountain, the cry merging with the water murmur. His longing for her now was as an ache in him. She watched him come to her and made no attempt to move; when he touched her she was trembling, her skin tight with the vibration of the water; her hair floating out dark and shining, the petals of a flower tangled into it, turned over and over by the run of the water.

Where the pool emptied, it ran over sand. He led her there and pressed her down so that she lay half-submerged in the shallow, bubbling water.

Chapter 32

Now, with returning strength, came thoughts of their future. Slater was sure that Seyawa felt they must go on to another island. Several times he noticed her set aside things that would be needed in the canoe. Nuts she selected carefully, flicking them with her fingers and listening to the sound they made; those which satisfied her she husked and set to one side. She collected ripe breadfruits and buried them in the ground to ferment; this she told them would make *madrai*, and though the process would not be nearly completed by the time they were ready to leave, it would nevertheless be nourishing food.

Now Slater's knowledge of the language grew quickly. Barber, though he tried hard enough, had little ear for it. Seeing Barber's slowness, Seyawa began to learn a few English words and phrases, using them to address him. Barber smiled with pleasure at her attempts and encouraged her, for he declared that for Seyawa to learn English was a far better thing than for Slater to learn her language.

They had now been on Koro for eight days, and Slater saw the need to make a decision about their future. Shortly after the meal next morning he mentioned it to Barber.

"Ye say the girl's set on us leavin' here," said Barber.

"She is."

"Now I wonder why. She knows we've to build a boat, an'

231

could ye find a better place to build a boat than what we've chanced on here? There's as much timber as we'd need, and it's close to the work, and there's a capital place for settin' the boat up, under shade with an easy launch when she's ready."

"I see all that," said Slater, "but she must have a reason."

"Does she know where we'd go if we was to leave?"

"She talks of a big land, Vanua Levu, she calls it."

"Aye," said Barber, nodding his head. "I could well believe it, for I've seen it."

"Ye've seen it?"

"Why I forgot to tell ye I can't say, but ye'll remember the day we did the caulkin'? I went walking in the afternoon, ye'll mind, and I went round the western tip here"—he pointed in the direction of the stream—"went a fair way round, Sir, an' I saw land. 'Twas a good day for seein', an' though 'twas mighty faint, I'd say it was land. Nor'-west, she lay."

"How far away?"

"Lord only knows. 'Twas very faint, hard to separate from the clouds. What was the name she gave it?"

"Vanua Levu. It means Big Land."

Now there was not so much need to draw in the earth; Slater knew many of the basic words he needed. Barber sat and watched them and followed most of it. They must go on because she had heard Koro spoken of many times in her father's house; she had heard tales of fighting, and of how once a canoe sent by the Tui Nayau came here, but before it reached its destination Tongans—*kai Toga*, she called them—swept out upon it, overwhelmed the crew and slaughtered all but one boy who dived overboard and escaped.

"Aye, then, we mind that," said Barber. "But ask her this: does she think we're going to find any more friendly people on this big island?"

She did not know.

"Nay, nor do we," said Barber.

"I'm hopeful we may, Sam."

"Hopeful, aye. But what are the chances?"

"Now, look ye. Remember when we landed first on Oneata? The people were friendly then."

"After we'd showed 'em what a musket ball could do, aye. But had our powder been damp 'twould have been a different story. Nay, Sir, let us stay here, where we've not been seen, and get on with the boat. 'Tis a lonely place, Mr. Slater, as lonely as ye'd find."

But Seyawa would have none of it. Once she understood what Barber meant, she shook her head vigorously, spoke too quickly for Slater to follow, but she left no doubt about her meaning.

They fell silent. Then Slater looked up at Barber. "Sam, 'tis a decision which could mean either success or failure. Most decisions do, for castaways, but this seems a particularly important one. Seein' it is, an' as 'tis your skin as much as mine. I'll put it to ye this way: what would ye say if I told ye 'twas m'mind to follow what Seyawa says?"

"I'd say," Barber said slowly, but with no hesitation, "that if 'twere that way the wind blew I'd take it as an order an' do as ye said. Mind, I wouldn't do it willingly, but I'd do it. Ye're the cap'n, Mr. Slater."

"Thank ye, Barber. Thank ye."

"I take it ye've decided."

"Aye. We go on to the other island."

Chapter 33

At first light next day they finished work on the canoe, loaded it and made away to the north-west again. A fresh breeze blew them through a short, choppy sea; but, rested and much stronger, using their weight as ballast, they drove the canoe as they had not been able to before they reached Koro.

The day passed uneventfully, a day of thin, grey clouds and intermittent bursts of sun, and by evening the wind had risen until it gusted, occasionally uncertain in direction and strong, but for most of the night it was astern of them and made for fair sailing. That night as he sat at his steering-paddle and searched the sky for the elusive stars, Slater wondered about the boat.

It was not the making of it that worried him, but how to navigate it when they had it. By losing the instruments they had lost the means to navigate. He was afraid to steer alone by the stars and the sun and the moon for five hundred leagues. That way they might be searching for land when their water ran out. He could see them building the boat, shaping wood, sawing, clinching, dowelling, tree-nailing, bending it. He could see it rigged, ready for sea, Barber prepared to stand his watch, not doubting that the course would be true. That night Slater came to see the boat as something impotent. Could he make Barber see that—and keep his faith in him? Barber, any man, could easily misunderstand and see not his fear, but only his preoccupation with a woman who destroyed his desire to return to civilisation.

Could they find their way? He had heard of a compass being made at sea, from a sail needle magnetised by being beaten against an iron bar. But if they did succeed in making a needle, and a card, and in some way suspending it, he still did not know the position of Port Jackson, nor had he the means of finding his own. Their one fantastically slim chance would be to put to sea, sail to the south-west, and hope to find a ship, whatever there might be in those waters. . . .

God, he thought, what a fool a man would be to harbour such a hope in this part of the world!

The next day was a greyer day, but they blessed the cloud, for it meant no sun. The wind fell and they paddled, driving the canoe against a long swell. They saw whales and watched them blow, and for much of that day seafowl followed them, swift-moving creatures against the grey sky, swooping low over them.

Rain came that day and water enveloped them. It drove at them solid and hard; it thrashed on to the surface of the sea and flattened it, filling the canoe, and they baled as they never had before. They lost direction and drifted. Day ended and night began and still it rained, and all that next day it rained, a windless world of pouring water. The sores that had started to heal opened and the rain drummed upon their skins until Slater wondered how much more of it they could stand. They tried to use the canoe's mat sail as an awning, but its sodden weight defeated them. Their own sails they could not touch without wetting their powder and meat and biscuit.

Where they drifted they knew not until the fifth morning dawned.

The rain stopped some time after midnight. There was still no wind and not a star to be seen. After the rain it was startlingly quiet, just the wash of the sea about them, catching, sucking at the parts of the canoe. They did not paddle, but slept, each an hour or two, waiting for the dawn and the wind.

But the dawn brought more than wind. It brought the sight of a misted shape over their starboard bow. This, then, Slater said, was Vanua Levu, and Seyawa stood and muttered to herself in her excitement. As they gazed at it, they knew that among these mountains and valleys they would find the means of leaving these islands, or death. For the first time since leaving Oneata, Slater remembered the sandalwood.

By the middle of the morning the wind had failed them and before noon a drizzling rain set in, falling so gently that they barely felt it. Then the wind returned, a breeze from the land, and with the dusk there came the faintest smell of wood smoke. That night there was again no wind and they paddled slowly, making just enough way to keep their heading.

In the morning they saw reef to the west and north of them. There was now a big swell from the south-east, and as the hours slid by and they neared this reef, they saw several passages through it. Tide and wind combined to raise some high surf along the reef edge. On the other side was calm water as far as they could see. As they came closer in they found their course was taking them towards what looked like a pass they might weather. But close to it they saw its shallowness; a wave broke over it and the wind whipped the top from the sea and blew it in over the lagoon, a mist of salt rolling and sparkling in a burst of sun.

But they soon found deeper water and slid through it into a lagoon so calm it was barely ruffled, and for some distance only a fathom or two deep. Now, still sailing north-west, they could see beyond the western end of this great island another, smaller one, faint and blue. On they sailed until they reached the southernmost tip of the land, where they altered course to make along its coast, in deeper water now, with the wind from the land. They headed more to the west in order to clear a mangrove-covered point which ran out ahead of them and behind which reared a humped mountain, patchy with green-grey scrub and trees and great areas of red and brown earth To starboard the mountains rose in layered chains, the farthest cloud-capped. Several times Barber pointed to tiny inlets in the mangrove-fringed shore and suggested they find a way in through one of them, but Slater had decided they would see what lay behind the point ahead.

As they neared the point, they saw that it ended in a stand of tall coconuts. A current set them close in, off a narrow beach of bright sand. The sun beat down, and the wind fell.

"Out paddles," cried Slater, and as they cleared the point they saw a wide bay off their starboard bow. Stretched across the bay in snaking lines floated mangrove leaves yellow-gold in the sunlight.

It was several minutes before they spoke. Then Slater said: " 'Tis all of eight, ten miles across."

"Aye, it is," said Barber, nodding his head. "An' ye'll notice there seems no sign o' natives."

"That northern side is too far away to tell. An' Lord knows what's behind the mangrove on that flat country over there." Slater was pointing north-east. "But it looks deserted enough."

At the back of the mangrove which fringed the coast were low hills, wide valleys and low-lying plains; behind this first section were more hills, rising gently and merging into the mountains. Their impression was of a dry, thinly-timbered country cut with valleys of richer soil where grew big, spreading trees.

"Well," said Barber, turning about to Slater and grinning, "we go in, eh?"

"Aye. 'Twill be as well to set sail. There's wind enough." Seyawa leaned out across the deck platform for the mast. Barber half stood and helped her raise it while Slater hauled on the backstay. The mast was half-way up when the lashing at the junction of the after main spar and the outrigger strut carried away. The outrigger, free now at its after end, swung out as a wave passed the canoe and the trailing edge of the deck platform above it drove down the now unsupported strut. They felt it first as a sudden drag, then as an uneasy roll as the next wave ran under them. Slater gave a shout, and letting the backstay go kicked forward against the spar, trying to hold against the pressure of the water. But the end of it was soon buried, a long crack appearing in it near its union with the gunwale. The gear on the deck began to slide astern, packing up against the the tucked-under after edge of the sail, the trailing edge of the deck soon well under water and the drag slewing the canoe to port. Seyawa dropped the mast and, throwing herself out over the deck, grabbed for the sail and the gear that was cached in it; the water filled the belly of the folded-under canvas and swirled about her arms. Then Barber recovered from his surprise and, cursing, went out after her, his great hands clawing at the canvas.

With water slopping in over the port gunwale, the mast and mat sail floating off but held by its vine and sennit rigging, the canoe wallowed sluggishly. Seyawa screamed as she felt the load shift under her and the sea pluck the sail from her hands. A musket slipped and disappeared in the broken water curling about the submerged end of the deck platform. Then the aftermost bundle slipped. She moved to hold it and cried out as she felt it going, but Slater shouted: "Let it go. Keep to the sail. Keep to the sail, Seyawa. Barber, d'ye hear, keep to the sail!"

A moment of desperate grasping and the sail was held, with gear caught in it, all but the aftermost bundle, which, free now, rolled over and over in the bubbling water, caught by the surge of the sea. They got the sail back and worked it forward, where its weight was better placed over the leading spar, and, while Seyawa baled, Barber hauled in the mast and rigging, hacked at the vine and used a length of it to lash the gear. Slater buried his paddle deep, striving to keep the swell astern of them.

But he saw the float working and fretting at its forward lashings and saw it would not be long before it tore from them; unsupported the narrow canoe would capsize immediately.

"Sam, a length o' the vine! Quick, man!"

Barber's knife slashed at it.

"Seyawa," cried Slater, pointing out towards the strut end, "out along the deck!" He spoke in English but she saw his meaning.

"Under the float end wi' it," said Barber.

"Aye. Here, girl, the vine."

She took it from Barber, but turned away from the outrigger, and Slater shouted at her, pointing: "This side. This, Seyawa."

"She don't understand ye," called Barber, and Slater shouted again. She did not seem to hear him but, drawing a deep breath and then expelling it, she stood straight for a second, bent from her hips and dived overboard, the vine whipping after her. Slater saw her turn and pass under the canoe. She reappeared treading water at the after end of the outrigger. With one hand she grasped the strut, with the other she led the outrigger back to it. Soon she had the vine about the float butting it up against the strut once more. She passed the end of the vine to Slater, who belayed it about the inboard end of the spar.

They helped her back aboard. She stood laughing a moment, then tears came and she half laughed, half cried, throwing back her head, her hair snapping wet about her shoulders. She remained standing, the water globules bright against her skin, the strands of her *liku* moulded about her buttocks. Slater watched her, filled with longing for her. They stepped the mast and set the sail. On course again, the canoe ran sweetly across the bay that lay under the green-brown hills.

In the dusk they found a river with three mouths and slipped into it, the mangrove close about them, its flowers hanging unmoving in the stillness, and their ears filled with the shrill singing of a thousand nesting birds.